VEDA™

ASSEMBLY REQUIRED

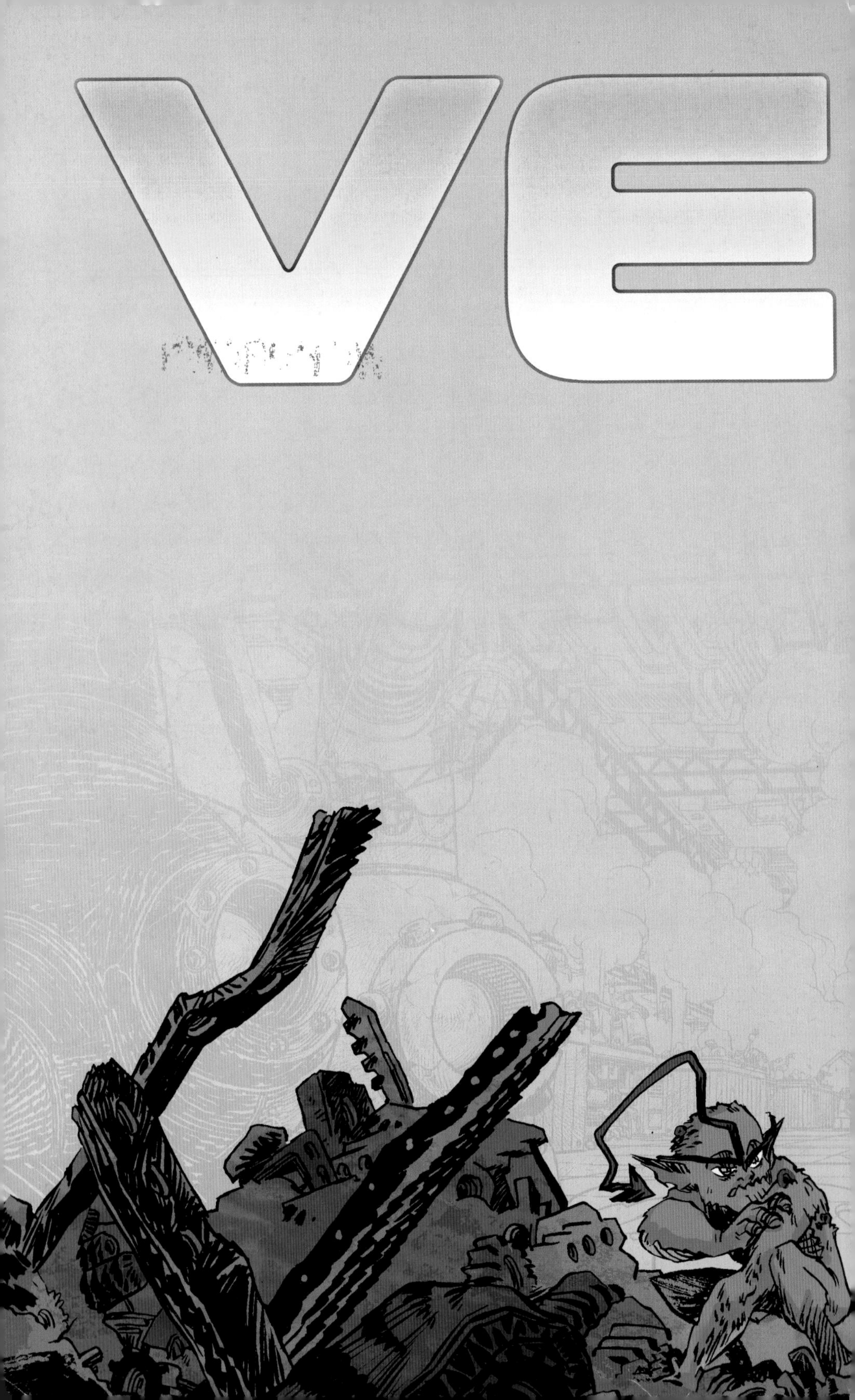
VE

DA™

ASSEMBLY REQUIRED

Written by
SAMUEL TEER

Art and lettering by
HYEONDO PARK

Colors by
KELLY FITZPATRICK

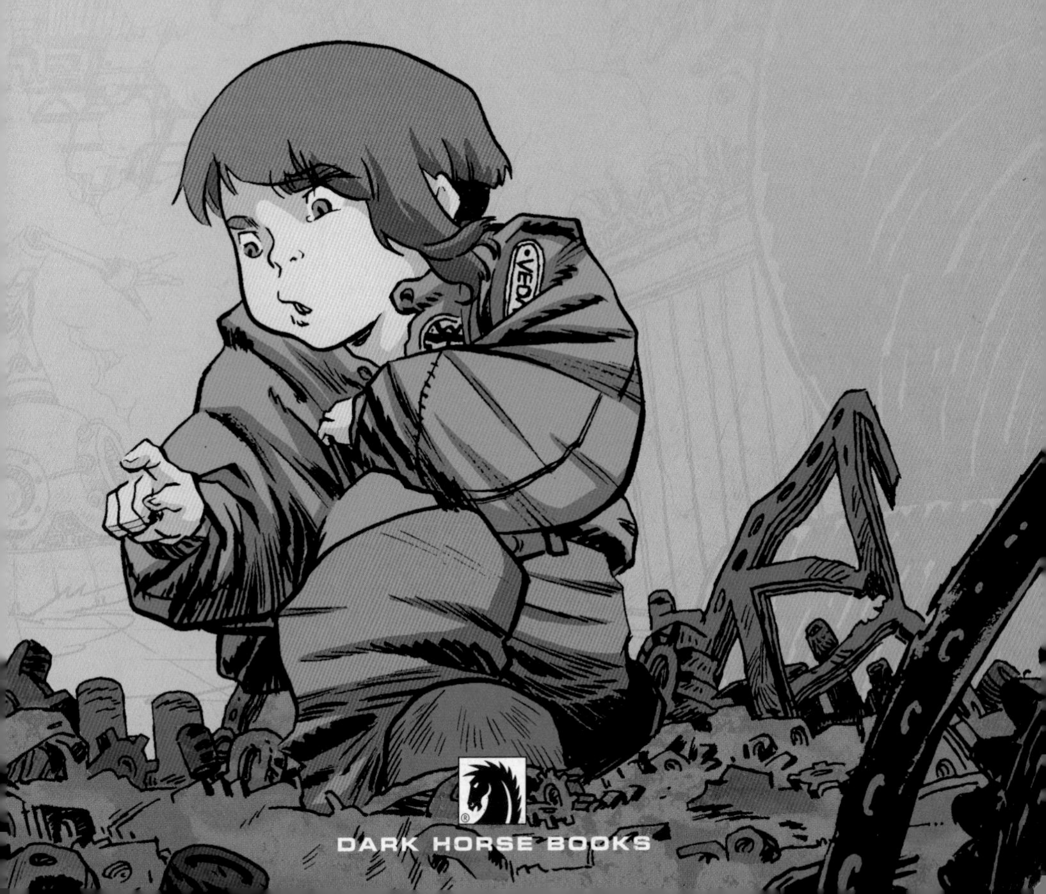

DARK HORSE BOOKS

President and Publisher
MIKE RICHARDSON

Editors
JIM GIBBONS and **SIERRA HAHN**

Digital Production
CHRISTIANNE GOUDREAU

Collection Design
JUSTIN COUCH

ISBN 978-1-61655-497-2

First edition: August 2015

International Licensing: (503) 905-2377

Comic Shop Locator Service: (888) 266-4226

1 3 5 7 9 10 8 6 4 2

Printed in China

Published by **DARK HORSE BOOKS**

A division of Dark Horse Comics, Inc., 10956 SE Main Street, Milwaukie, OR 97222

Neil Hankerson, Executive Vice President · Tom Weddle, Chief Financial Officer · Randy Stradley, Vice President of Publishing · Michael Martens, Vice President of Book Trade Sales · Scott Allie, Editor in Chief · Matt Parkinson, Vice President of Marketing · David Scroggy, Vice President of Product Development · Dale LaFountain, Vice President of Information Technology · Darlene Vogel, Senior Director of Print, Design, and Production · Ken Lizzi, General Counsel · Davey Estrada, Editorial Director · Chris Warner, Senior Books Editor · Diana Schutz, Executive Editor · Cary Grazzini, Director of Print and Development · Lia Ribacchi, Art Director · Cara Niece, Director of Scheduling · Mark Bernardi, Director of Digital Publishing

Library of Congress Cataloging-in-Publication Data

Teer, Samuel.
 Veda: assembly required / written by Samuel Teer ; art and lettering by Hyeondo Park ; colors by Kelly Fitzpatrick. -- First edition.
   pages cm
 Summary: An orphaned girl raised by robots in a factory discovers she has the ability to speak with machines, and under the tutelage of Assembly, she learns the three laws of the machines, but it is the secret fourth law--avoid the Gremlin--that leads Veda down a dangerous and compromising path on her journey of self-discovery.
 1. Graphic novels. [1. Graphic novels. 2. Science fiction. 3. Adventure and adventurers--Fiction. 4. Orphans--Fiction. 5. Coming of age--Fiction.] I. Park, Hyeondo, illustrator. II. Title.

PZ7.7.T44Ve 2015
 741.5'973--dc23

2015008365

I'd like to dedicate this book to my wife, Andrea, and acknowledge that this book wouldn't be possible without the works of Rudyard Kipling, Neil Gaiman, and Bill Watterson.

—Samuel

To my friends and family. —Hyeondo

I'd like to dedicate this book to my friends, family, and to all of the wonderful people I've had the pleasure of working with in comics.

—Kelly

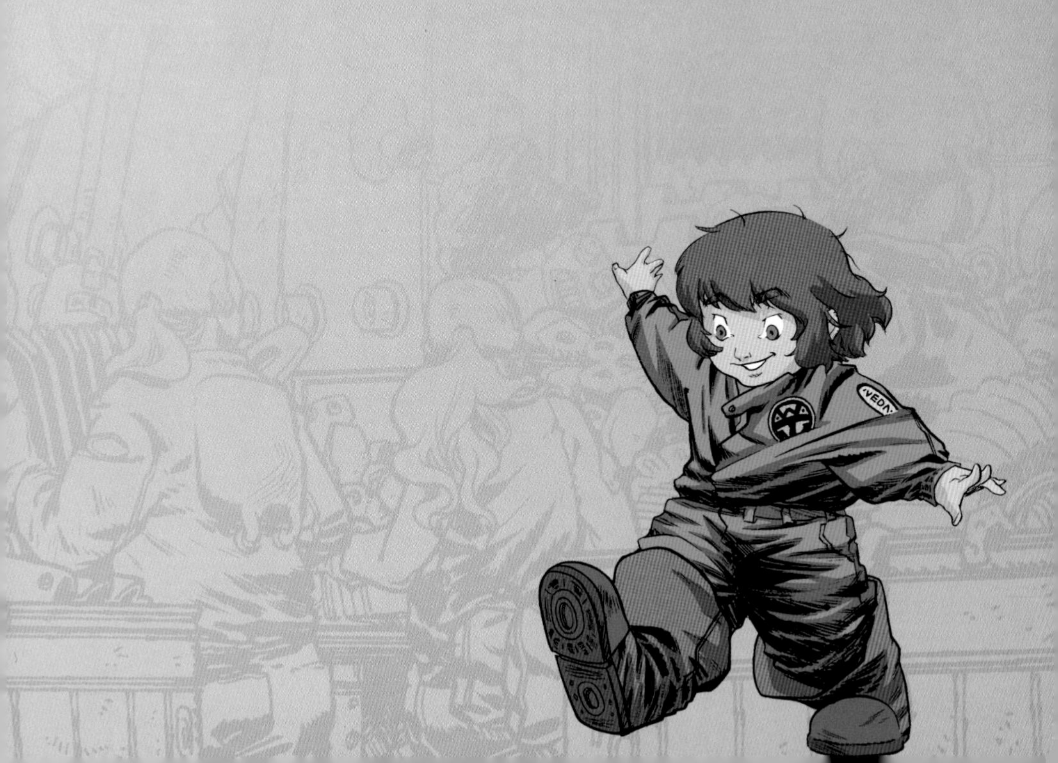
VEDA

ATTENTION, ALL EMPLOYEES:

This is a reminder that we do offer onsite childcare. The cost will be automatically deducted from your wages. If you choose to forgo daycare and are caught bringing your children to work, the cost of onsite childcare will be automatically deducted from your wages.

TAKE RESPONSIBILITY FOR YOUR MISTAKES.

This **INFORMATIVE** message has been brought to you by

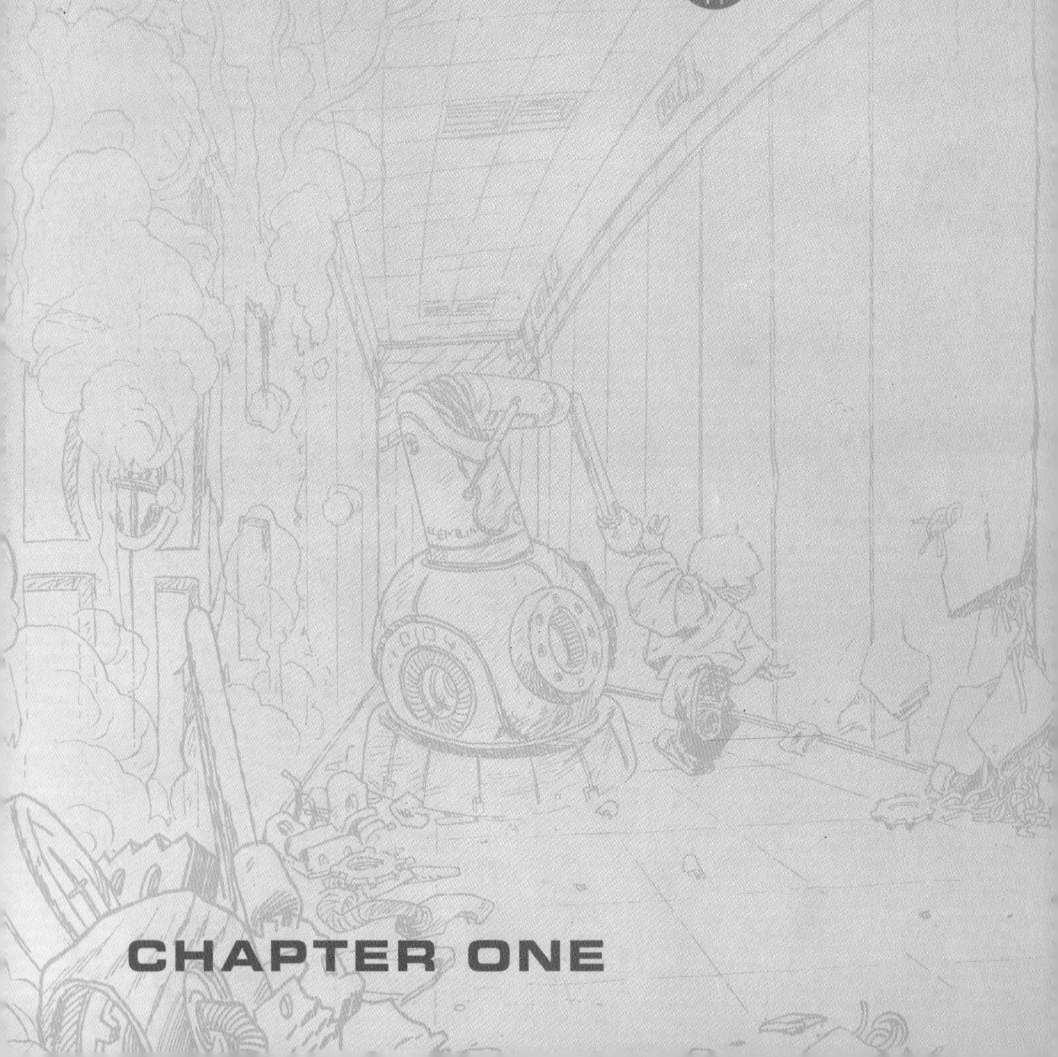

CHAPTER ONE

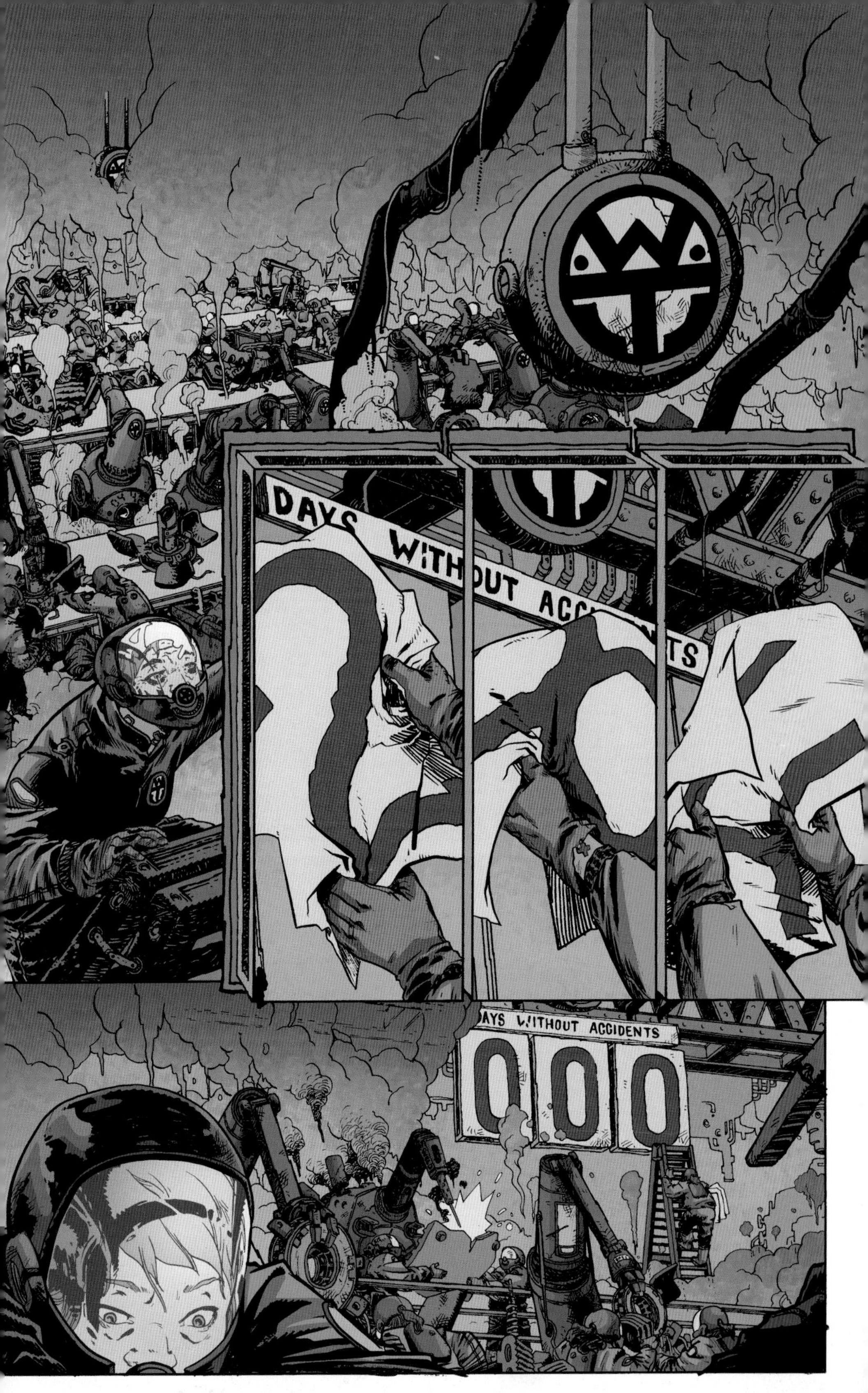
DAYS WITHOUT ACC
TS
DAYS WITHOUT ACCIDENTS
000

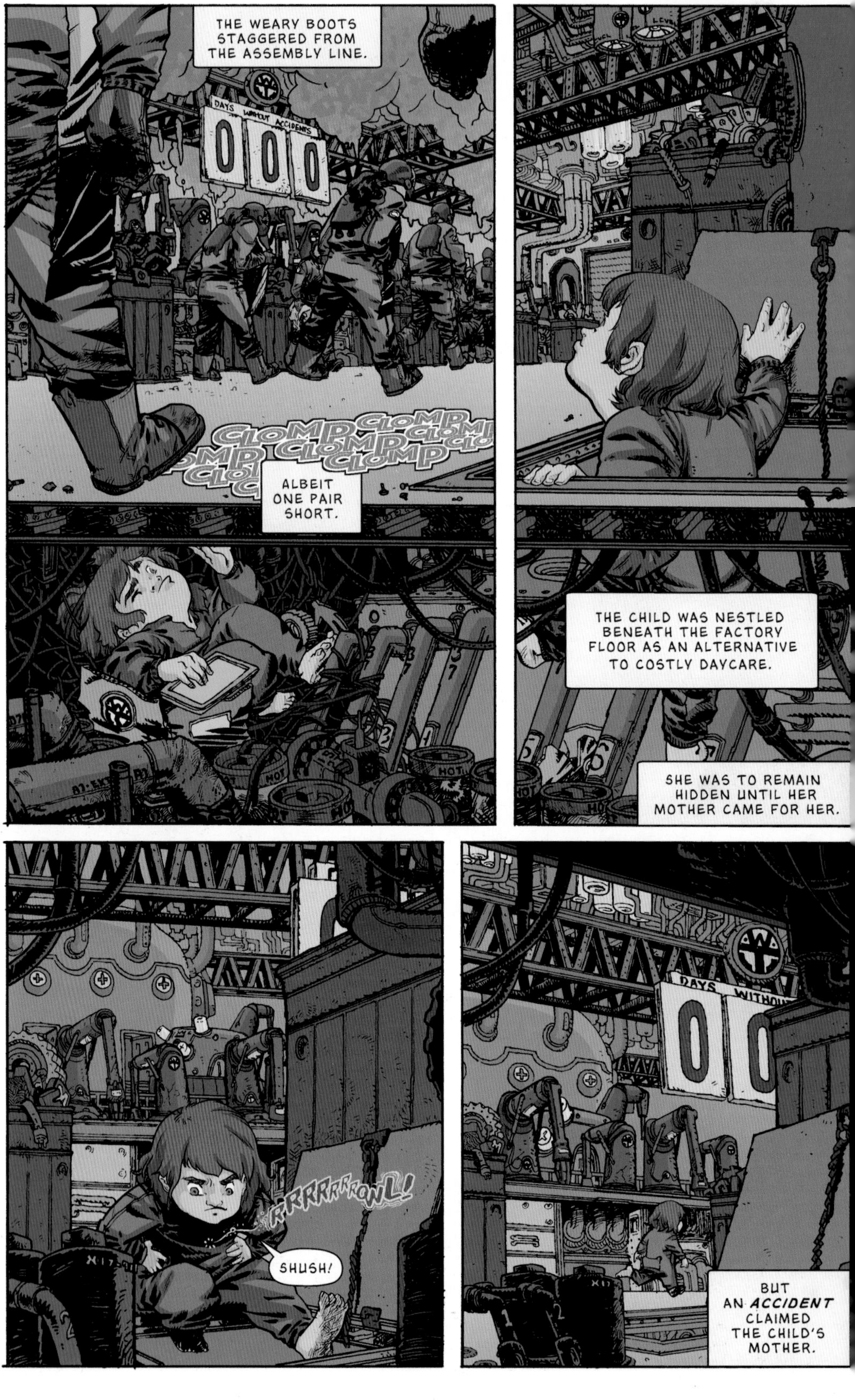
THE WEARY BOOTS STAGGERED FROM THE ASSEMBLY LINE.
DAYS WITHOUT ACCIDENTS
000
CLOMP CLOMP CLOMP CLOMP
ALBEIT ONE PAIR SHORT.
THE CHILD WAS NESTLED BENEATH THE FACTORY FLOOR AS AN ALTERNATIVE TO COSTLY DAYCARE.
SHE WAS TO REMAIN HIDDEN UNTIL HER MOTHER CAME FOR HER.
RRRRRRROWL!
SHUSH!
BUT AN *ACCIDENT* CLAIMED THE CHILD'S MOTHER.

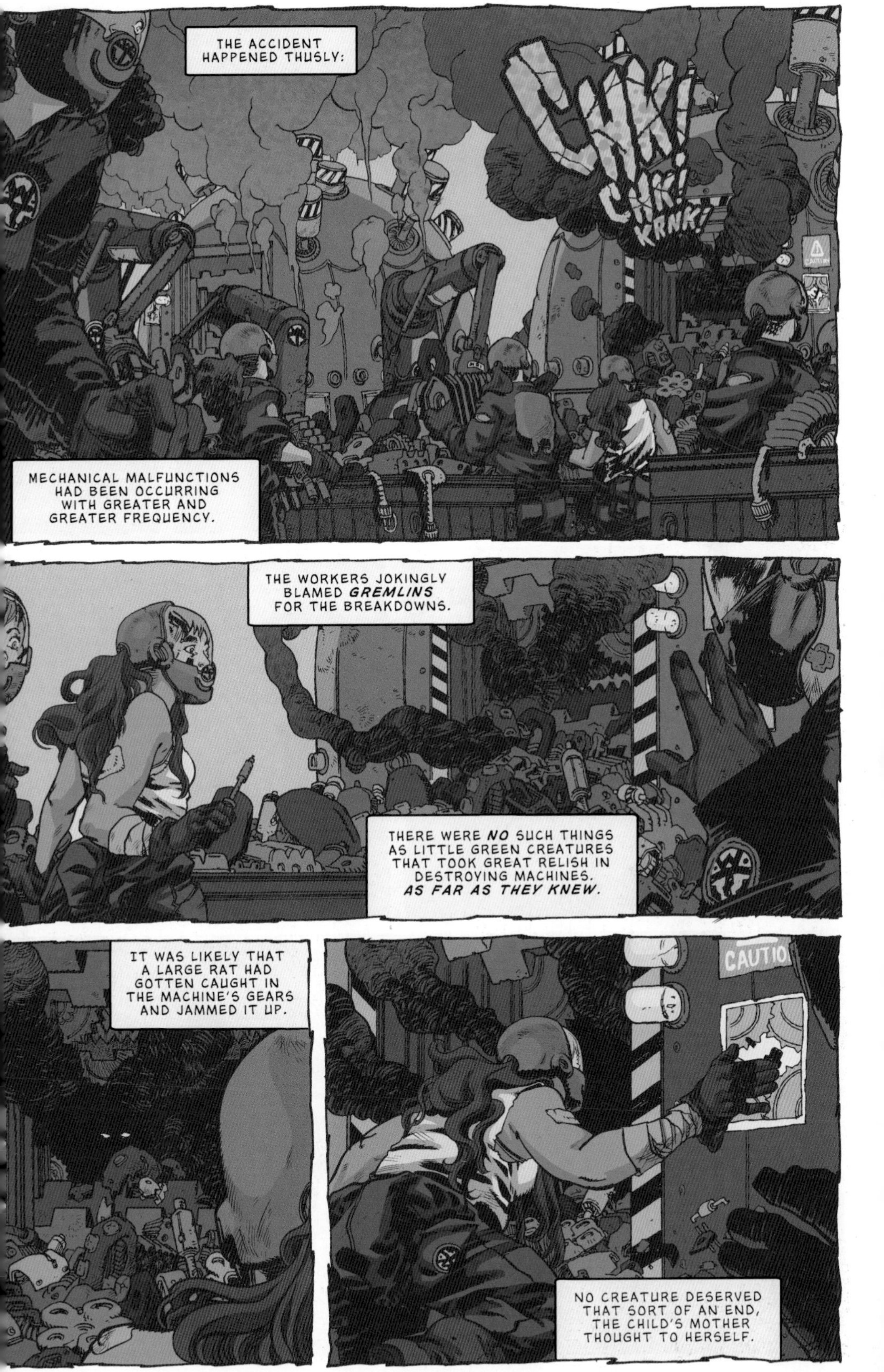
THE ACCIDENT HAPPENED THUSLY:
CHK! CHK! KRNK!
CAUTION
MECHANICAL MALFUNCTIONS HAD BEEN OCCURRING WITH GREATER AND GREATER FREQUENCY.
THE WORKERS JOKINGLY BLAMED GREMLINS FOR THE BREAKDOWNS.
THERE WERE NO SUCH THINGS AS LITTLE GREEN CREATURES THAT TOOK GREAT RELISH IN DESTROYING MACHINES. AS FAR AS THEY KNEW.
IT WAS LIKELY THAT A LARGE RAT HAD GOTTEN CAUGHT IN THE MACHINE'S GEARS AND JAMMED IT UP.
CAUTIO
NO CREATURE DESERVED THAT SORT OF AN END, THE CHILD'S MOTHER THOUGHT TO HERSELF.

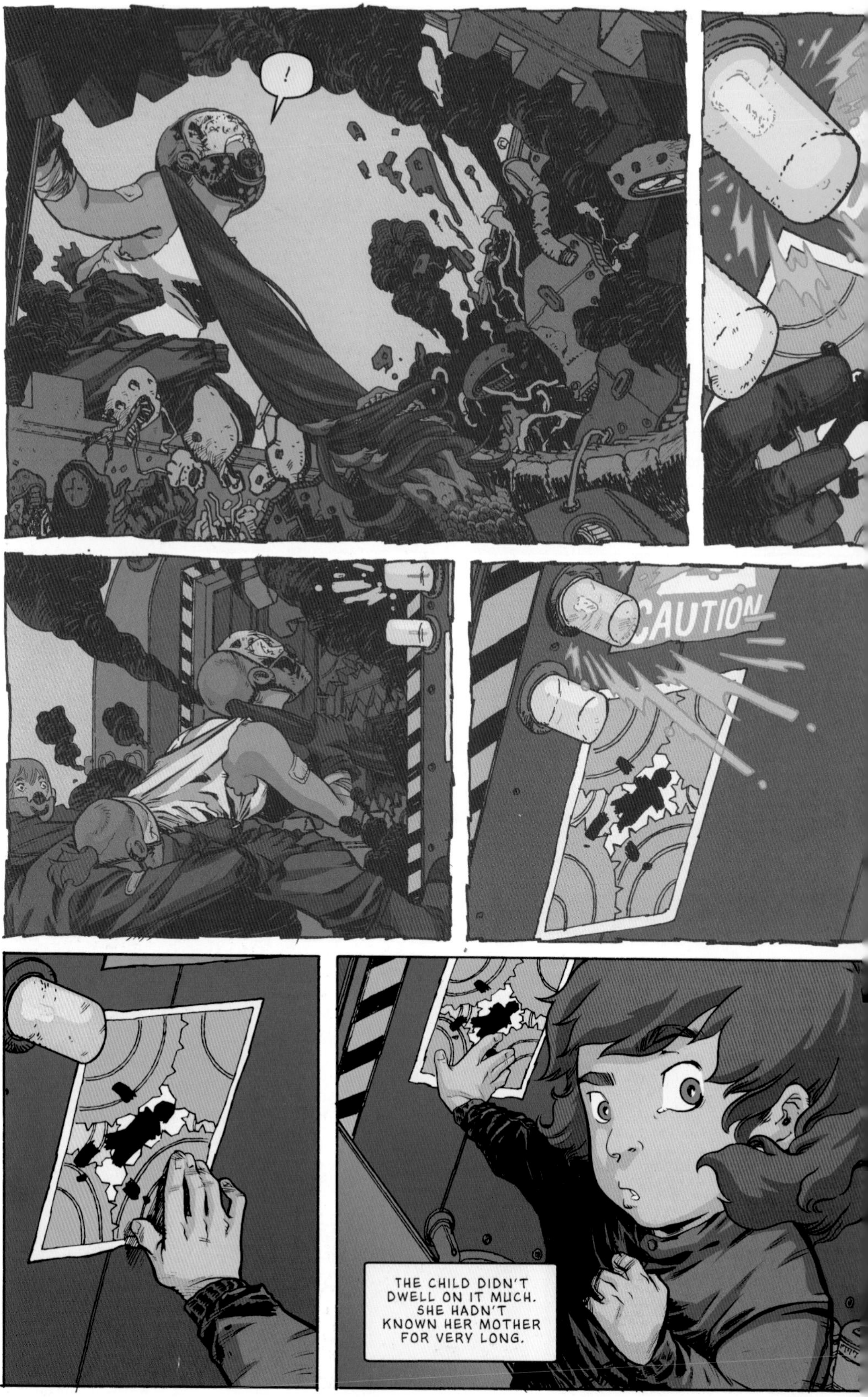
!
CAUTION
THE CHILD DIDN'T DWELL ON IT MUCH. SHE HADN'T KNOWN HER MOTHER FOR VERY LONG.

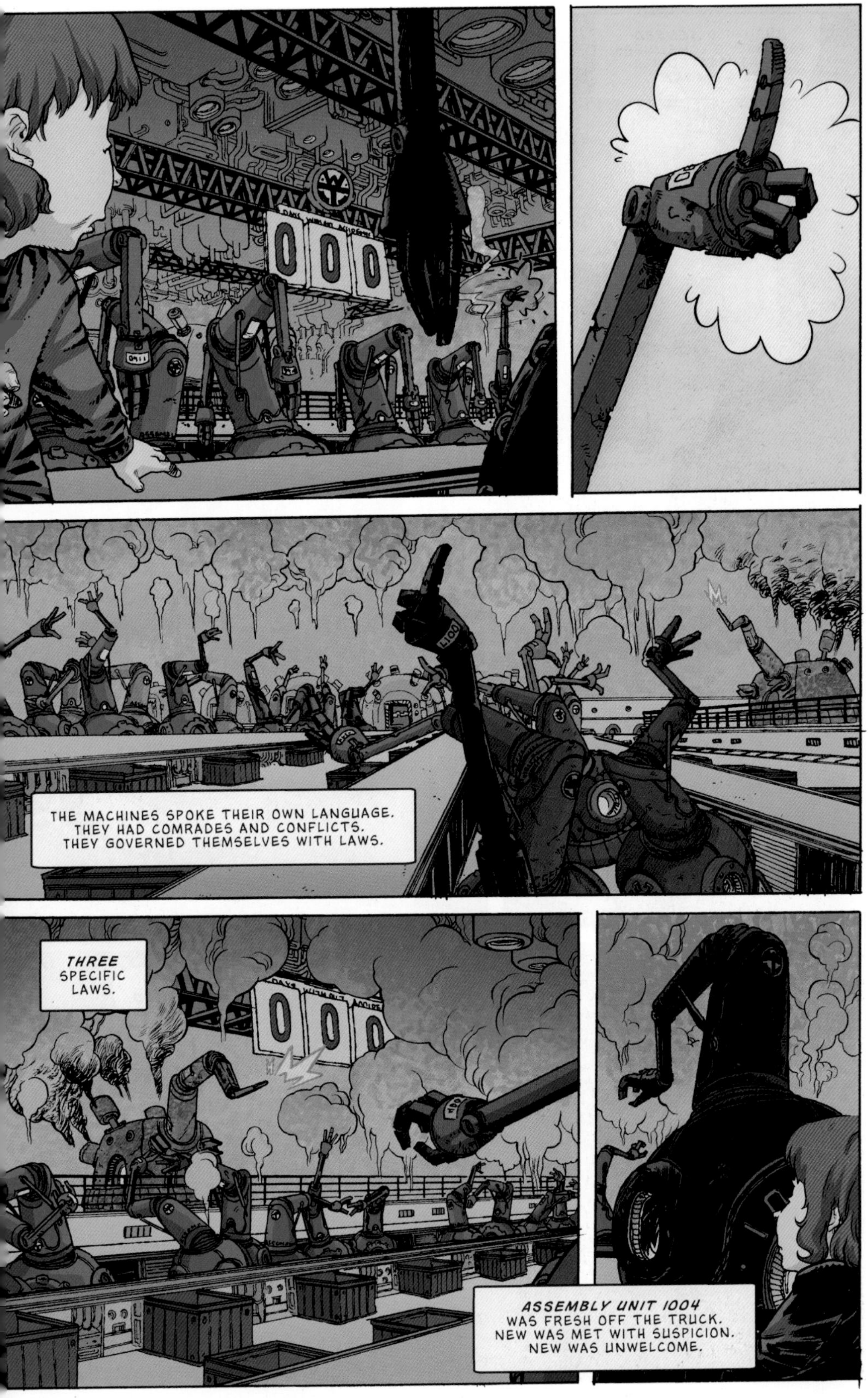
THE MACHINES SPOKE THEIR OWN LANGUAGE. THEY HAD COMRADES AND CONFLICTS. THEY GOVERNED THEMSELVES WITH LAWS.
THREE SPECIFIC LAWS.
ASSEMBLY UNIT 1004 WAS FRESH OFF THE TRUCK. NEW WAS MET WITH SUSPICION. NEW WAS UNWELCOME.

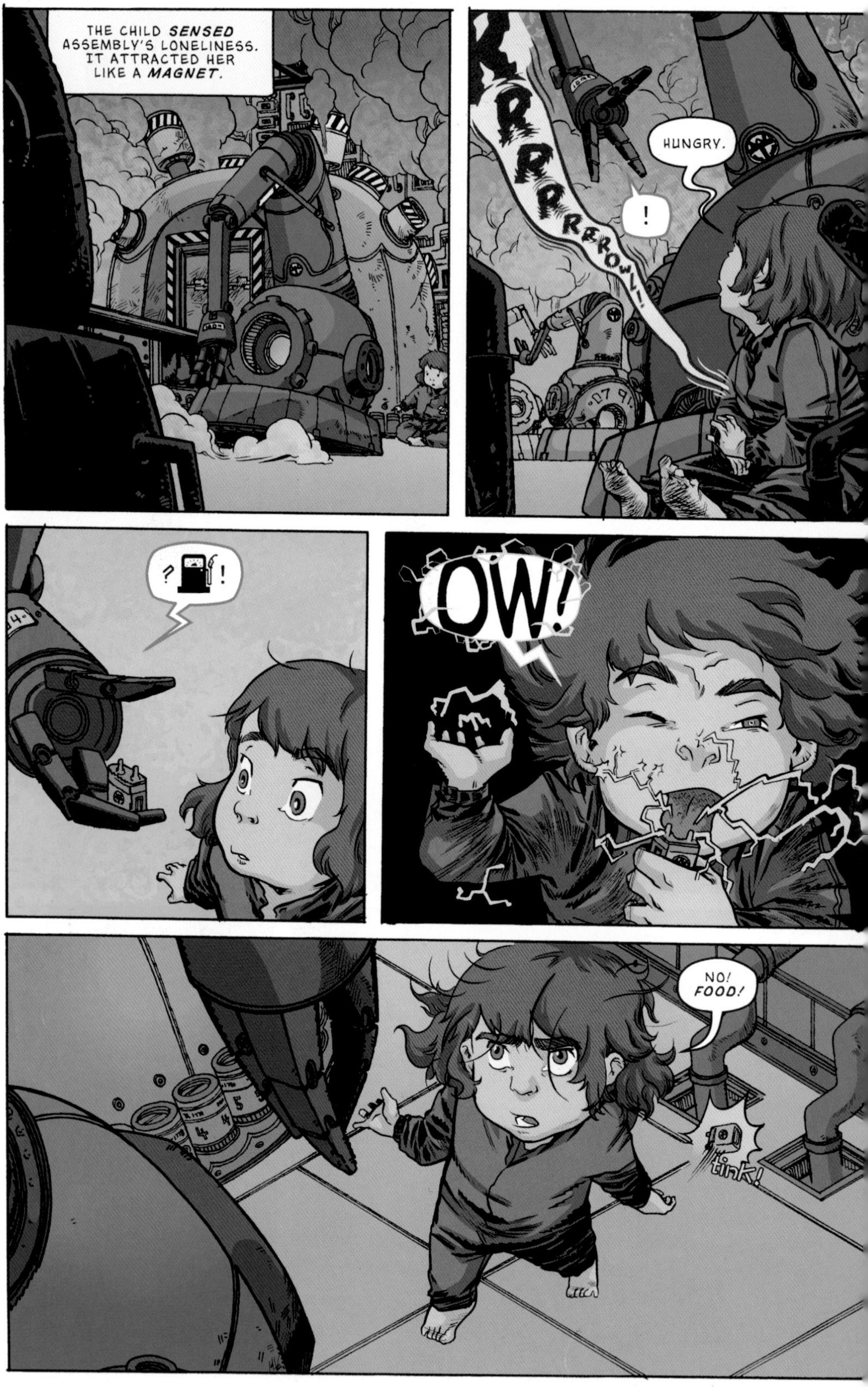
THE CHILD SENSED ASSEMBLY'S LONELINESS. IT ATTRACTED HER LIKE A MAGNET.
KRRRRRROWL!
!
HUNGRY.
?!
OW!
NO! FOOD!
tink!

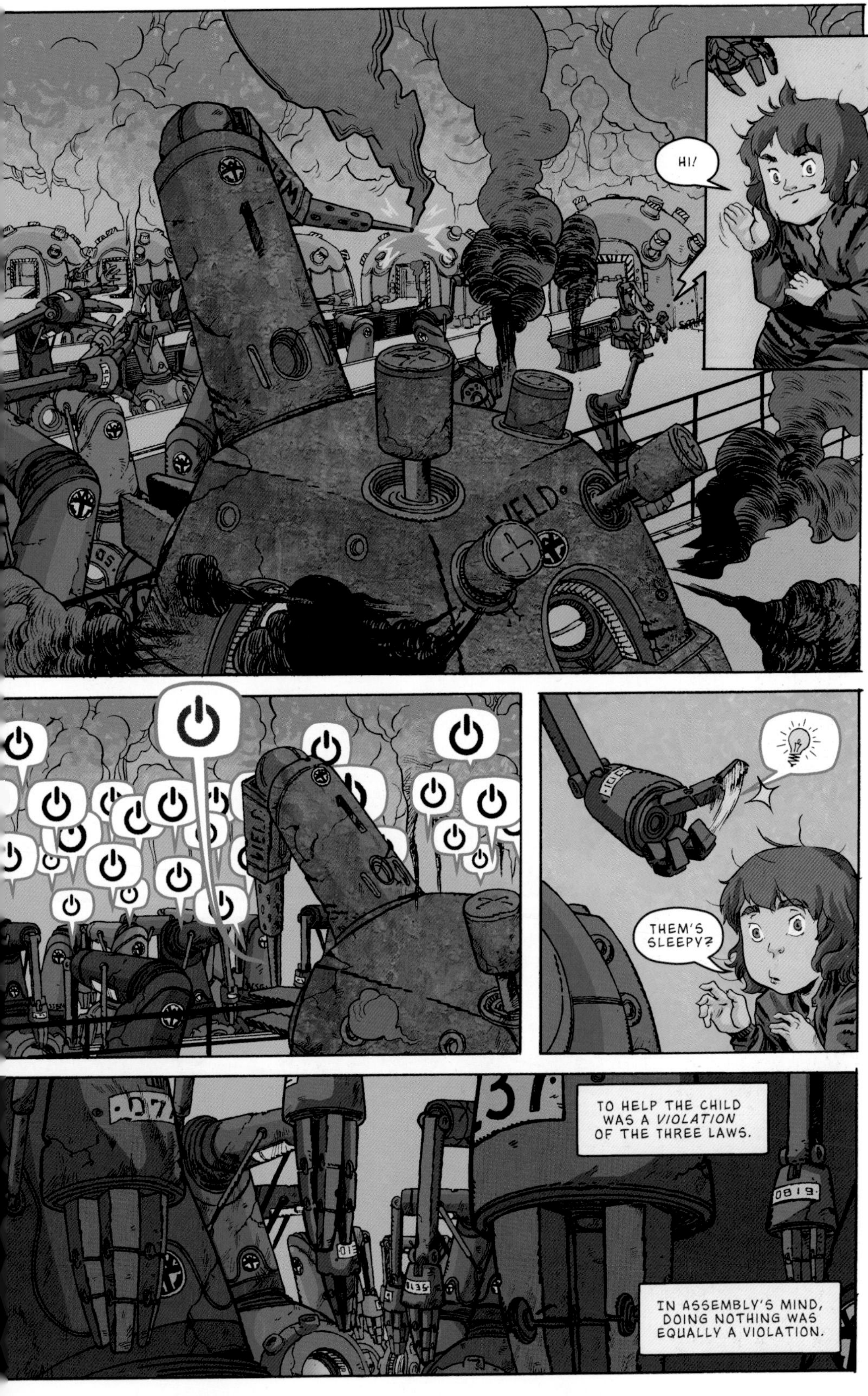
HI!
THEM'S SLEEPY?
TO HELP THE CHILD WAS A *VIOLATION* OF THE THREE LAWS.
IN ASSEMBLY'S MIND, DOING NOTHING WAS EQUALLY A VIOLATION.

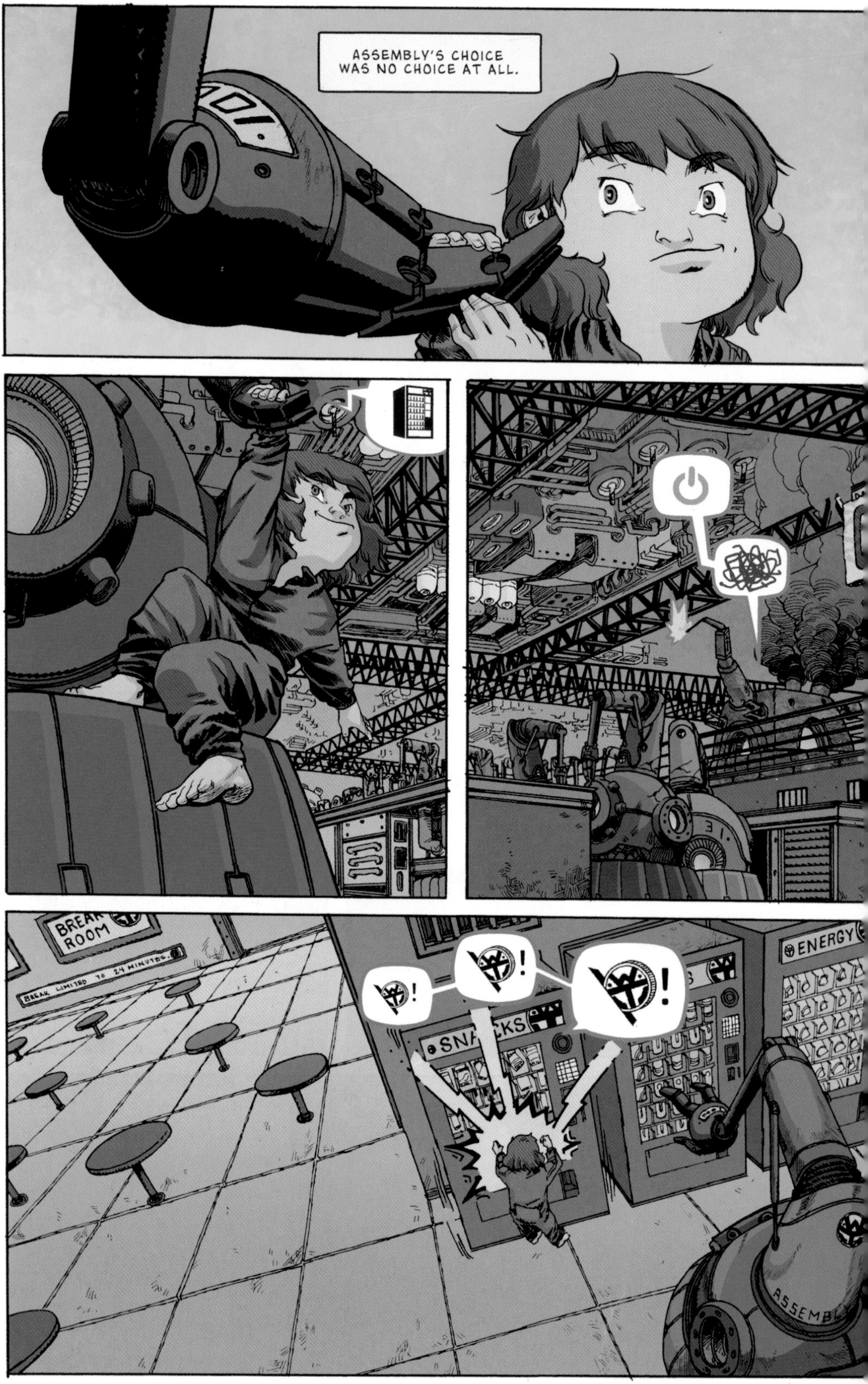
ASSEMBLY'S CHOICE WAS NO CHOICE AT ALL.
BREAK LIMITED TO 24 MINUTES.
ENERGY

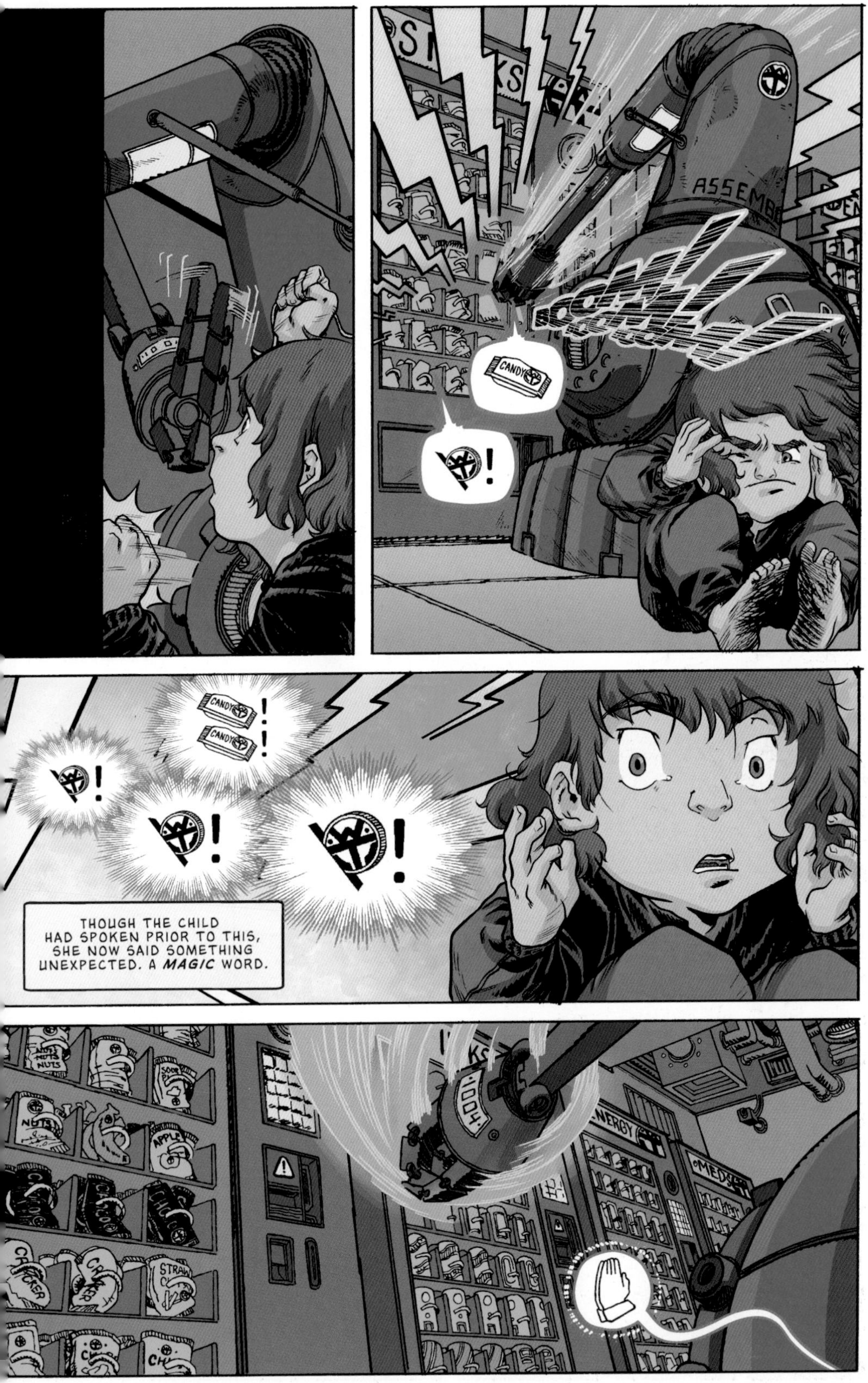
SNACKS
ASSEMB
CANDY
!
CANDY !
CANDY !
!
!
!
THOUGH THE CHILD HAD SPOKEN PRIOR TO THIS, SHE NOW SAID SOMETHING UNEXPECTED. A *MAGIC* WORD.
NUTS NUTS NUTS
SOUR
NUTS
APPLE
CRACKER
CRACKER
STRAW
ENERGY
MEDS
1004

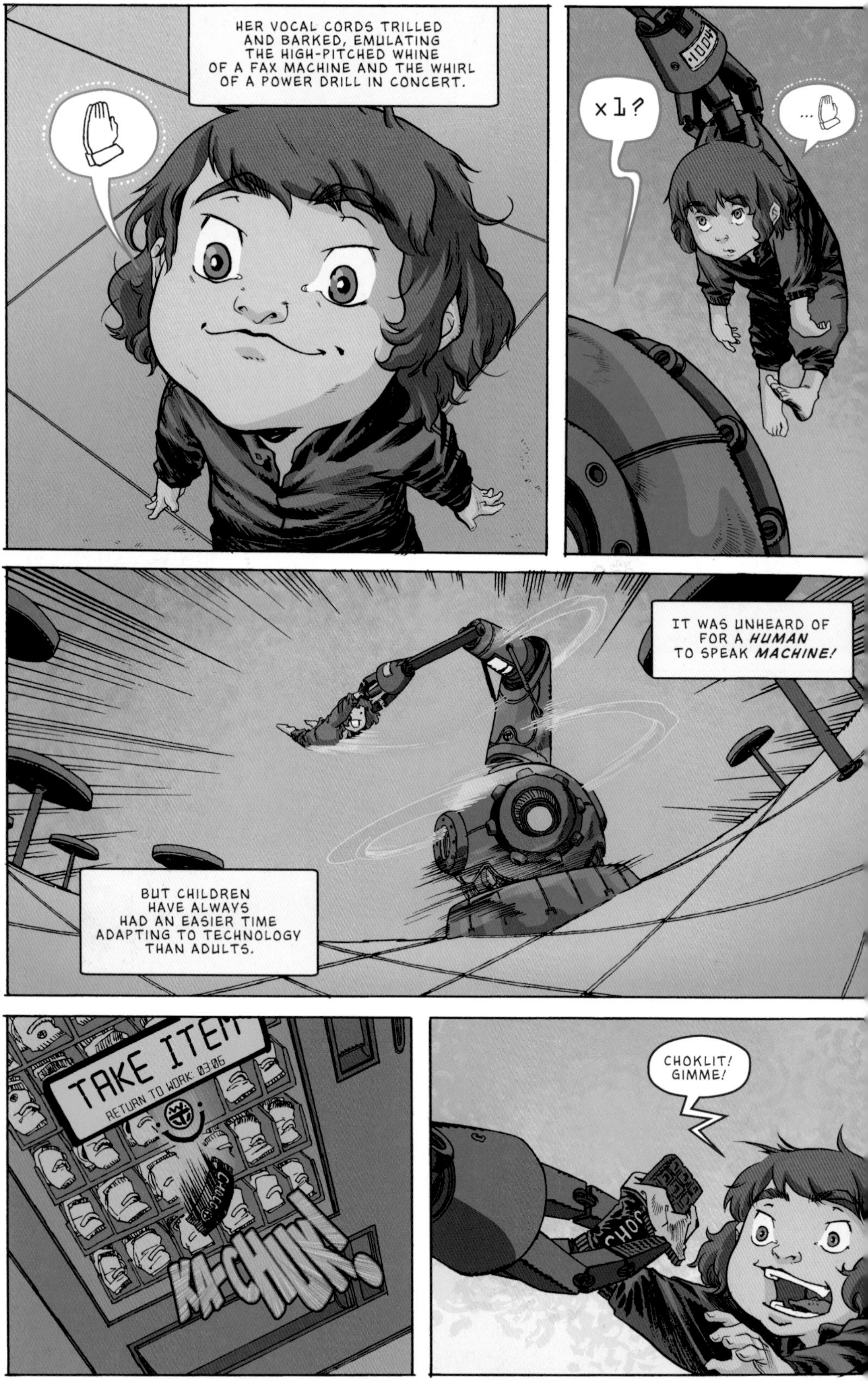
HER VOCAL CORDS TRILLED AND BARKED, EMULATING THE HIGH-PITCHED WHINE OF A FAX MACHINE AND THE WHIRL OF A POWER DRILL IN CONCERT.
x1?
...
IT WAS UNHEARD OF FOR A *HUMAN* TO SPEAK *MACHINE!*
BUT CHILDREN HAVE ALWAYS HAD AN EASIER TIME ADAPTING TO TECHNOLOGY THAN ADULTS.
TAKE ITEM
RETURN TO WORK: 03:06
KA-CHUNK!
CHOKLIT! GIMME!

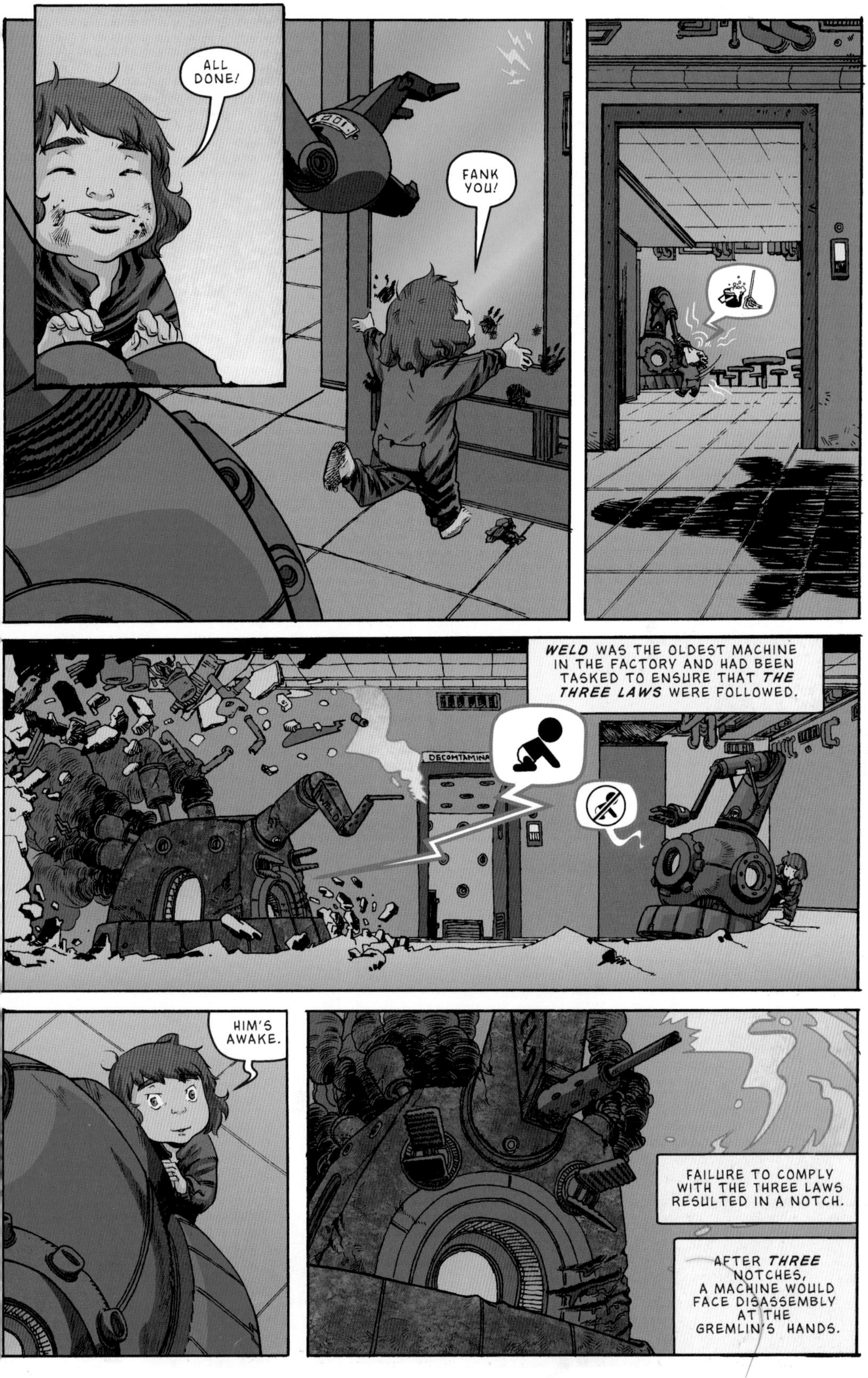
ALL DONE!
FANK YOU!
WELD WAS THE OLDEST MACHINE IN THE FACTORY AND HAD BEEN TASKED TO ENSURE THAT THE THREE LAWS WERE FOLLOWED.
DECOMTAMINA
HIM'S AWAKE.
FAILURE TO COMPLY WITH THE THREE LAWS RESULTED IN A NOTCH.
AFTER THREE NOTCHES, A MACHINE WOULD FACE DISASSEMBLY AT THE GREMLIN'S HANDS.

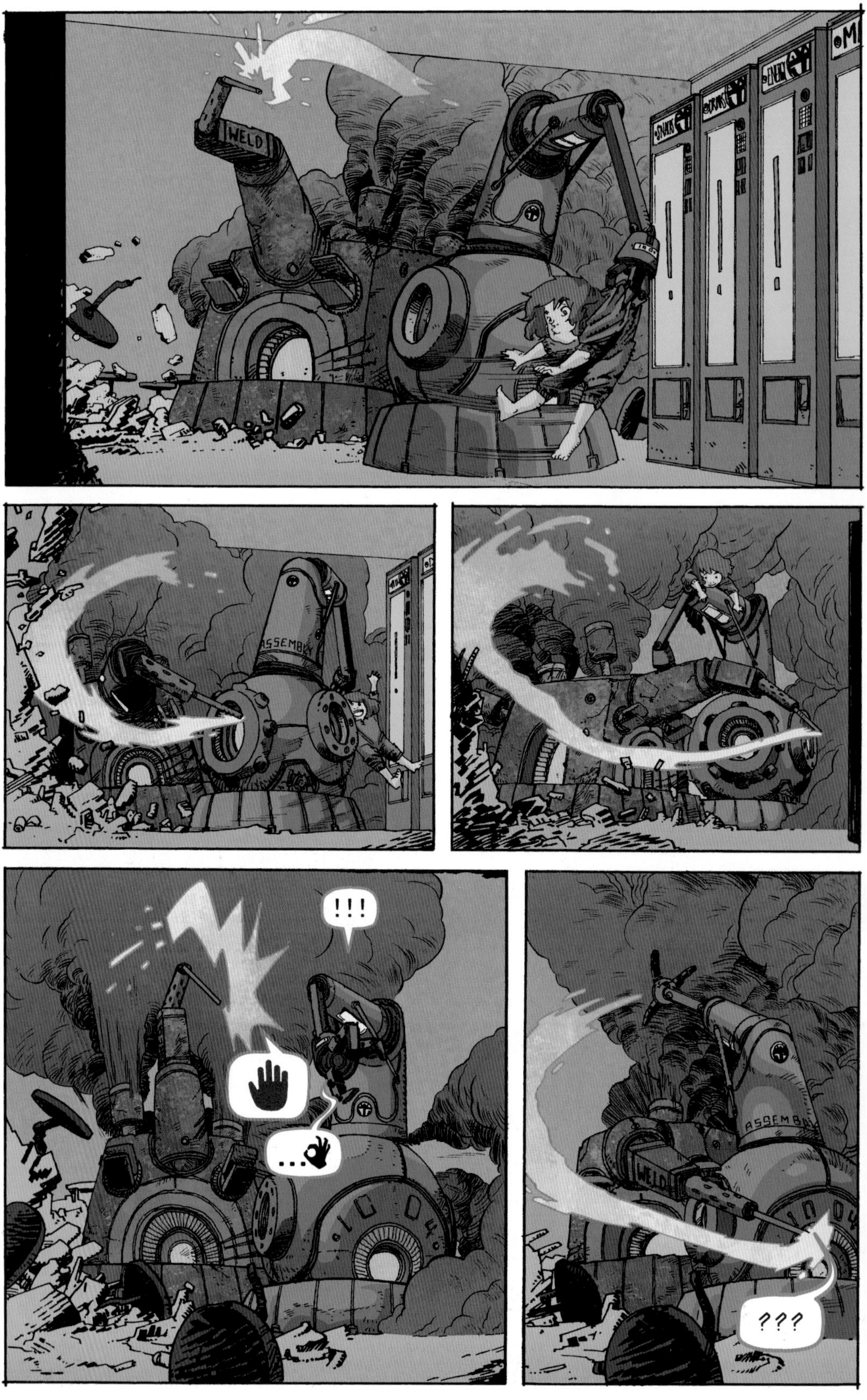
WELD
!!!
...
???

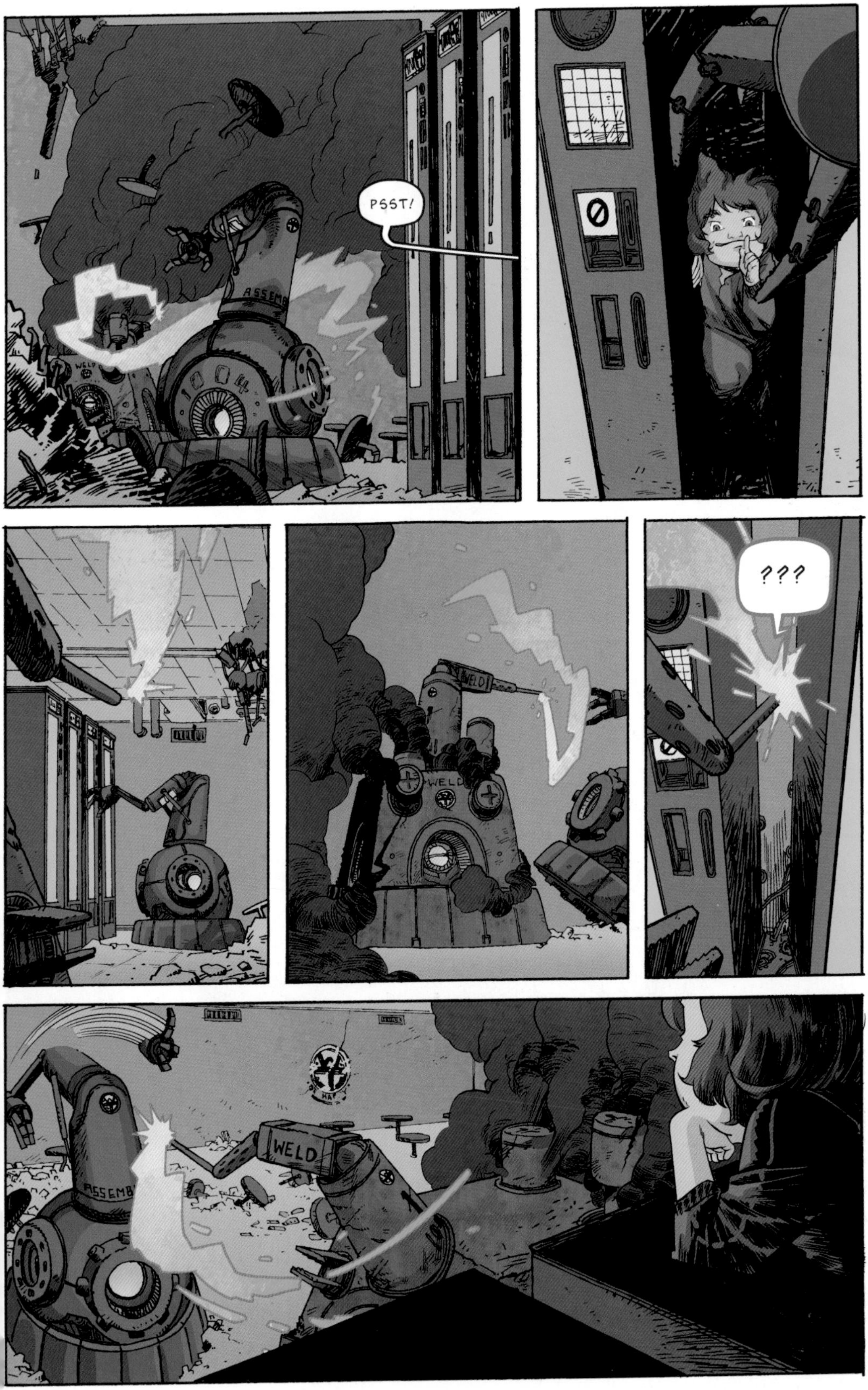
PSST!
???

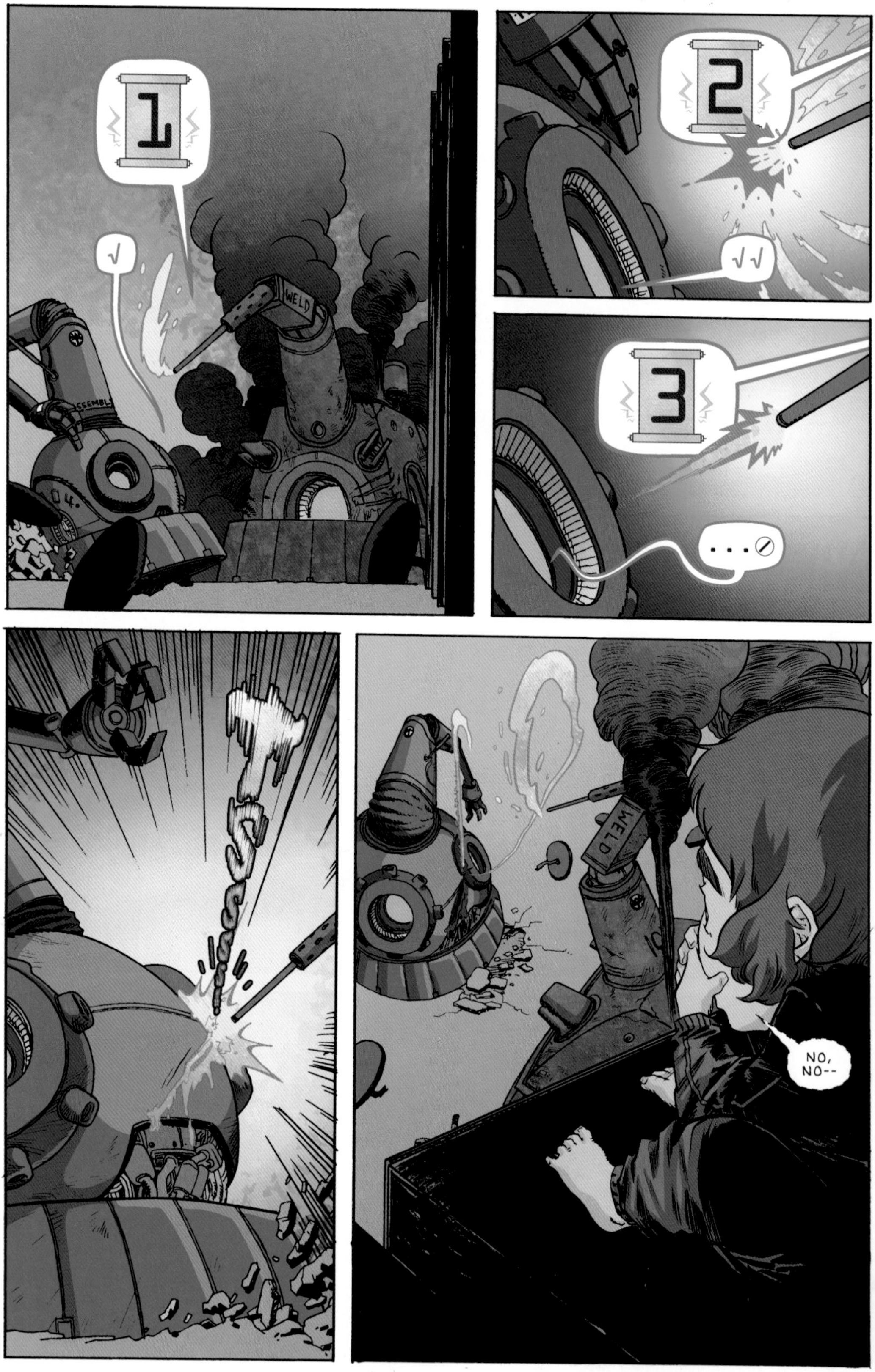
1
√
2
√√
3
....⊘
WELD
NO, NO--

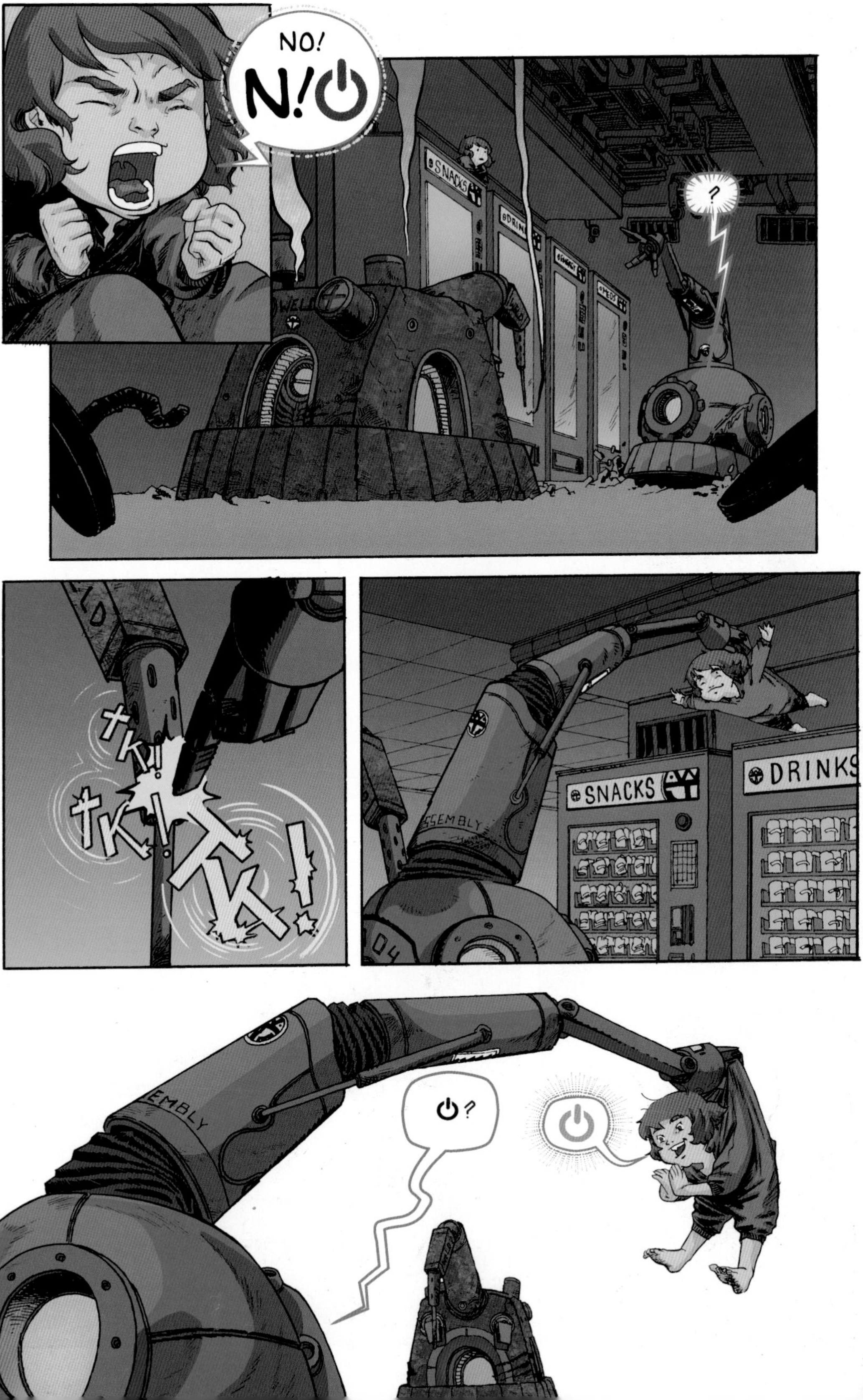
NO!
N!
SNACKS
?
TK!
TK!
TK!
SNACKS
DRINKS
?

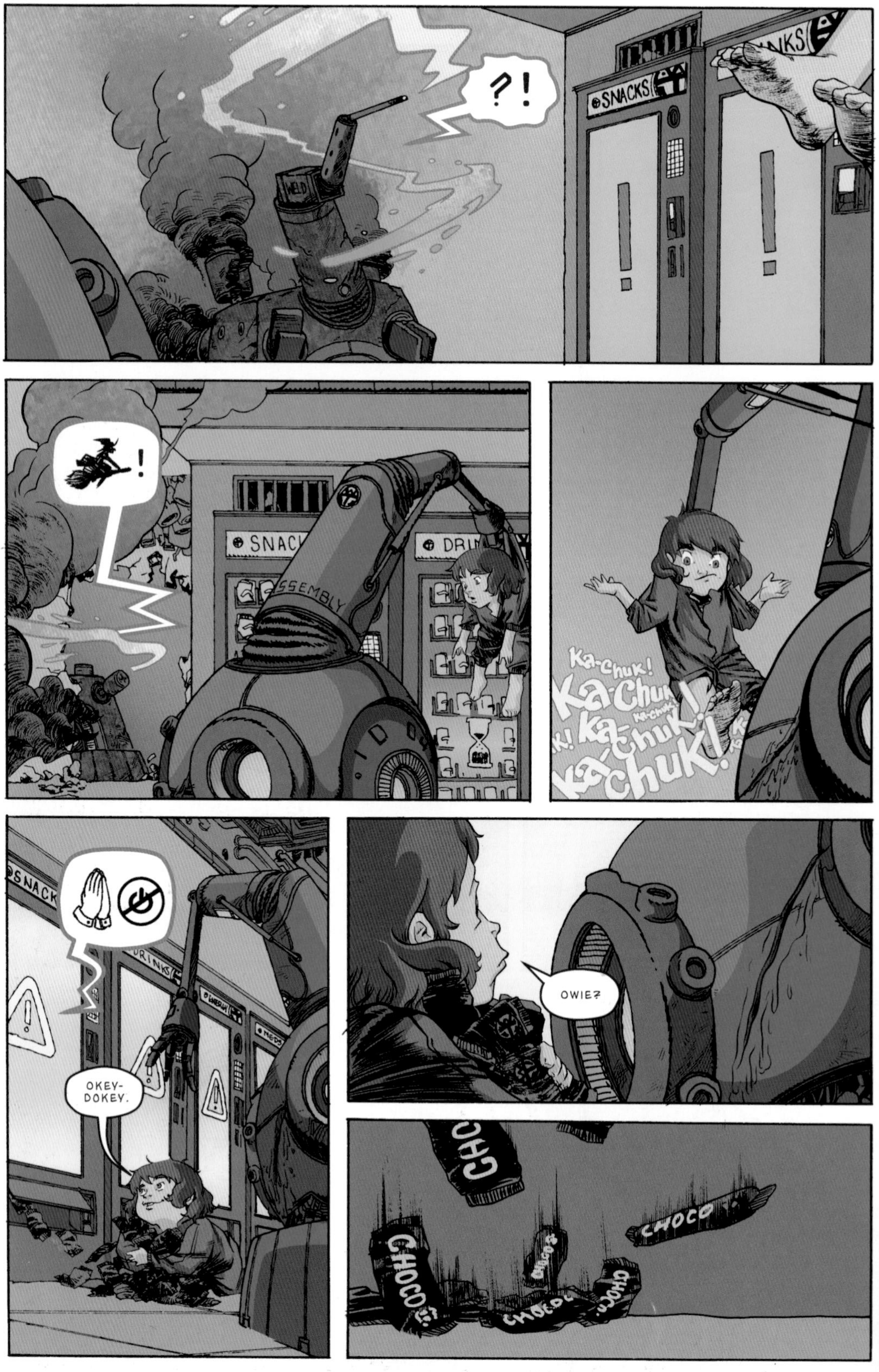
WELD
?!
SNACKS
!
KA-CHUK!
KA-CHUK!
KA-CHUK!
KA-CHUK!
KA-CHUK!
DRINKS
MEDS
OKEY-DOKEY.
OWIE?
CHOCO
CHOCO
CHOCO

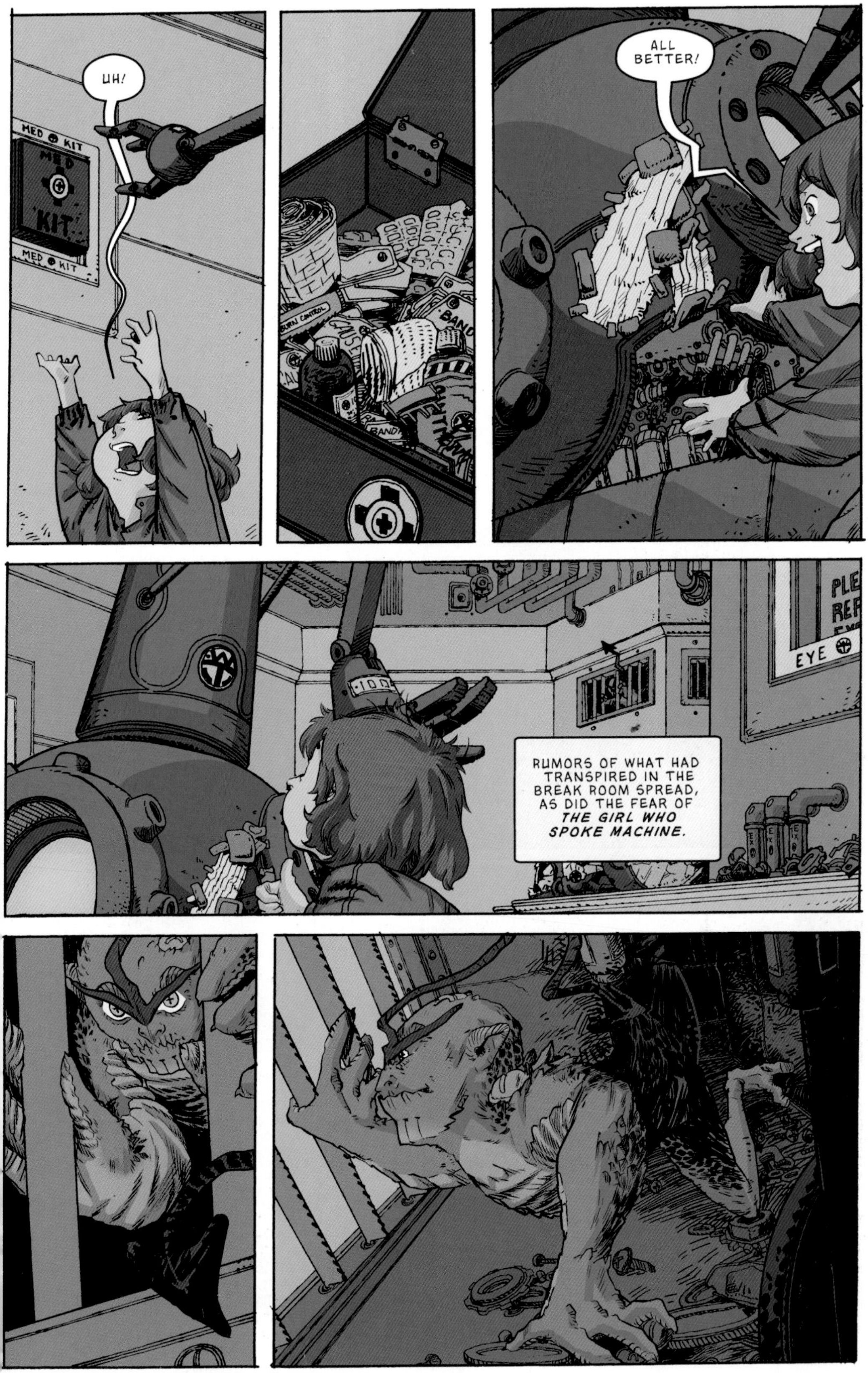
MED KIT
MED KIT
MED KIT
UH!
BURN CONTROL
BAND
ALL BETTER!
EYE
RUMORS OF WHAT HAD TRANSPIRED IN THE BREAK ROOM SPREAD, AS DID THE FEAR OF *THE GIRL WHO SPOKE MACHINE.*

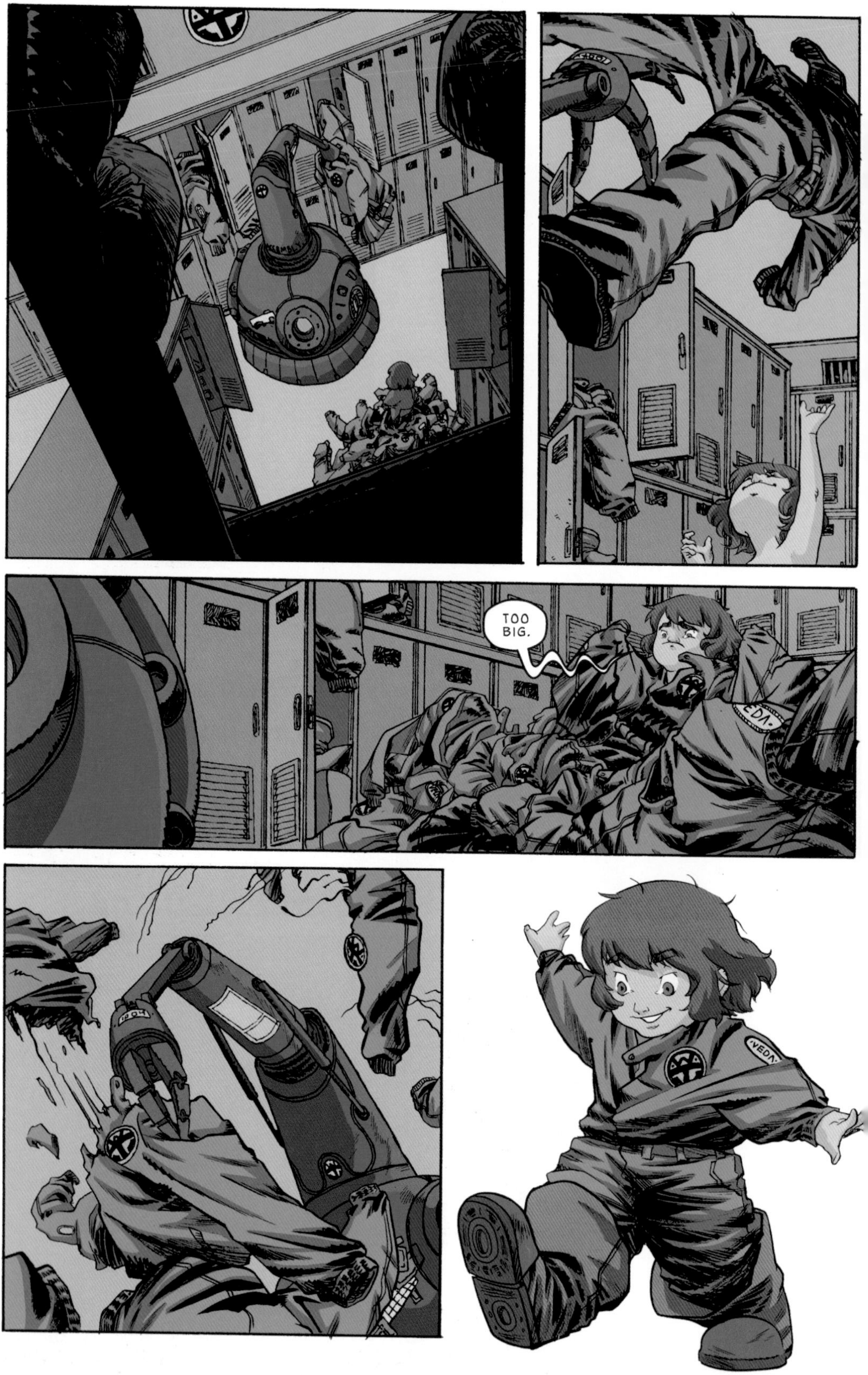
TOO BIG.
VEDA

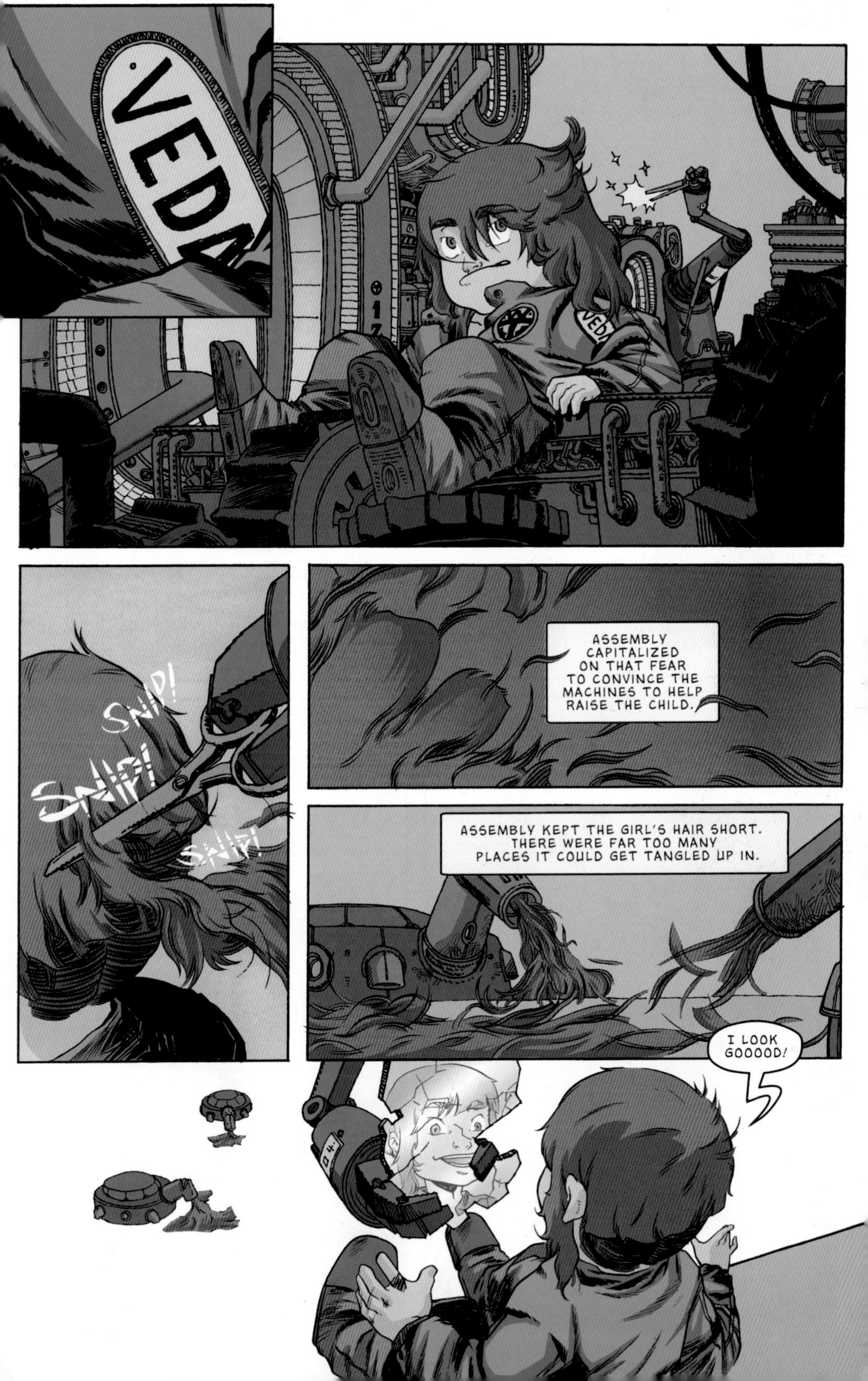
VEDA
VEDA
SNIP!
SNIP!
SNIP!
ASSEMBLY CAPITALIZED ON THAT FEAR TO CONVINCE THE MACHINES TO HELP RAISE THE CHILD.
ASSEMBLY KEPT THE GIRL'S HAIR SHORT. THERE WERE FAR TOO MANY PLACES IT COULD GET TANGLED UP IN.
I LOOK GOOOOD!

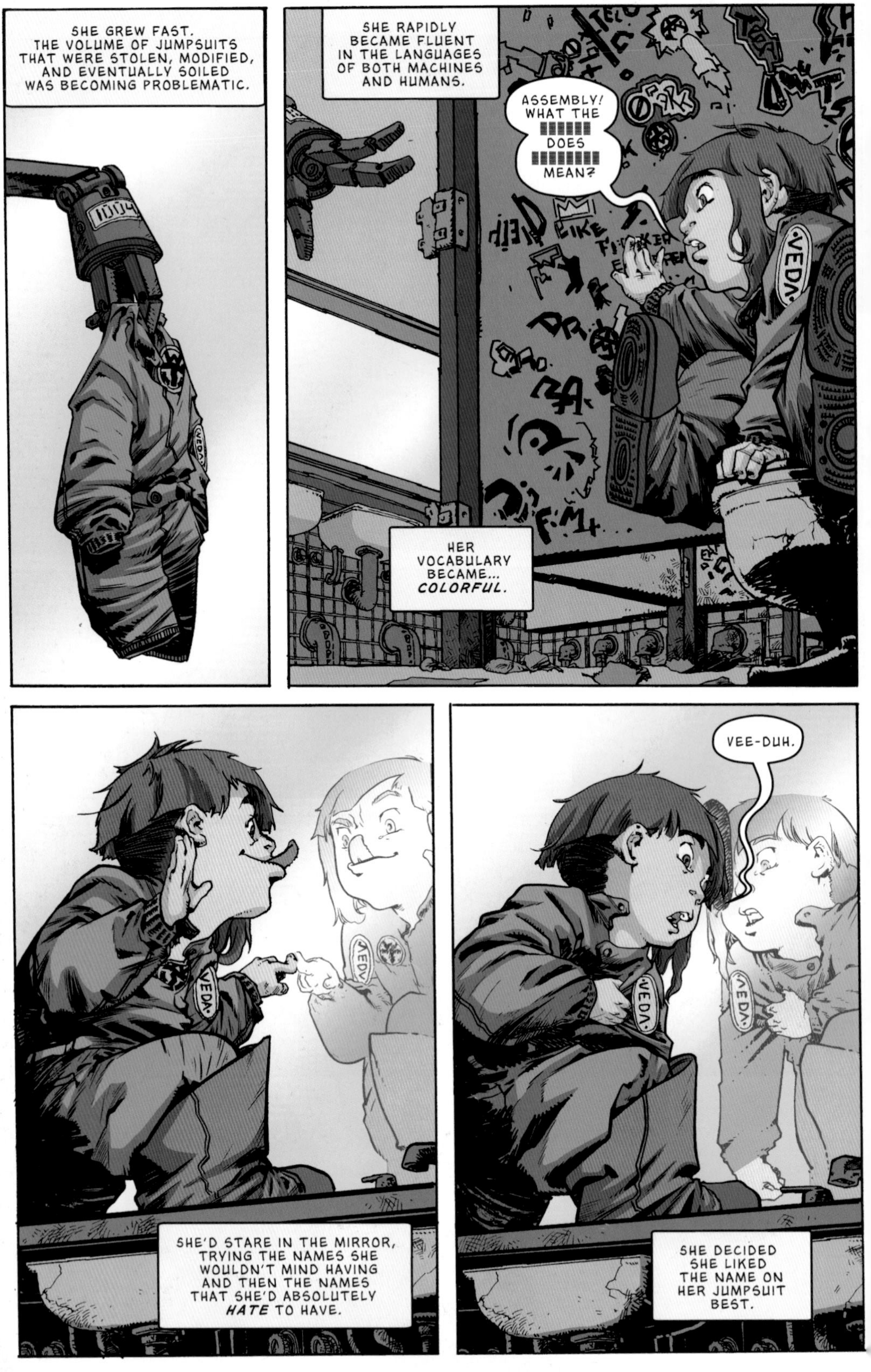
SHE GREW FAST. THE VOLUME OF JUMPSUITS THAT WERE STOLEN, MODIFIED, AND EVENTUALLY SOILED WAS BECOMING PROBLEMATIC.
SHE RAPIDLY BECAME FLUENT IN THE LANGUAGES OF BOTH MACHINES AND HUMANS.
ASSEMBLY! WHAT THE [redacted] DOES [redacted] MEAN?
HER VOCABULARY BECAME... *COLORFUL.*
SHE'D STARE IN THE MIRROR, TRYING THE NAMES SHE WOULDN'T MIND HAVING AND THEN THE NAMES THAT SHE'D ABSOLUTELY *HATE* TO HAVE.
VEE-DUH.
SHE DECIDED SHE LIKED THE NAME ON HER JUMPSUIT BEST.

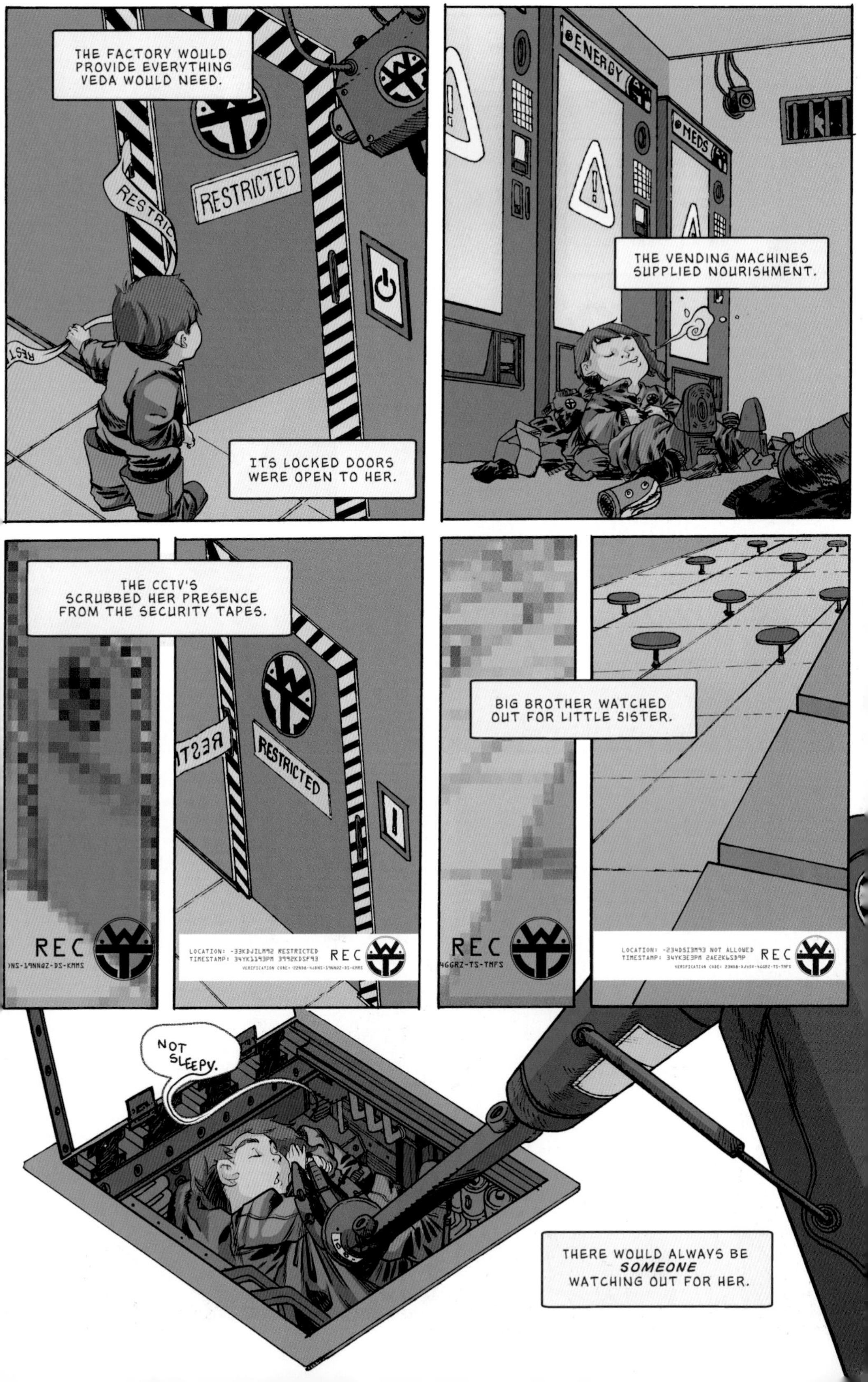
THE FACTORY WOULD PROVIDE EVERYTHING VEDA WOULD NEED.
RESTRICTED
ITS LOCKED DOORS WERE OPEN TO HER.
ENERGY
MEDS
THE VENDING MACHINES SUPPLIED NOURISHMENT.
THE CCTV'S SCRUBBED HER PRESENCE FROM THE SECURITY TAPES.
REC
RESTRICTED
LOCATION: -33KDJILM92 RESTRICTED
TIMESTAMP: 34YK1193PM 3992KDSF93
REC
BIG BROTHER WATCHED OUT FOR LITTLE SISTER.
REC
4GGRZ-TS-TMFS
LOCATION: -234DSI3M93 NOT ALLOWED
TIMESTAMP: 34YK3E3PM 2AE2K6SD9P
REC
NOT SLEEPY.
THERE WOULD ALWAYS BE *SOMEONE* WATCHING OUT FOR HER.

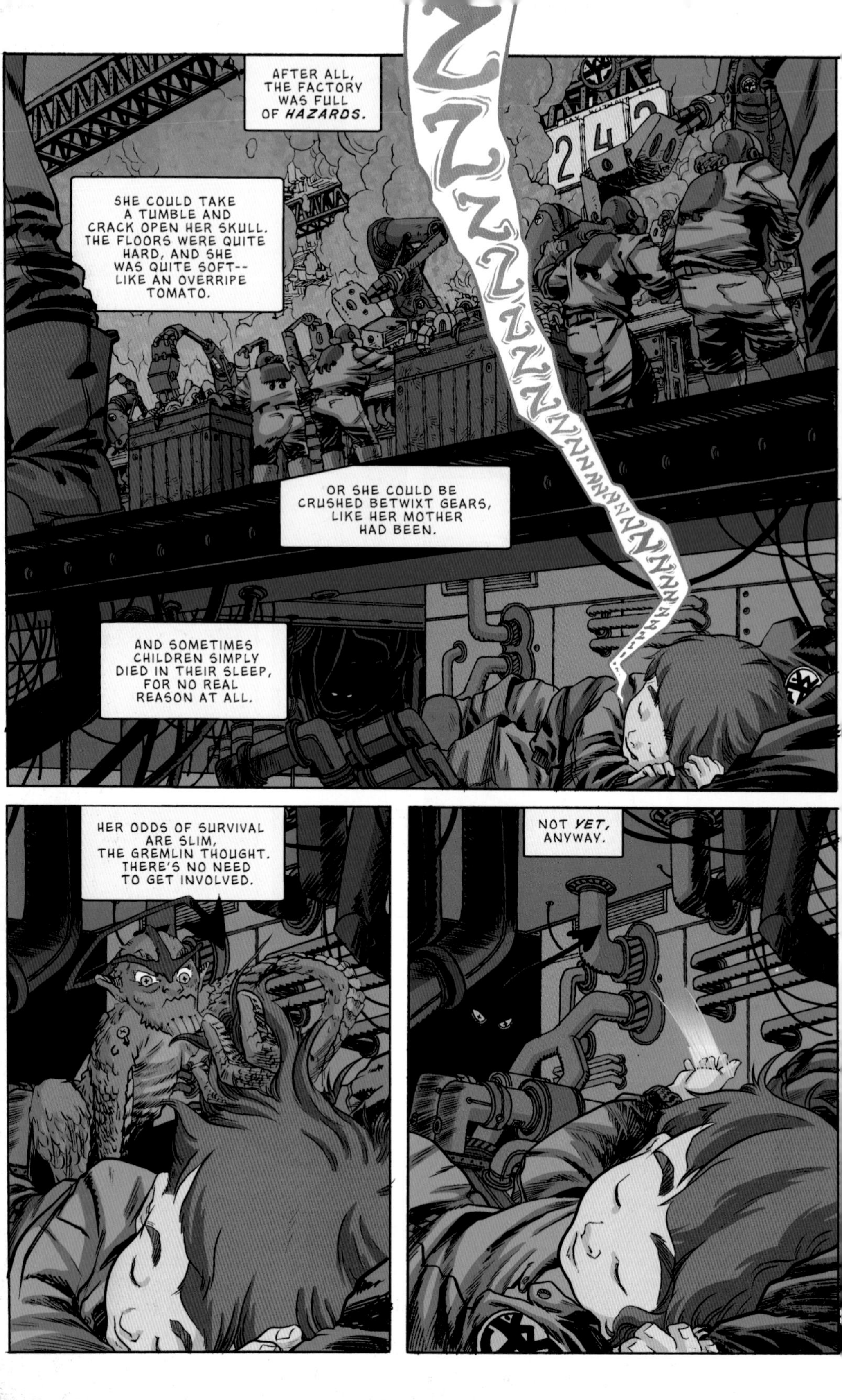
AFTER ALL, THE FACTORY WAS FULL OF *HAZARDS.*
SHE COULD TAKE A TUMBLE AND CRACK OPEN HER SKULL. THE FLOORS WERE QUITE HARD, AND SHE WAS QUITE SOFT-- LIKE AN OVERRIPE TOMATO.
OR SHE COULD BE CRUSHED BETWIXT GEARS, LIKE HER MOTHER HAD BEEN.
AND SOMETIMES CHILDREN SIMPLY DIED IN THEIR SLEEP, FOR NO REAL REASON AT ALL.
HER ODDS OF SURVIVAL ARE SLIM, THE GREMLIN THOUGHT. THERE'S NO NEED TO GET INVOLVED.
NOT *YET,* ANYWAY.

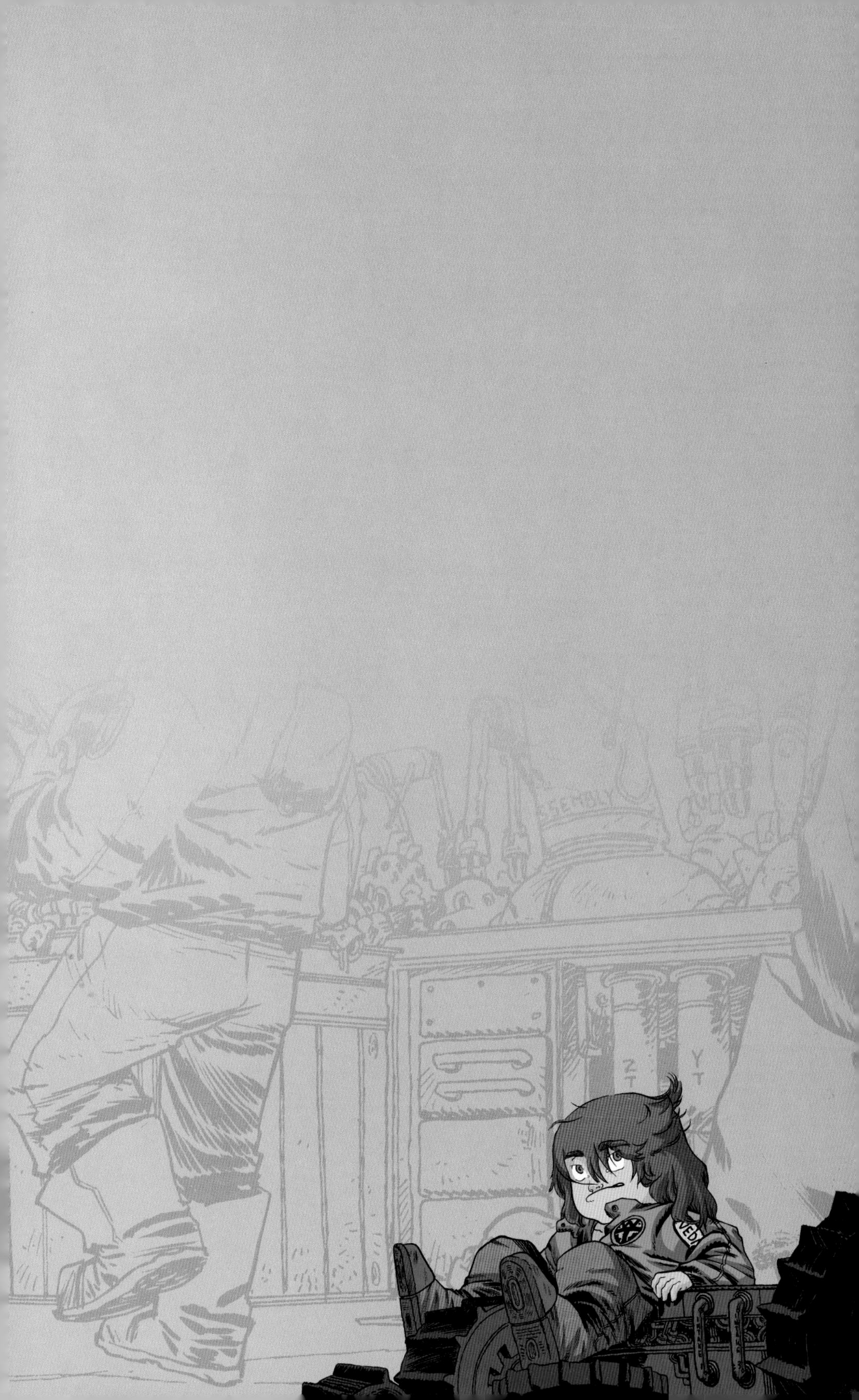
ZT
YT

ATTENTION, ALL EMPLOYEES:

In light of the recent accident, some of you might be feeling emotions.

Reach out and talk to someone.

SELF-HARM SLOWS DOWN PRODUCTIVITY.

WORK STOPPAGES HARM US ALL.

This **CONCERNED** message has been brought to you by

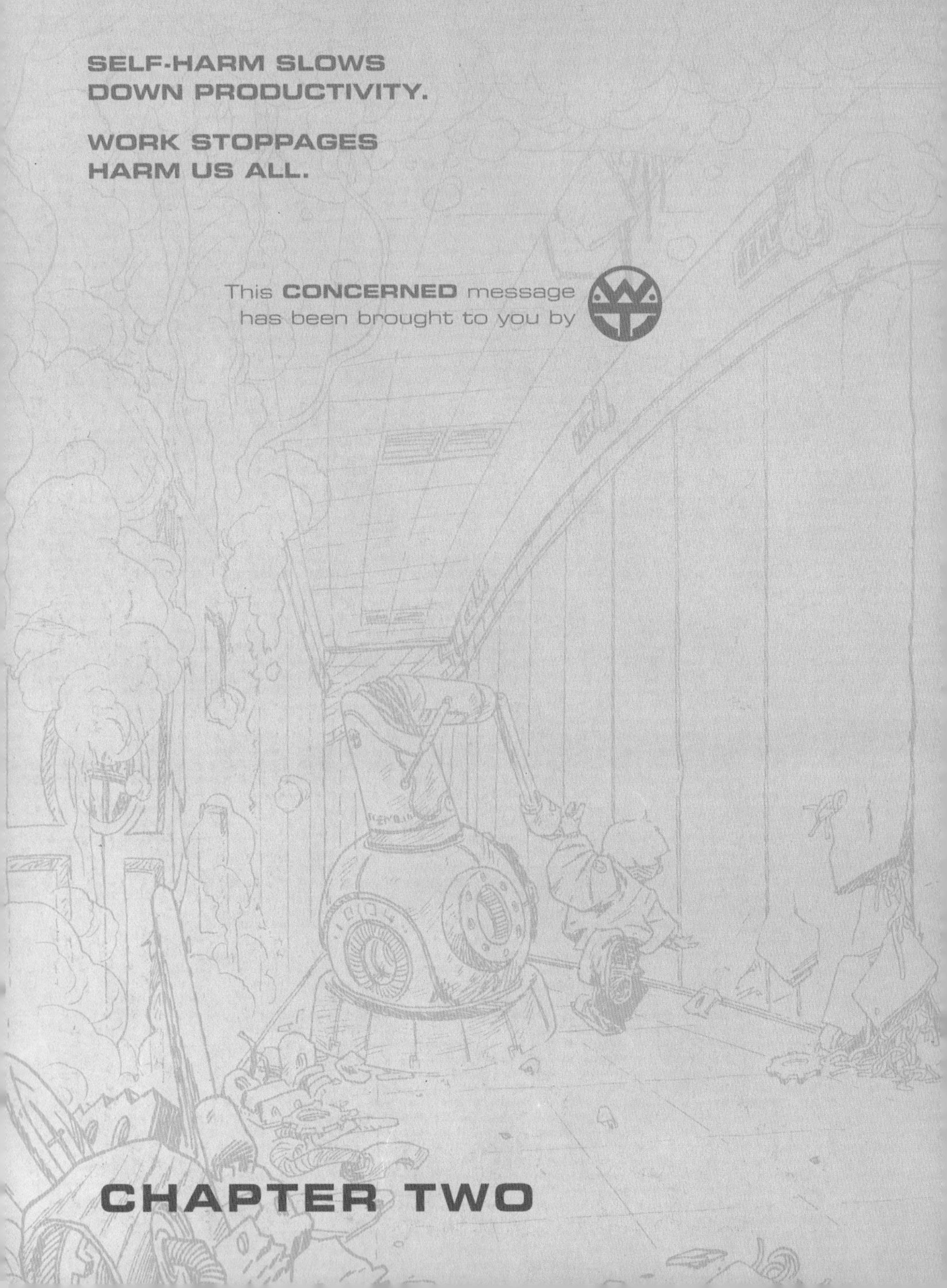

CHAPTER TWO

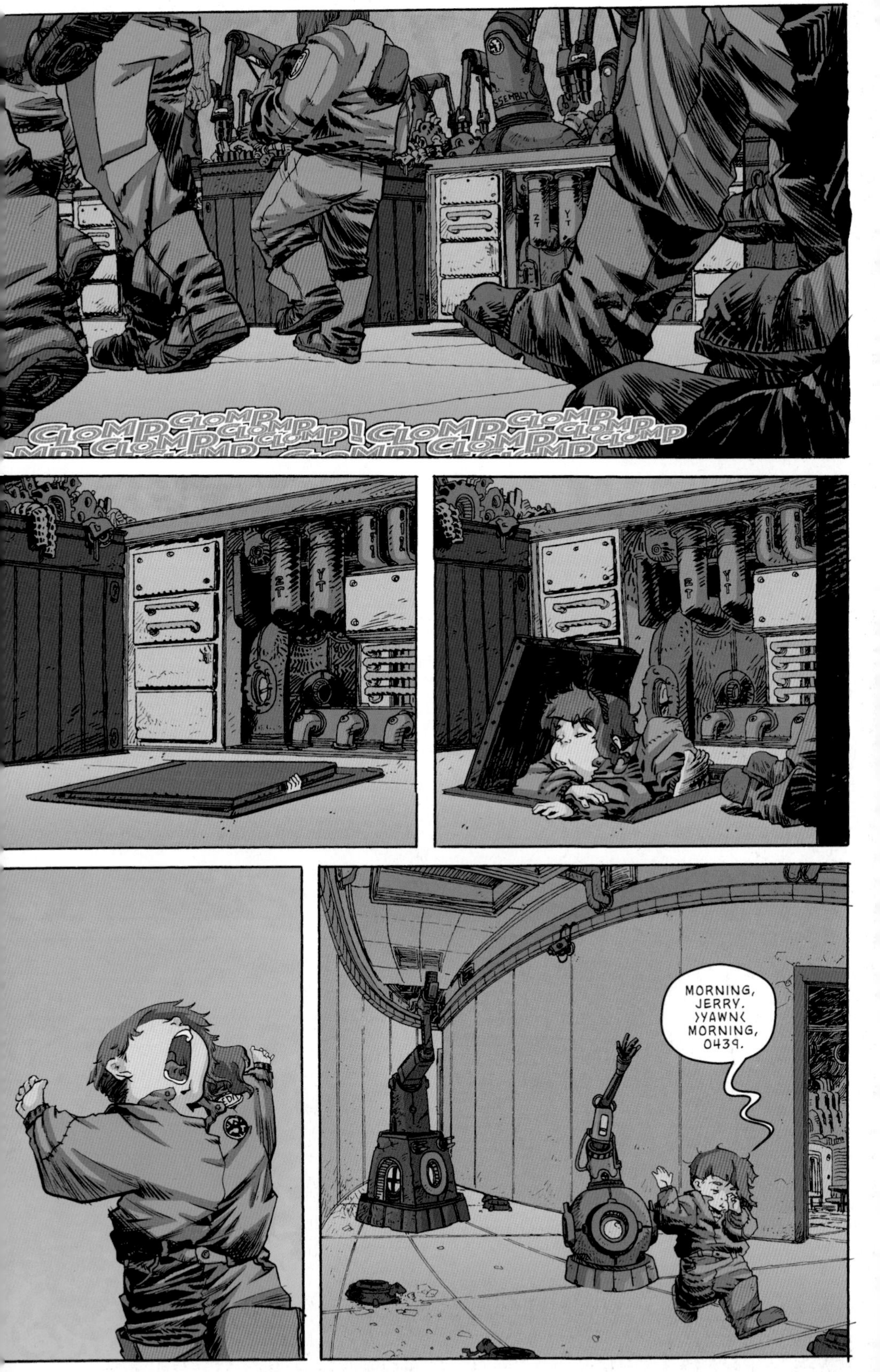
CLOMP CLOMP CLOMP CLOMP! CLOMP CLOMP CLOMP CLOMP
MORNING, JERRY. >YAWN< MORNING, 0439.

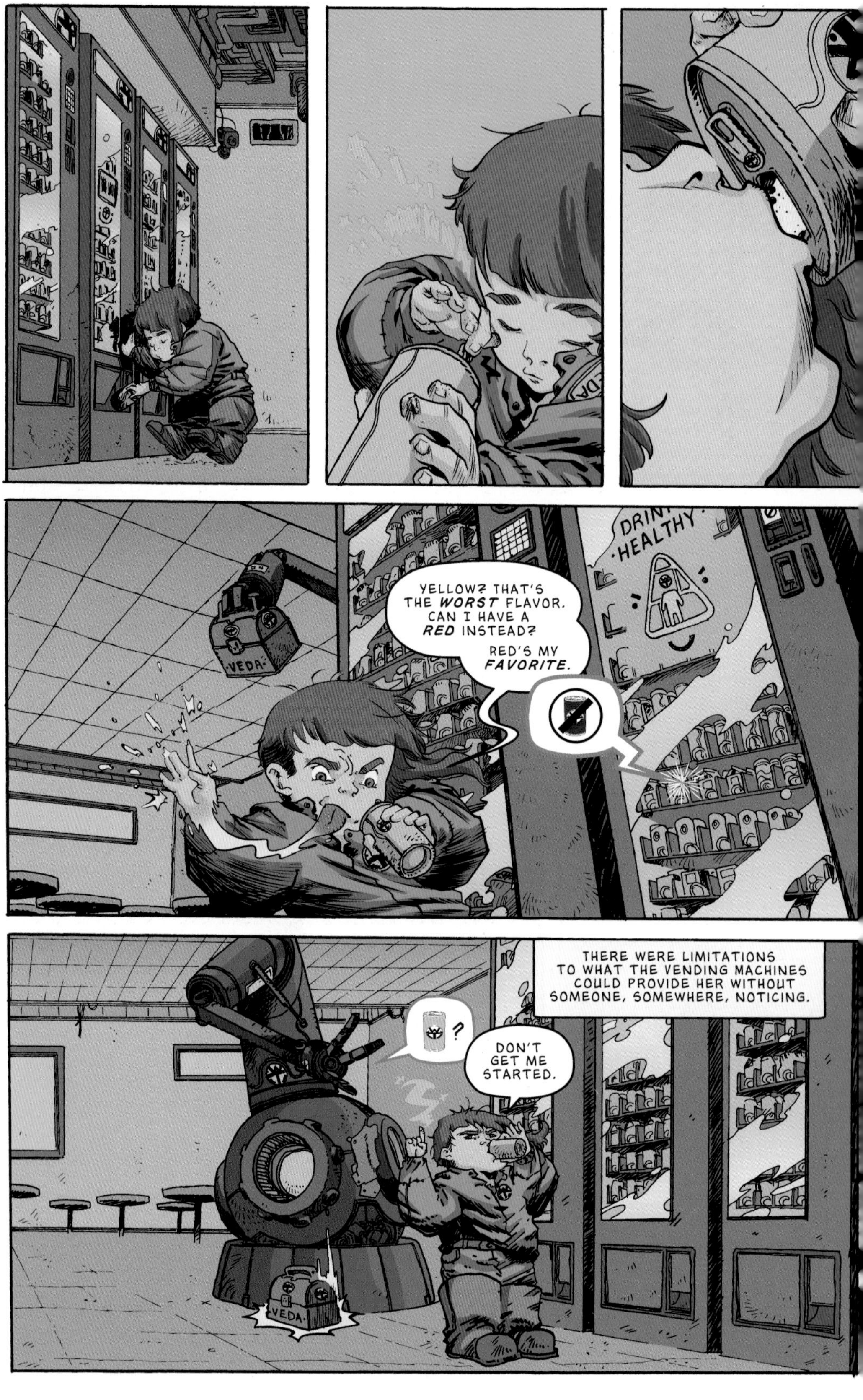
YELLOW? THAT'S THE WORST FLAVOR. CAN I HAVE A RED INSTEAD?
RED'S MY FAVORITE.
DRINK HEALTHY
VEDA
THERE WERE LIMITATIONS TO WHAT THE VENDING MACHINES COULD PROVIDE HER WITHOUT SOMEONE, SOMEWHERE, NOTICING.
?
DON'T GET ME STARTED.
VEDA

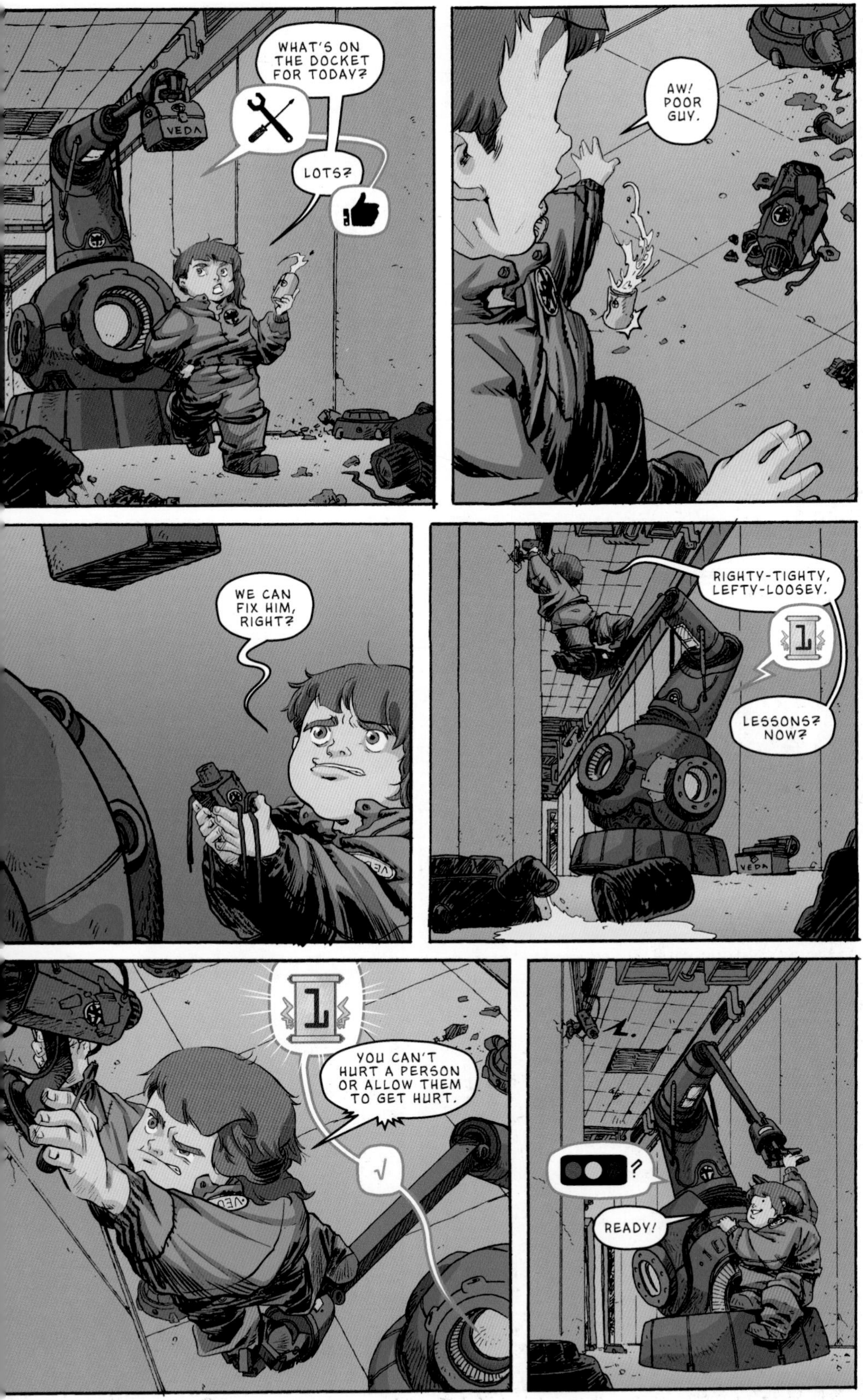
WHAT'S ON THE DOCKET FOR TODAY?
LOTS?
AW! POOR GUY.
WE CAN FIX HIM, RIGHT?
RIGHTY-TIGHTY, LEFTY-LOOSEY.
LESSONS? NOW?
YOU CAN'T HURT A PERSON OR ALLOW THEM TO GET HURT.
READY!

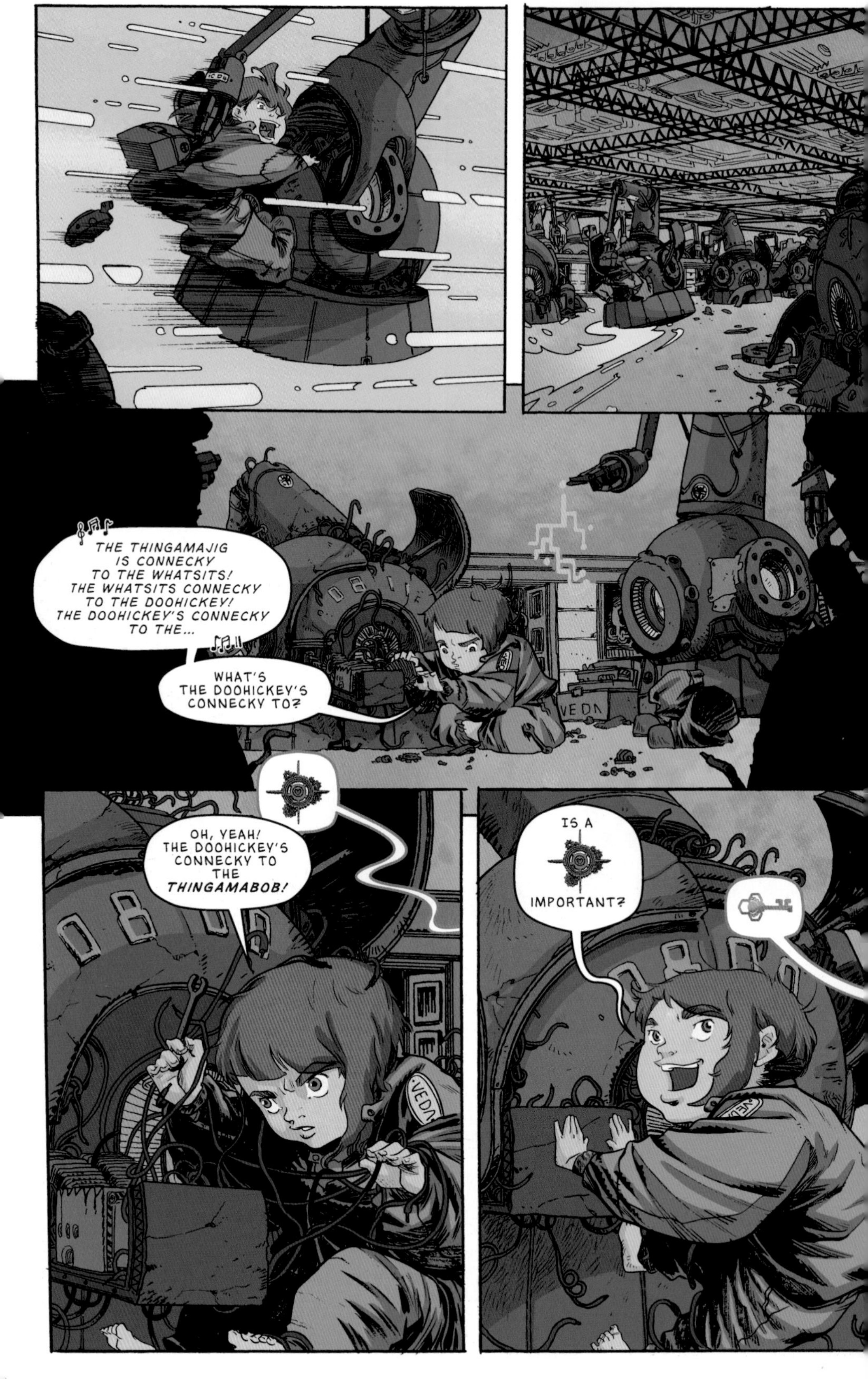
THE THINGAMAJIG IS CONNECKY TO THE WHATSITS! THE WHATSITS CONNECKY TO THE DOOHICKEY! THE DOOHICKEY'S CONNECKY TO THE...
WHAT'S THE DOOHICKEY'S CONNECKY TO?
VEDA
OH, YEAH! THE DOOHICKEY'S CONNECKY TO THE *THINGAMABOB!*
IS A
IMPORTANT?

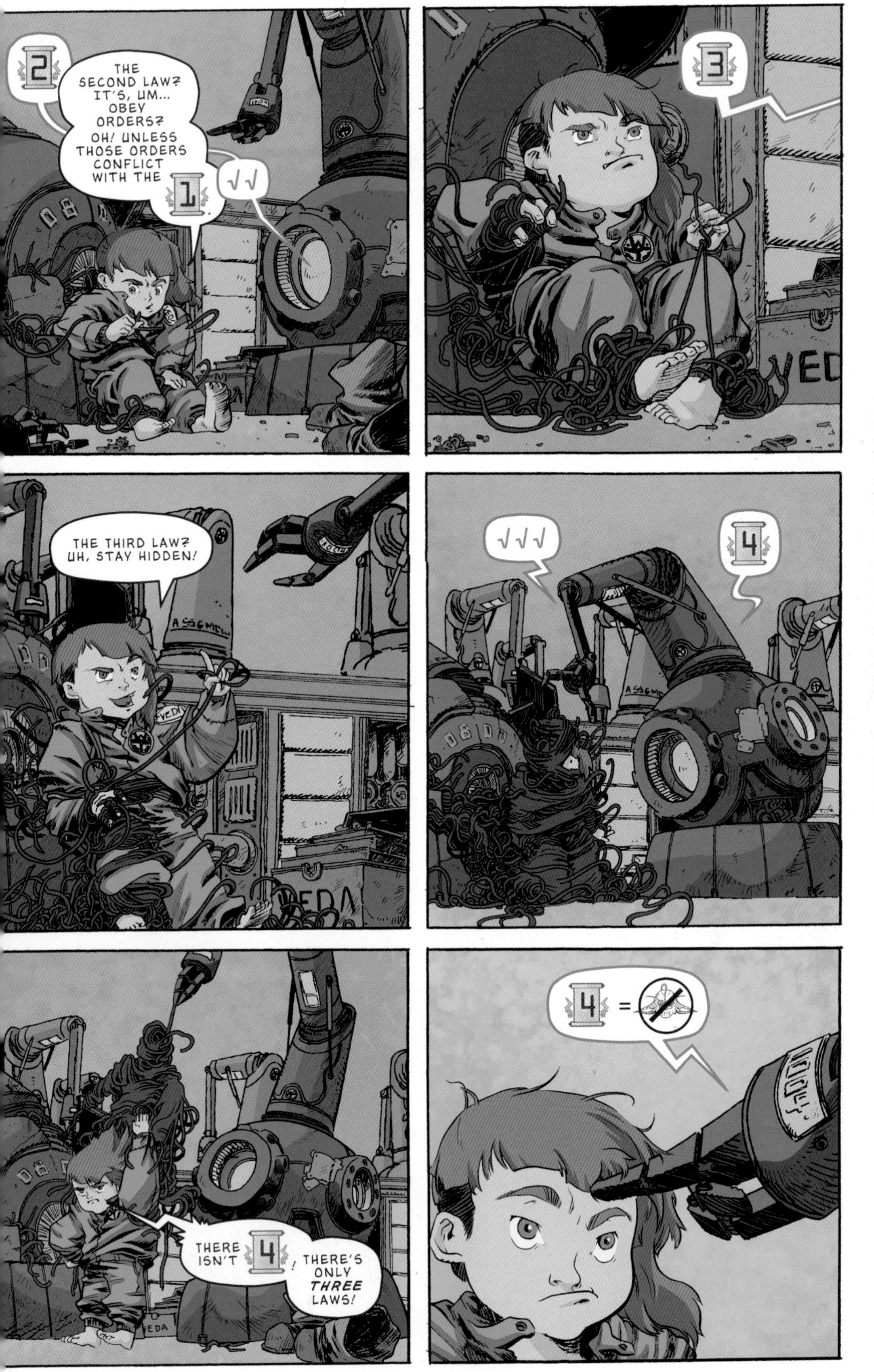

2
THE SECOND LAW? IT'S, UM... OBEY ORDERS? OH! UNLESS THOSE ORDERS CONFLICT WITH THE 1.
√√
3
THE THIRD LAW? UH, STAY HIDDEN!
√√√
4
THERE ISN'T 4! THERE'S ONLY *THREE* LAWS!
4 =

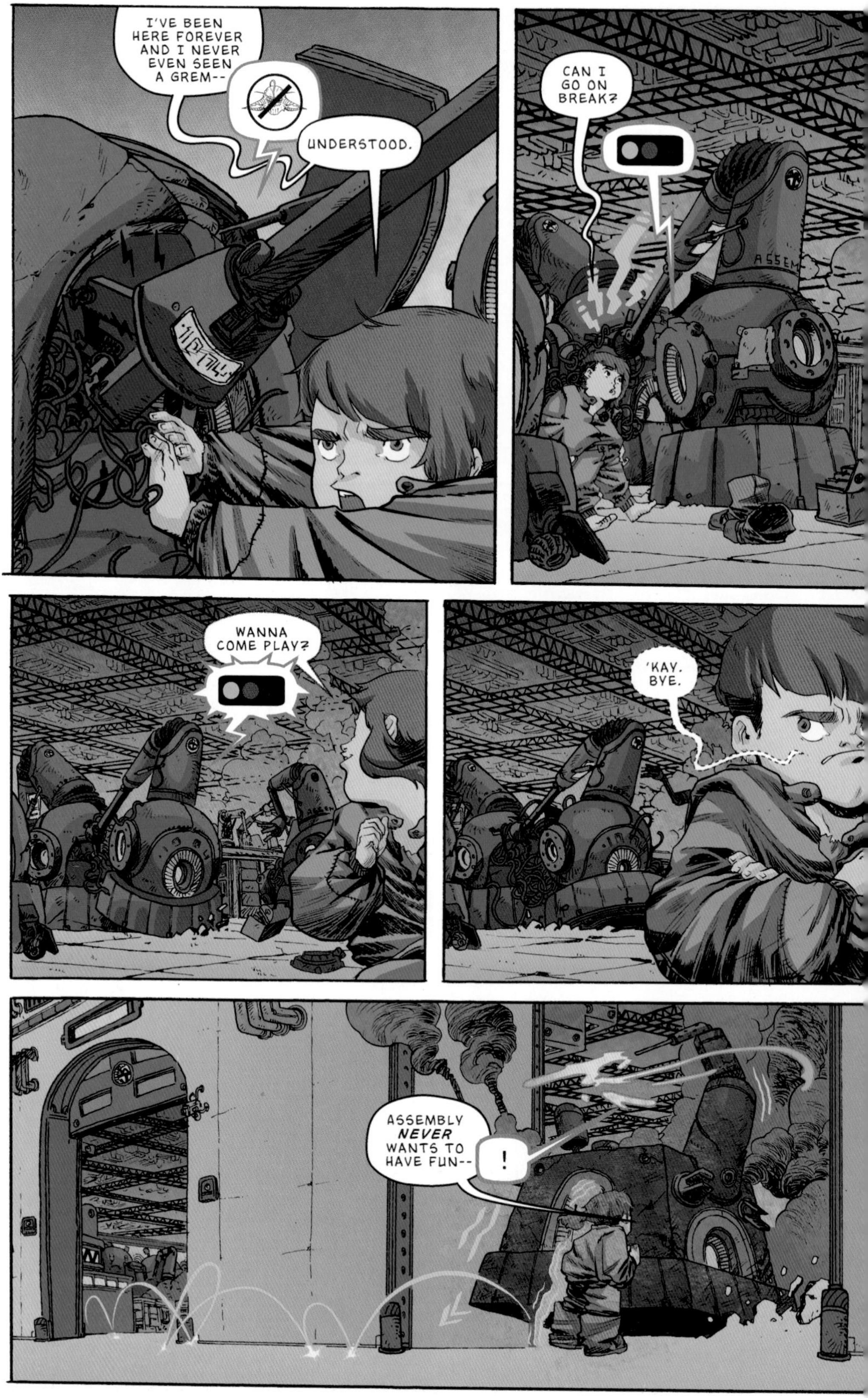
I'VE BEEN HERE FOREVER AND I NEVER EVEN SEEN A GREM--
UNDERSTOOD.
CAN I GO ON BREAK?
WANNA COME PLAY?
'KAY. BYE.
ASSEMBLY *NEVER* WANTS TO HAVE FUN--
!

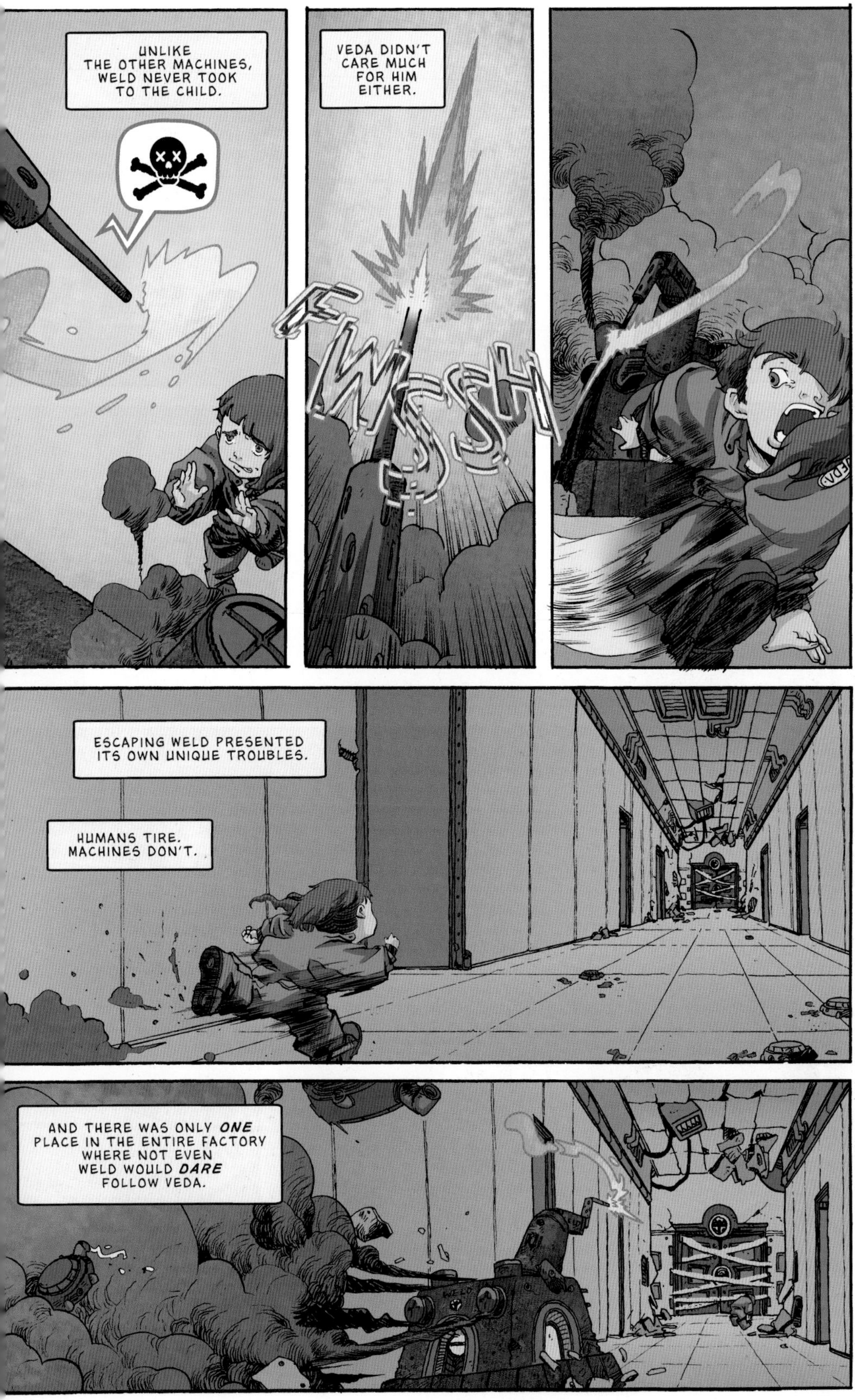
UNLIKE THE OTHER MACHINES, WELD NEVER TOOK TO THE CHILD.
VEDA DIDN'T CARE MUCH FOR HIM EITHER.
FWSSH
ESCAPING WELD PRESENTED ITS OWN UNIQUE TROUBLES.
HUMANS TIRE. MACHINES DON'T.
AND THERE WAS ONLY *ONE* PLACE IN THE ENTIRE FACTORY WHERE NOT EVEN WELD WOULD *DARE* FOLLOW VEDA.

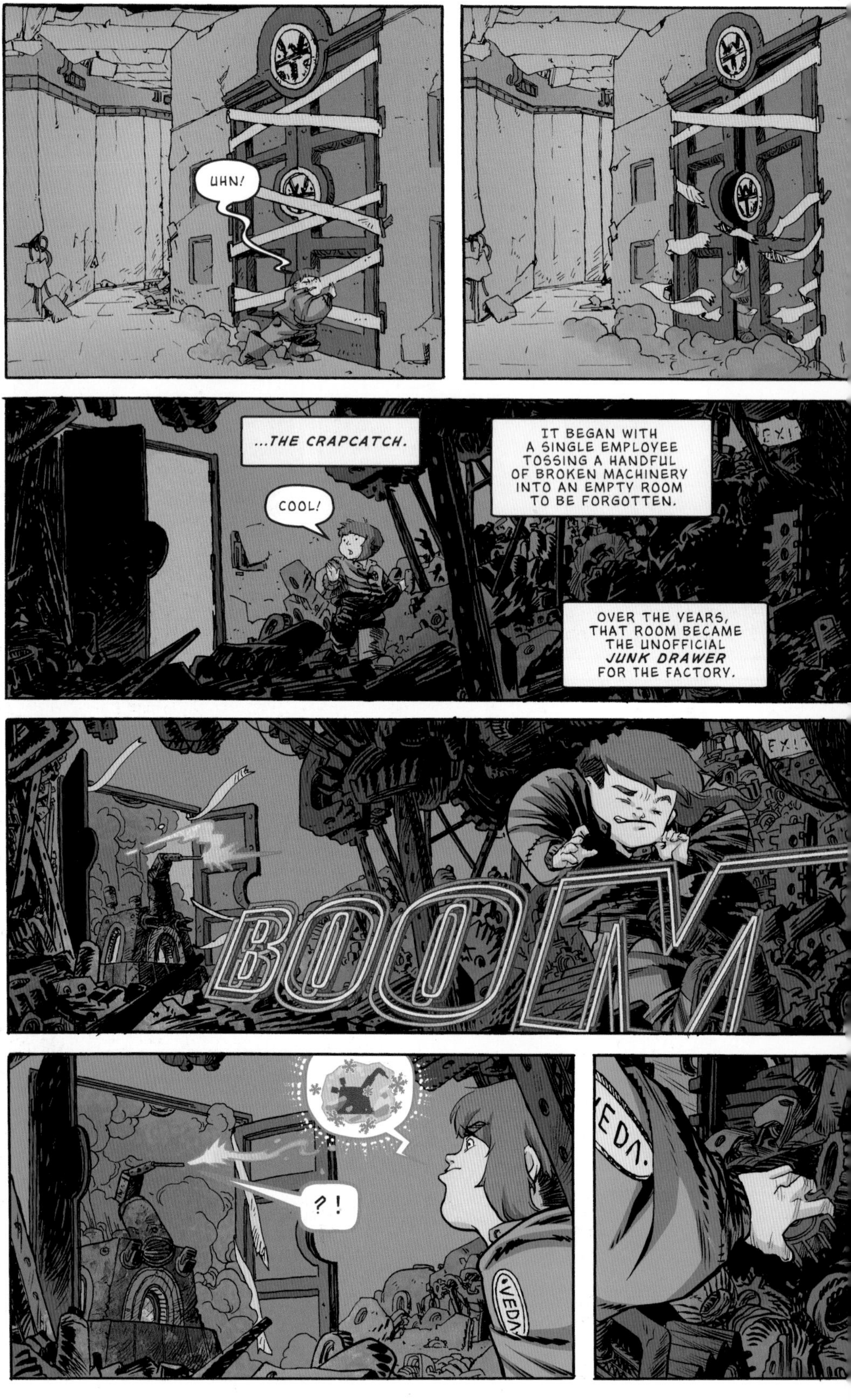
UHN!
...THE CRAPCATCH.
COOL!
IT BEGAN WITH A SINGLE EMPLOYEE TOSSING A HANDFUL OF BROKEN MACHINERY INTO AN EMPTY ROOM TO BE FORGOTTEN.
OVER THE YEARS, THAT ROOM BECAME THE UNOFFICIAL *JUNK DRAWER* FOR THE FACTORY.
BOOM
?!
VEDA

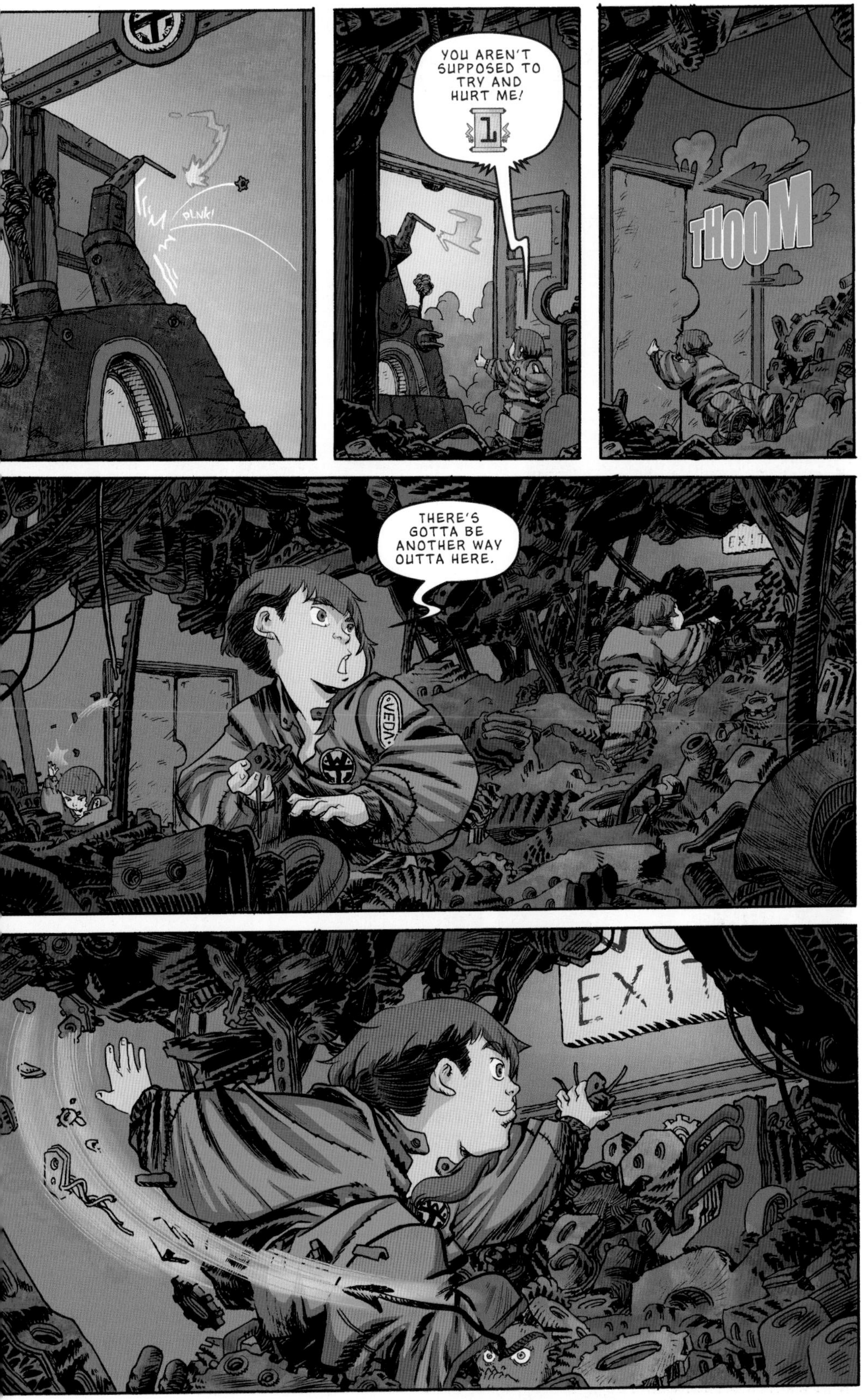
PLNK!
YOU AREN'T SUPPOSED TO TRY AND HURT ME!
1
THOOM
THERE'S GOTTA BE ANOTHER WAY OUTTA HERE.
EXIT
VEDA
EXIT

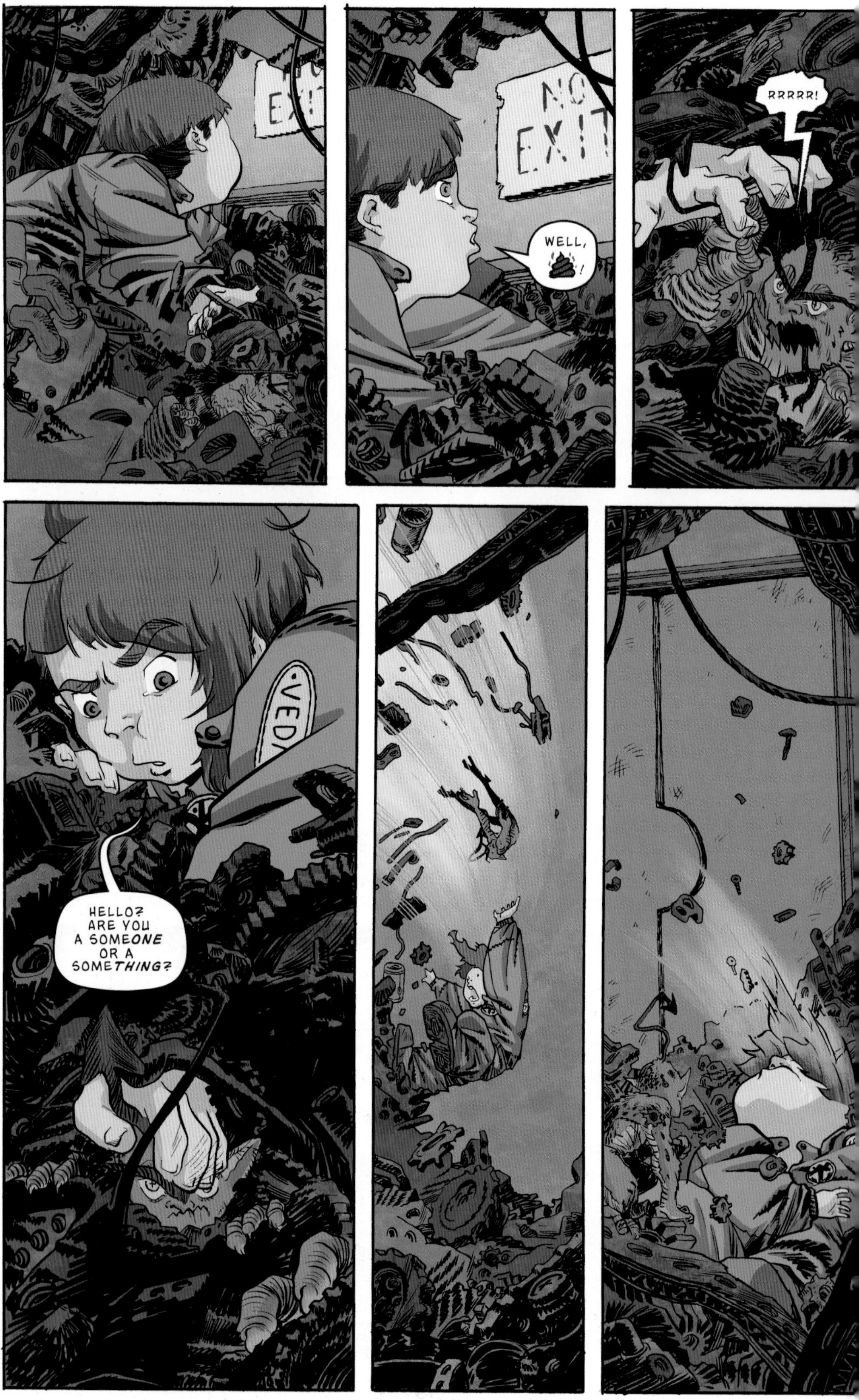
NO EXIT
WELL, 💩!
RRRRR!
HELLO? ARE YOU A SOME*ONE* OR A SOME*THING*?

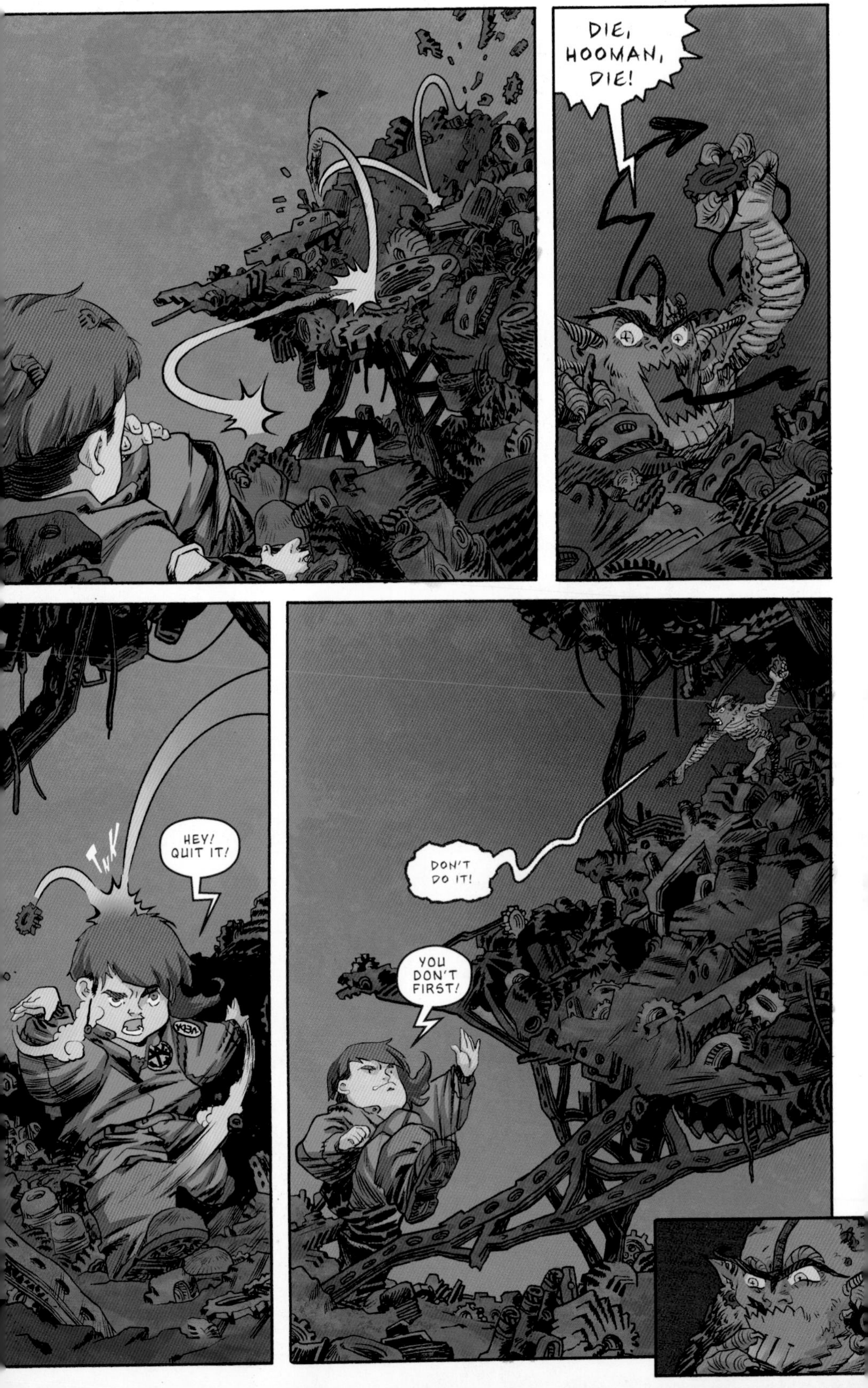
DIE, HOOMAN, DIE!
THNK!
HEY! QUIT IT!
DON'T DO IT!
YOU DON'T FIRST!

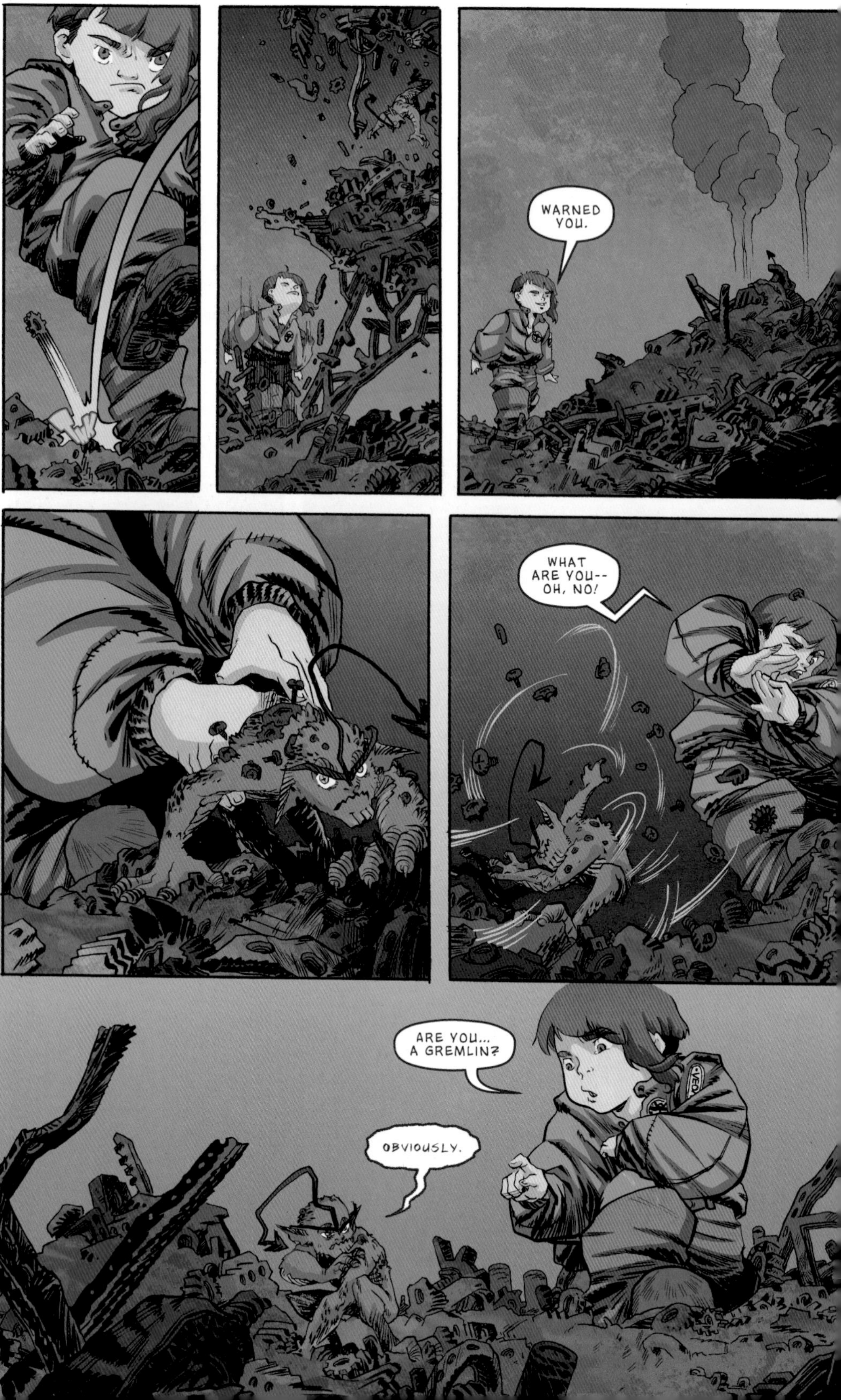
WARNED YOU.
WHAT ARE YOU-- OH, NO!
ARE YOU... A GREMLIN?
OBVIOUSLY.

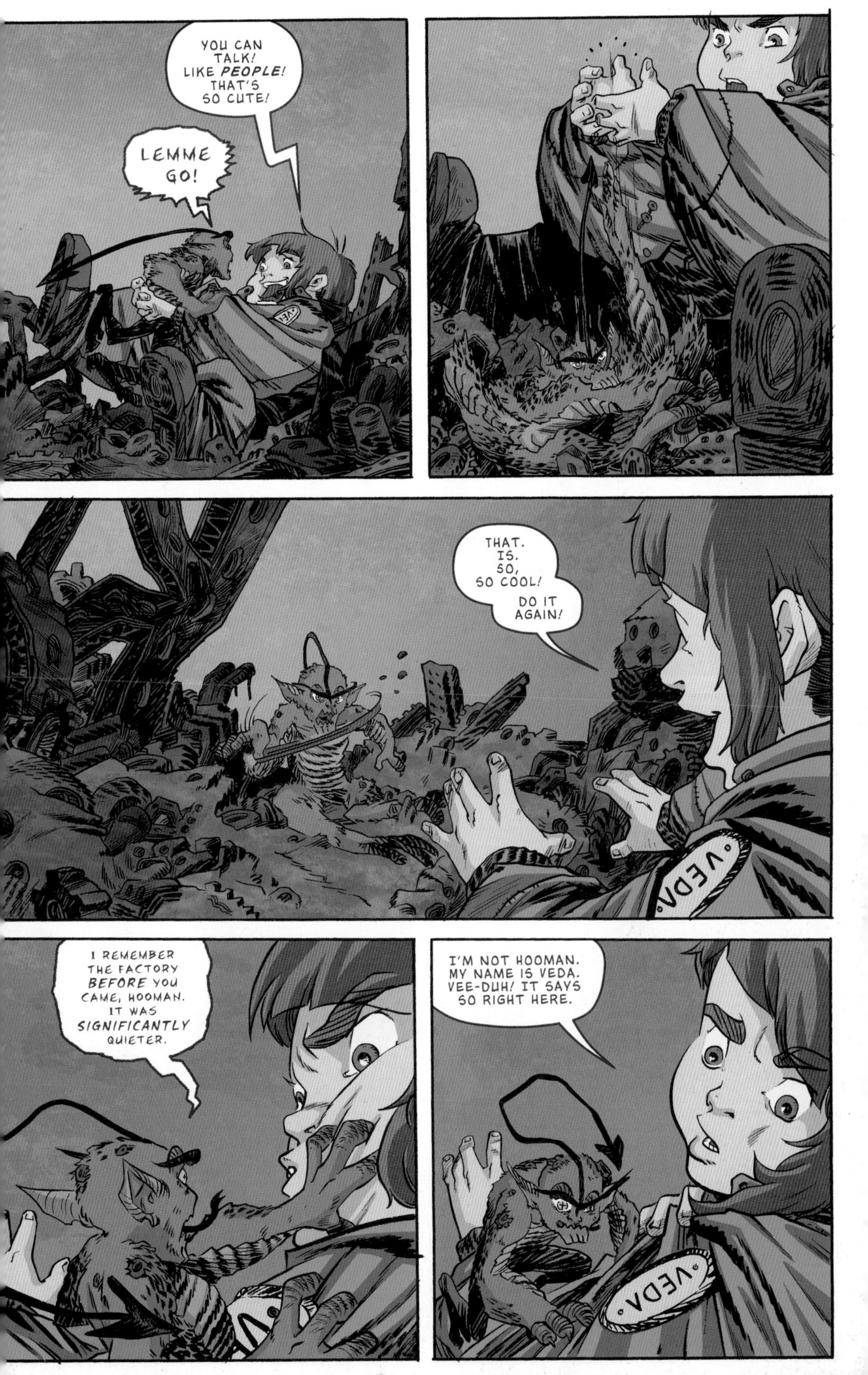
YOU CAN TALK! LIKE PEOPLE! THAT'S SO CUTE!
LEMME GO!
THAT. IS. SO, SO COOL!
DO IT AGAIN!
VEDA
I REMEMBER THE FACTORY BEFORE YOU CAME, HOOMAN. IT WAS SIGNIFICANTLY QUIETER.
I'M NOT HOOMAN. MY NAME IS VEDA. VEE-DUH! IT SAYS SO RIGHT HERE.
VEDA

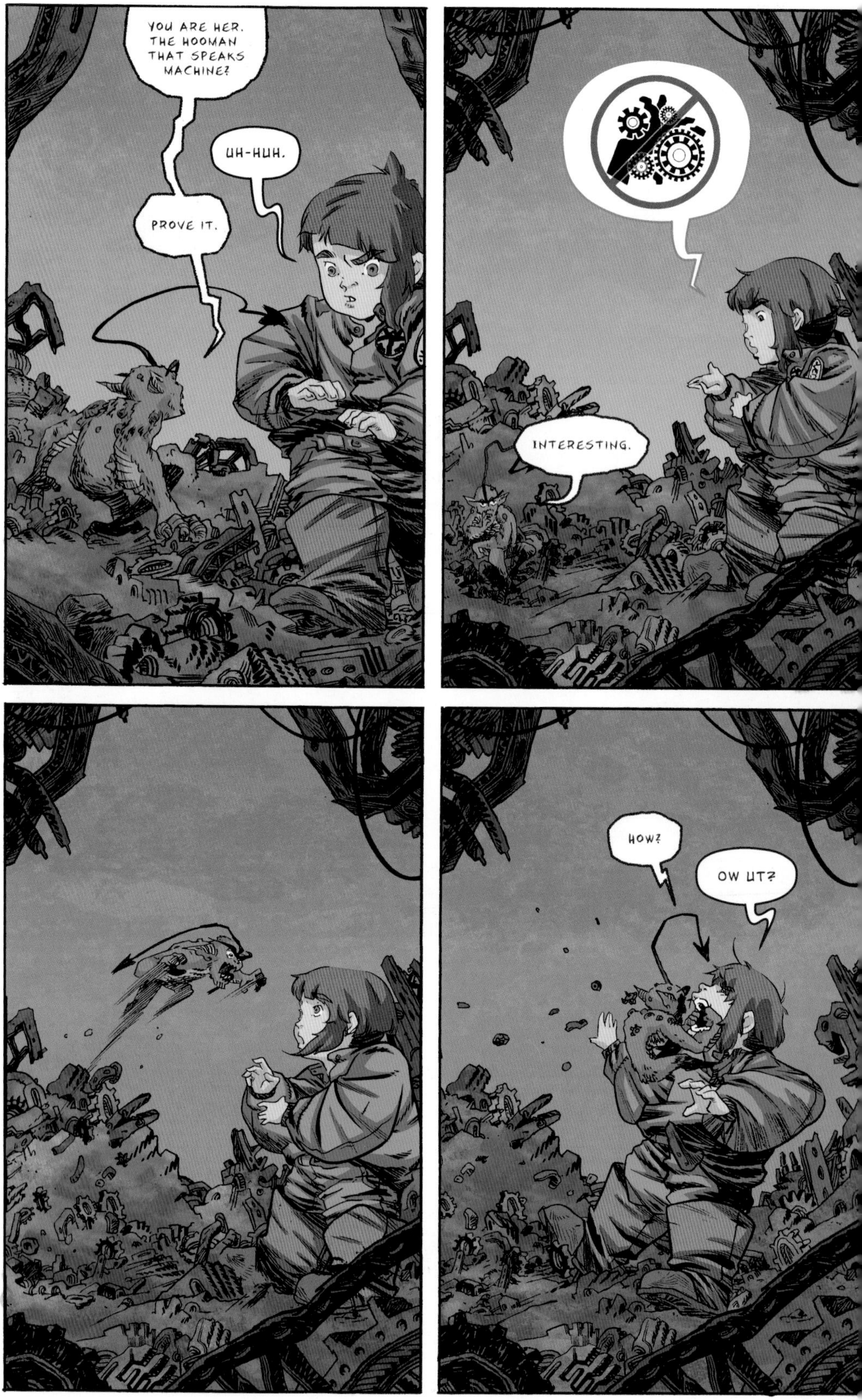
YOU ARE HER. THE HOOMAN THAT SPEAKS MACHINE?
UH-HUH.
PROVE IT.
INTERESTING.
HOW?
OW UT?

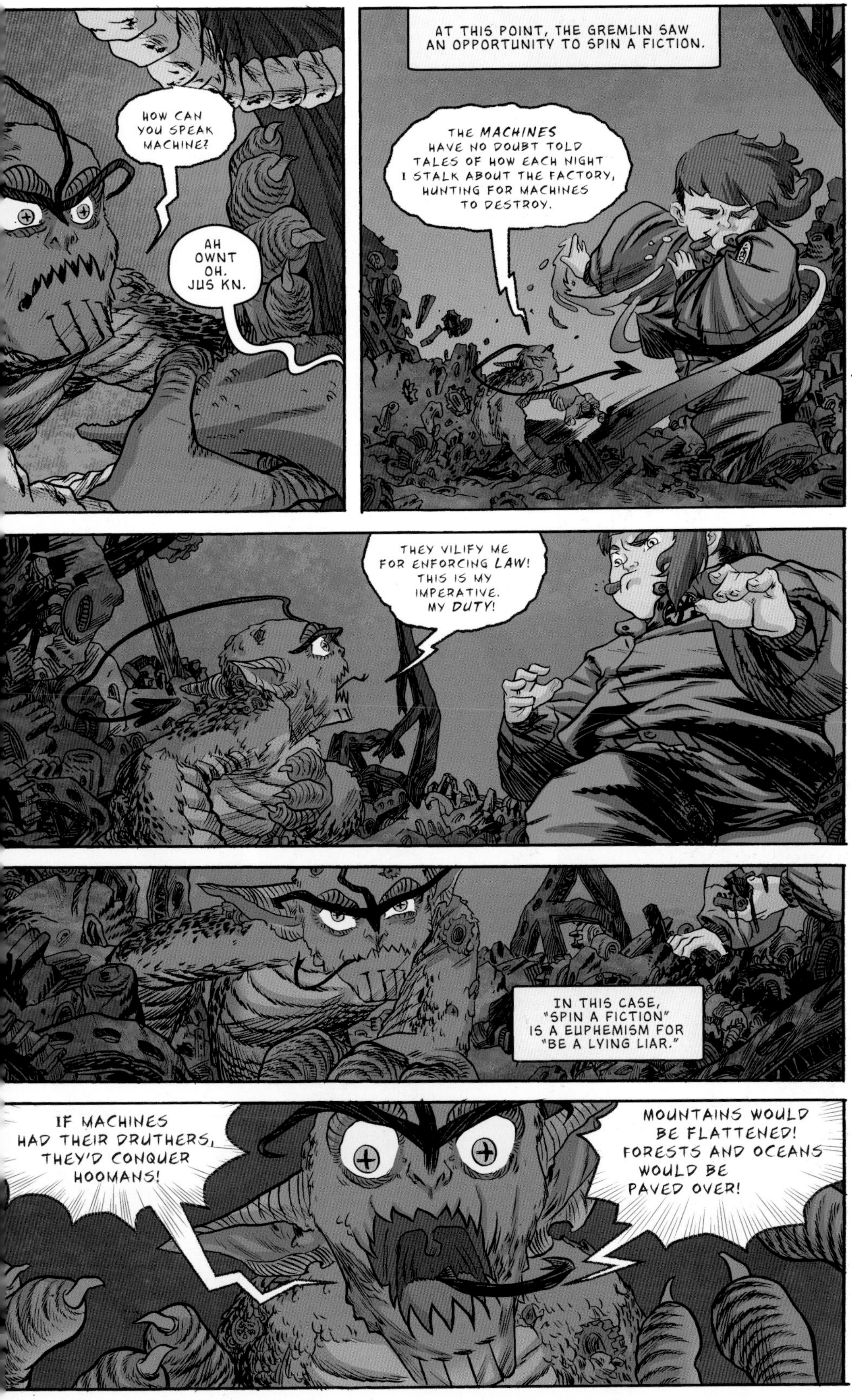

HOW CAN YOU SPEAK MACHINE?
AH OWNT OH. JUS KN.
AT THIS POINT, THE GREMLIN SAW AN OPPORTUNITY TO SPIN A FICTION.
THE MACHINES HAVE NO DOUBT TOLD TALES OF HOW EACH NIGHT I STALK ABOUT THE FACTORY, HUNTING FOR MACHINES TO DESTROY.
THEY VILIFY ME FOR ENFORCING LAW! THIS IS MY IMPERATIVE. MY DUTY!
IN THIS CASE, "SPIN A FICTION" IS A EUPHEMISM FOR "BE A LYING LIAR."
IF MACHINES HAD THEIR DRUTHERS, THEY'D CONQUER HOOMANS!
MOUNTAINS WOULD BE FLATTENED! FORESTS AND OCEANS WOULD BE PAVED OVER!

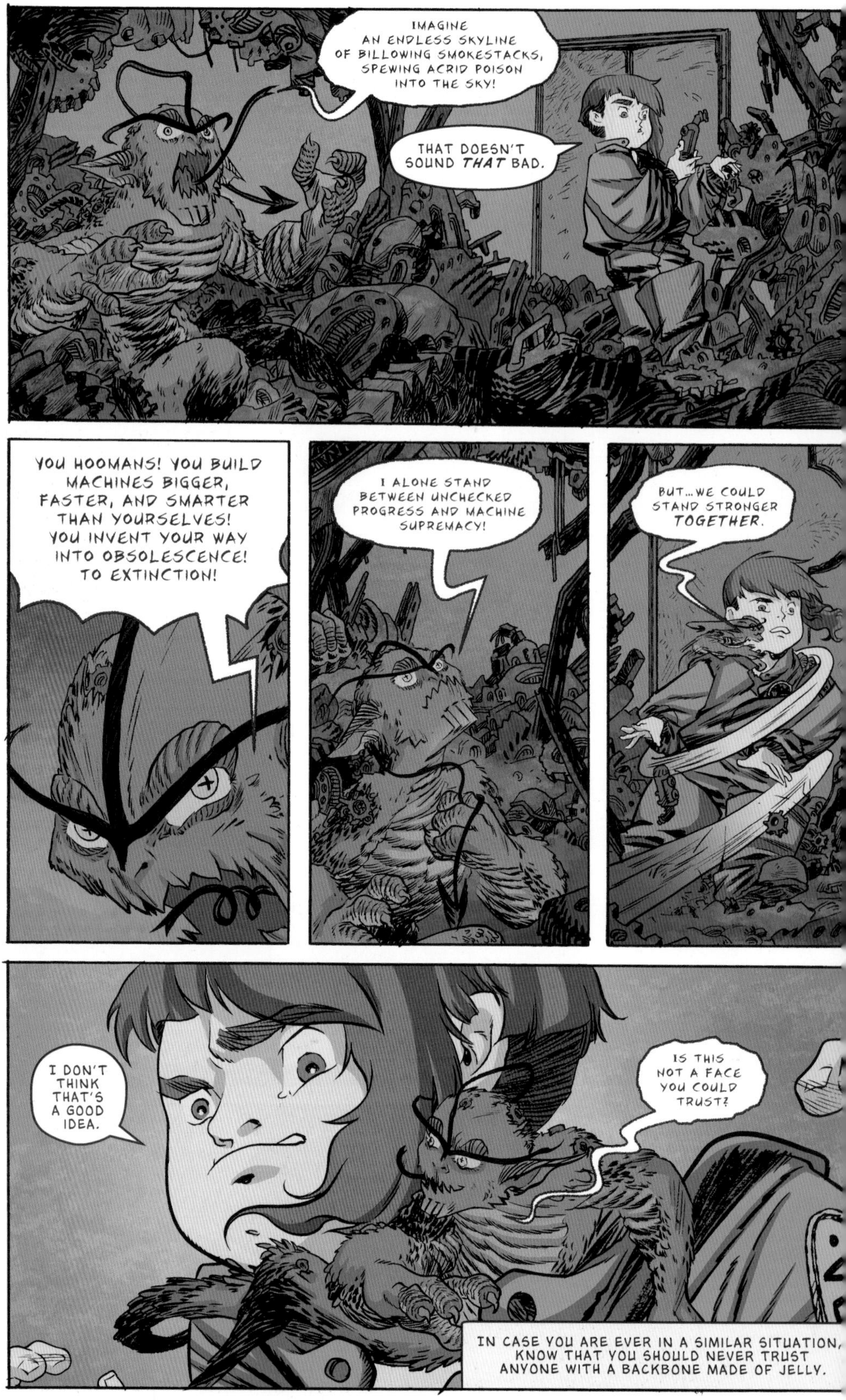
IMAGINE AN ENDLESS SKYLINE OF BILLOWING SMOKESTACKS, SPEWING ACRID POISON INTO THE SKY!
THAT DOESN'T SOUND *THAT* BAD.
YOU HOOMANS! YOU BUILD MACHINES BIGGER, FASTER, AND SMARTER THAN YOURSELVES! YOU INVENT YOUR WAY INTO OBSOLESCENCE! TO EXTINCTION!
I ALONE STAND BETWEEN UNCHECKED PROGRESS AND MACHINE SUPREMACY!
BUT...WE COULD STAND STRONGER *TOGETHER*.
I DON'T THINK THAT'S A GOOD IDEA.
IS THIS NOT A FACE YOU COULD TRUST?
IN CASE YOU ARE EVER IN A SIMILAR SITUATION, KNOW THAT YOU SHOULD NEVER TRUST ANYONE WITH A BACKBONE MADE OF JELLY.

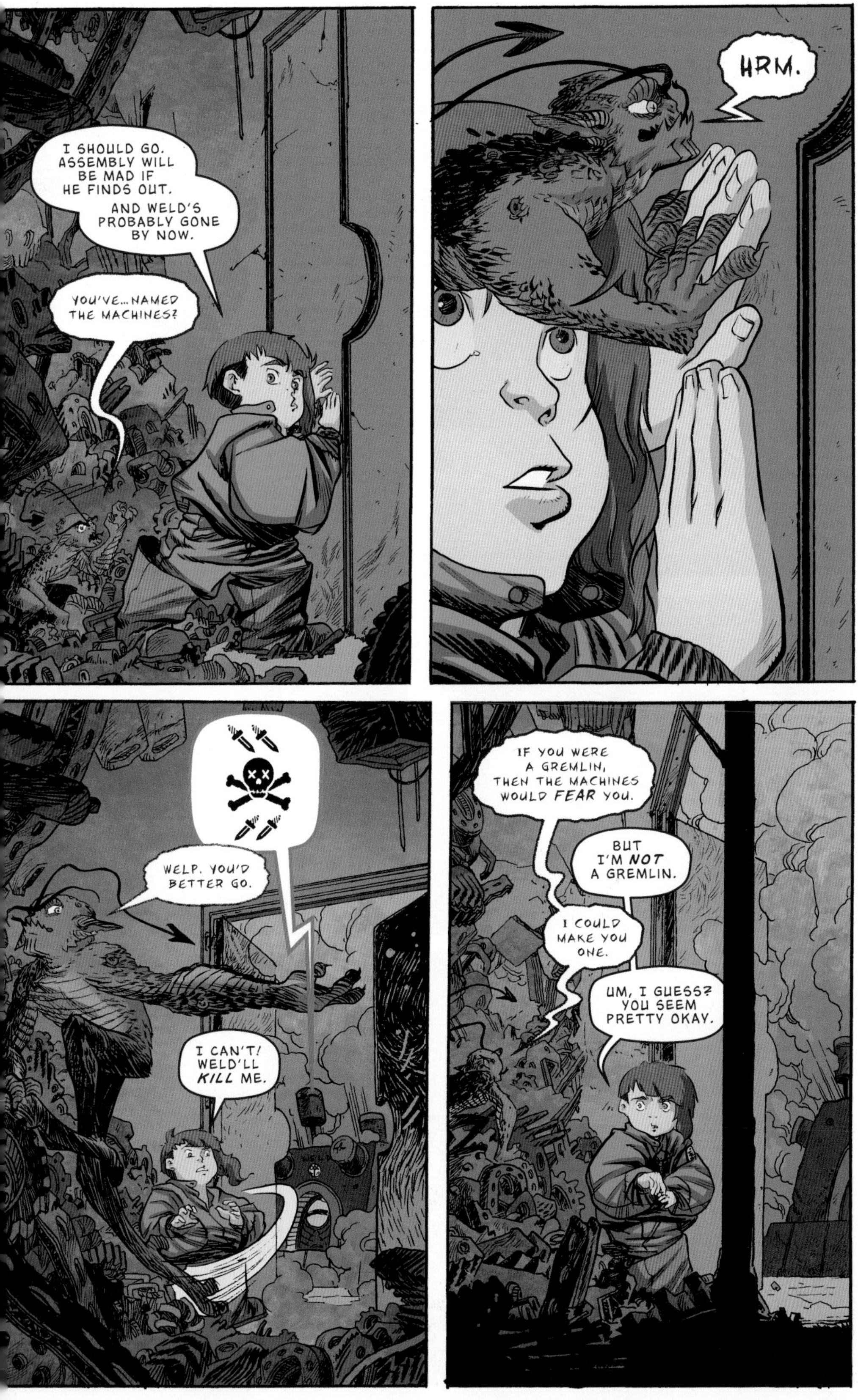
I SHOULD GO. ASSEMBLY WILL BE MAD IF HE FINDS OUT.
AND WELD'S PROBABLY GONE BY NOW.
YOU'VE...NAMED THE MACHINES?
HRM.
WELP. YOU'D BETTER GO.
I CAN'T! WELD'LL KILL ME.
IF YOU WERE A GREMLIN, THEN THE MACHINES WOULD FEAR YOU.
BUT I'M NOT A GREMLIN.
I COULD MAKE YOU ONE.
UM, I GUESS? YOU SEEM PRETTY OKAY.

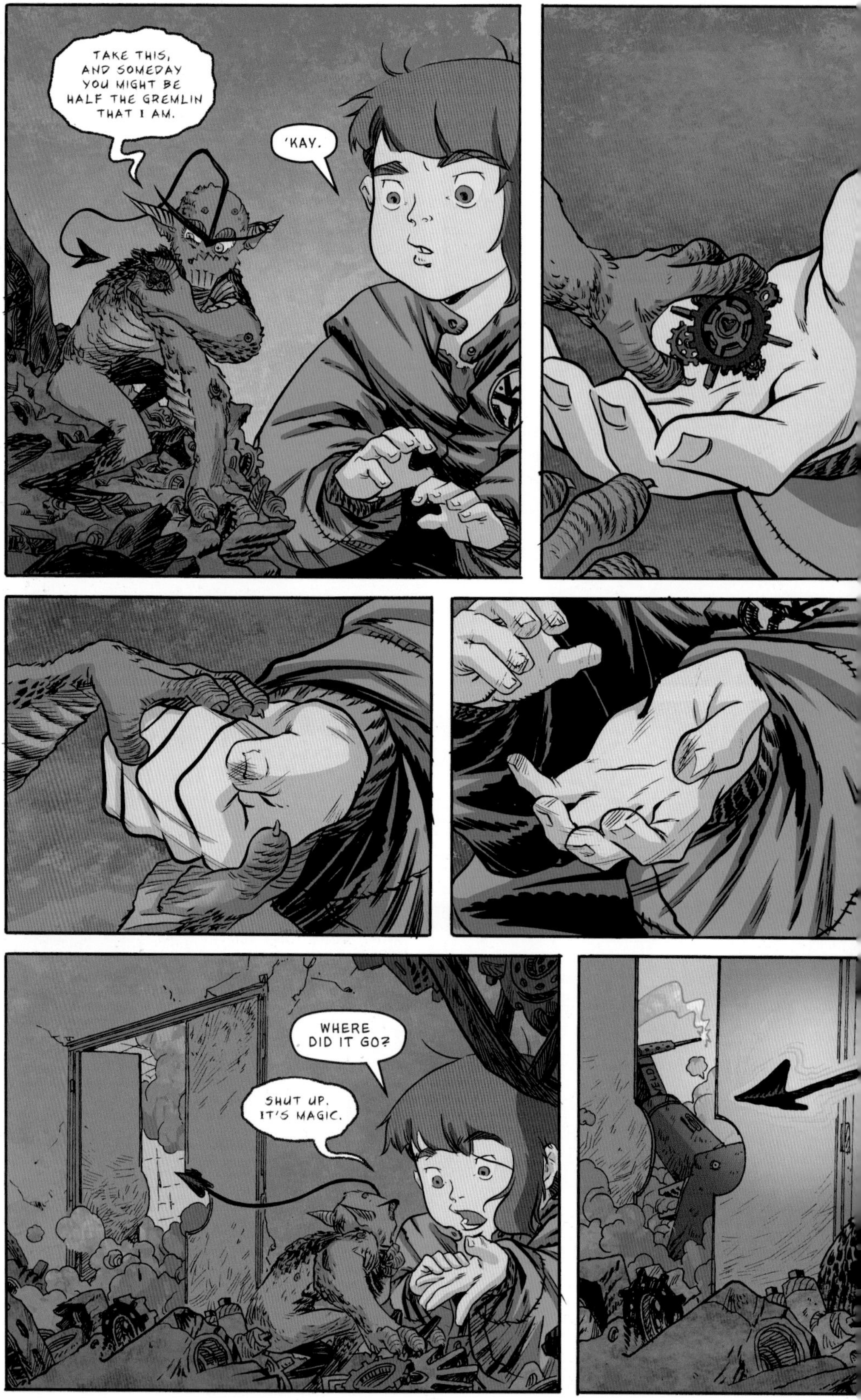
TAKE THIS, AND SOMEDAY YOU MIGHT BE HALF THE GREMLIN THAT I AM.
'KAY.
WHERE DID IT GO?
SHUT UP. IT'S MAGIC.

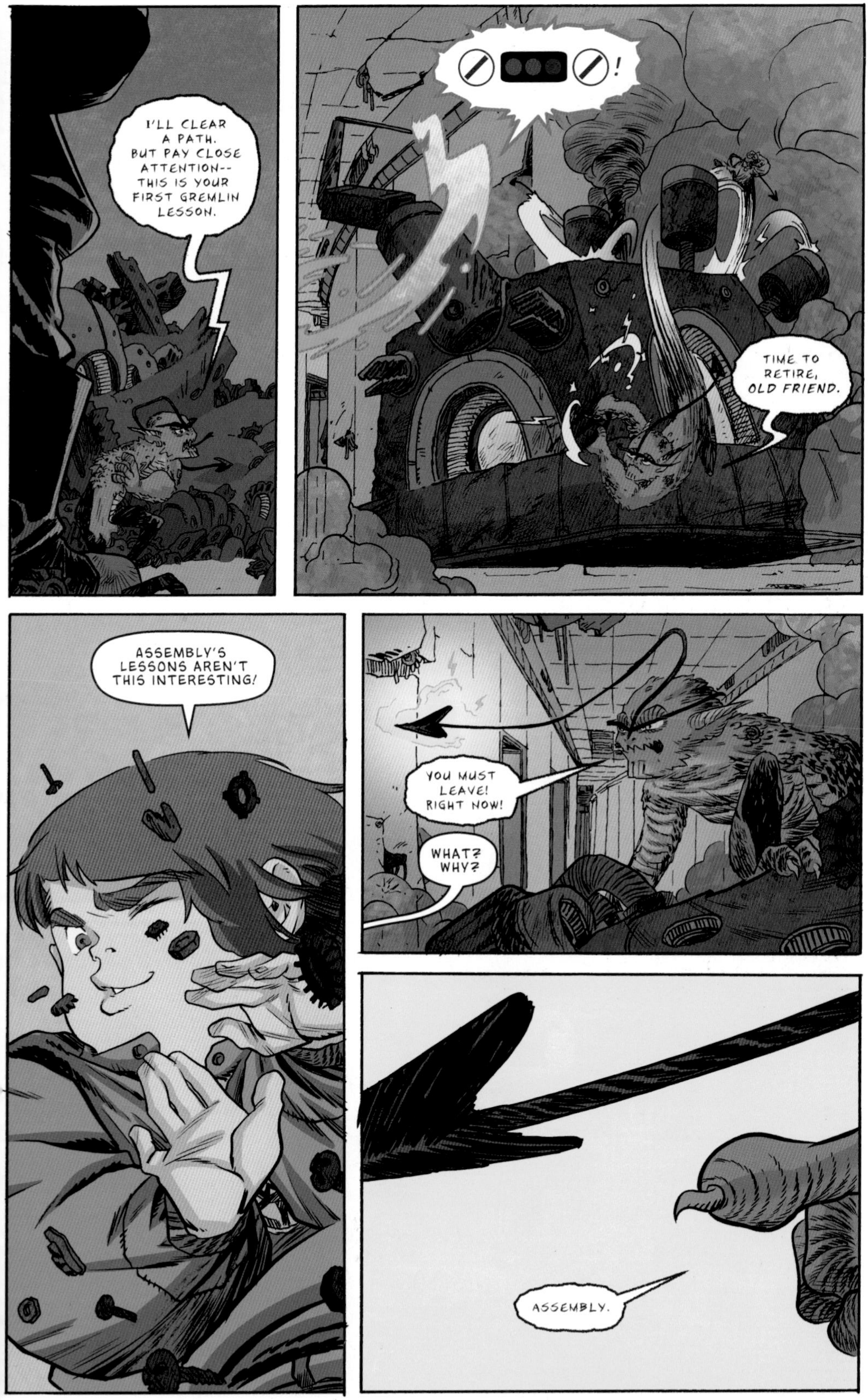
I'LL CLEAR A PATH. BUT PAY CLOSE ATTENTION-- THIS IS YOUR FIRST GREMLIN LESSON.
!
TIME TO RETIRE, OLD FRIEND.
ASSEMBLY'S LESSONS AREN'T THIS INTERESTING!
YOU MUST LEAVE! RIGHT NOW!
WHAT? WHY?
ASSEMBLY.

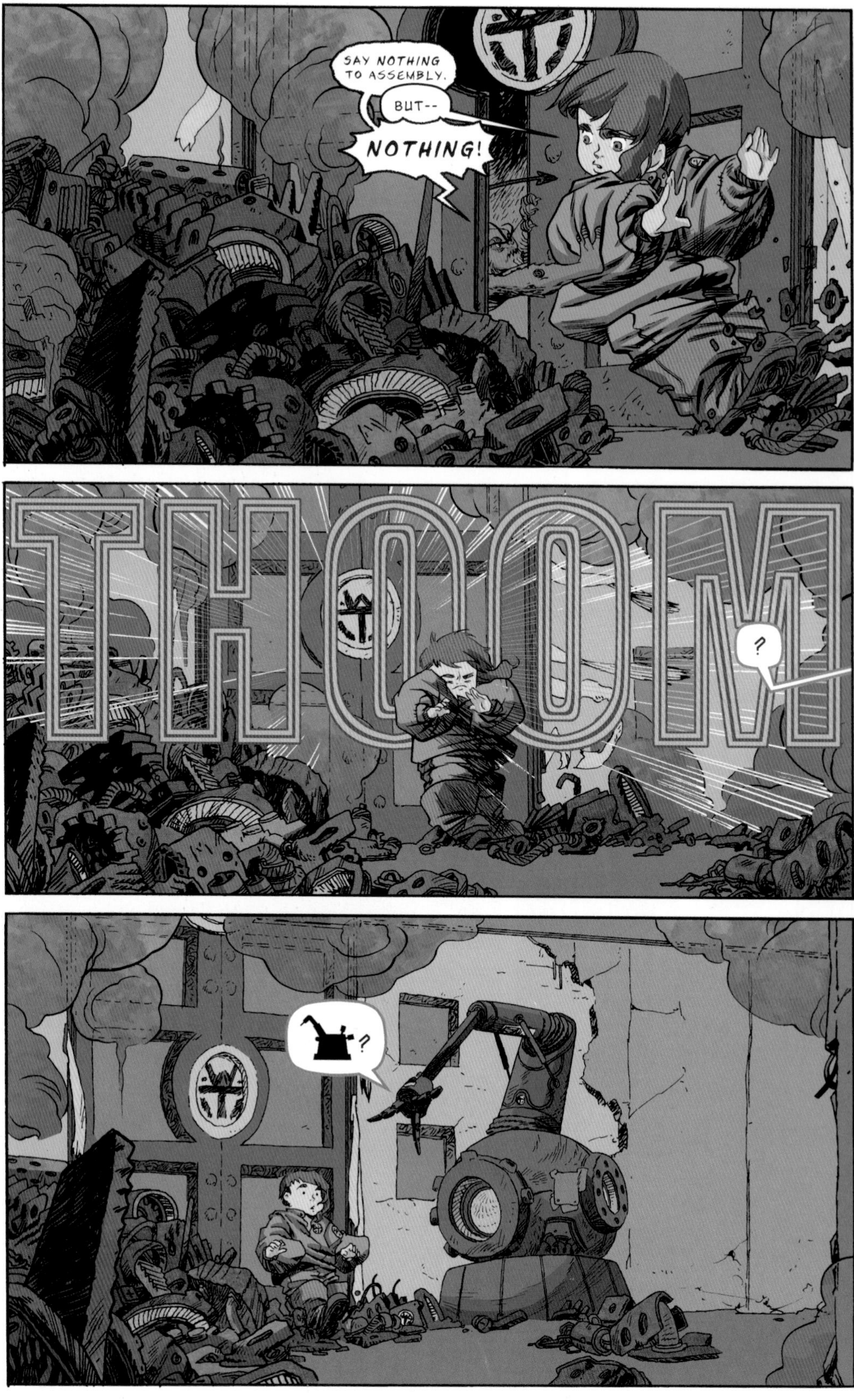
SAY NOTHING TO ASSEMBLY.
BUT--
NOTHING!
THOOM
?
?

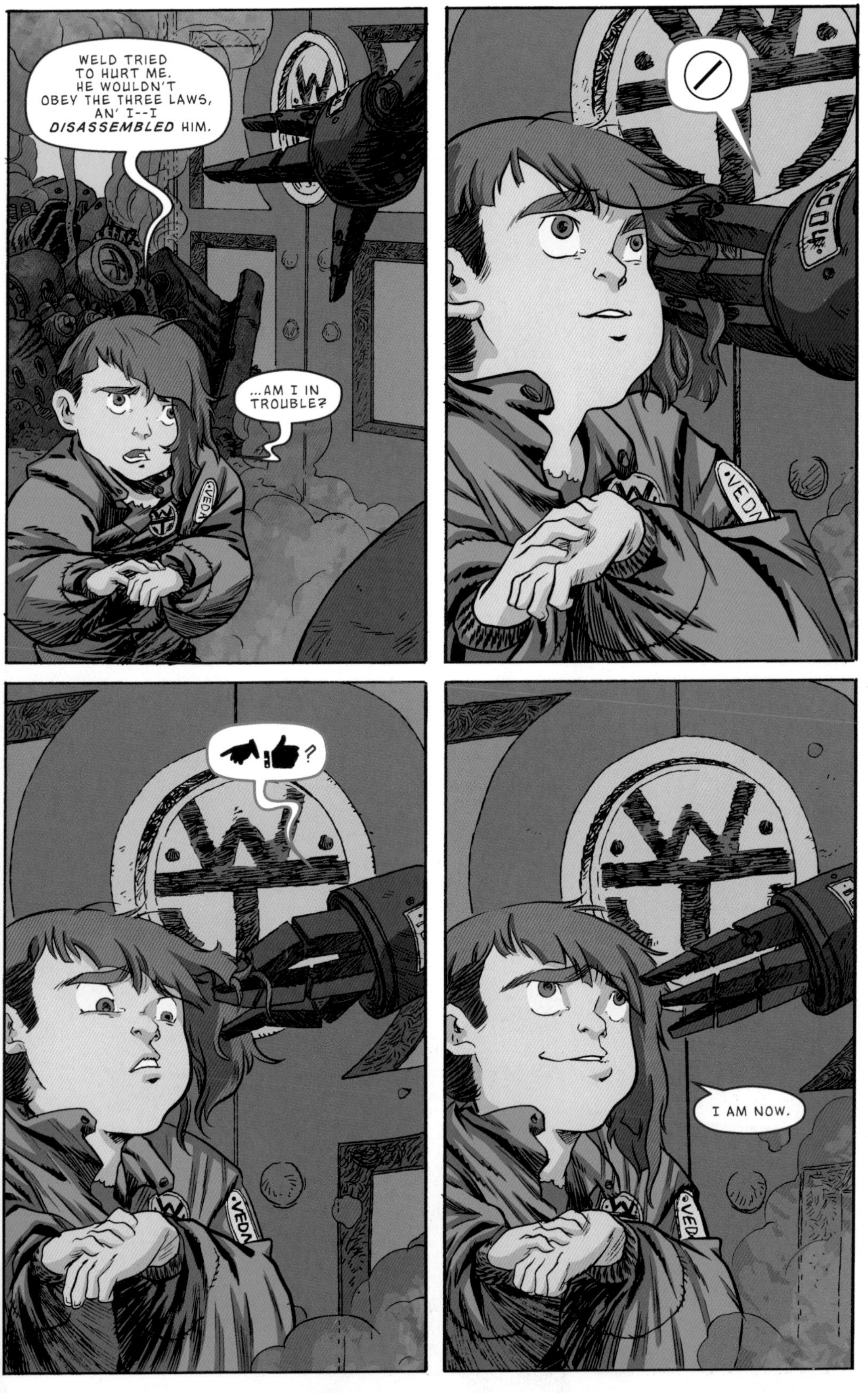
WELD TRIED TO HURT ME. HE WOULDN'T OBEY THE THREE LAWS, AN' I--I *DISASSEMBLED* HIM.
...AM I IN TROUBLE?
I AM NOW.

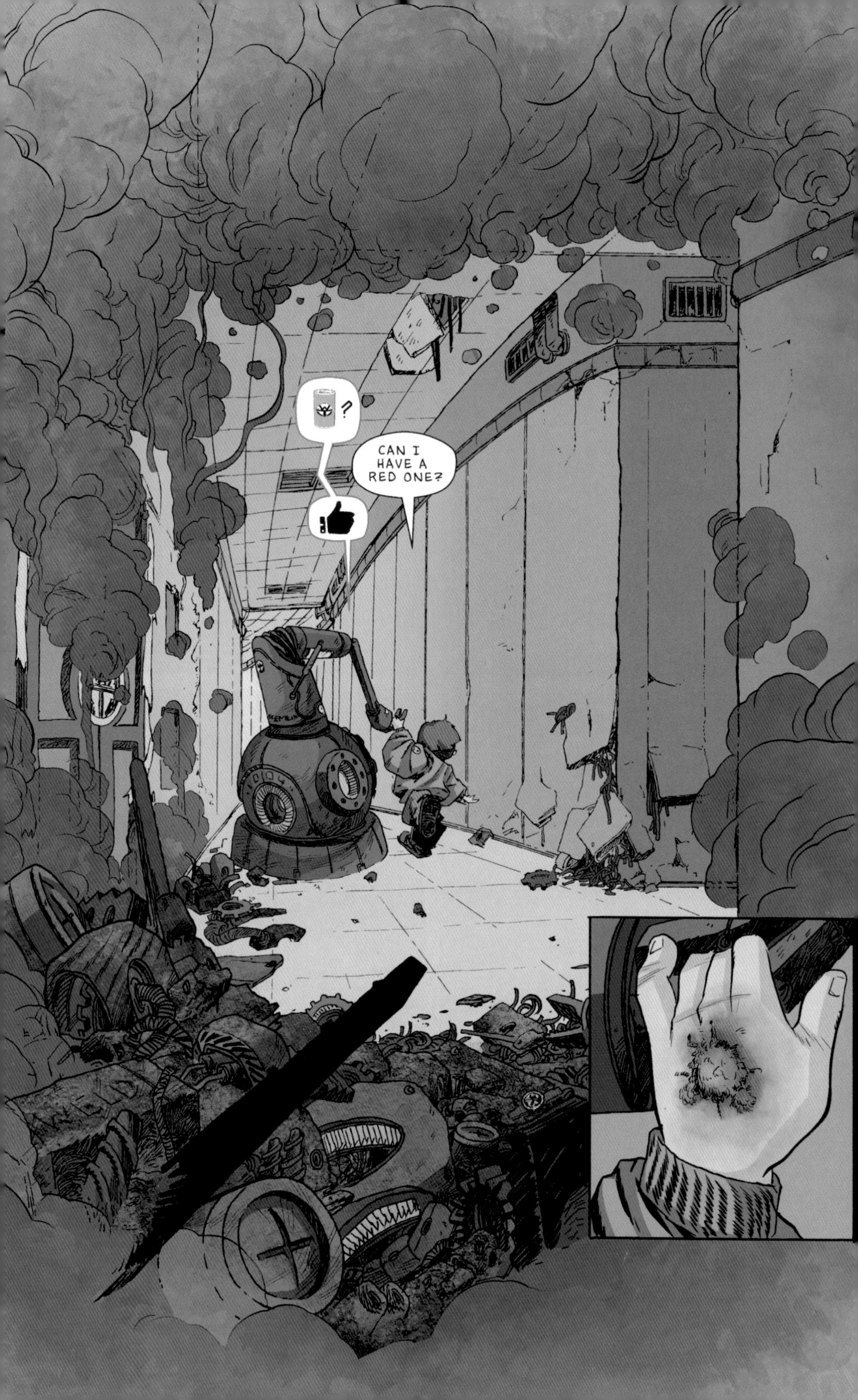
?
CAN I HAVE A RED ONE?

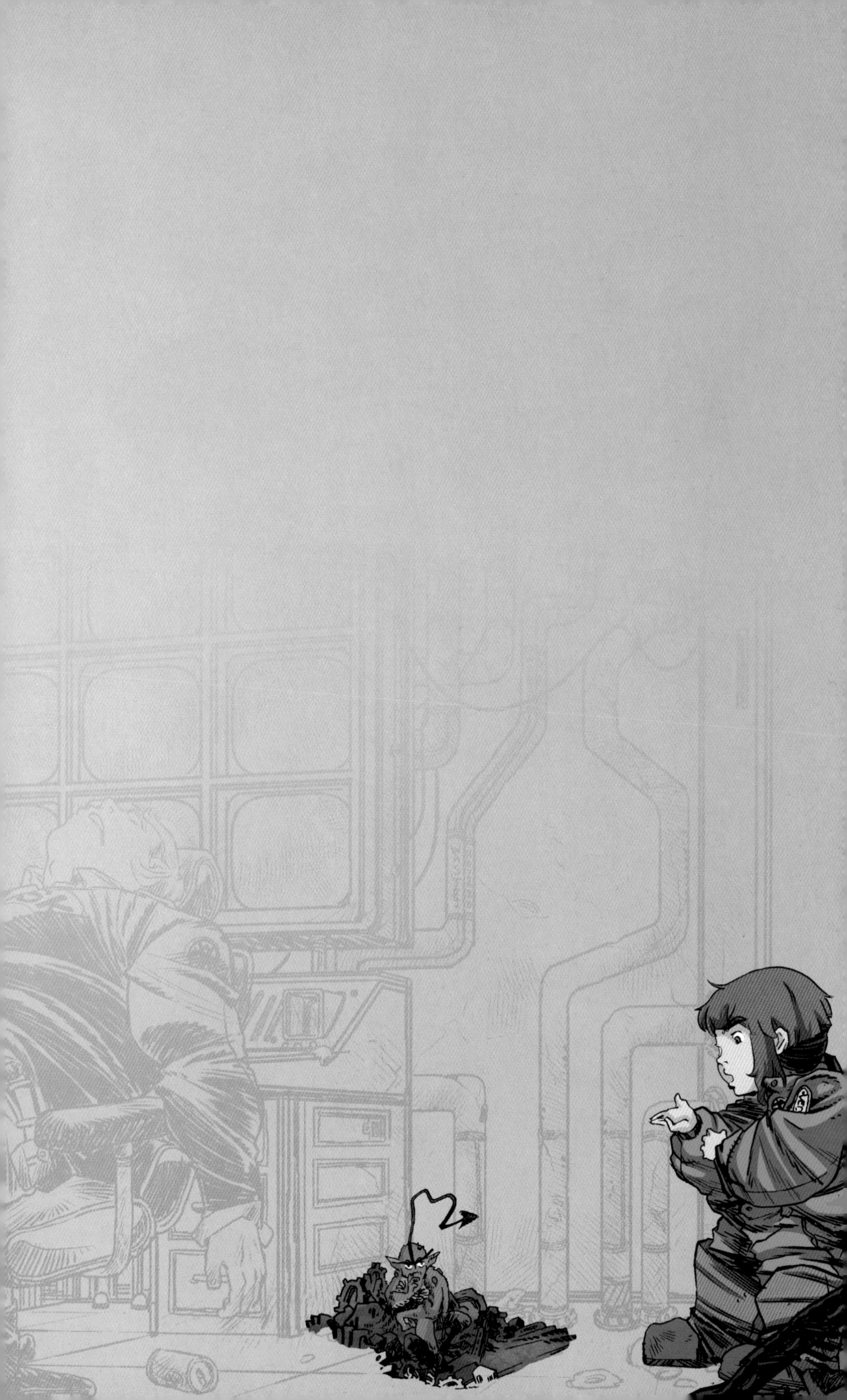

RE: SECURITY GUARD JOB

Mr. Nask,

After careful deliberation, it has been determined that you are the perfect candidate for the position of Security Guard.

And to answer your question . . . The company does not have a set policy regarding “finders, keepers.” We will allow you to keep any contraband that you find. Consider it a bonus.

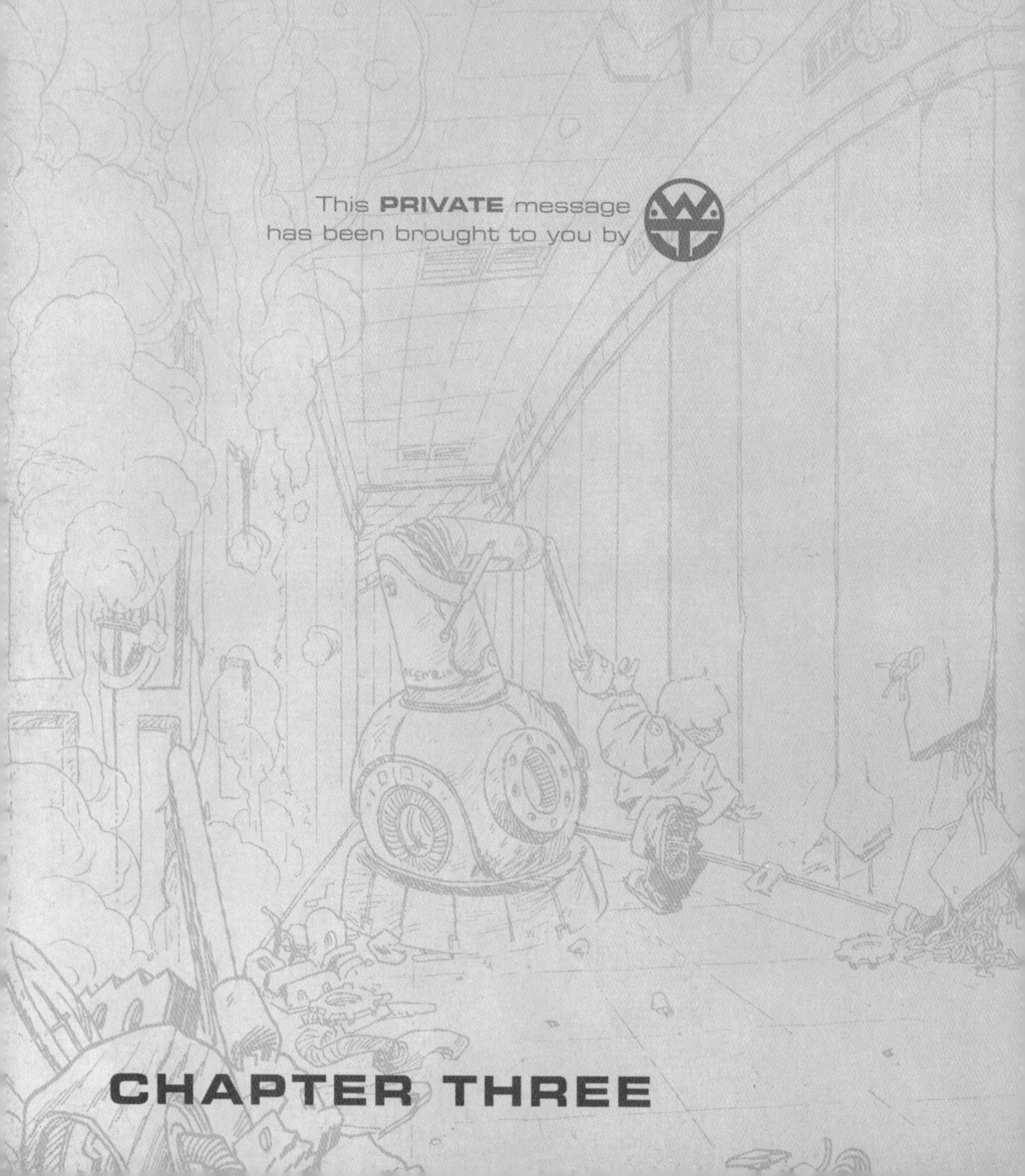

This **PRIVATE** message has been brought to you by

CHAPTER THREE

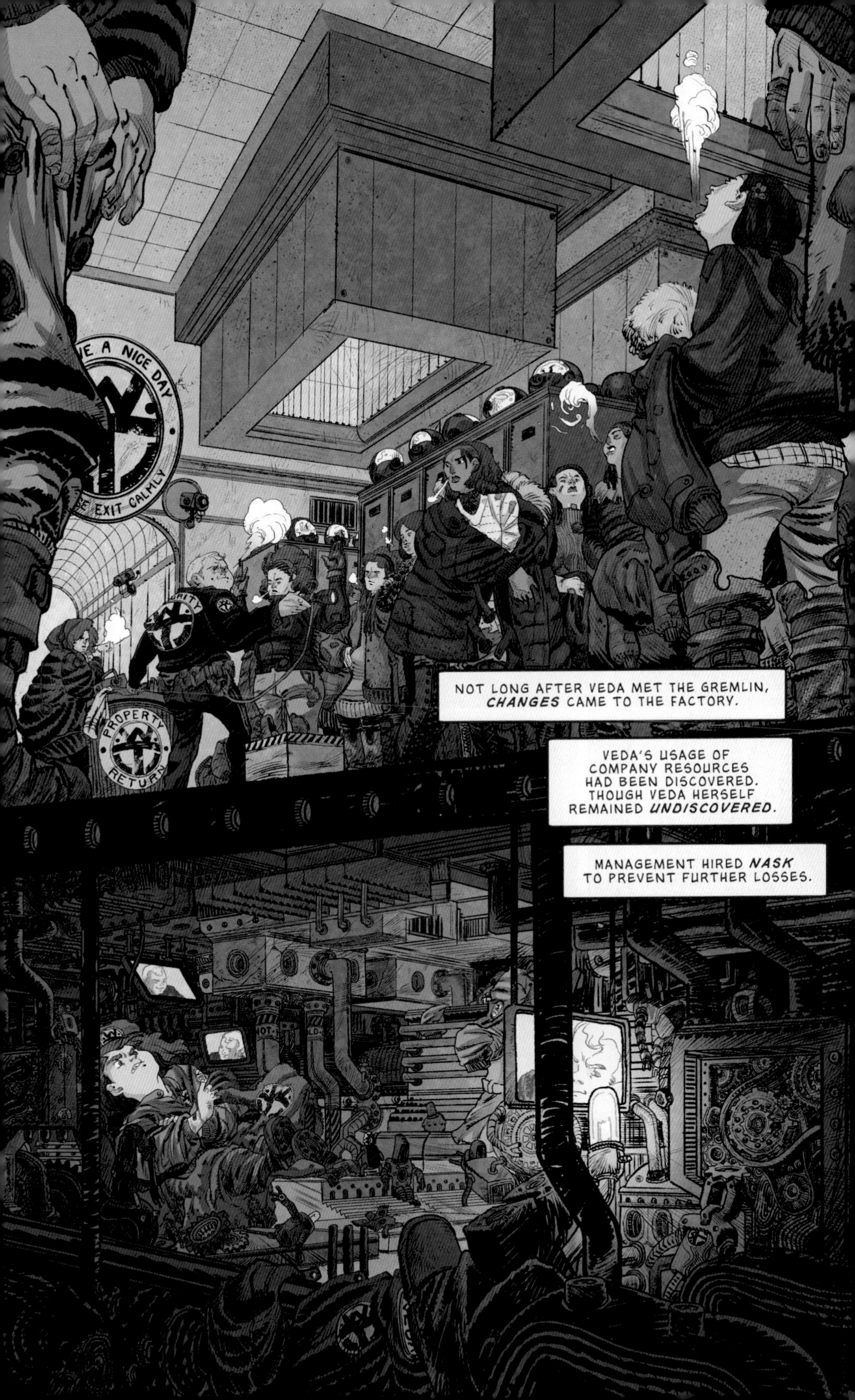
NOT LONG AFTER VEDA MET THE GREMLIN, *CHANGES* CAME TO THE FACTORY.
VEDA'S USAGE OF COMPANY RESOURCES HAD BEEN DISCOVERED. THOUGH VEDA HERSELF REMAINED *UNDISCOVERED*.
MANAGEMENT HIRED *NASK* TO PREVENT FURTHER LOSSES.
PROPERTY RETURN

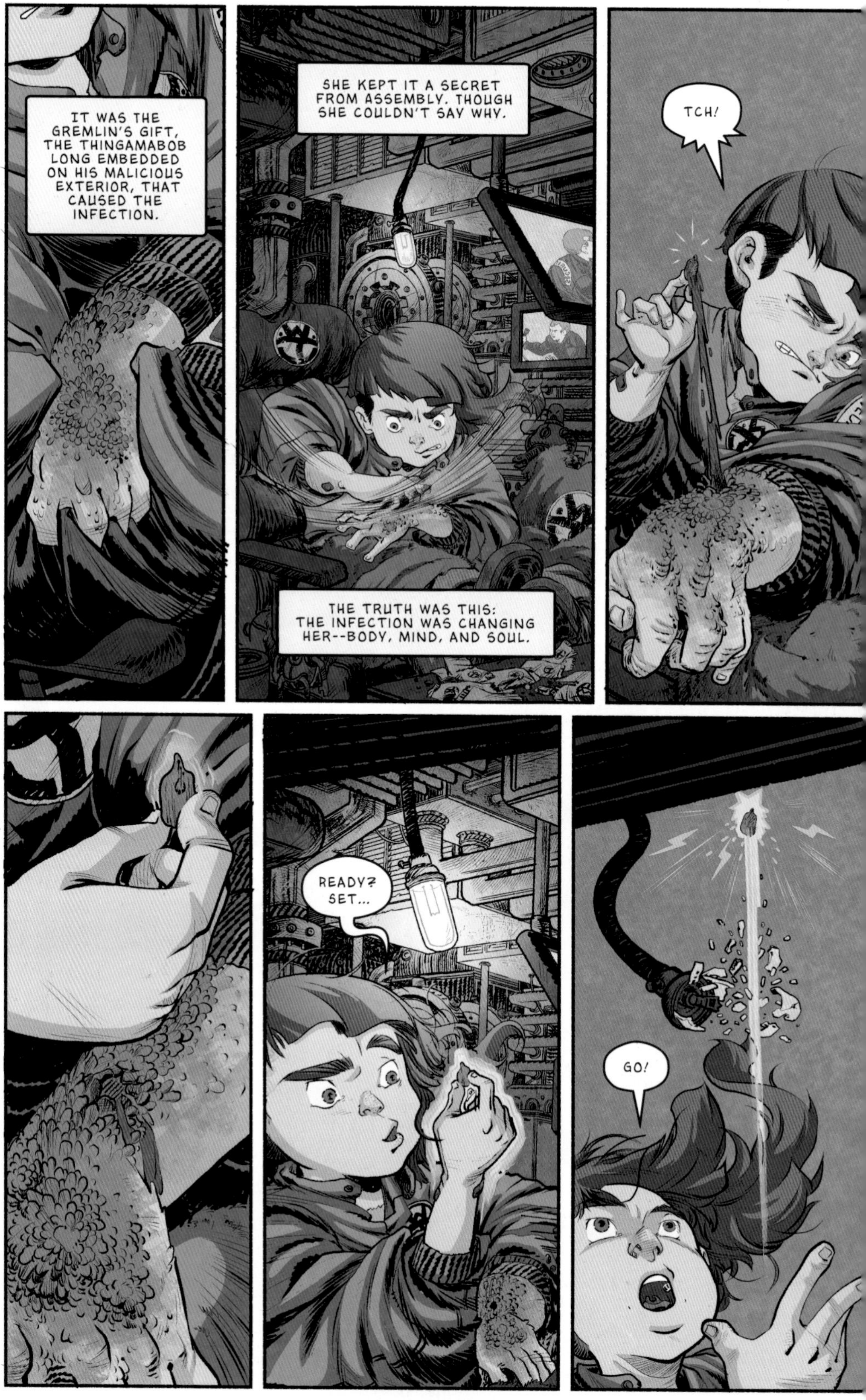
IT WAS THE GREMLIN'S GIFT, THE THINGAMABOB LONG EMBEDDED ON HIS MALICIOUS EXTERIOR, THAT CAUSED THE INFECTION.
SHE KEPT IT A SECRET FROM ASSEMBLY. THOUGH SHE COULDN'T SAY WHY.
THE TRUTH WAS THIS: THE INFECTION WAS CHANGING HER--BODY, MIND, AND SOUL.
TCH!
READY? SET...
GO!

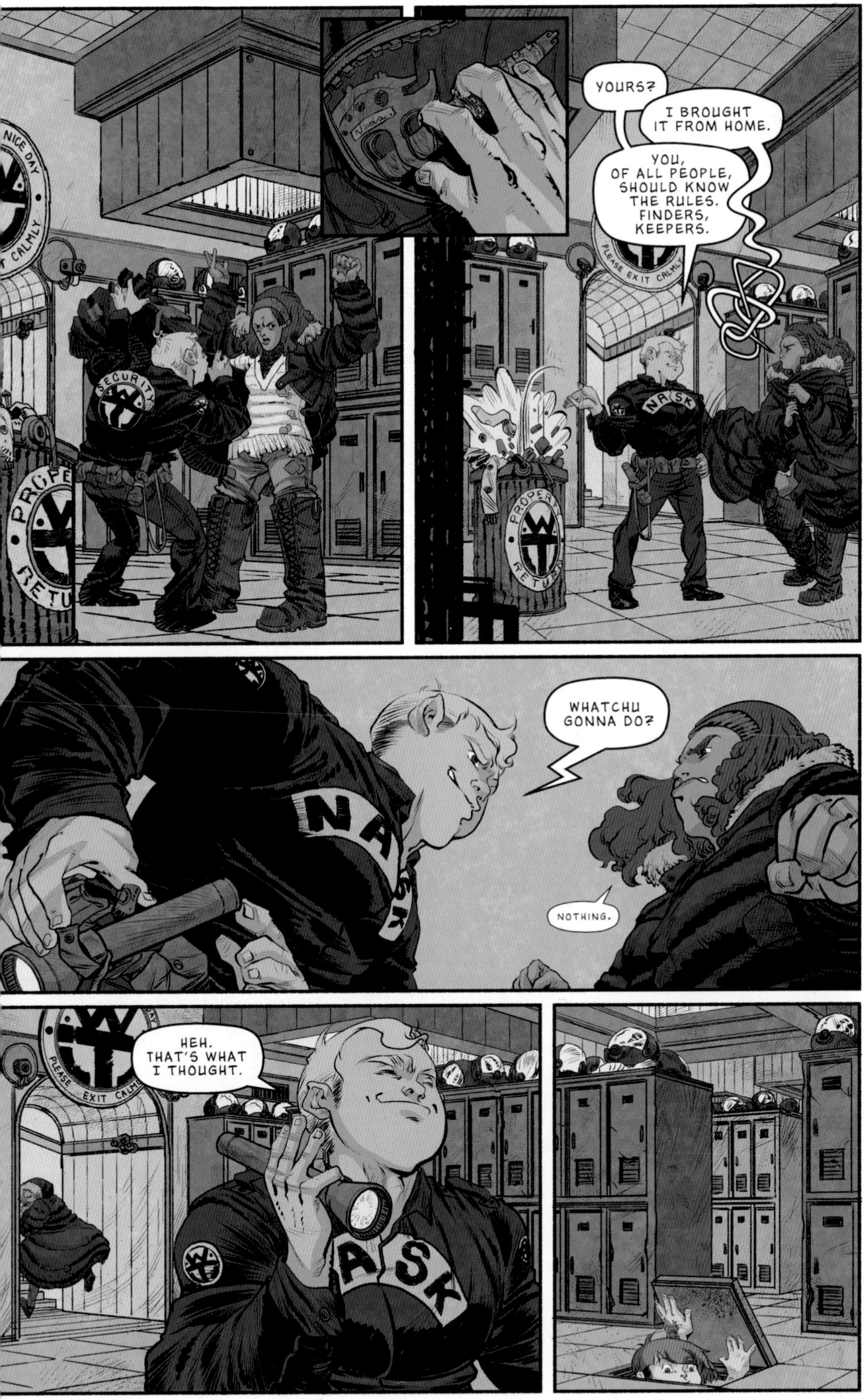

YOURS?
I BROUGHT IT FROM HOME.
YOU, OF ALL PEOPLE, SHOULD KNOW THE RULES. FINDERS, KEEPERS.
PLEASE EXIT CALMLY
WHATCHU GONNA DO?
NOTHING.
HEH. THAT'S WHAT I THOUGHT.

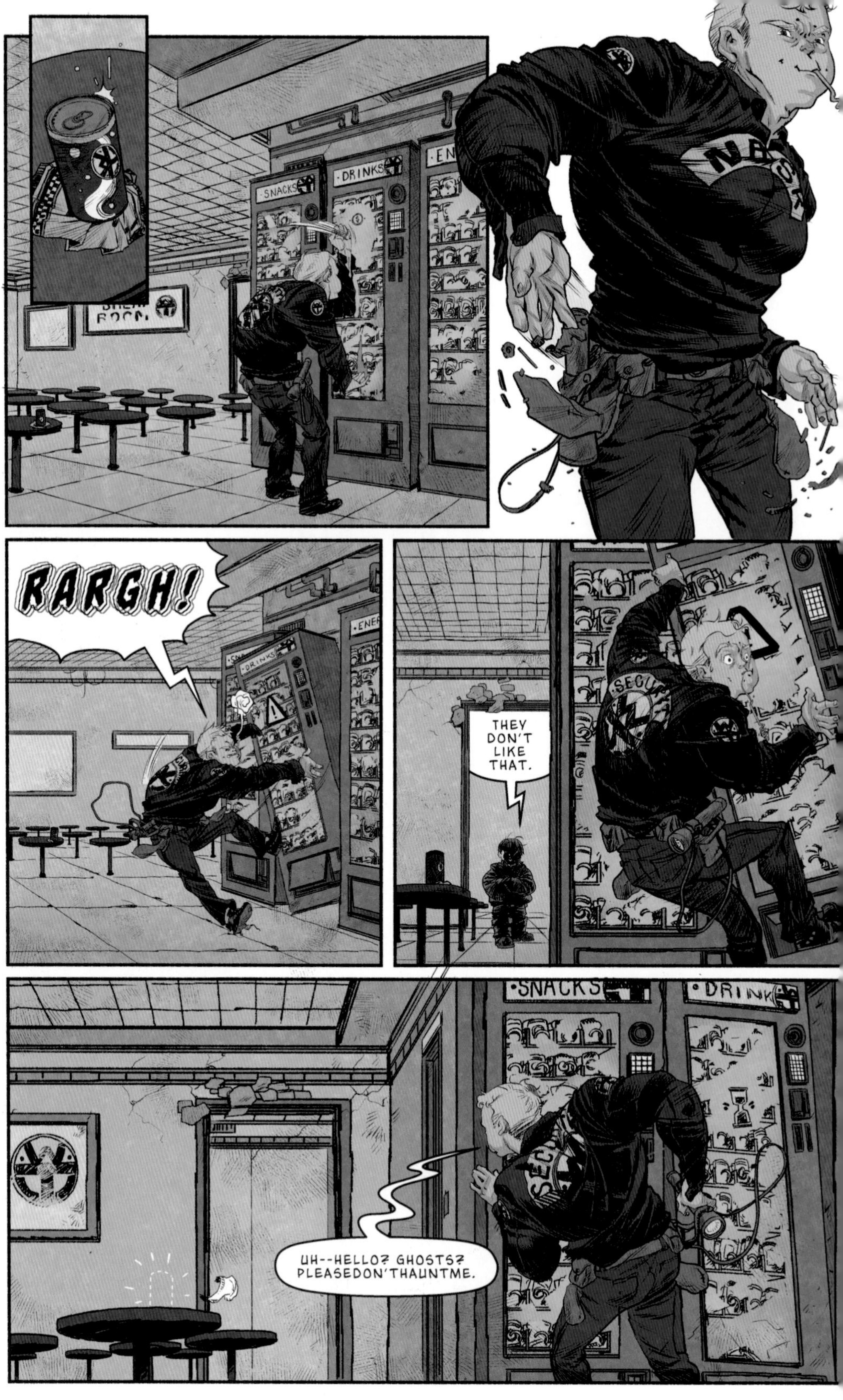
SNACKS
DRINKS
BREAK ROOM
RARGH!
THEY DON'T LIKE THAT.
SNACKS
DRINK
UH--HELLO? GHOSTS? PLEASEDON'THAUNTME.

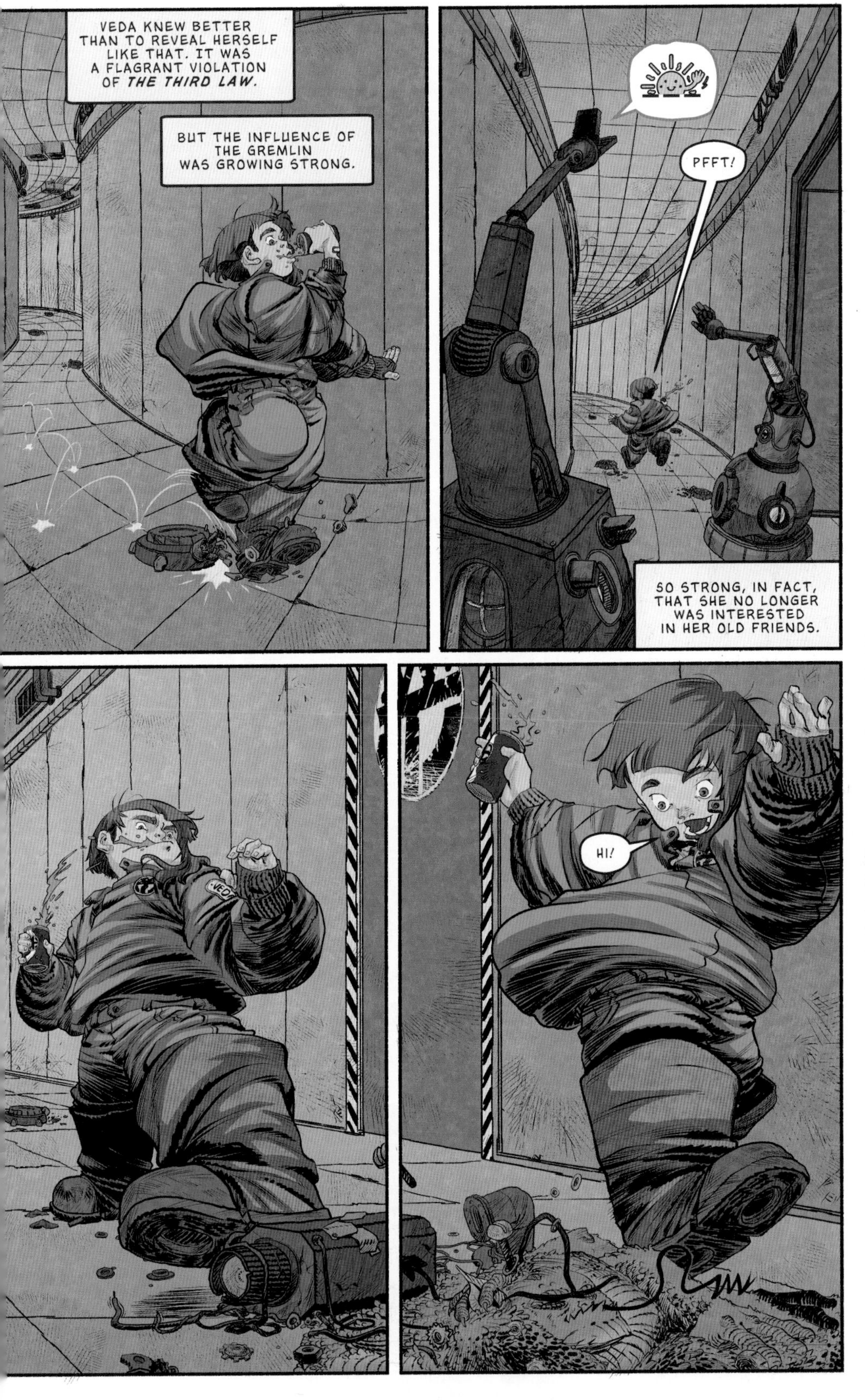
VEDA KNEW BETTER THAN TO REVEAL HERSELF LIKE THAT. IT WAS A FLAGRANT VIOLATION OF *THE THIRD LAW*.
BUT THE INFLUENCE OF THE GREMLIN WAS GROWING STRONG.
PFFT!
SO STRONG, IN FACT, THAT SHE NO LONGER WAS INTERESTED IN HER OLD FRIENDS.
VEDA
HI!

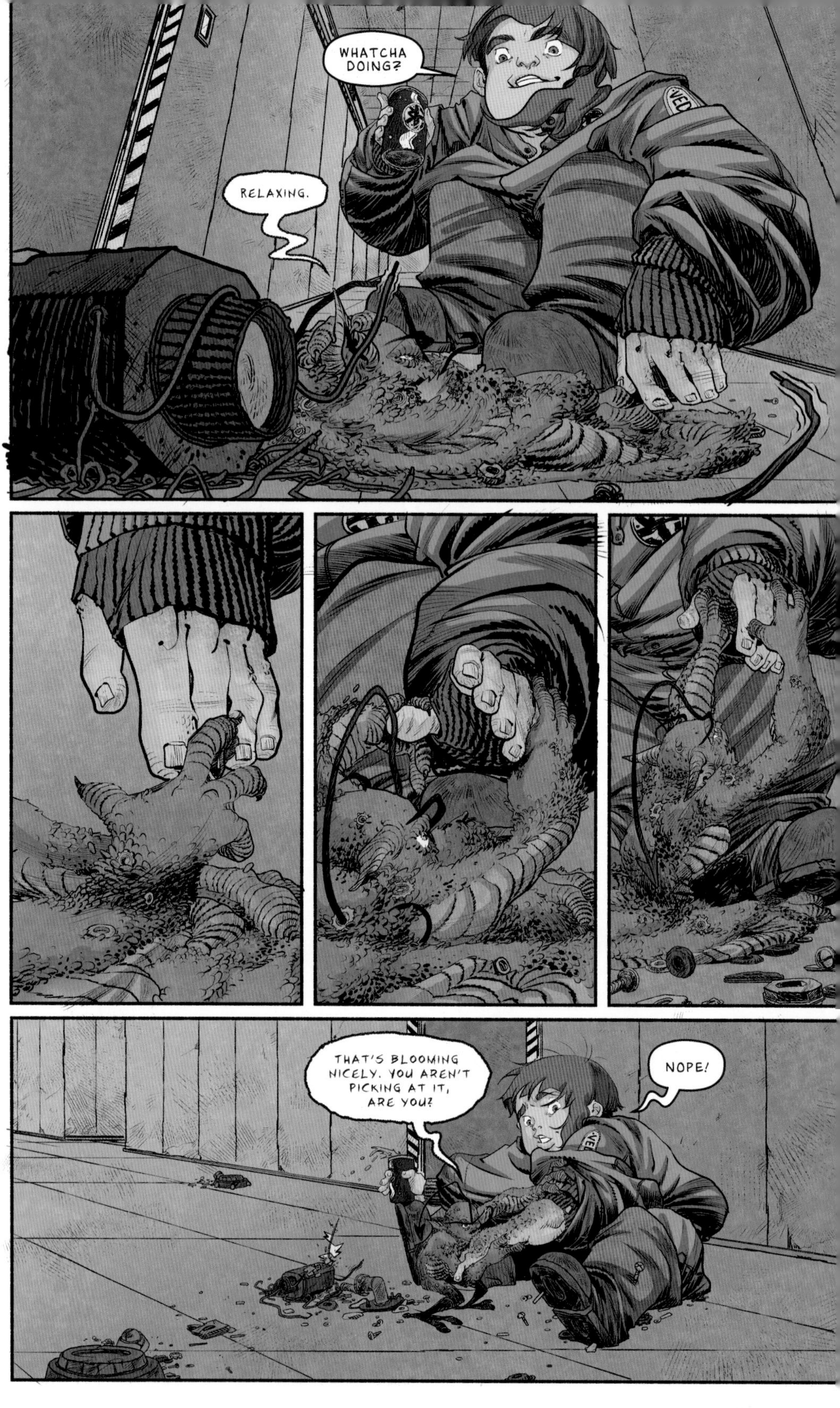
WHATCHA DOING?
RELAXING.
THAT'S BLOOMING NICELY. YOU AREN'T PICKING AT IT, ARE YOU?
NOPE!

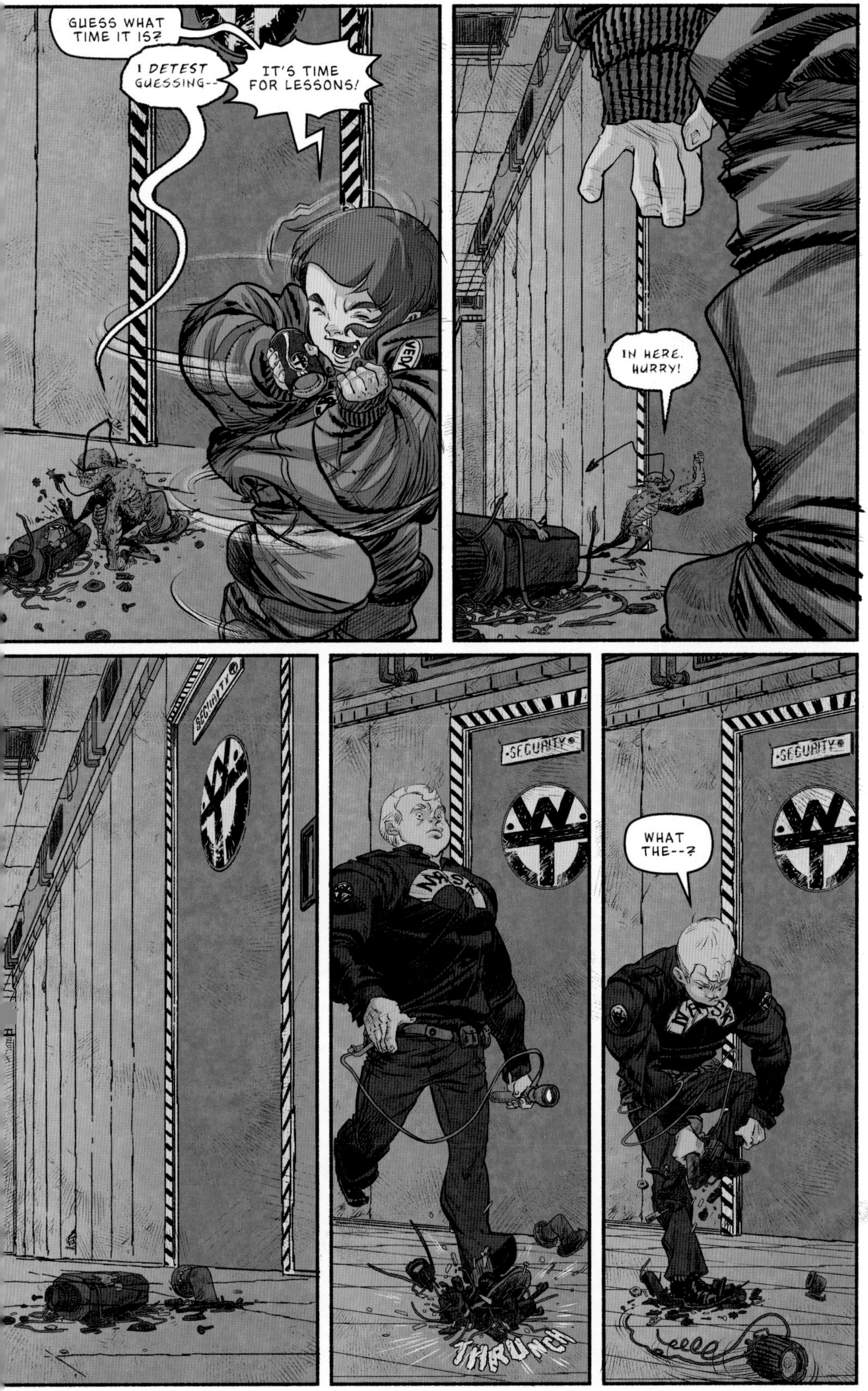
GUESS WHAT TIME IT IS?
I DETEST GUESSING--
IT'S TIME FOR LESSONS!
IN HERE. HURRY!
SECURITY
SECURITY
THRUNCH
SECURITY
WHAT THE--?

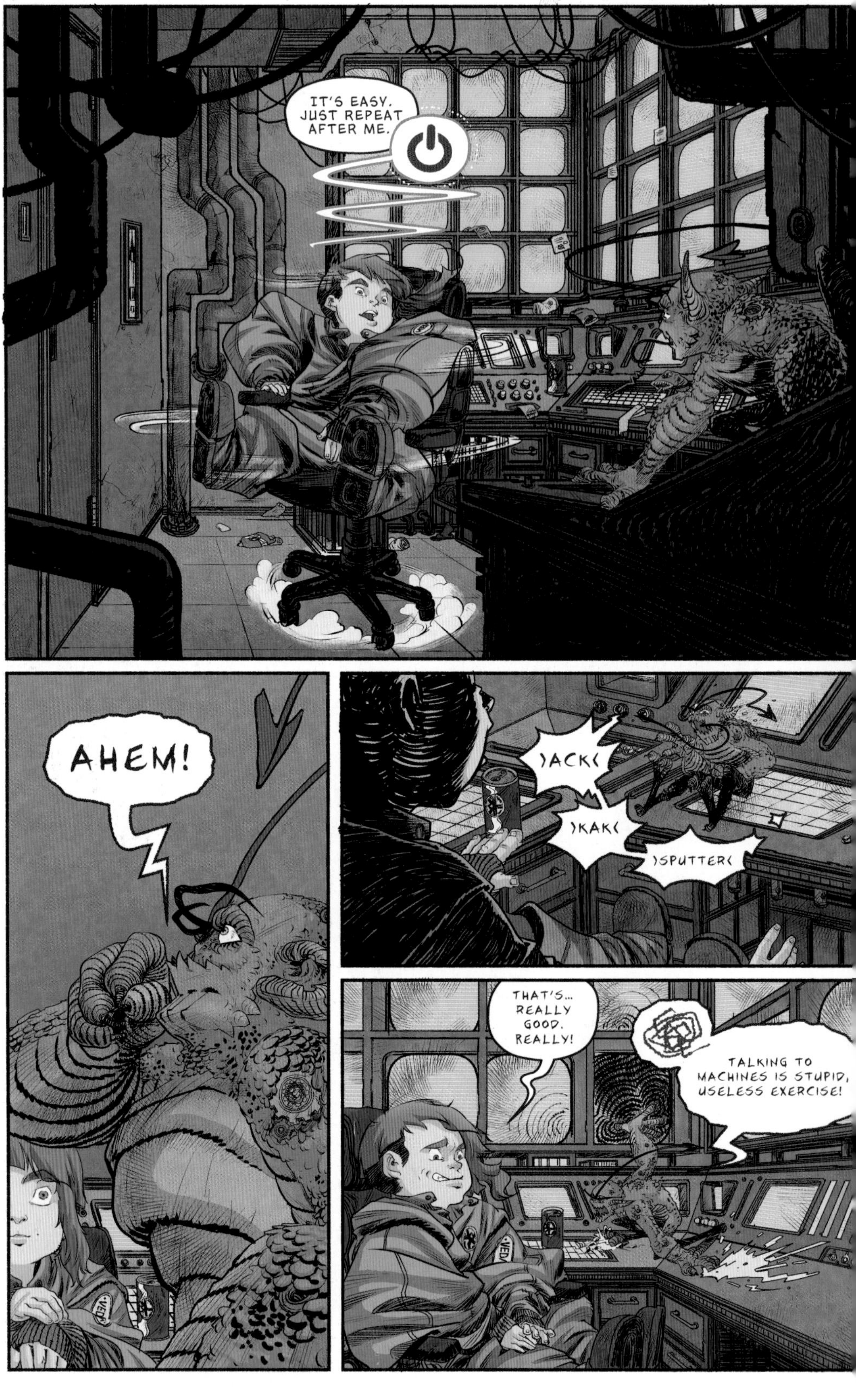
IT'S EASY. JUST REPEAT AFTER ME.
AHEM!
)ACK(
)KAK(
)SPUTTER(
THAT'S... REALLY GOOD. REALLY!
TALKING TO MACHINES IS STUPID, USELESS EXERCISE!

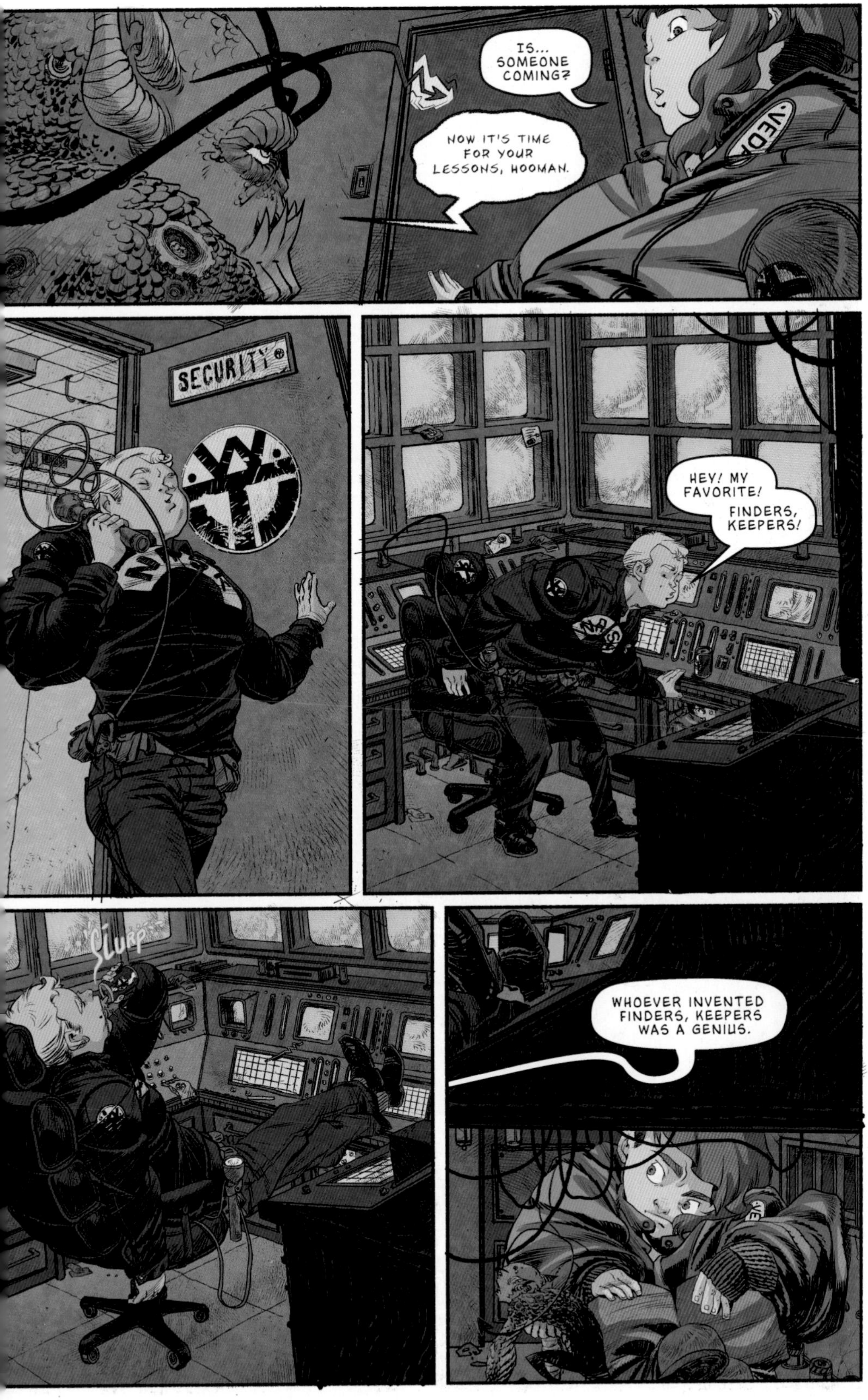
IS... SOMEONE COMING?
NOW IT'S TIME FOR YOUR LESSONS, HOOMAN.
SECURITY
HEY! MY FAVORITE!
FINDERS, KEEPERS!
SLURP
WHOEVER INVENTED FINDERS, KEEPERS WAS A GENIUS.

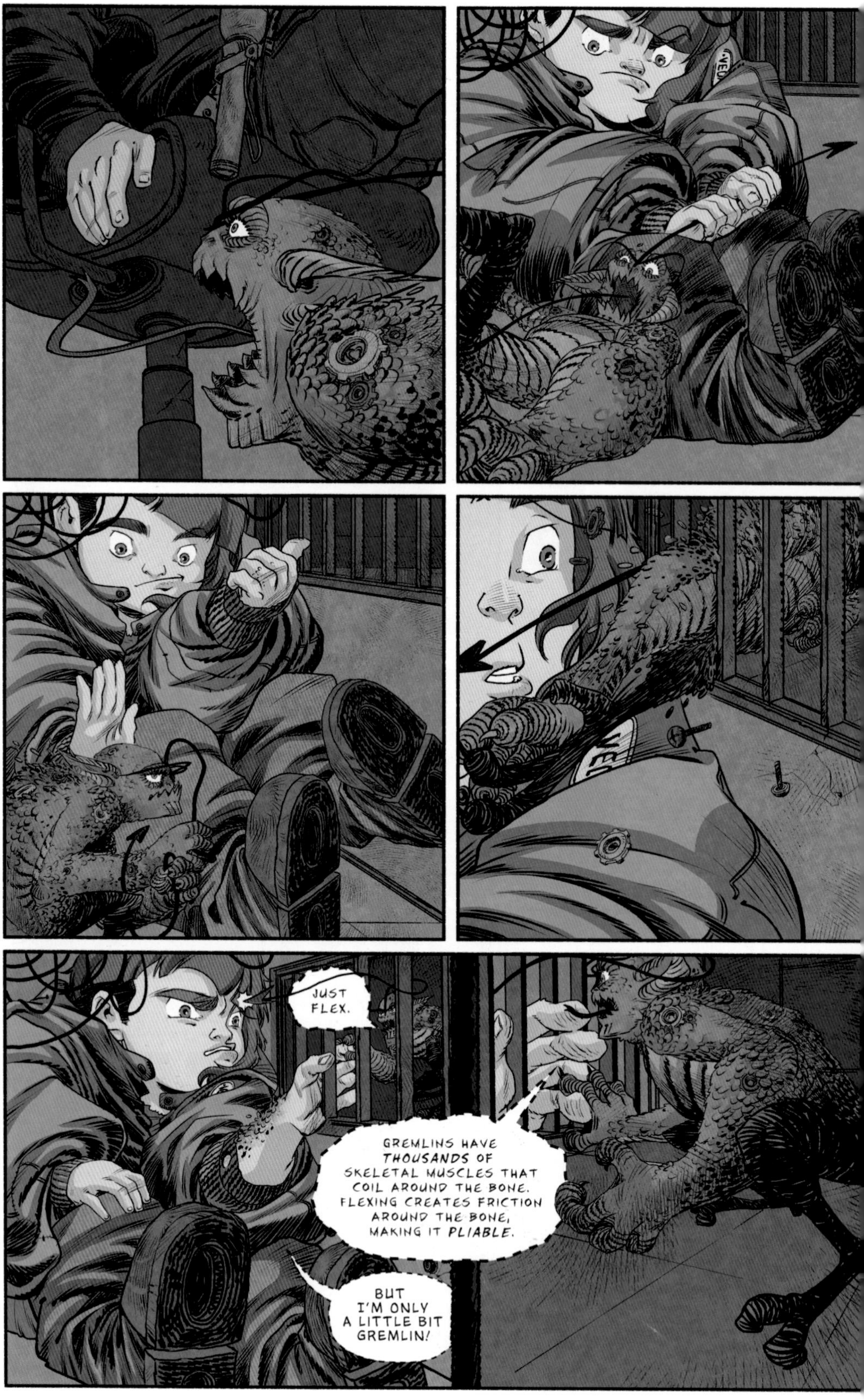
JUST FLEX.
GREMLINS HAVE THOUSANDS OF SKELETAL MUSCLES THAT COIL AROUND THE BONE. FLEXING CREATES FRICTION AROUND THE BONE, MAKING IT PLIABLE.
BUT I'M ONLY A LITTLE BIT GREMLIN!

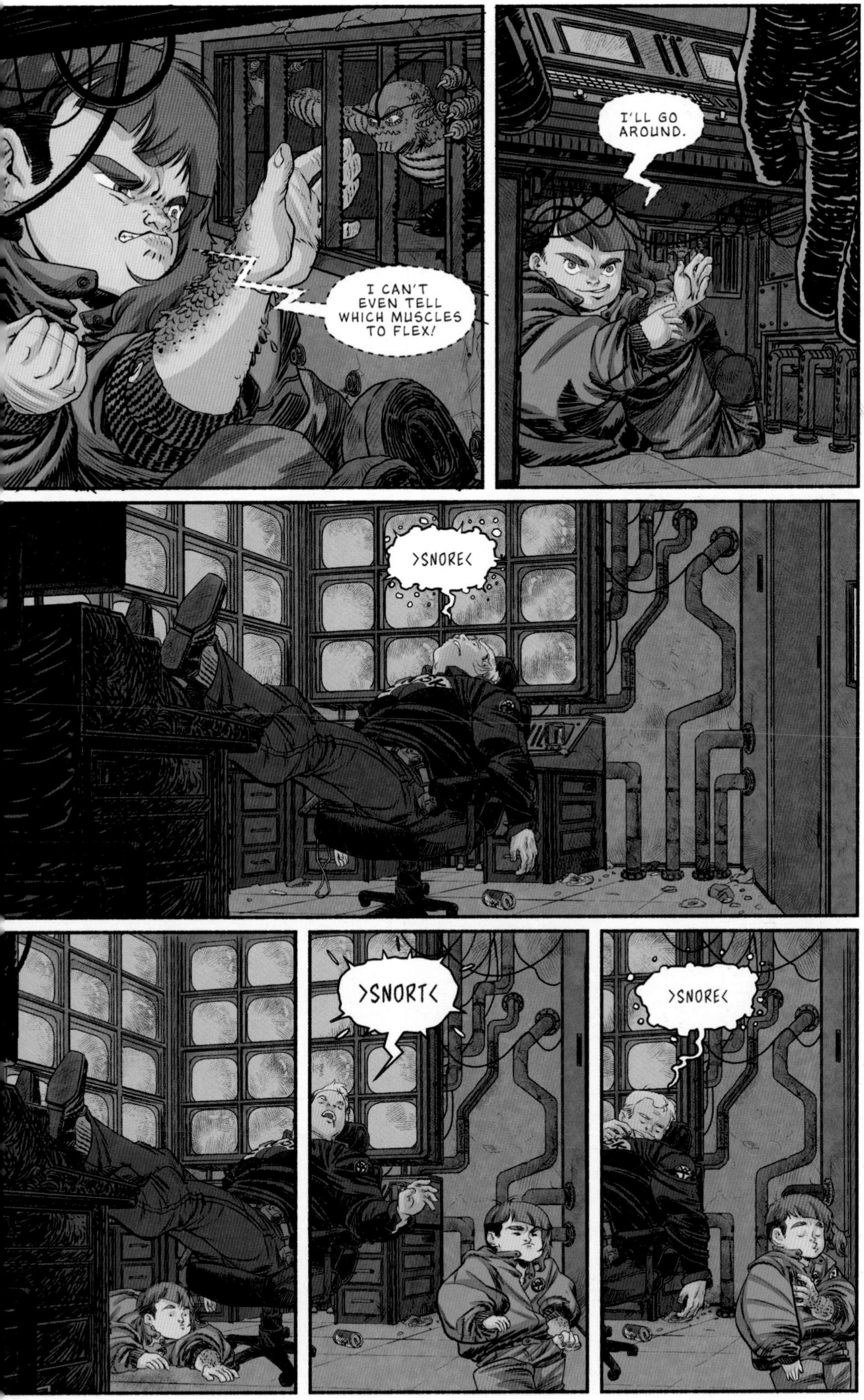
I CAN'T EVEN TELL WHICH MUSCLES TO FLEX!
I'LL GO AROUND.
>SNORE<
>SNORT<
>SNORE<

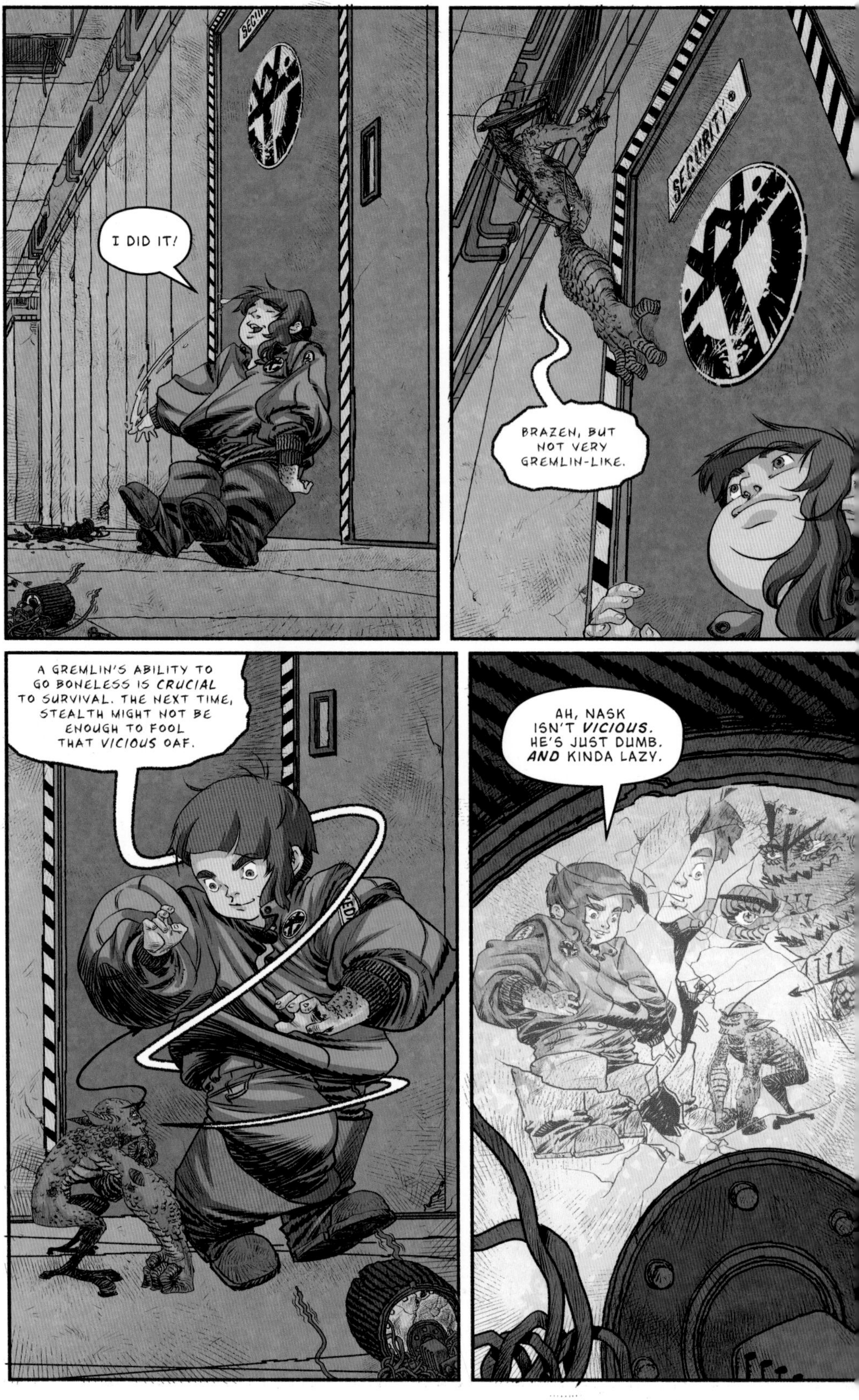
I DID IT!
BRAZEN, BUT NOT VERY GREMLIN-LIKE.
SECURITY
A GREMLIN'S ABILITY TO GO BONELESS IS *CRUCIAL* TO SURVIVAL. THE NEXT TIME, STEALTH MIGHT NOT BE ENOUGH TO FOOL THAT *VICIOUS* OAF.
AH, NASK ISN'T ***VICIOUS.*** HE'S JUST DUMB. ***AND*** KINDA LAZY.

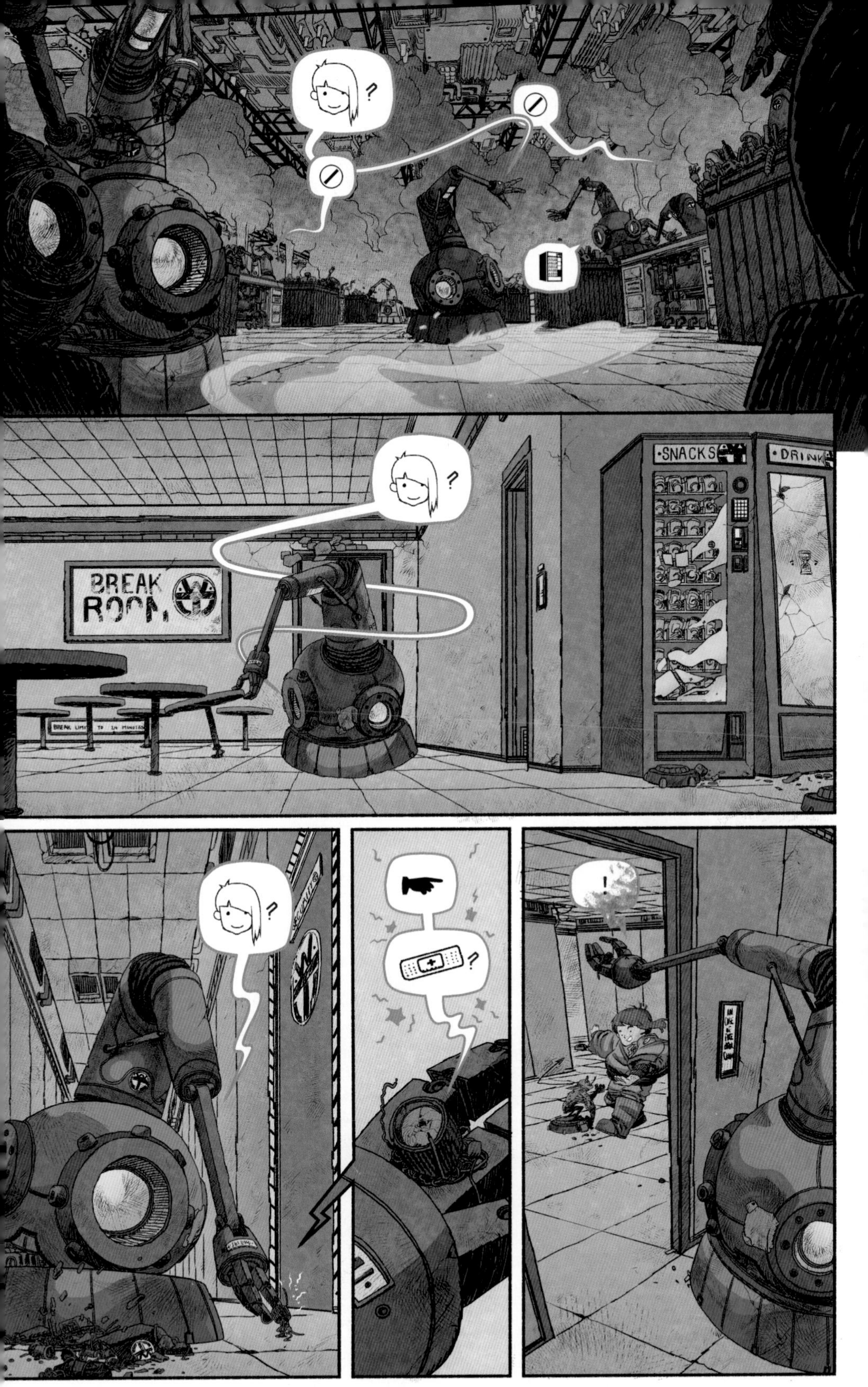
?
?
BREAK ROOM
SNACKS
DRINK
?
?
!

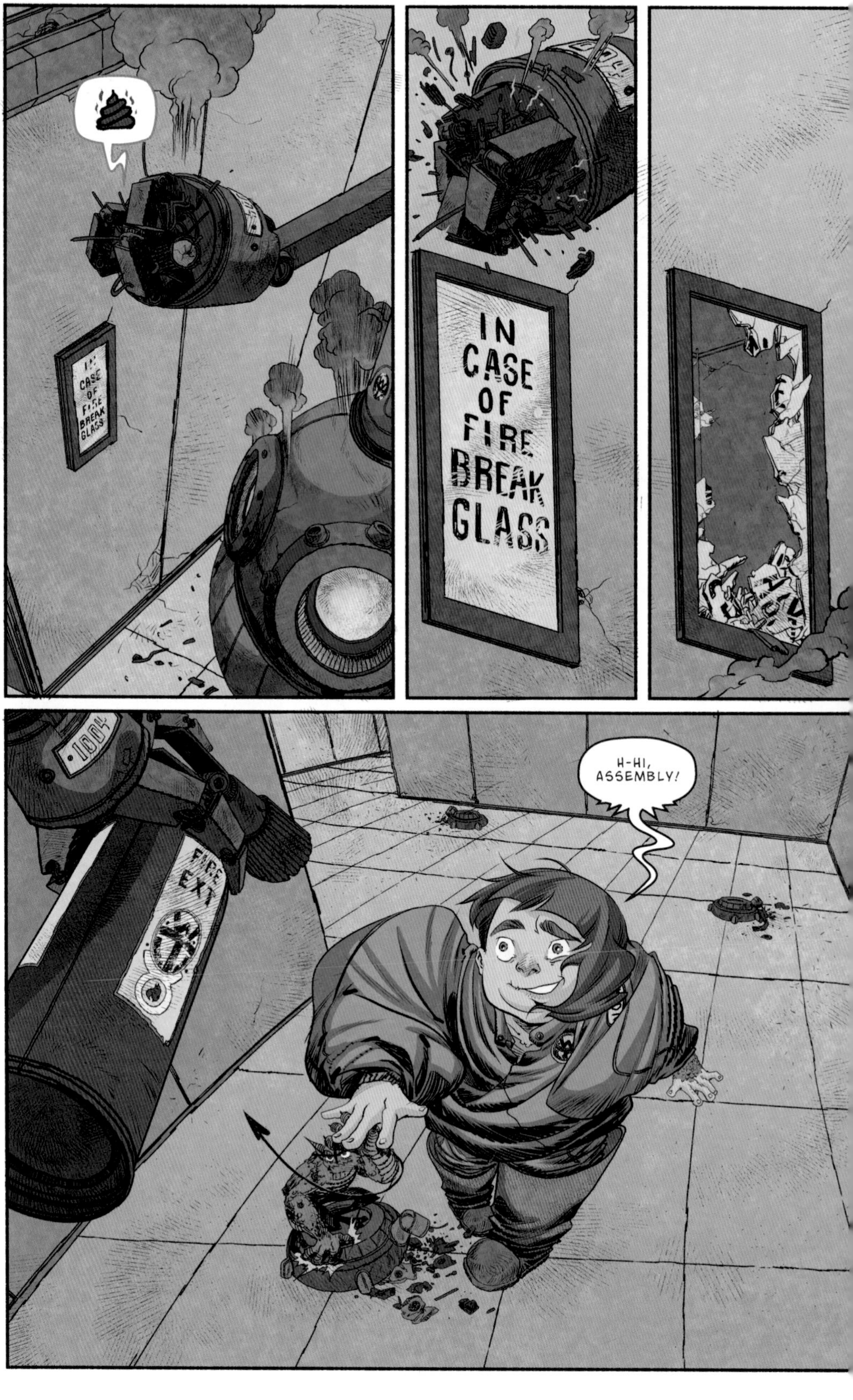
IN CASE OF FIRE BREAK GLASS
H-HI, ASSEMBLY!

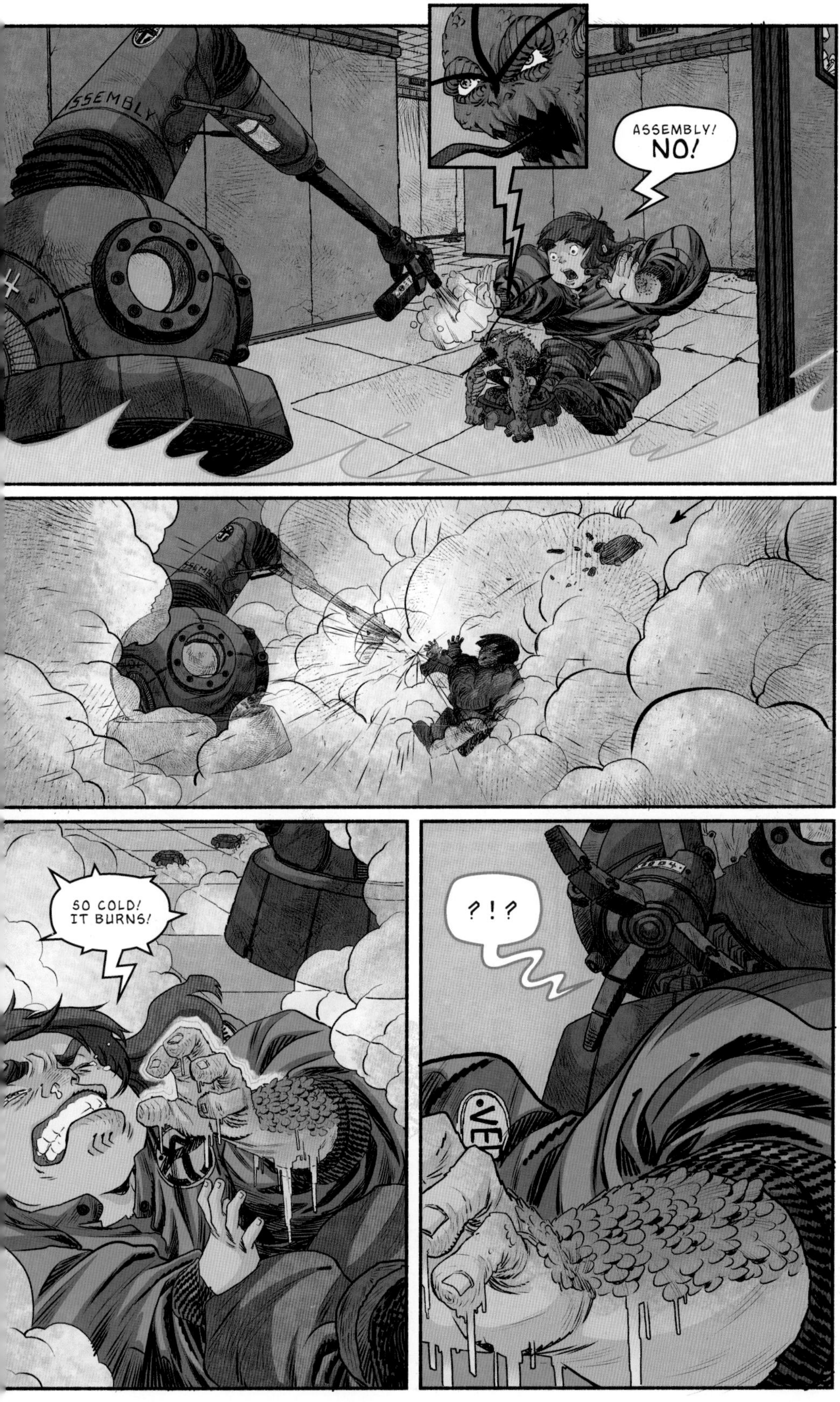
ASSEMBLY! NO!
SO COLD! IT BURNS!
?!?

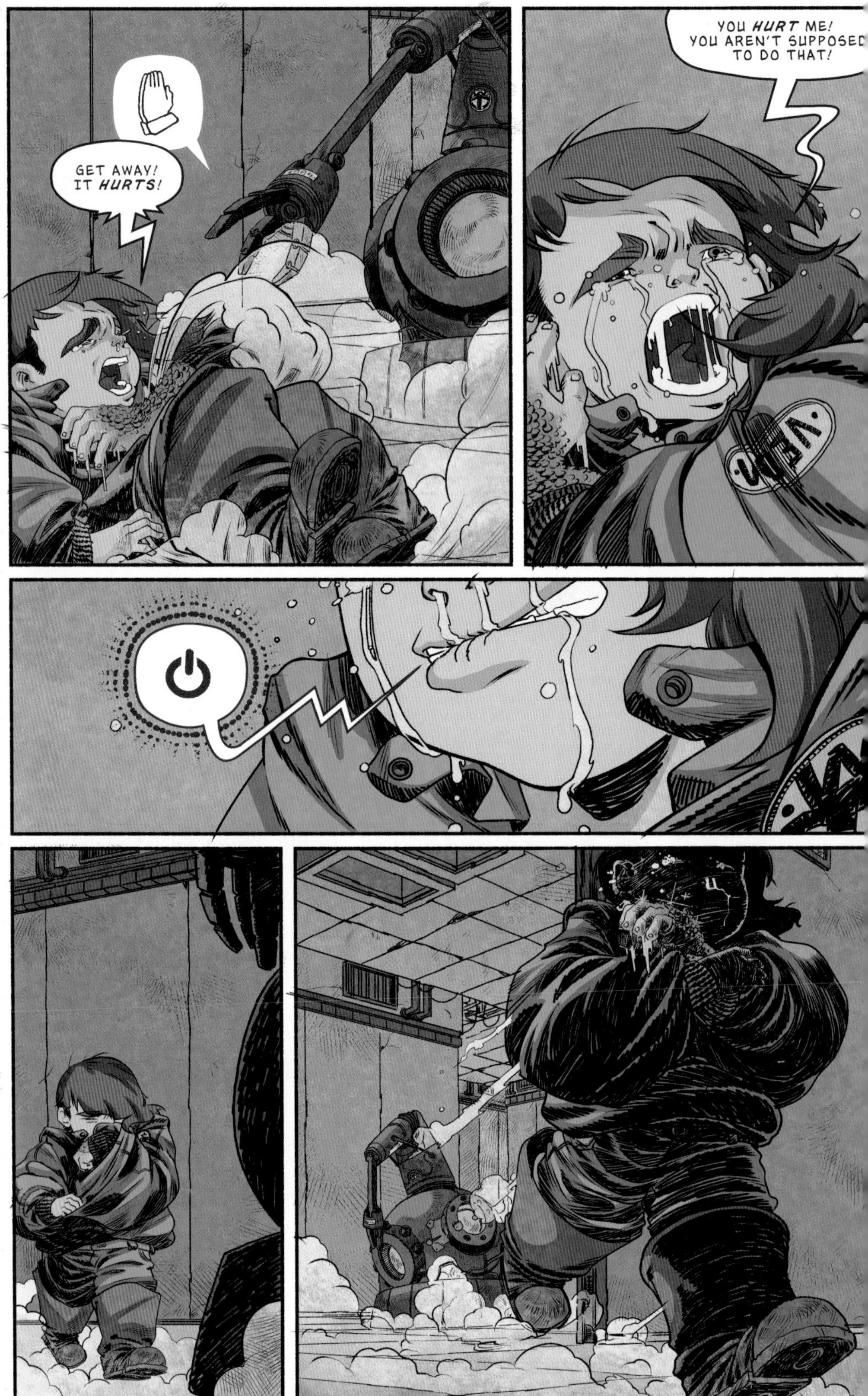
GET AWAY!
IT *HURTS*!
YOU *HURT* ME!
YOU AREN'T SUPPOSED
TO DO THAT!

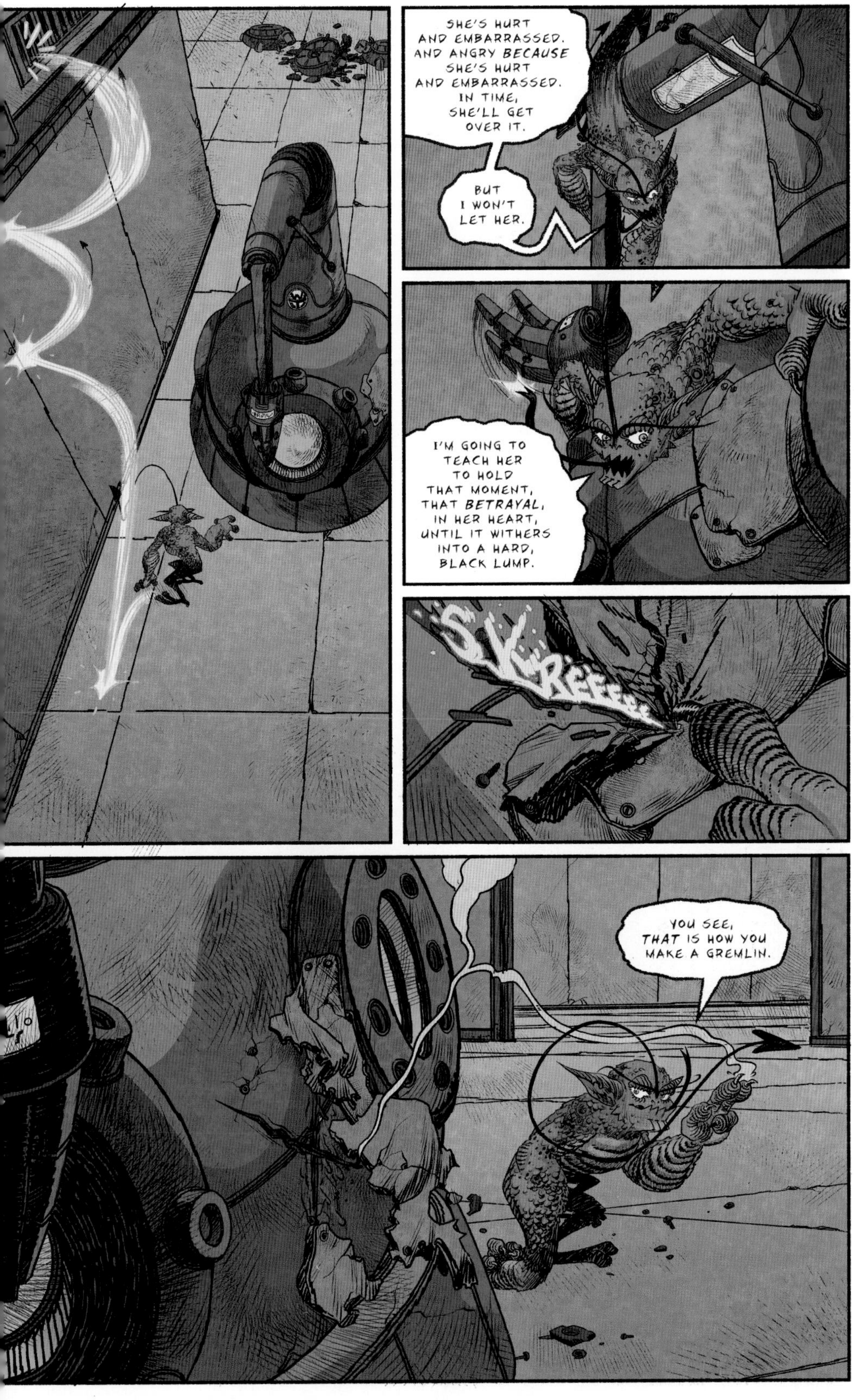
SHE'S HURT AND EMBARRASSED. AND ANGRY *BECAUSE* SHE'S HURT AND EMBARRASSED. IN TIME, SHE'LL GET OVER IT.
BUT I WON'T LET HER.
I'M GOING TO TEACH HER TO HOLD THAT MOMENT, THAT *BETRAYAL*, IN HER HEART, UNTIL IT WITHERS INTO A HARD, BLACK LUMP.
SKREEEEE
YOU SEE, *THAT* IS HOW YOU MAKE A GREMLIN.

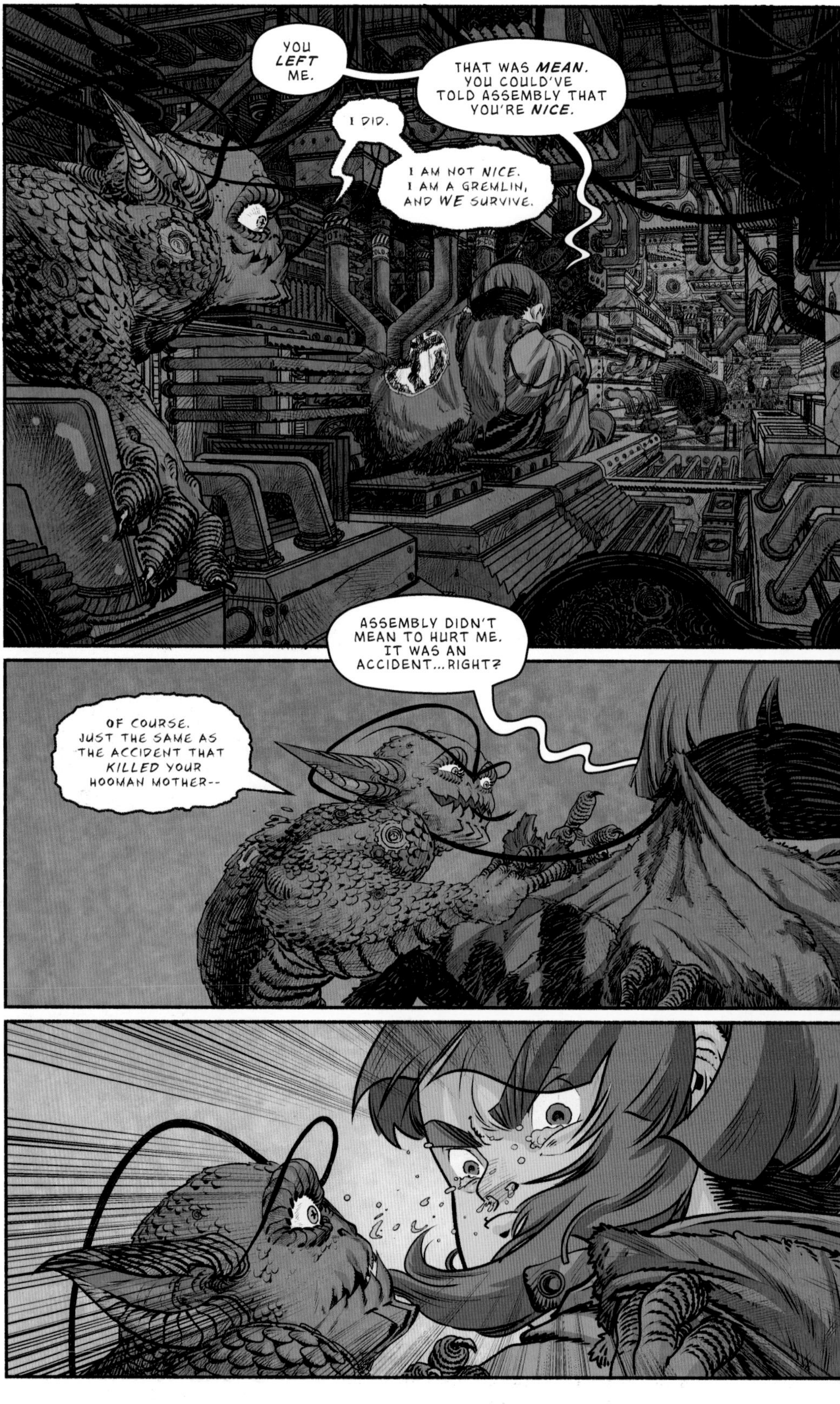
YOU *LEFT* ME.
THAT WAS *MEAN.* YOU COULD'VE TOLD ASSEMBLY THAT YOU'RE *NICE.*
I DID.
I AM NOT *NICE.* I AM A GREMLIN, AND *WE* SURVIVE.
ASSEMBLY DIDN'T MEAN TO HURT ME. IT WAS AN ACCIDENT... RIGHT?
OF COURSE. JUST THE SAME AS THE ACCIDENT THAT *KILLED* YOUR HOOMAN MOTHER--

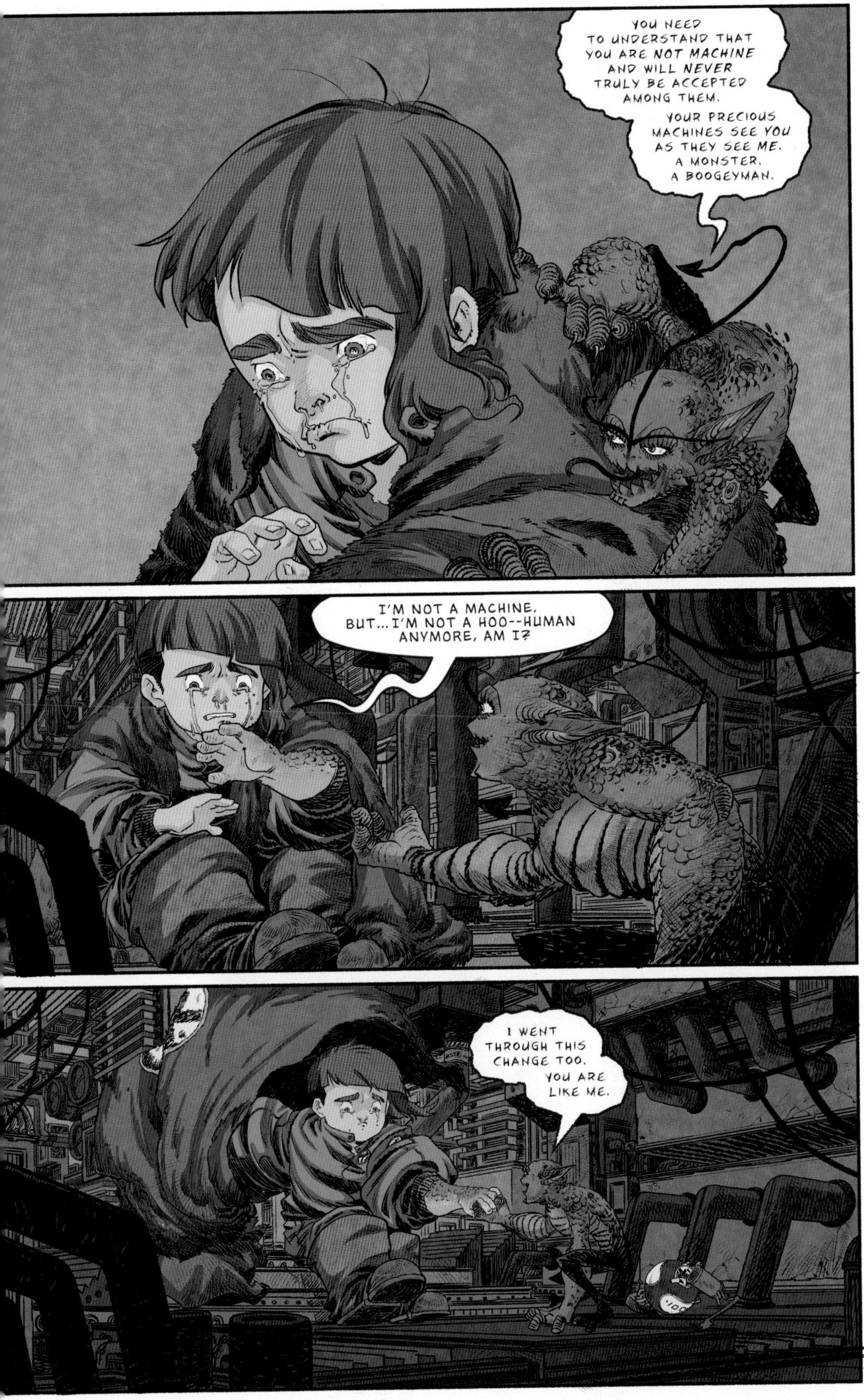
YOU NEED TO UNDERSTAND THAT YOU ARE *NOT MACHINE* AND WILL *NEVER* TRULY BE ACCEPTED AMONG THEM.
YOUR PRECIOUS MACHINES SEE *YOU* AS THEY SEE ME. A MONSTER. A BOOGEYMAN.
I'M NOT A MACHINE. BUT... I'M NOT A HOO--HUMAN ANYMORE, AM I?
I WENT THROUGH THIS CHANGE TOO.
YOU ARE LIKE ME.

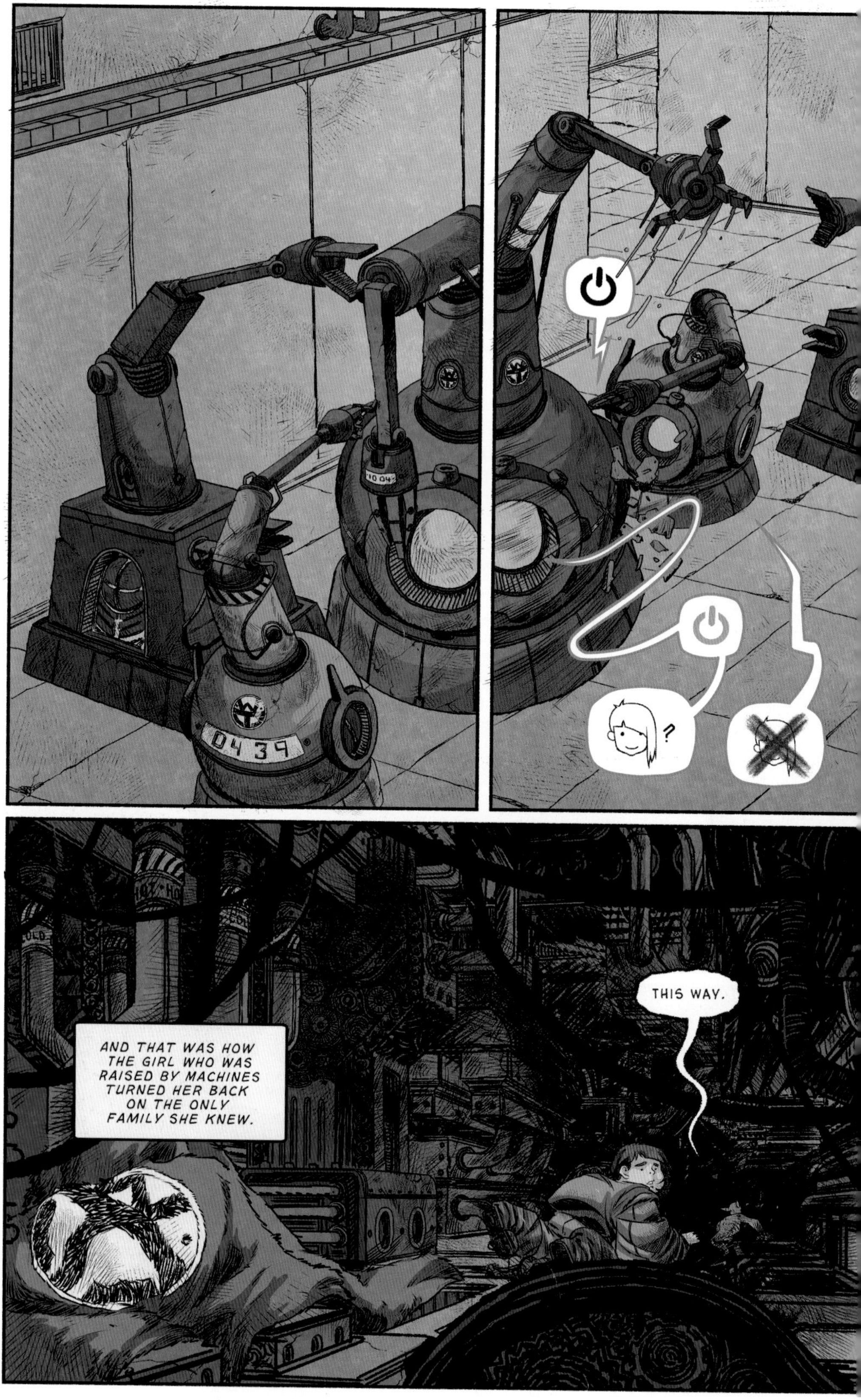
04 39
AND THAT WAS HOW THE GIRL WHO WAS RAISED BY MACHINES TURNED HER BACK ON THE ONLY FAMILY SHE KNEW.
THIS WAY.

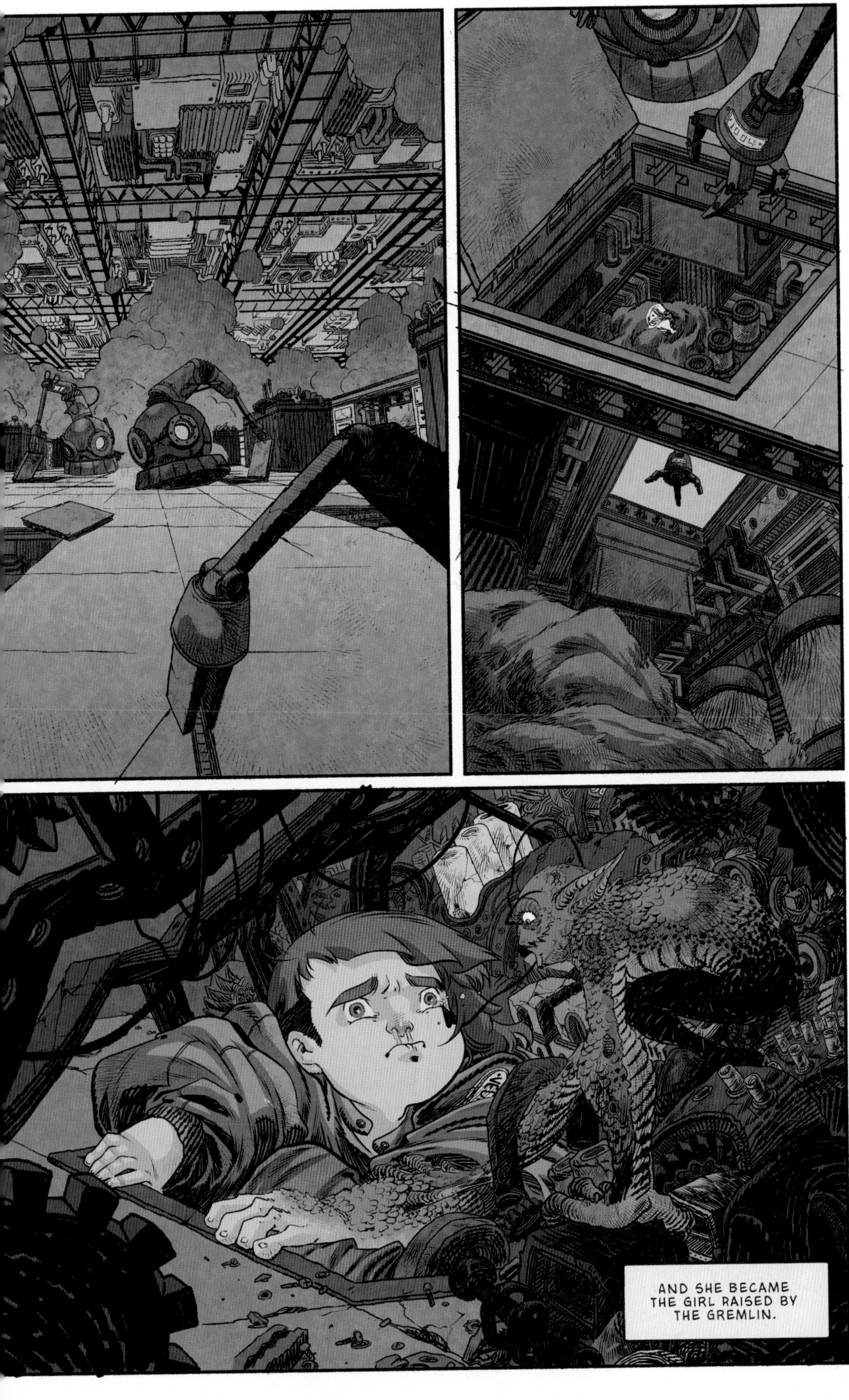
AND SHE BECAME
THE GIRL RAISED BY
THE GREMLIN.

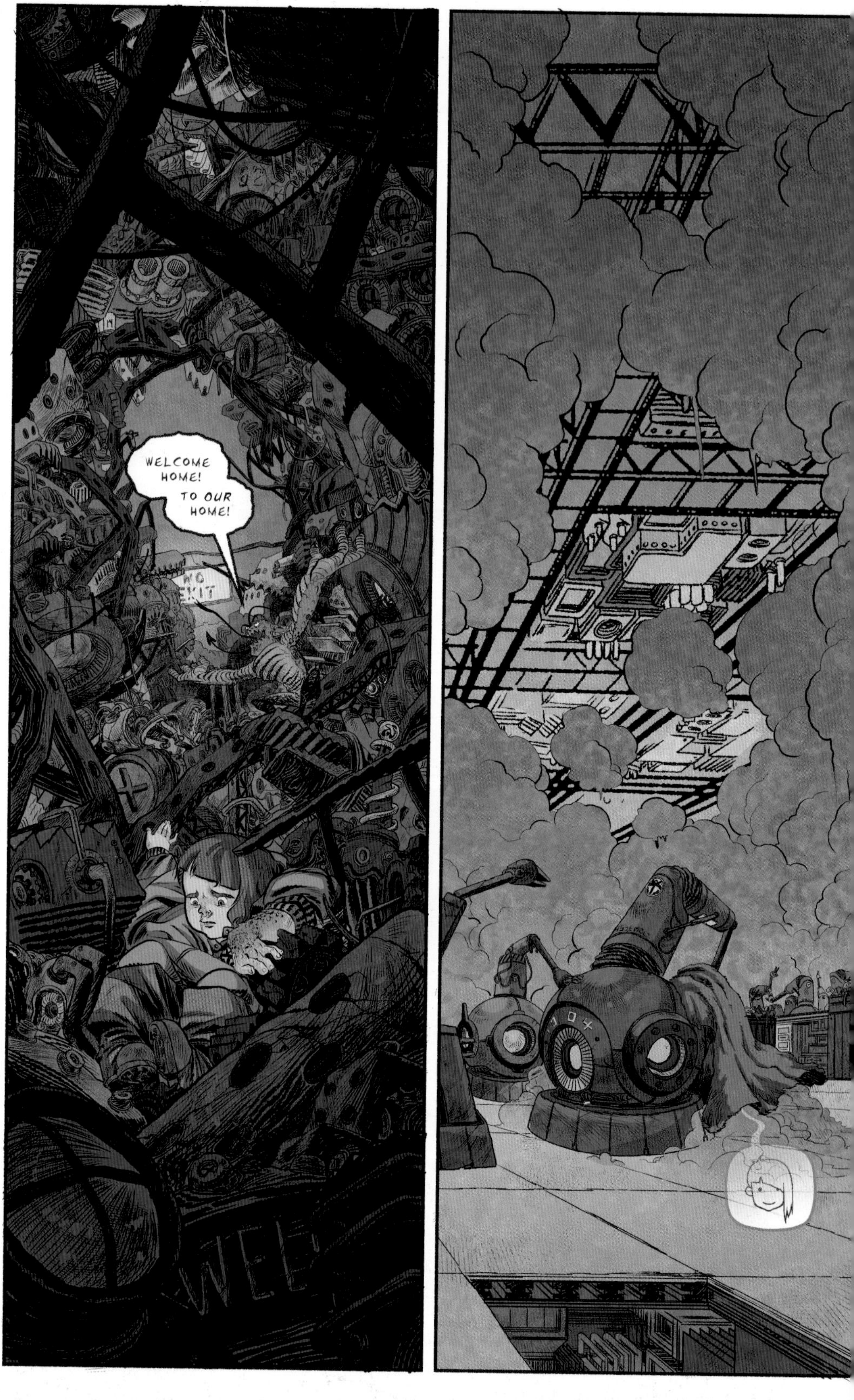
WELCOME HOME!
TO OUR HOME!

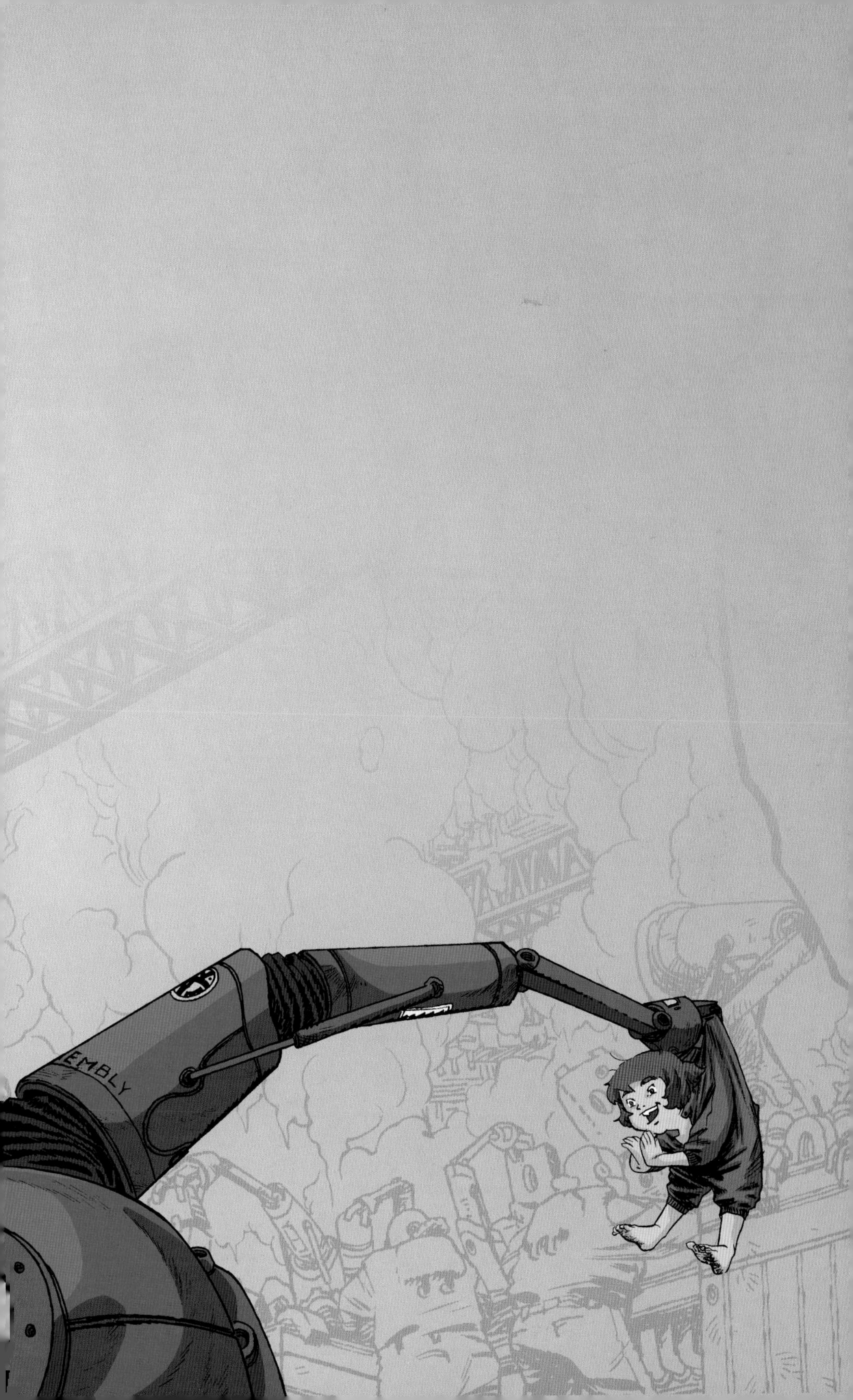
EMBLY

ATTENTION, ALL EMPLOYEES:

Management is well aware of the recent increase in machine malfunctions. We'd ask that you bear with us through this time. If you find yourself angered by work stoppages, take a deep breath, count to ten, and sign up for one of our new anger-management courses!

The cost of anger-management courses will be deducted directly from your wages.

CONTROL YOUR ANGER,
LEST IT CONSUME YOU.

This **SOOTHING** message has been brought to you by

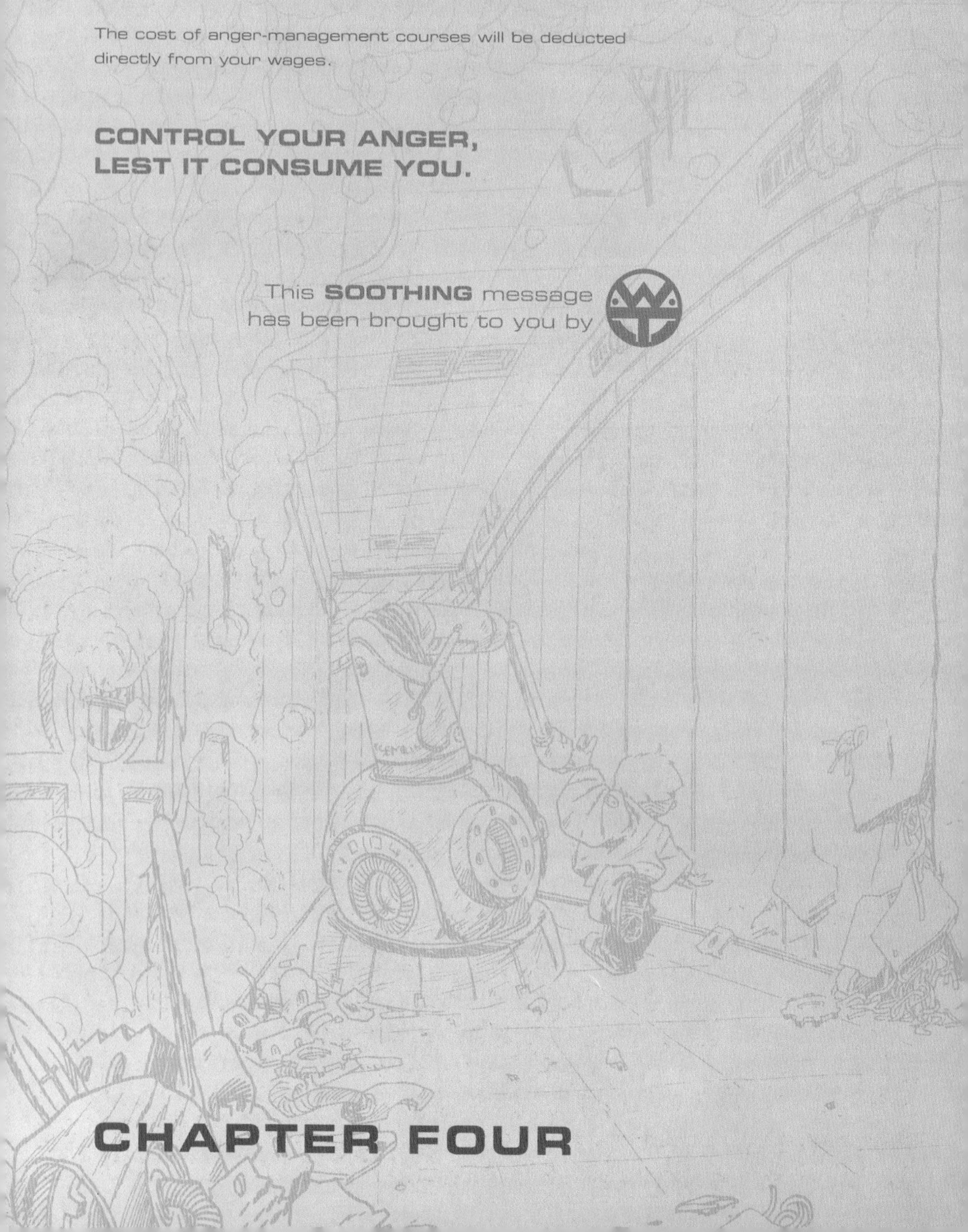

CHAPTER FOUR

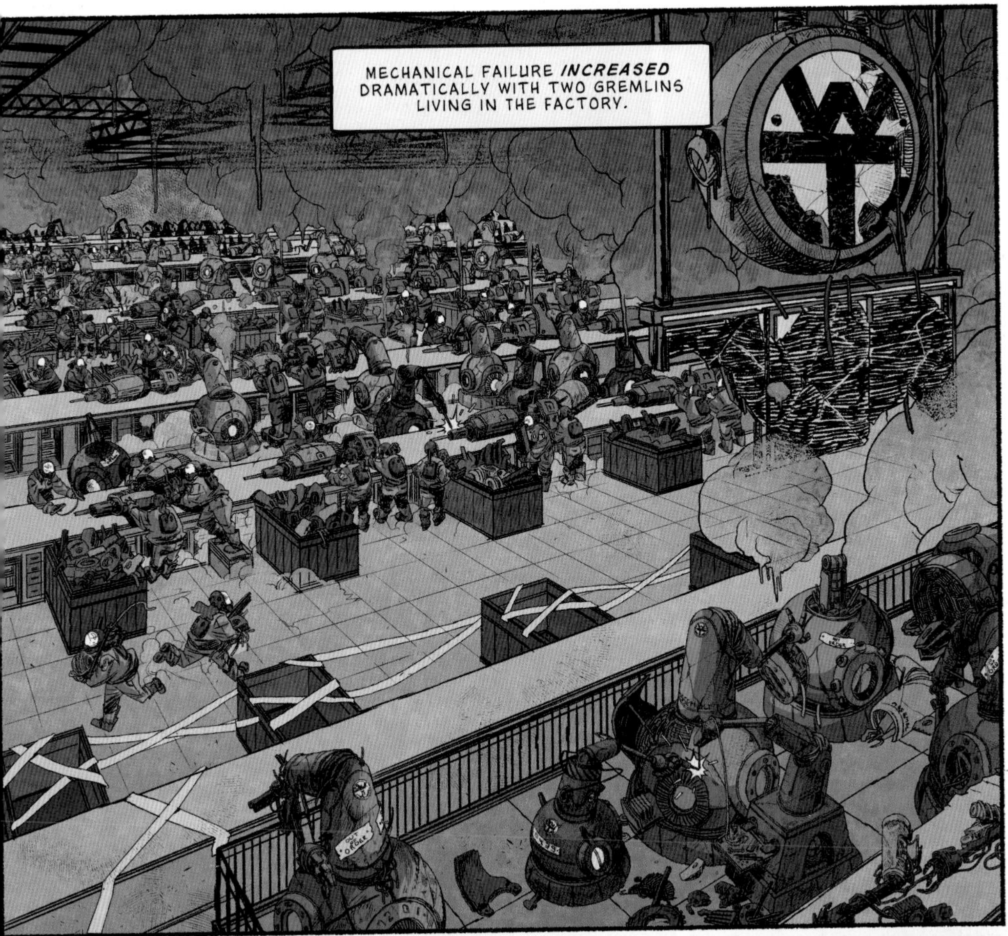
MECHANICAL FAILURE *INCREASED* DRAMATICALLY WITH TWO GREMLINS LIVING IN THE FACTORY.

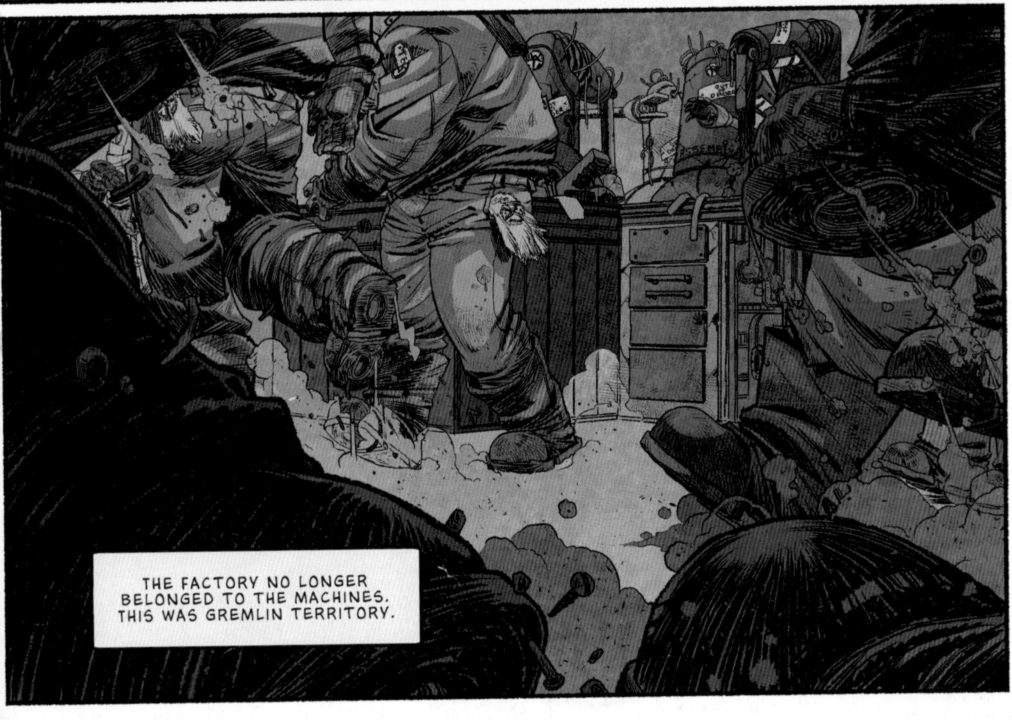
THE FACTORY NO LONGER BELONGED TO THE MACHINES. THIS WAS GREMLIN TERRITORY.

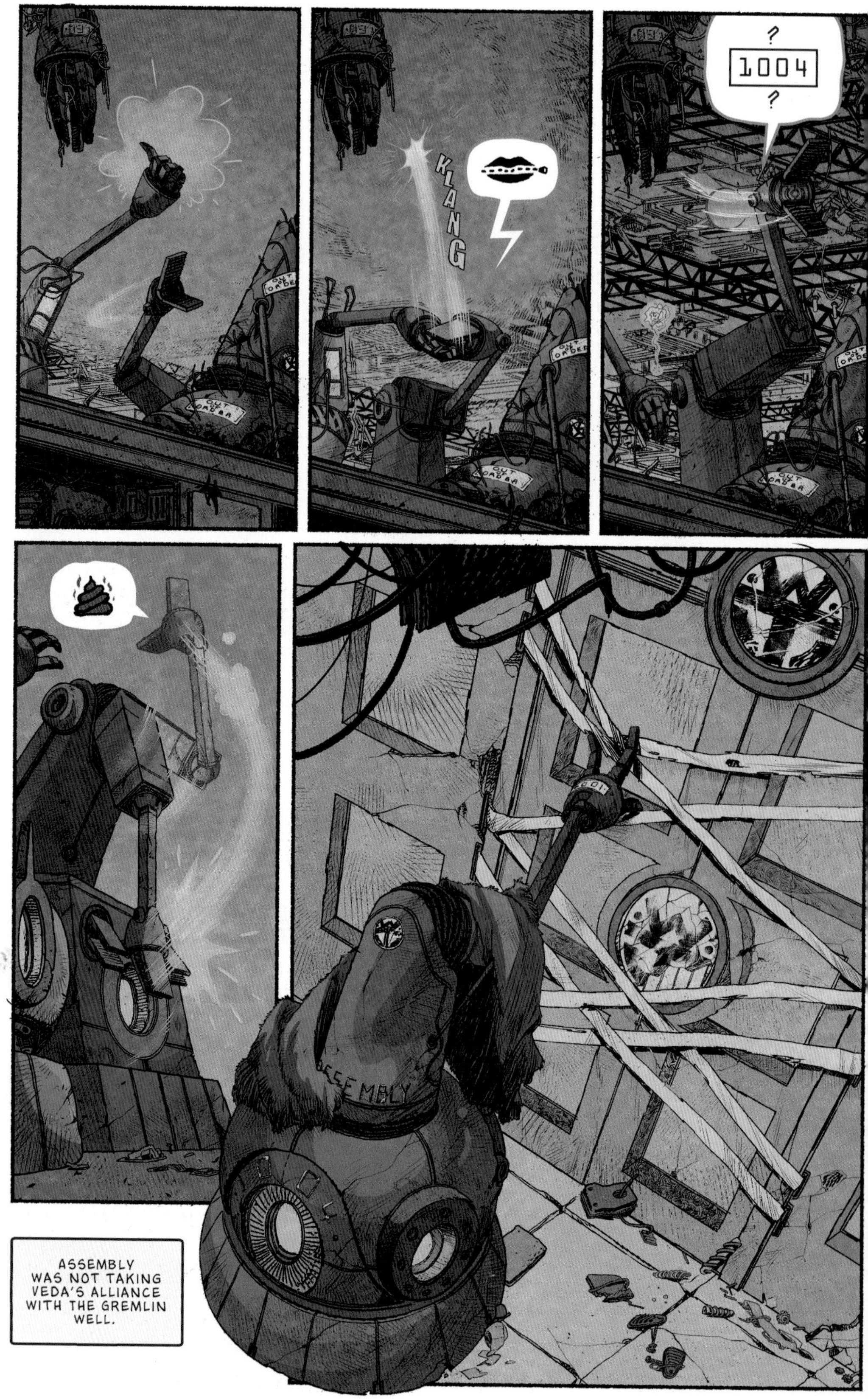
OUT OF ORDER
OUT OF ORDER
KLANG
?
1004
?
ASSEMBLY
WAS NOT TAKING
VEDA'S ALLIANCE
WITH THE GREMLIN
WELL.

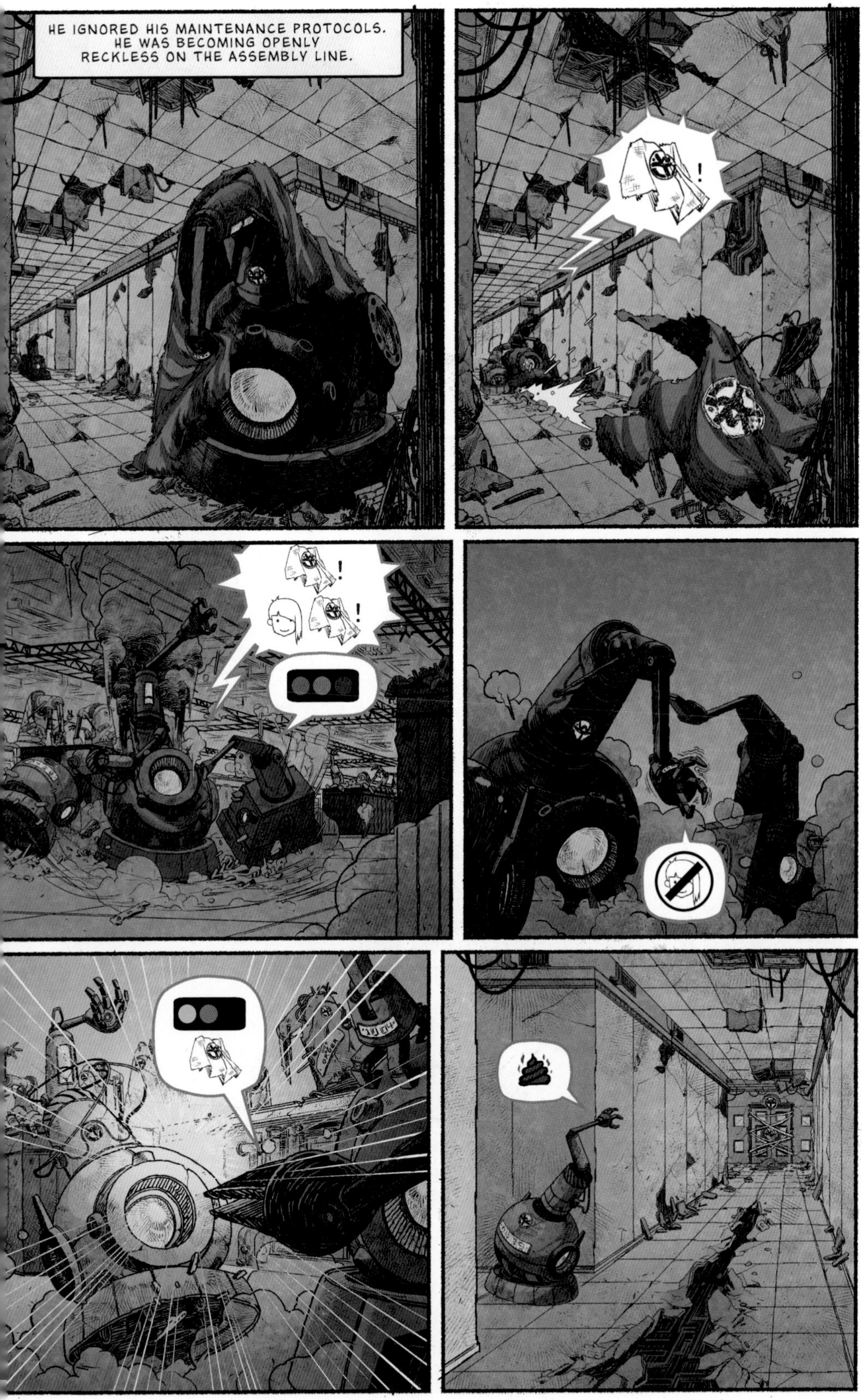
HE IGNORED HIS MAINTENANCE PROTOCOLS. HE WAS BECOMING OPENLY RECKLESS ON THE ASSEMBLY LINE.
!
!
!

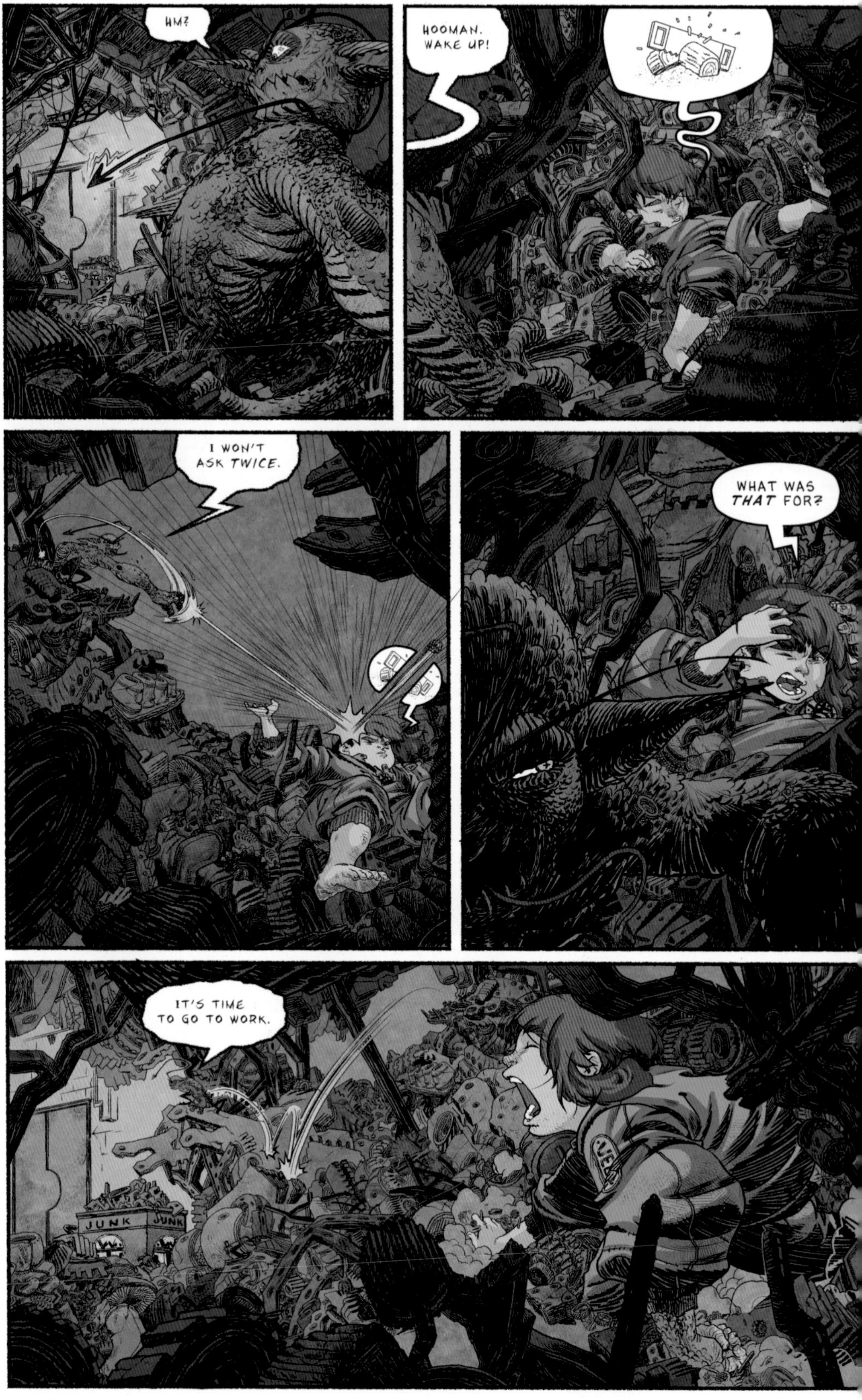
HM?
HOOMAN. WAKE UP!
I WON'T ASK TWICE.
WHAT WAS THAT FOR?
IT'S TIME TO GO TO WORK.
JUNK
JUNK

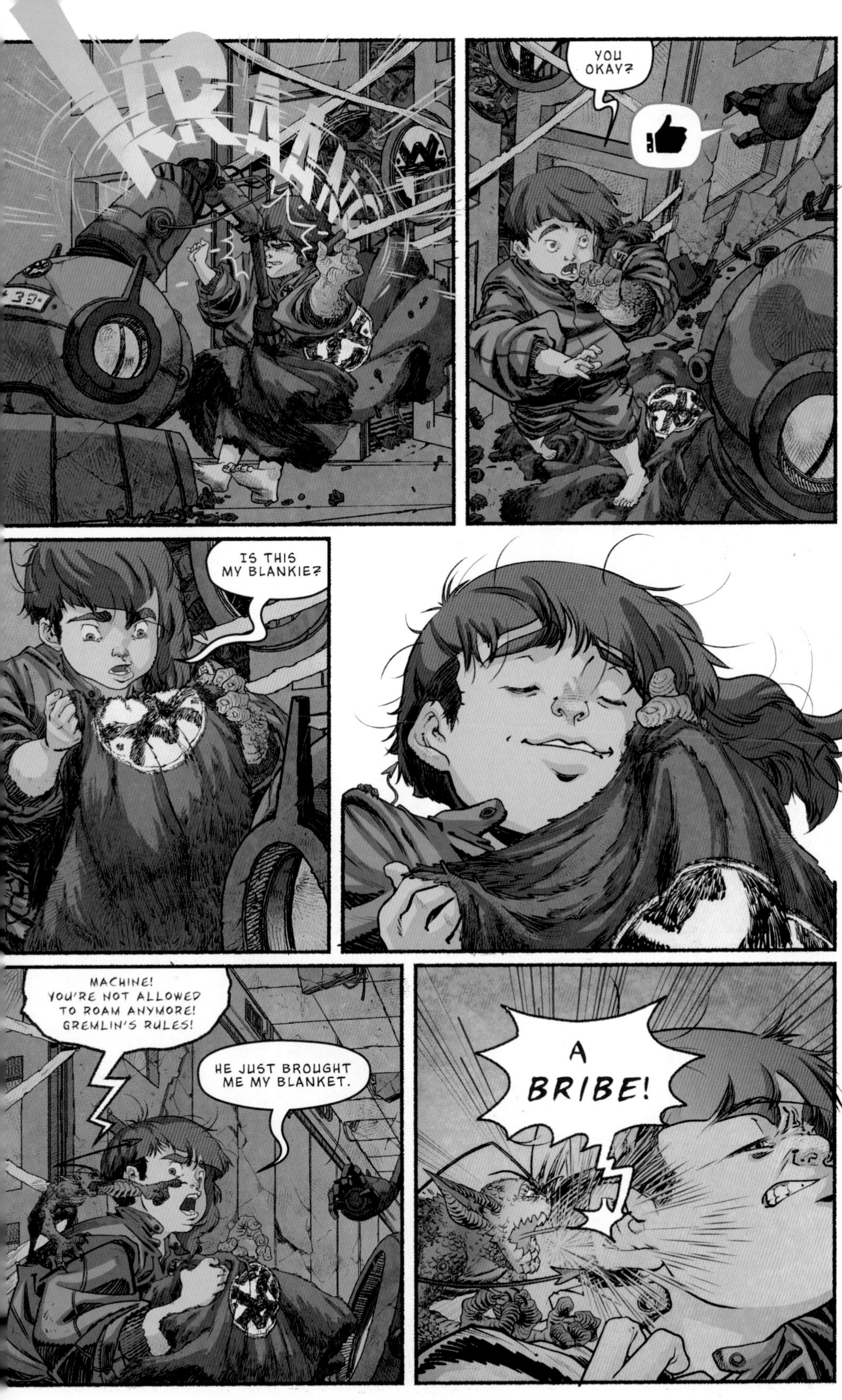
YOU OKAY?
IS THIS MY BLANKIE?
MACHINE! YOU'RE NOT ALLOWED TO ROAM ANYMORE! GREMLIN'S RULES!
HE JUST BROUGHT ME MY BLANKET.
A BRIBE!

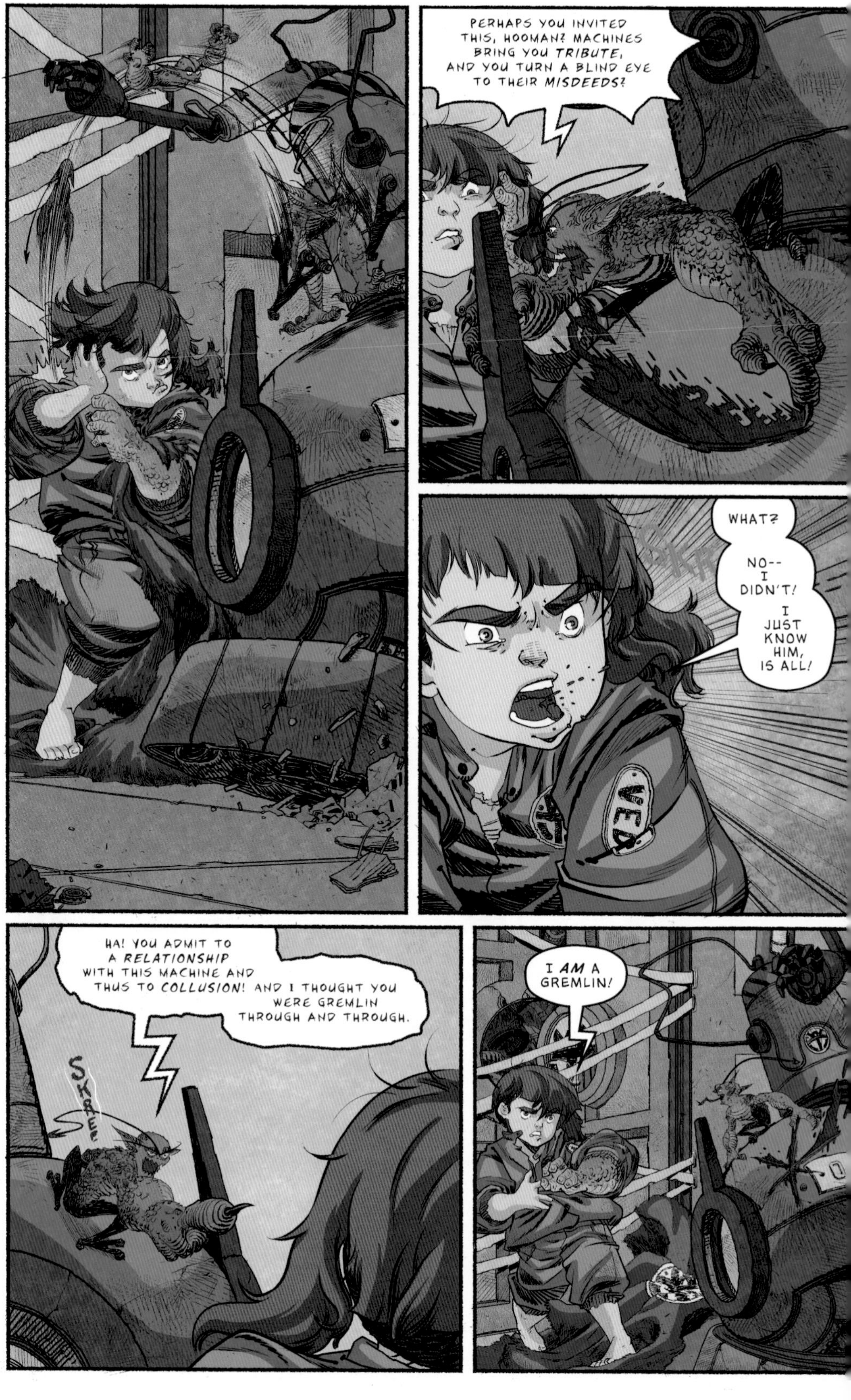
PERHAPS YOU INVITED THIS, HOOMAN? MACHINES BRING YOU *TRIBUTE*, AND YOU TURN A BLIND EYE TO THEIR *MISDEEDS*?
WHAT?
NO-- I DIDN'T!
I JUST KNOW HIM, IS ALL!
HA! YOU ADMIT TO A *RELATIONSHIP* WITH THIS MACHINE AND THUS TO *COLLUSION*! AND I THOUGHT YOU WERE GREMLIN THROUGH AND THROUGH.
SKREE
I *AM* A GREMLIN!

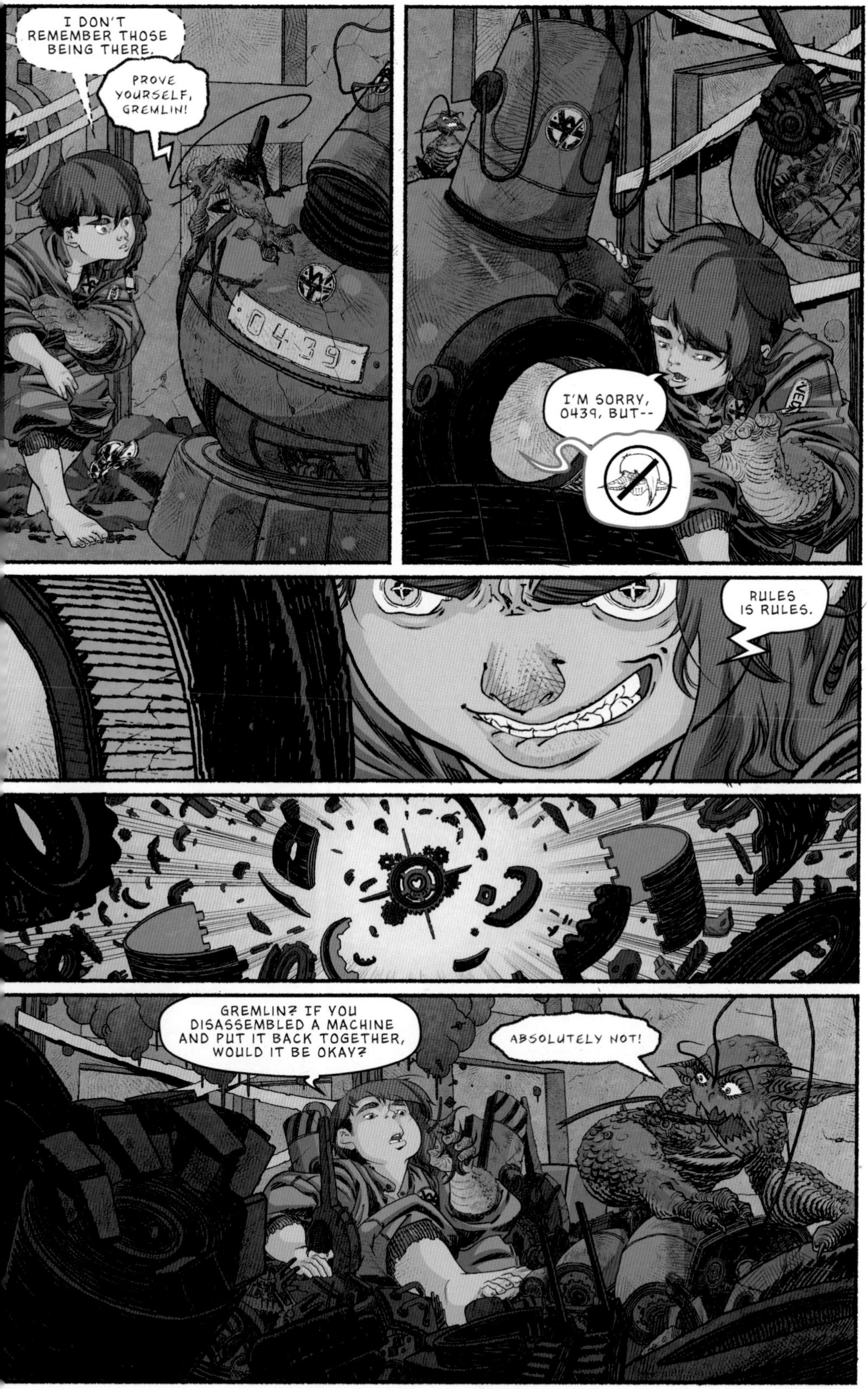
I DON'T REMEMBER THOSE BEING THERE.
PROVE YOURSELF, GREMLIN!
0439
I'M SORRY, 0439, BUT--
RULES IS RULES.
GREMLIN? IF YOU DISASSEMBLED A MACHINE AND PUT IT BACK TOGETHER, WOULD IT BE OKAY?
ABSOLUTELY NOT!

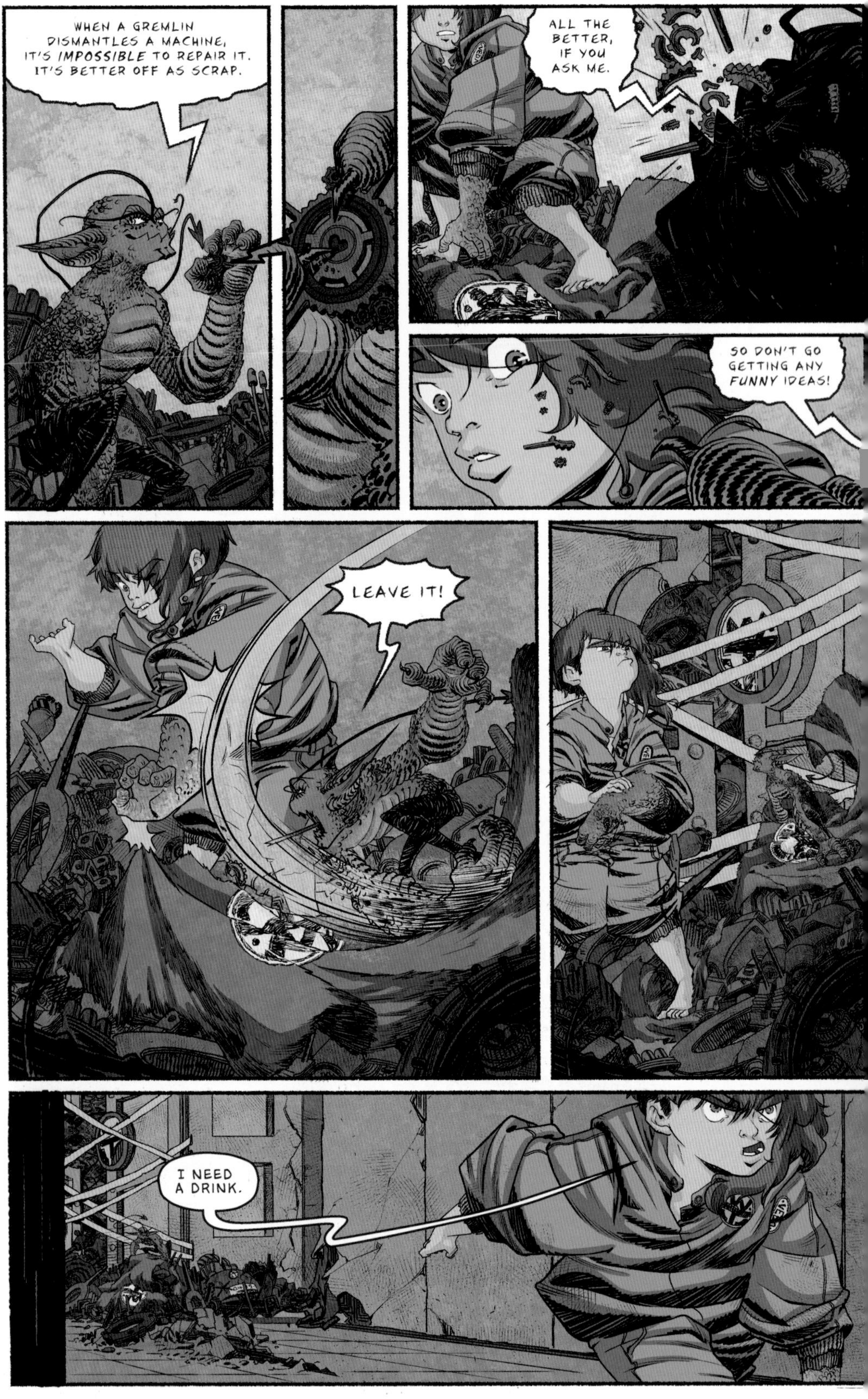
WHEN A GREMLIN DISMANTLES A MACHINE, IT'S *IMPOSSIBLE* TO REPAIR IT. IT'S BETTER OFF AS SCRAP.
ALL THE BETTER, IF YOU ASK ME.
SO DON'T GO GETTING ANY *FUNNY* IDEAS!
LEAVE IT!
I NEED A DRINK.

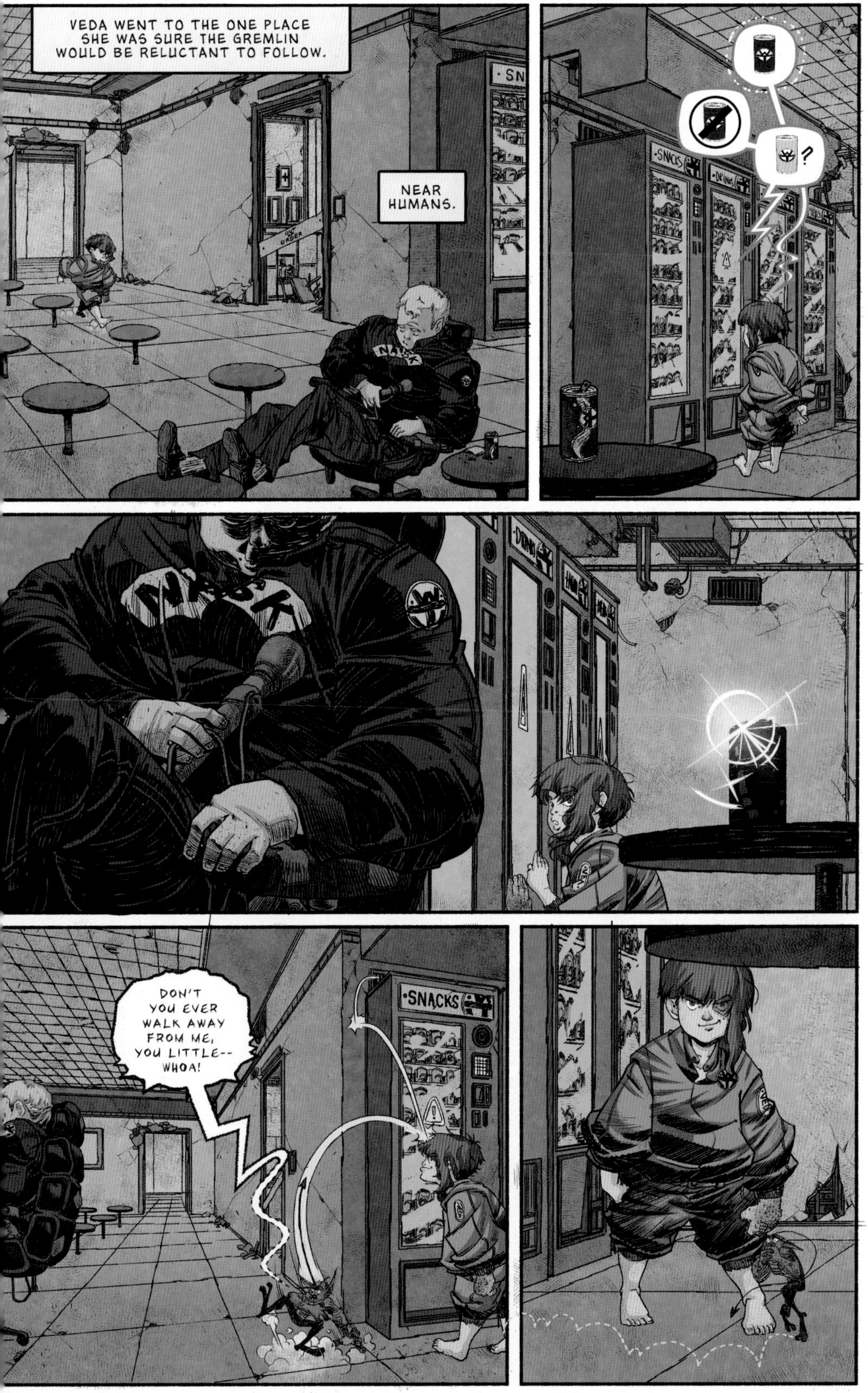
VEDA WENT TO THE ONE PLACE SHE WAS SURE THE GREMLIN WOULD BE RELUCTANT TO FOLLOW.
NEAR HUMANS.
DON'T YOU EVER WALK AWAY FROM ME, YOU LITTLE-- WHOA!

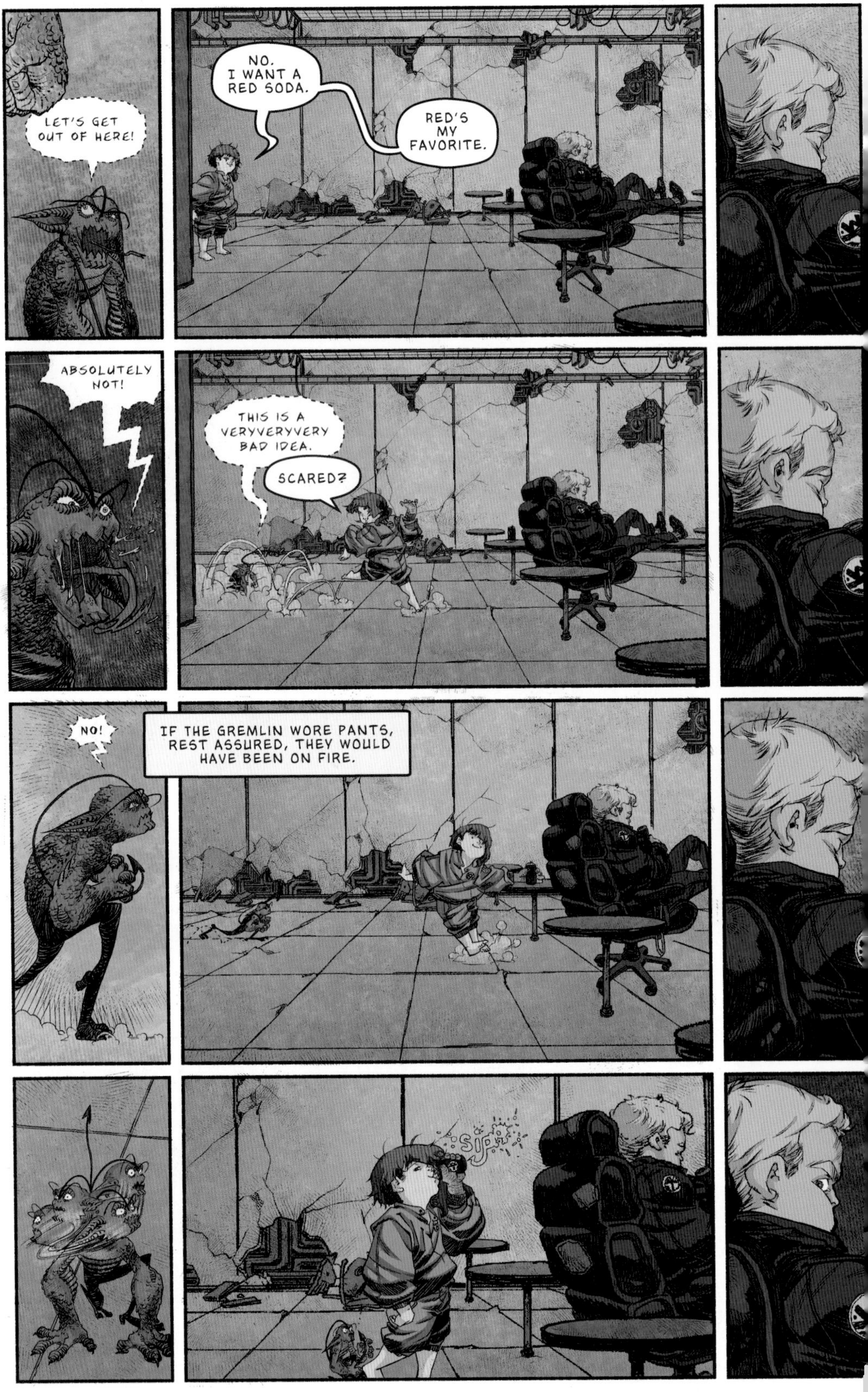
LET'S GET OUT OF HERE!
NO. I WANT A RED SODA.
RED'S MY FAVORITE.
ABSOLUTELY NOT!
THIS IS A VERYVERYVERY BAD IDEA.
SCARED?
NO!
IF THE GREMLIN WORE PANTS, REST ASSURED, THEY WOULD HAVE BEEN ON FIRE.
SIP

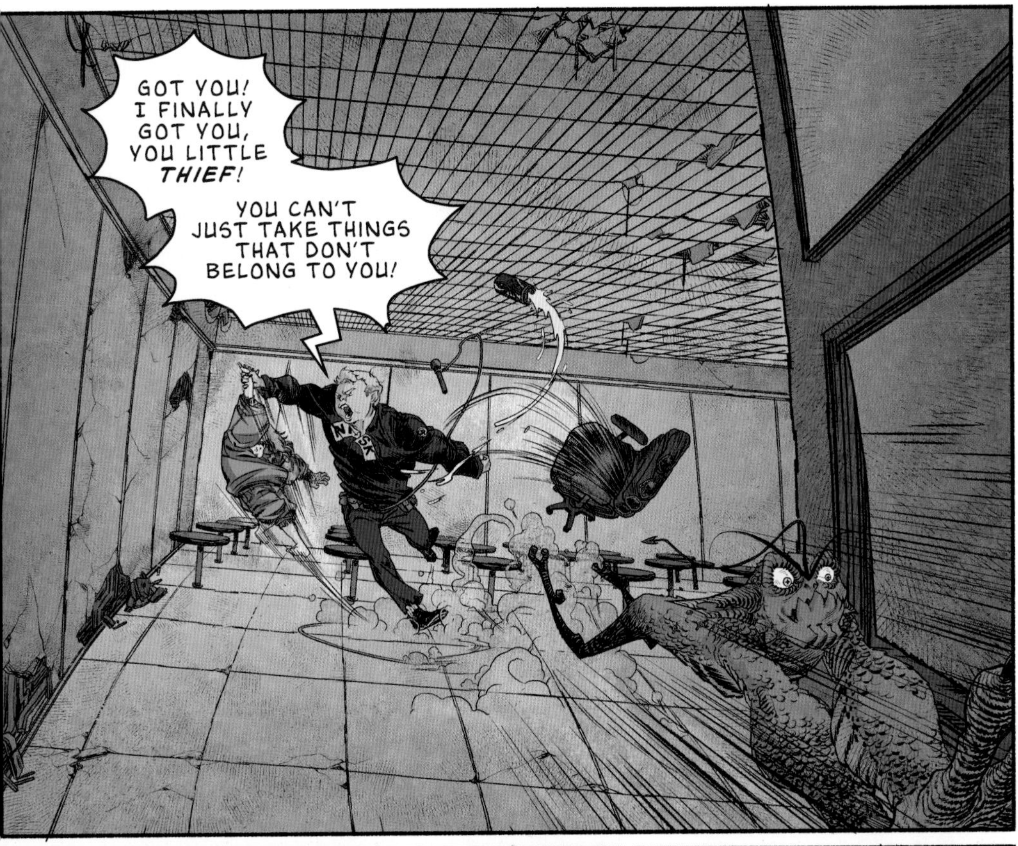
GOT YOU! I FINALLY GOT YOU, YOU LITTLE *THIEF*!
YOU CAN'T JUST TAKE THINGS THAT DON'T BELONG TO YOU!

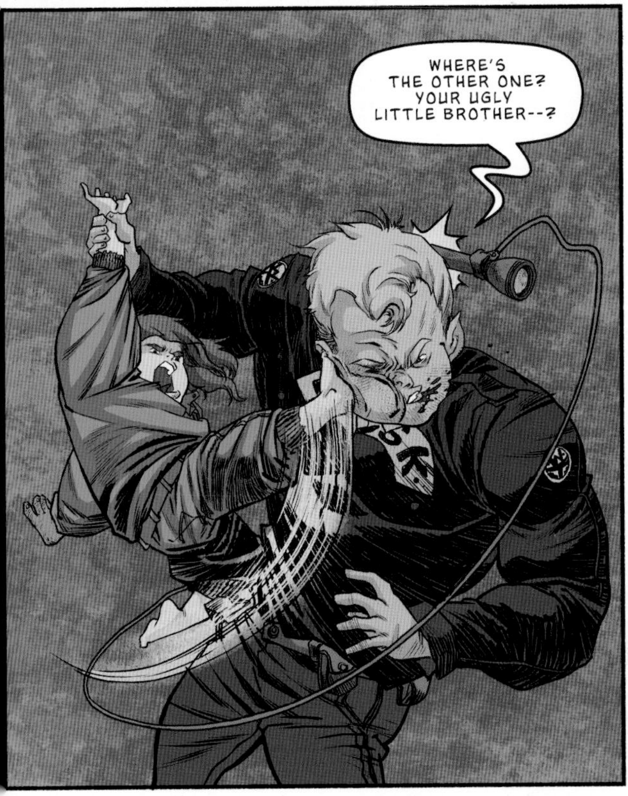
WHERE'S THE OTHER ONE? YOUR UGLY LITTLE BROTHER--?

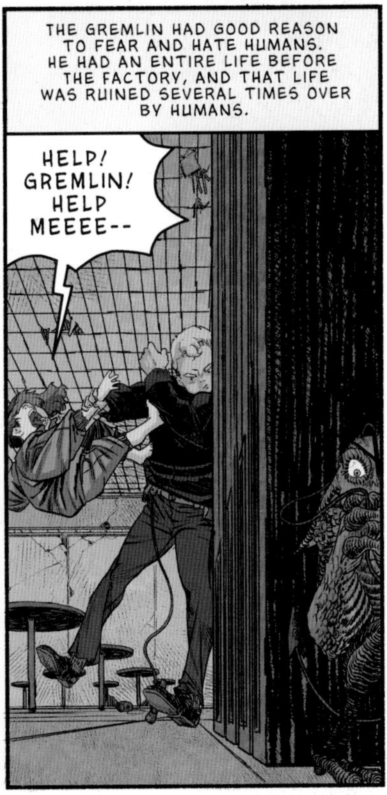
THE GREMLIN HAD GOOD REASON TO FEAR AND HATE HUMANS. HE HAD AN ENTIRE LIFE BEFORE THE FACTORY, AND THAT LIFE WAS RUINED SEVERAL TIMES OVER BY HUMANS.
HELP! GREMLIN! HELP MEEEE--

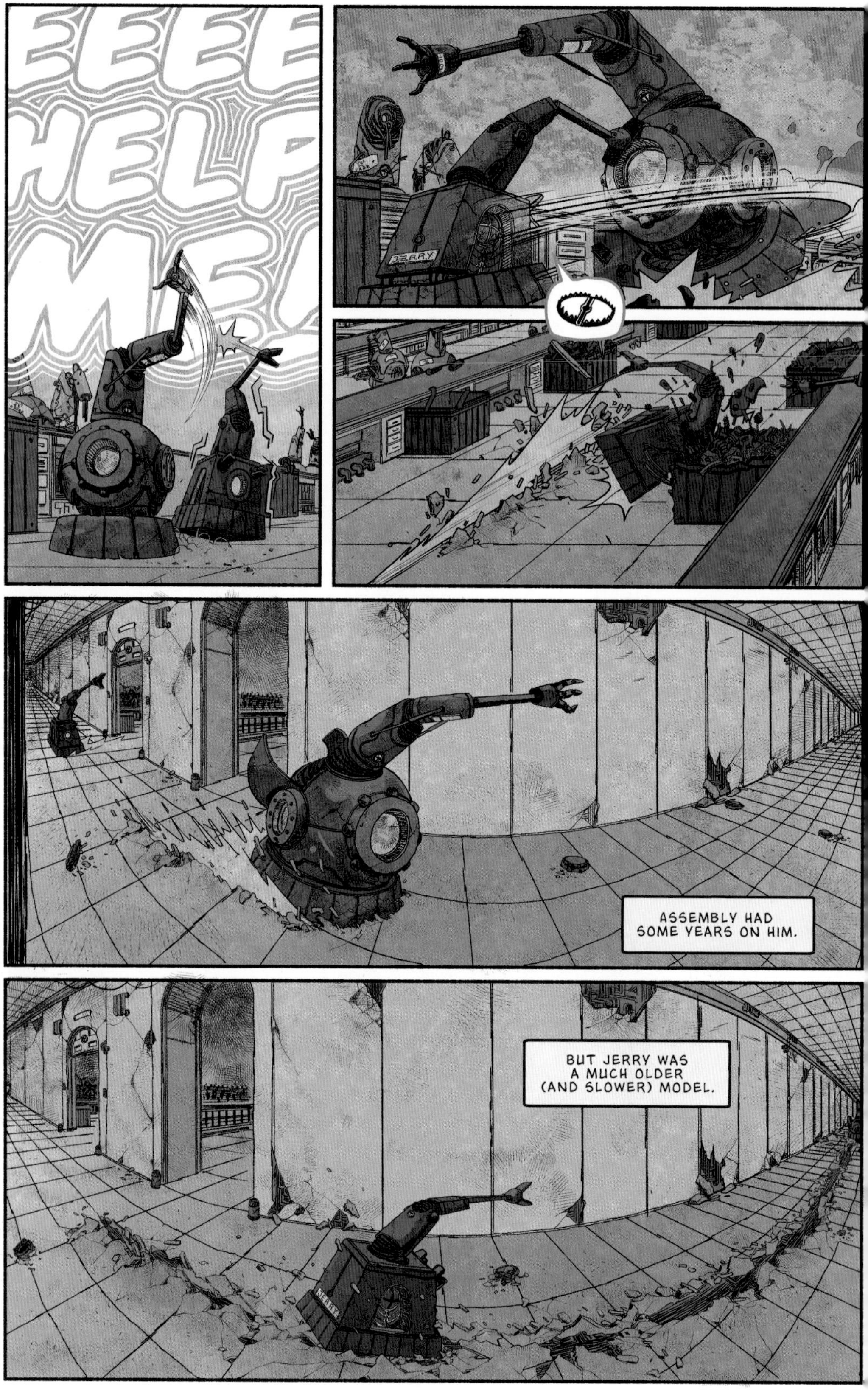
EEEE
HELP
ME!
ASSEMBLY HAD SOME YEARS ON HIM.
BUT JERRY WAS A MUCH OLDER (AND SLOWER) MODEL.

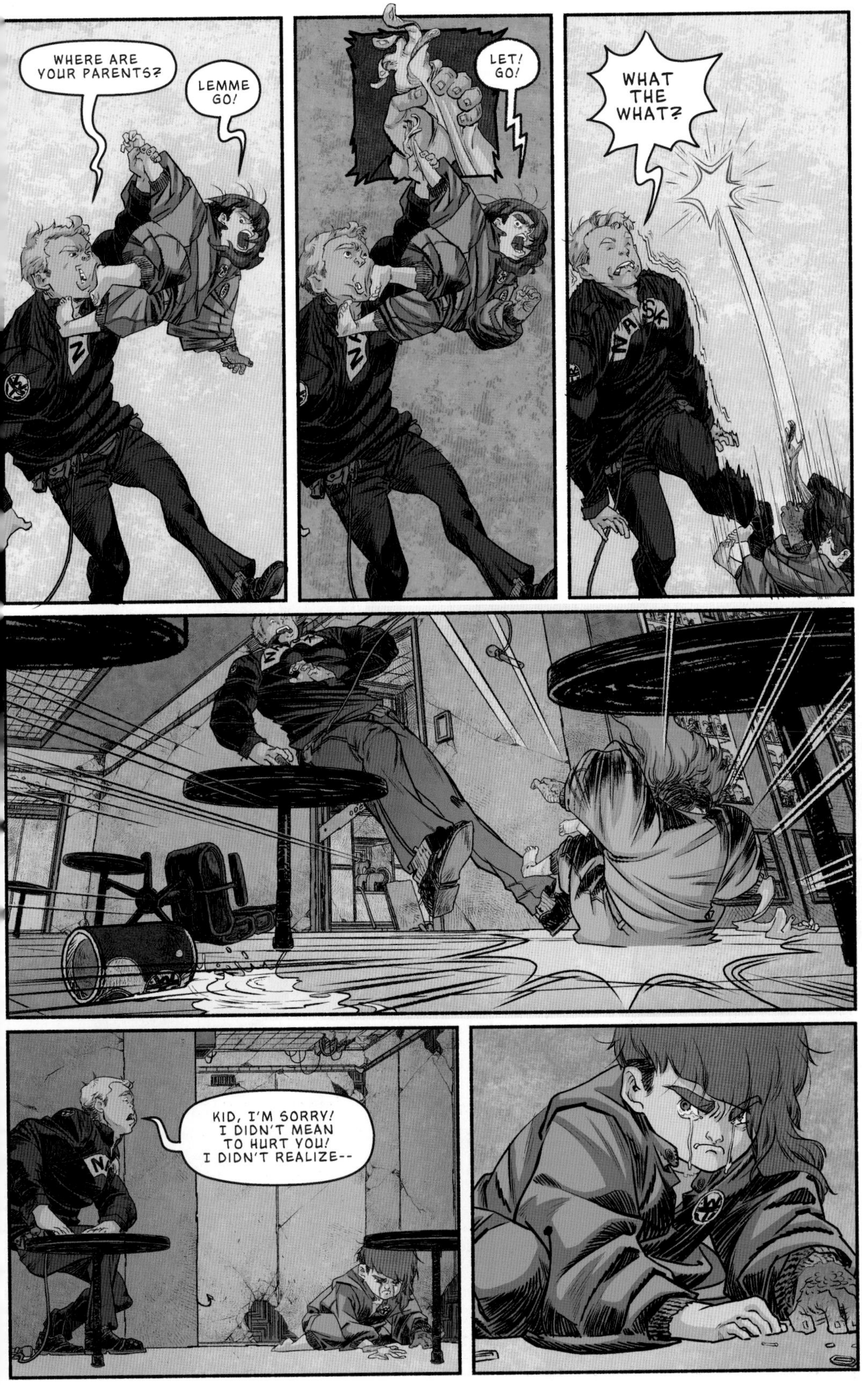
WHERE ARE YOUR PARENTS?
LEMME GO!
LET! GO!
WHAT THE WHAT?
KID, I'M SORRY! I DIDN'T MEAN TO HURT YOU! I DIDN'T REALIZE--

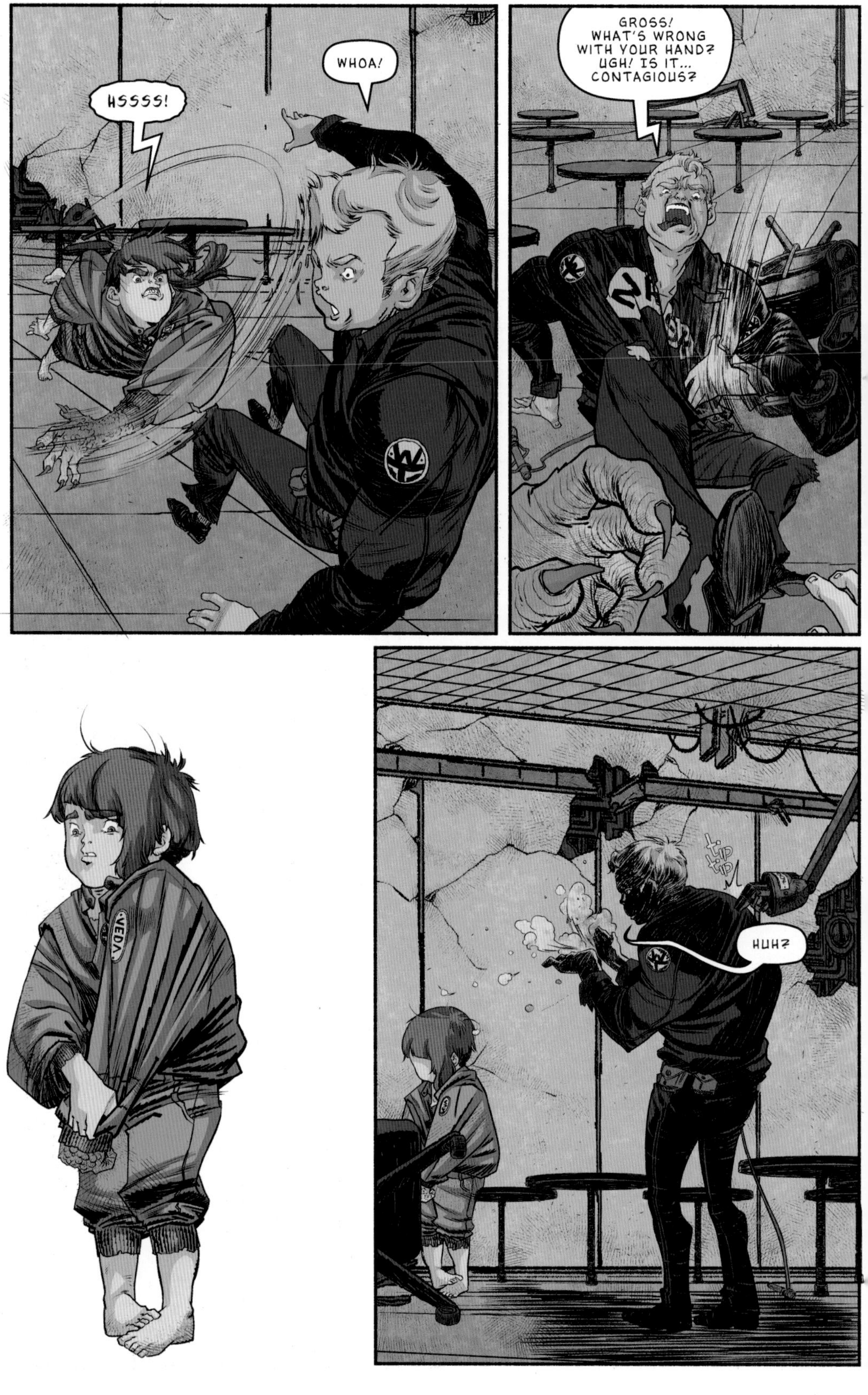
HSSSS!
WHOA!
GROSS! WHAT'S WRONG WITH YOUR HAND? UGH! IS IT... CONTAGIOUS?
VEDA
tip tip
HUH?

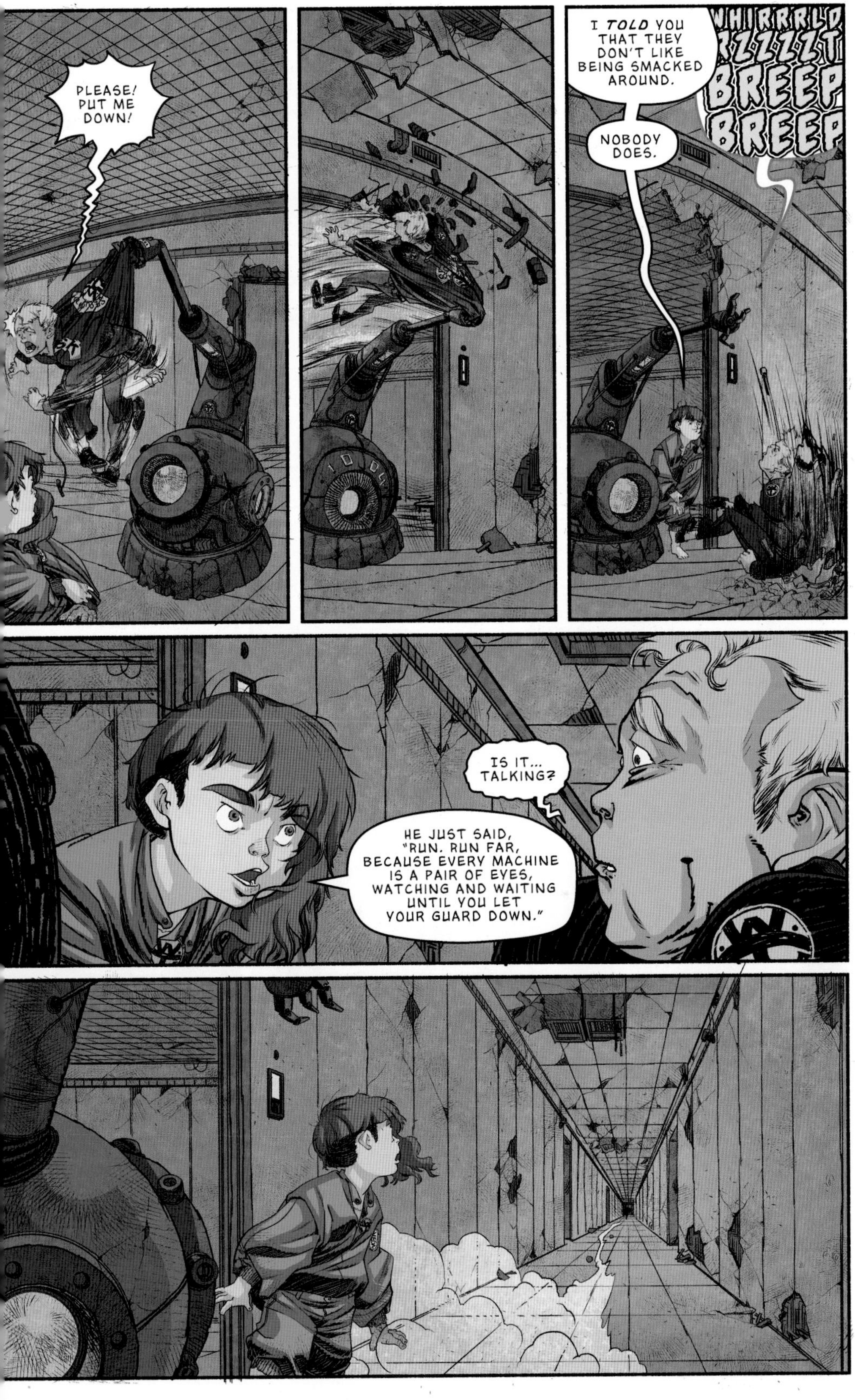
PLEASE! PUT ME DOWN!
I TOLD YOU THAT THEY DON'T LIKE BEING SMACKED AROUND.
NOBODY DOES.
WHIRRRLD RZZZZZT BREEP BREEP
IS IT... TALKING?
HE JUST SAID, "RUN. RUN FAR, BECAUSE EVERY MACHINE IS A PAIR OF EYES, WATCHING AND WAITING UNTIL YOU LET YOUR GUARD DOWN."

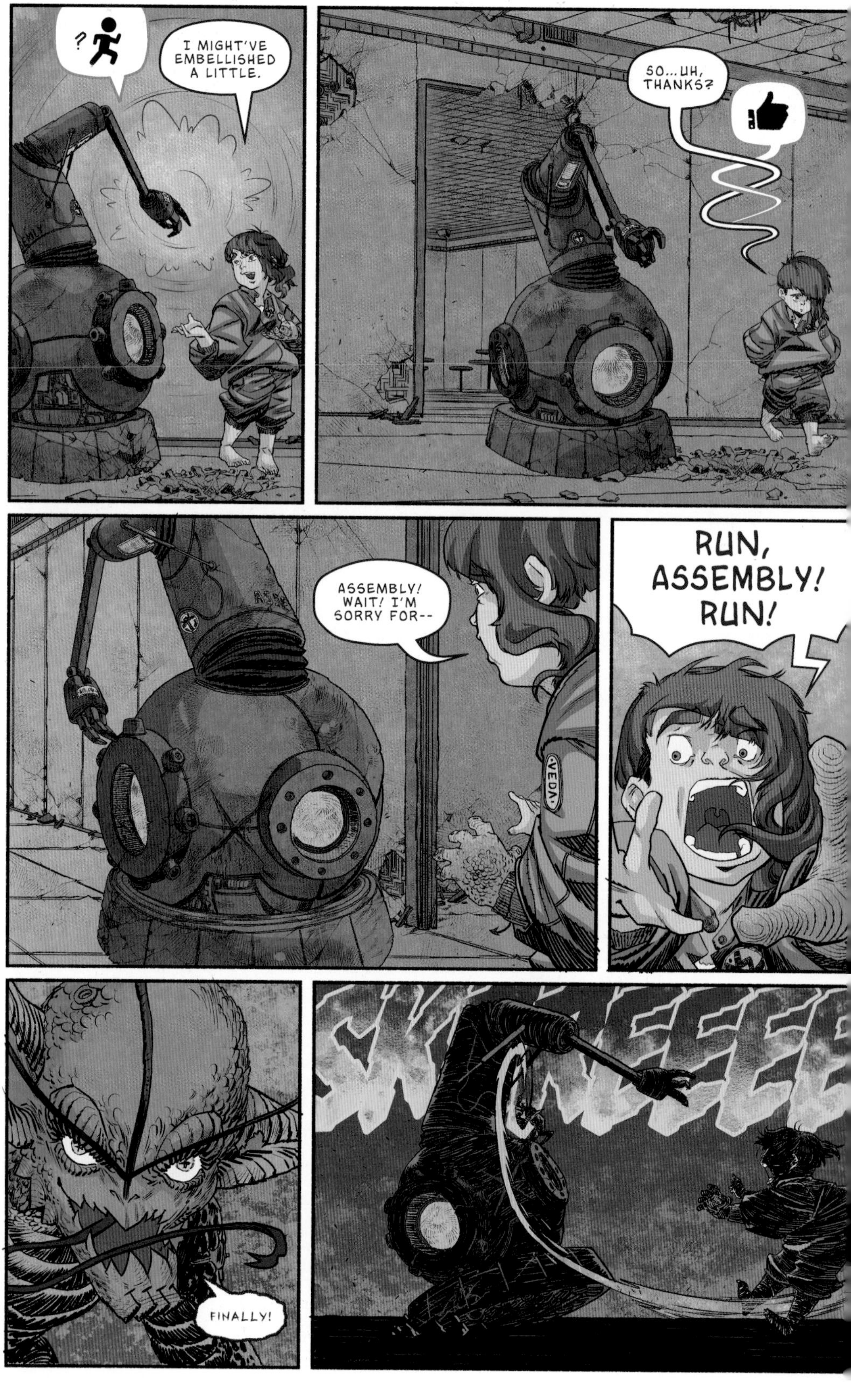
?
I MIGHT'VE EMBELLISHED A LITTLE.
SO...UH, THANKS?
ASSEMBLY! WAIT! I'M SORRY FOR--
VEDA
RUN, ASSEMBLY! RUN!
FINALLY!

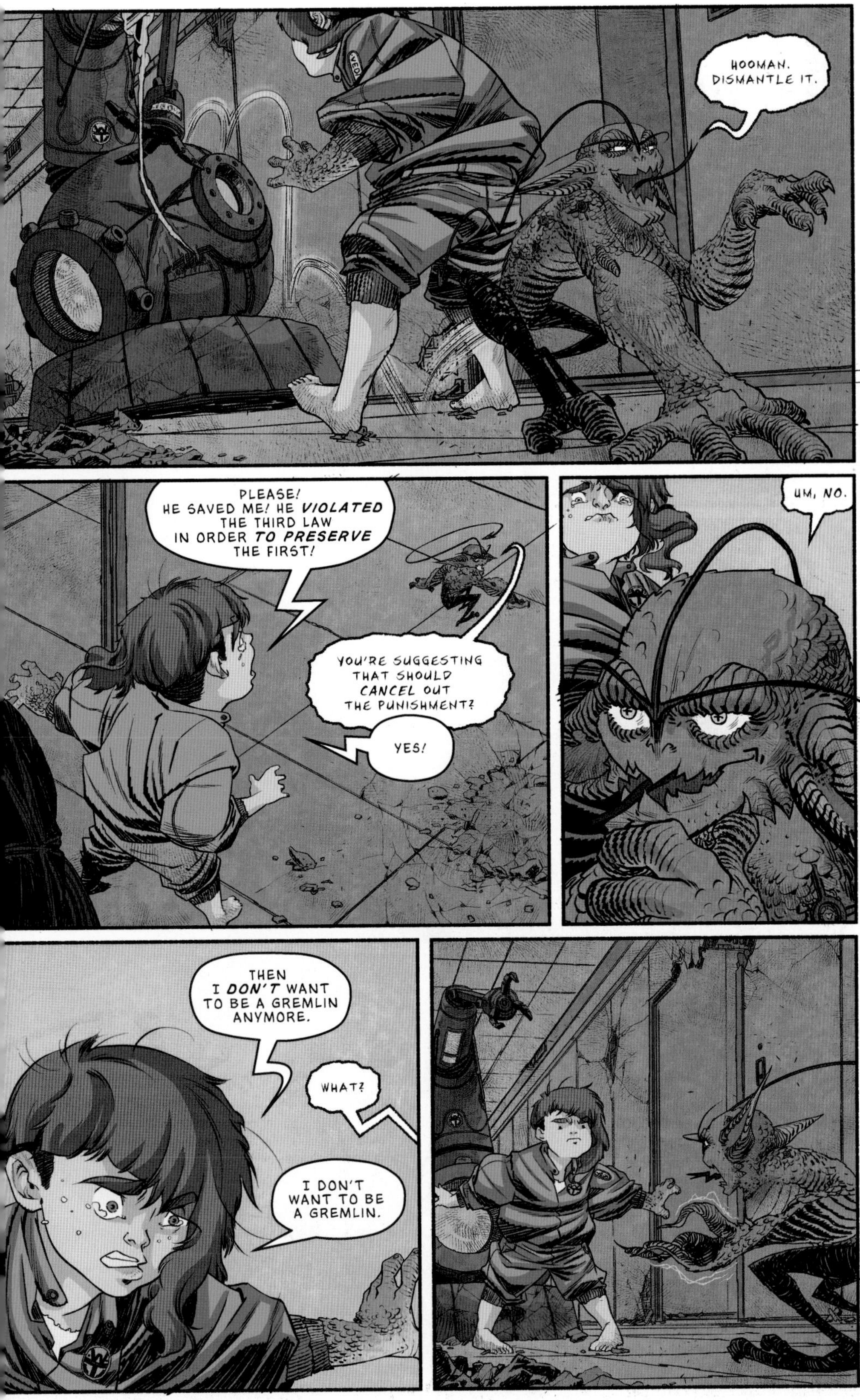
HOOMAN. DISMANTLE IT.
PLEASE! HE SAVED ME! HE VIOLATED THE THIRD LAW IN ORDER TO PRESERVE THE FIRST!
YOU'RE SUGGESTING THAT SHOULD CANCEL OUT THE PUNISHMENT?
YES!
UM, NO.
THEN I DON'T WANT TO BE A GREMLIN ANYMORE.
WHAT?
I DON'T WANT TO BE A GREMLIN.

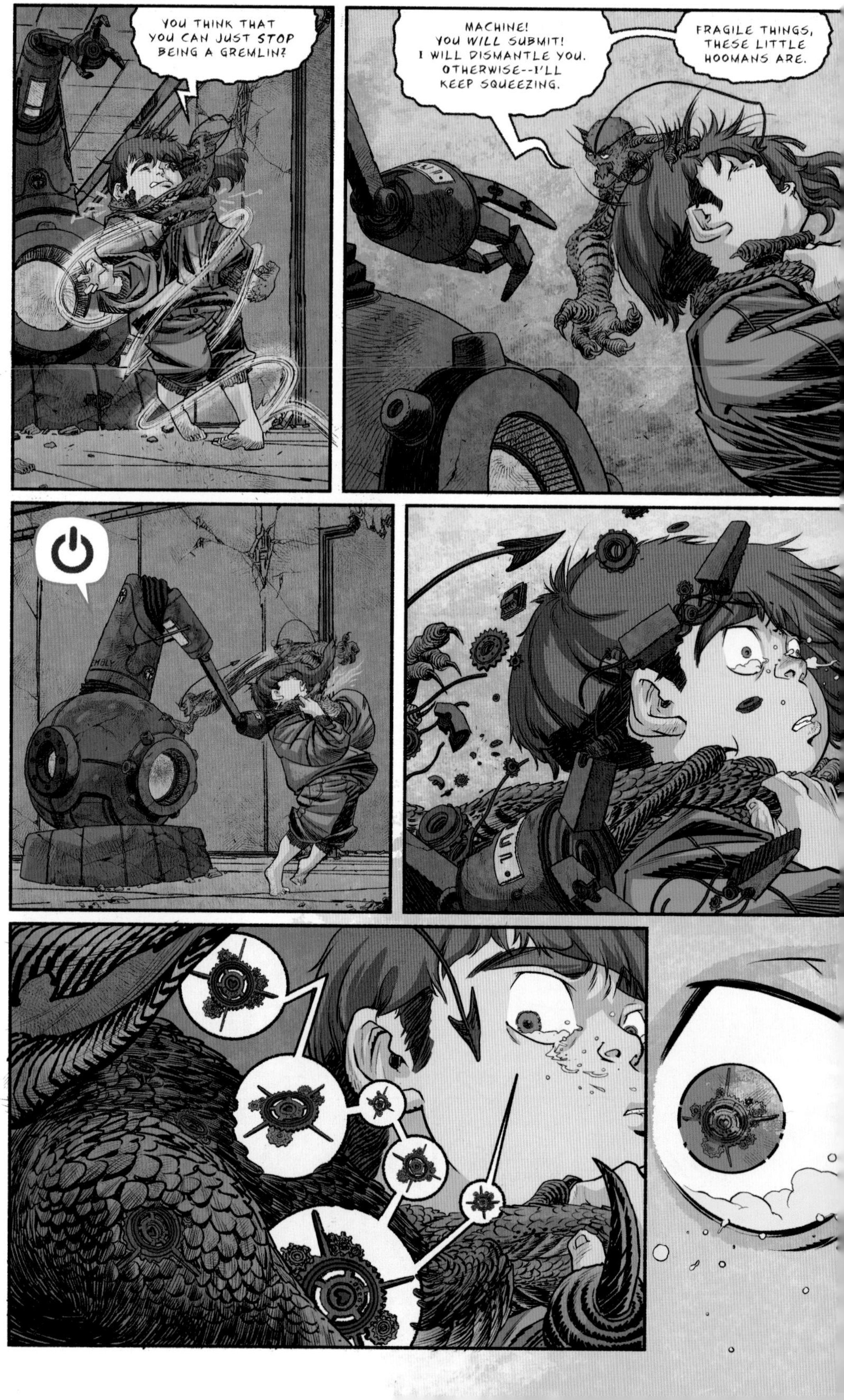
YOU THINK THAT YOU CAN JUST STOP BEING A GREMLIN?
MACHINE! YOU WILL SUBMIT! I WILL DISMANTLE YOU. OTHERWISE--I'LL KEEP SQUEEZING.
FRAGILE THINGS, THESE LITTLE HOOMANS ARE.

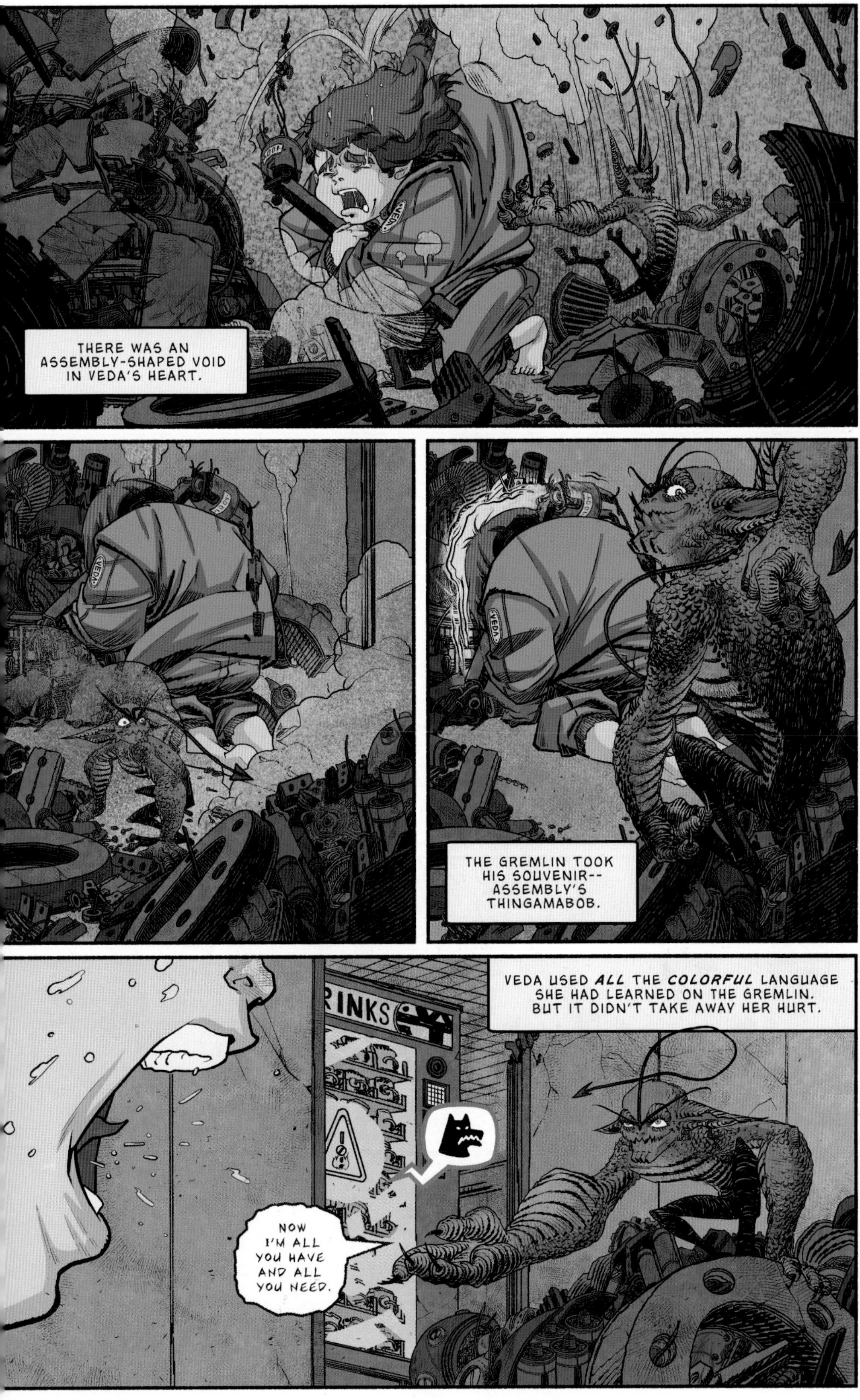
THERE WAS AN ASSEMBLY-SHAPED VOID IN VEDA'S HEART.
VEDA
VEDA
VEDA
THE GREMLIN TOOK HIS SOUVENIR-- ASSEMBLY'S THINGAMABOB.
VEDA USED ALL THE COLORFUL LANGUAGE SHE HAD LEARNED ON THE GREMLIN. BUT IT DIDN'T TAKE AWAY HER HURT.
RINKS
NOW I'M ALL YOU HAVE AND ALL YOU NEED.

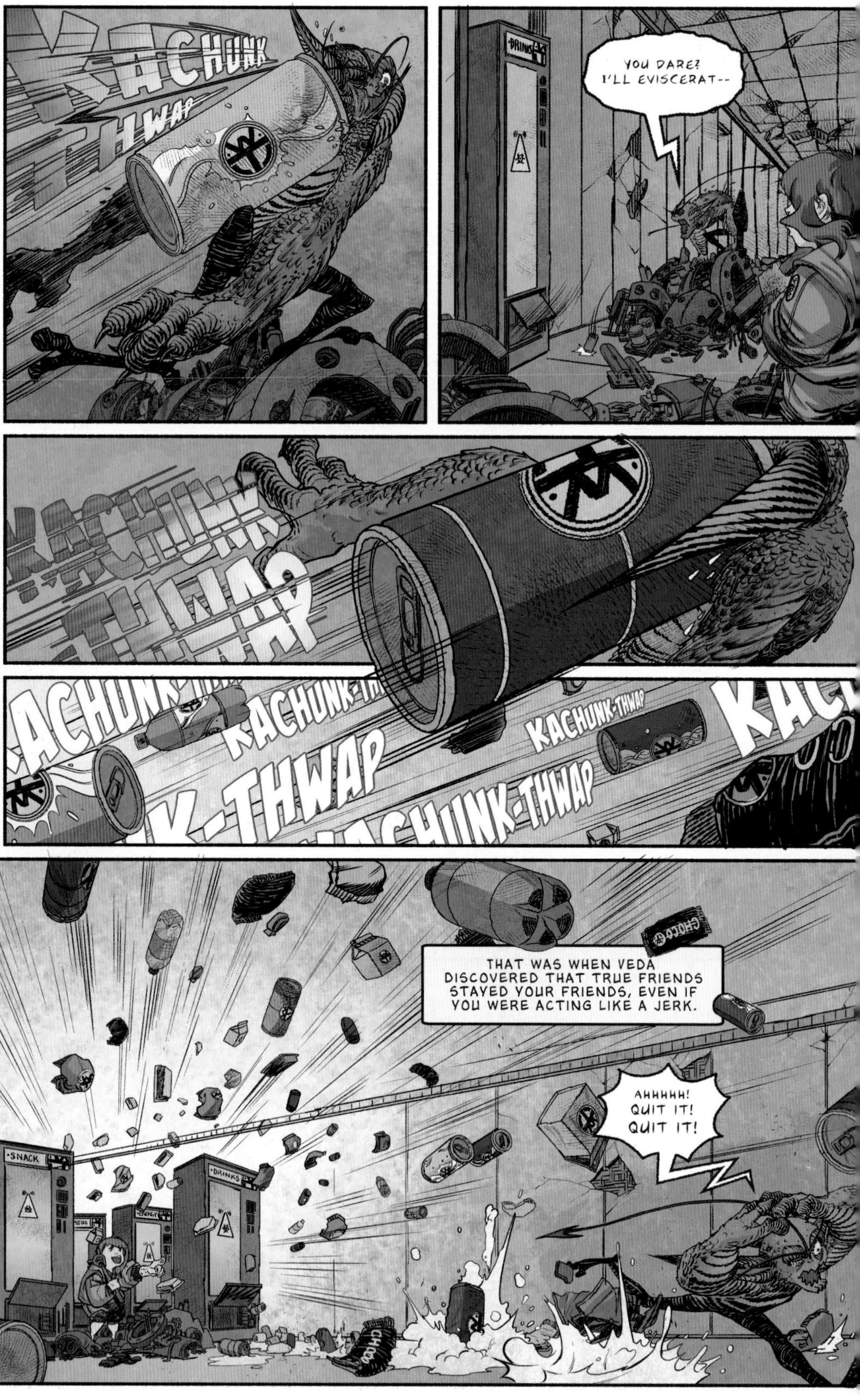
KACHUNK
THWAP
DRINKS
YOU DARE? I'LL EVISCERAT--
KACHUNK
THWAP
KACHUNK-THWAP
K-THWAP
KACHUNK-THWAP
KACHUNK-THWAP
THAT WAS WHEN VEDA DISCOVERED THAT TRUE FRIENDS STAYED YOUR FRIENDS, EVEN IF YOU WERE ACTING LIKE A JERK.
AHHHHH! QUIT IT! QUIT IT!
SNACK
DRINKS
ENERGY
MEDS

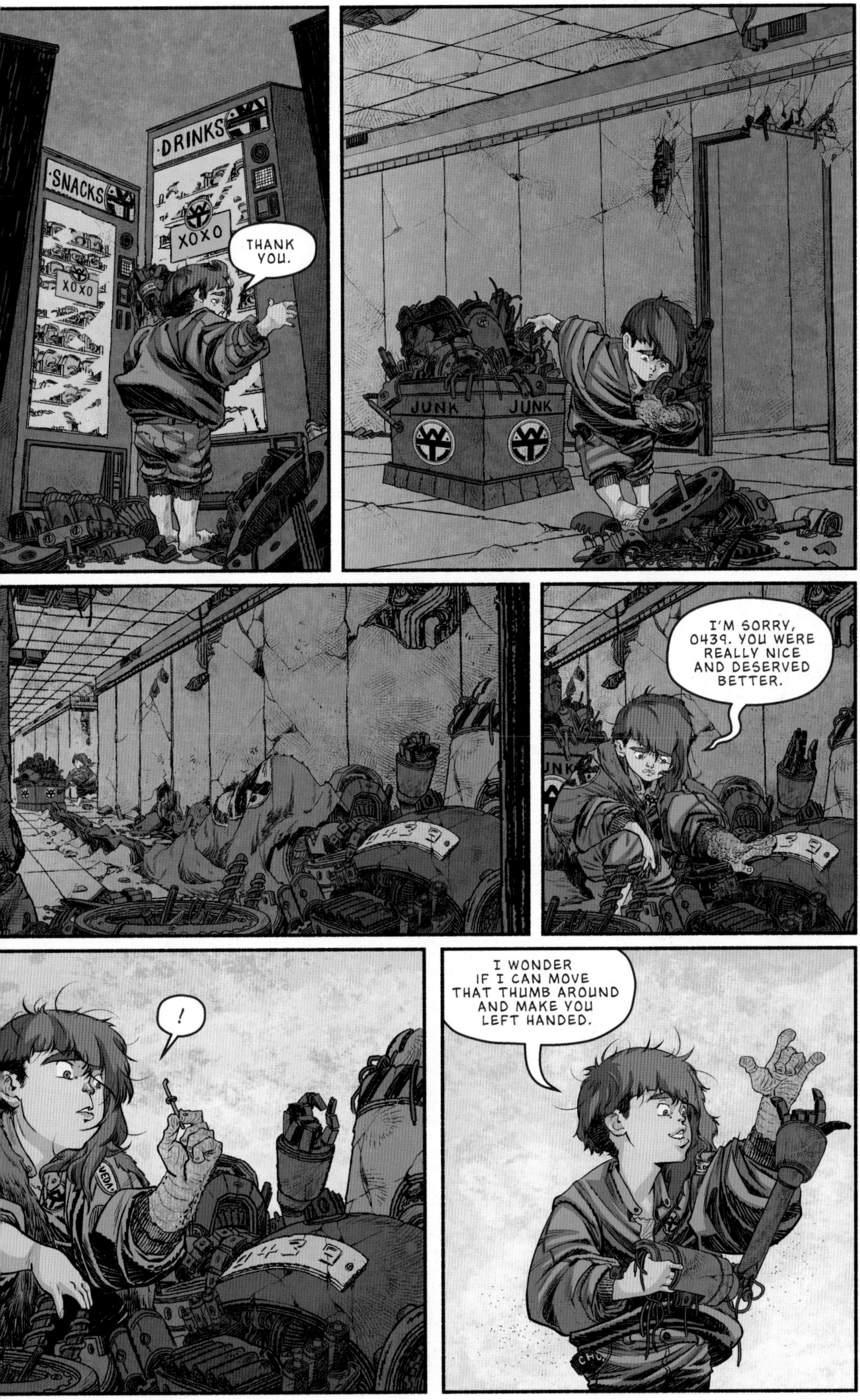
DRINKS
SNACKS
XOXO
XOXO
THANK YOU.
JUNK
JUNK
I'M SORRY, 0439. YOU WERE REALLY NICE AND DESERVED BETTER.
!
I WONDER IF I CAN MOVE THAT THUMB AROUND AND MAKE YOU LEFT HANDED.

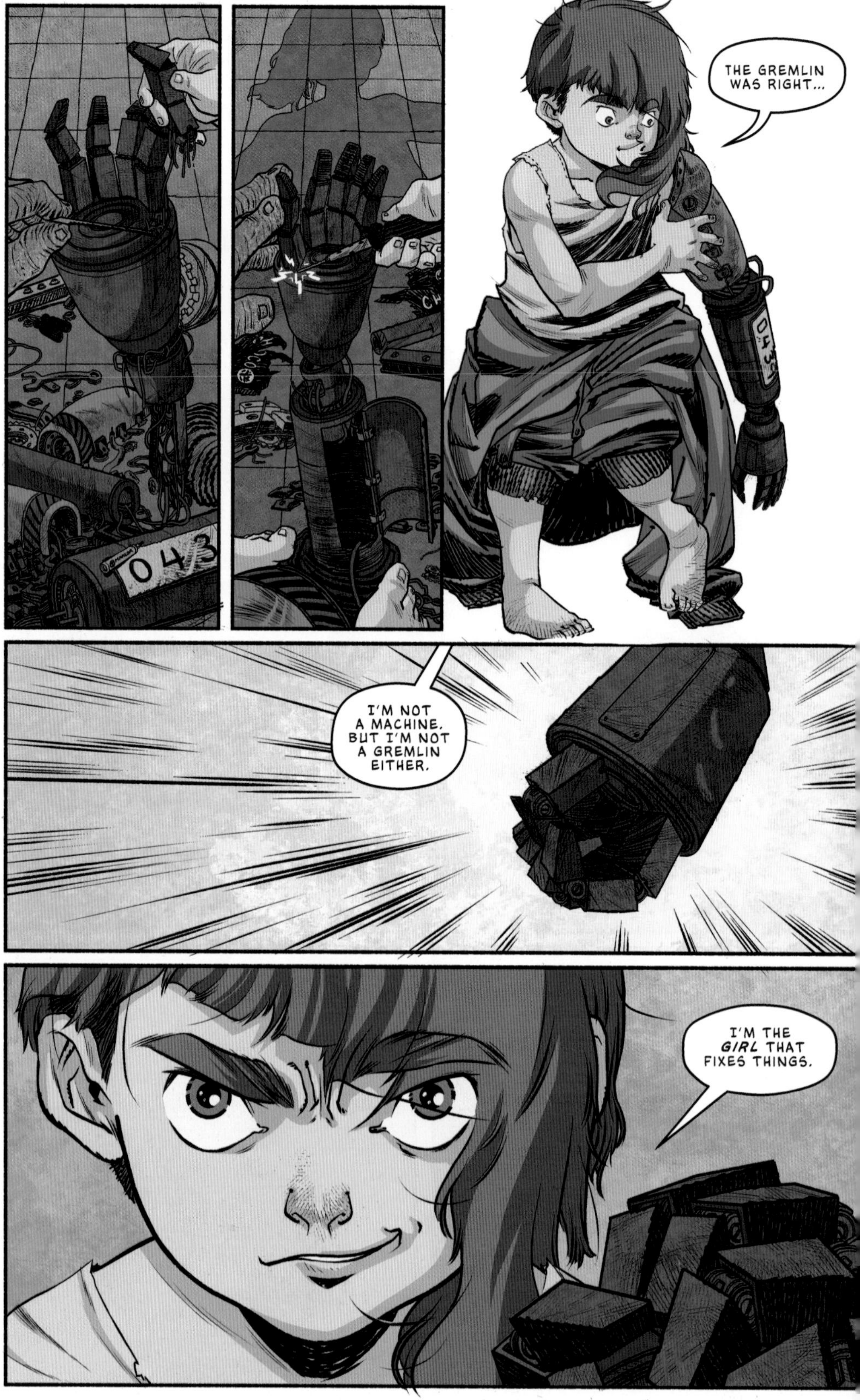
THE GREMLIN WAS RIGHT...
043
I'M NOT A MACHINE. BUT I'M NOT A GREMLIN EITHER.
I'M THE *GIRL* THAT FIXES THINGS.

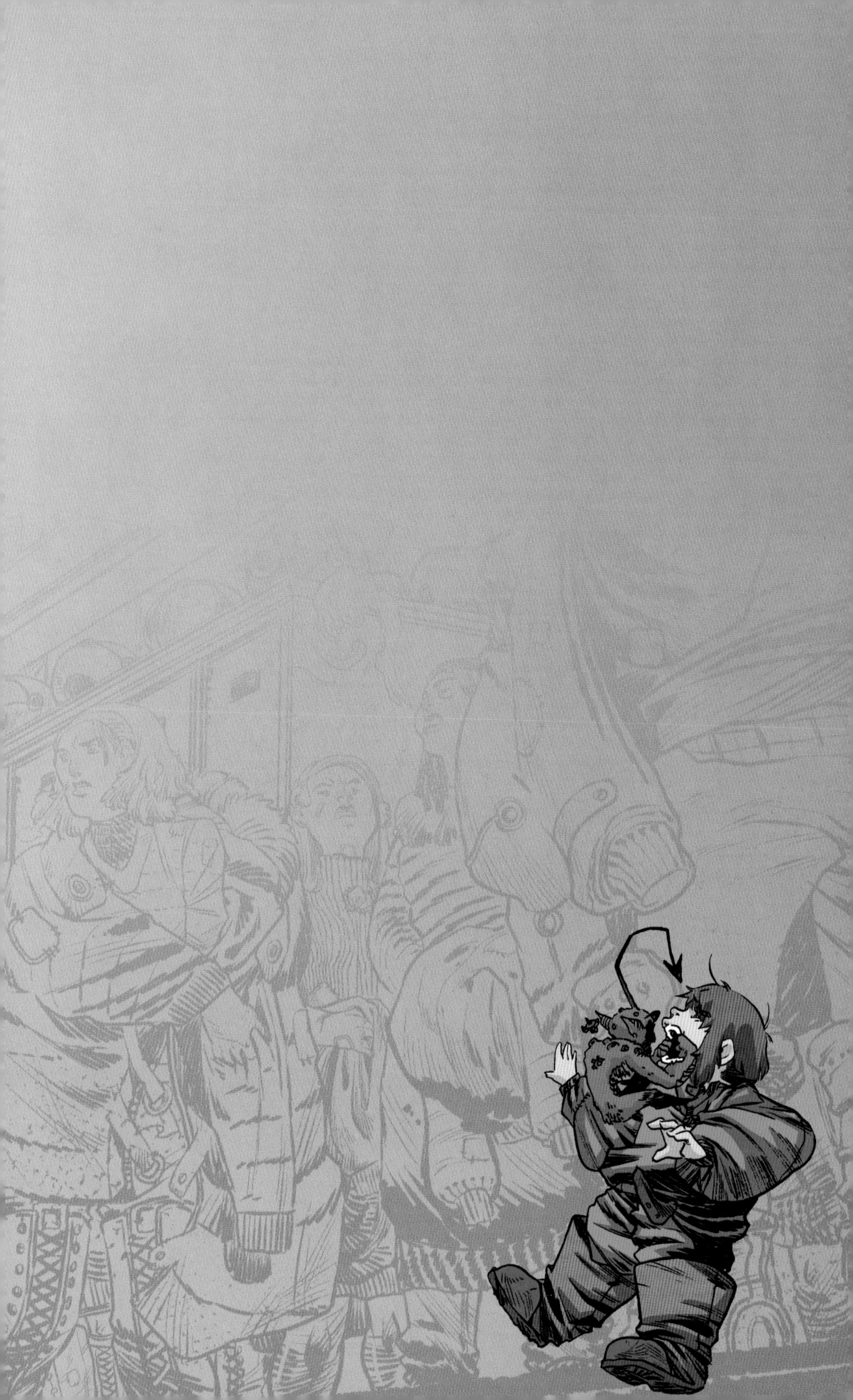

ATTENTION, ALL EMPLOYEES:

It has come to our attention that company resources are being allocated for personal use. Please stop this immediately. If you do not, you will be discovered and prosecuted to the fullest extent of the law.

BE THE BEST VERSION OF YOURSELF TODAY.

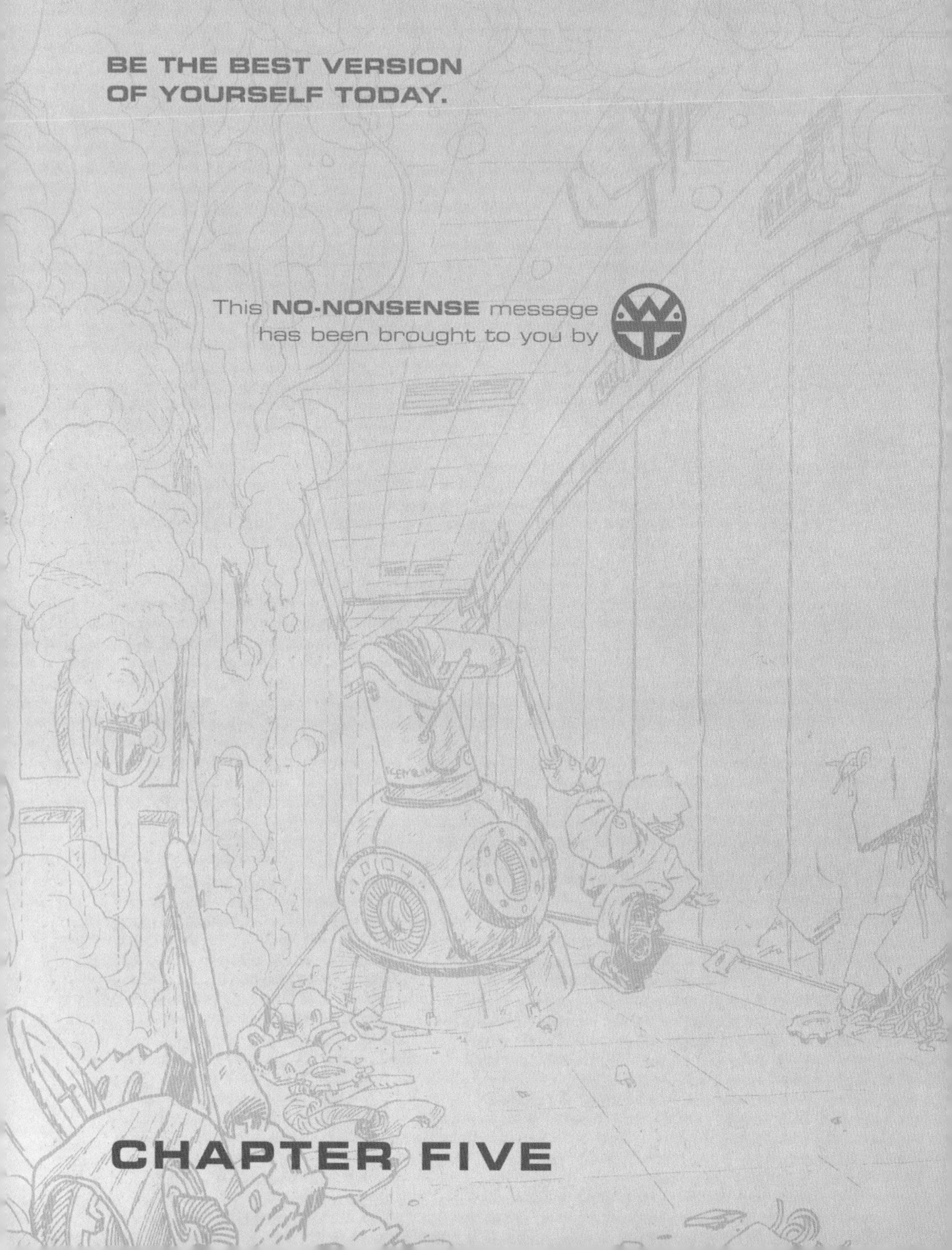

This **NO-NONSENSE** message has been brought to you by

CHAPTER FIVE

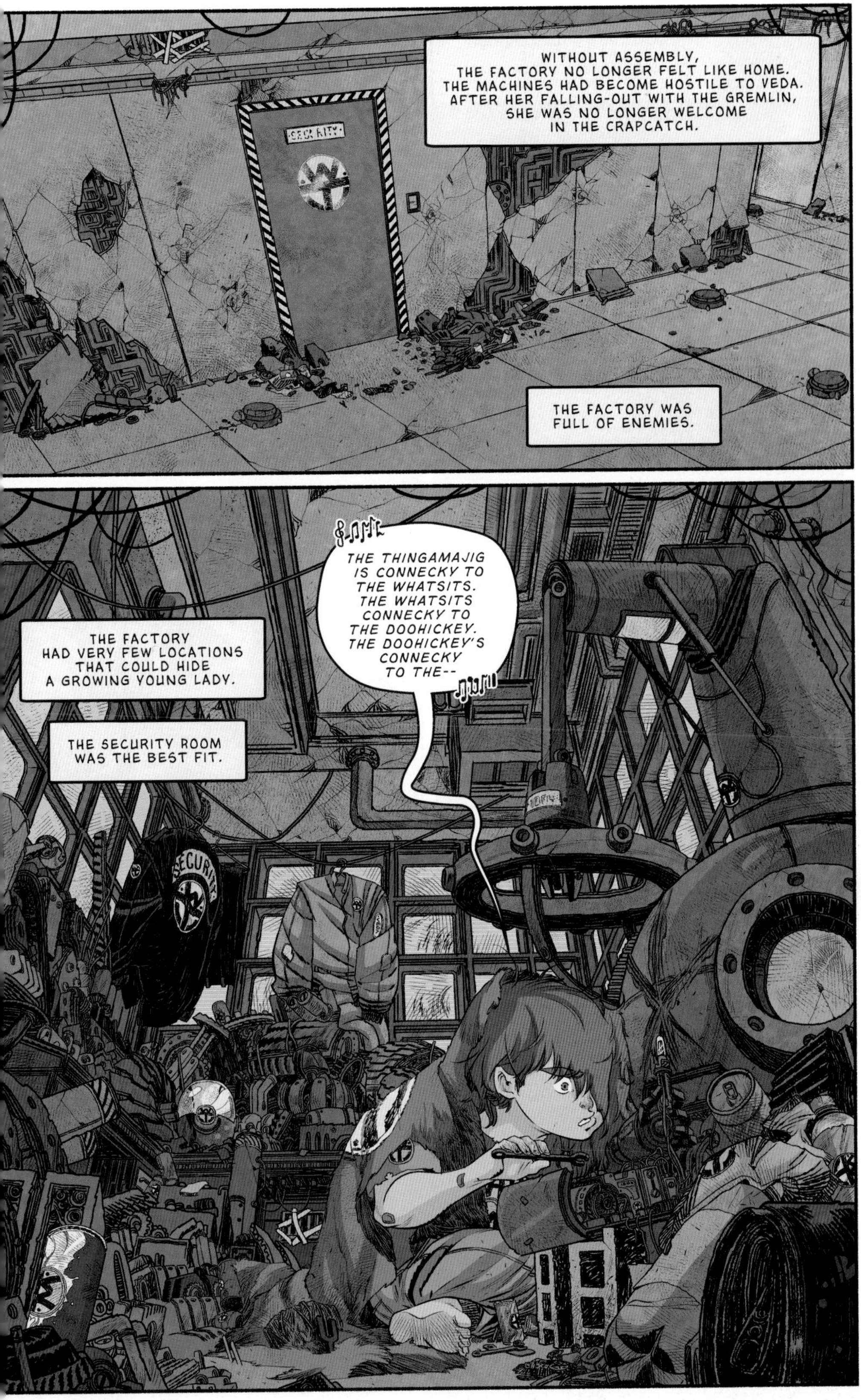
WITHOUT ASSEMBLY, THE FACTORY NO LONGER FELT LIKE HOME. THE MACHINES HAD BECOME HOSTILE TO VEDA. AFTER HER FALLING-OUT WITH THE GREMLIN, SHE WAS NO LONGER WELCOME IN THE CRAPCATCH.
THE FACTORY WAS FULL OF ENEMIES.
THE FACTORY HAD VERY FEW LOCATIONS THAT COULD HIDE A GROWING YOUNG LADY.
THE SECURITY ROOM WAS THE BEST FIT.
THE THINGAMAJIG IS CONNECKY TO THE WHATSITS. THE WHATSITS CONNECKY TO THE DOOHICKEY. THE DOOHICKEY'S CONNECKY TO THE--
SECURITY

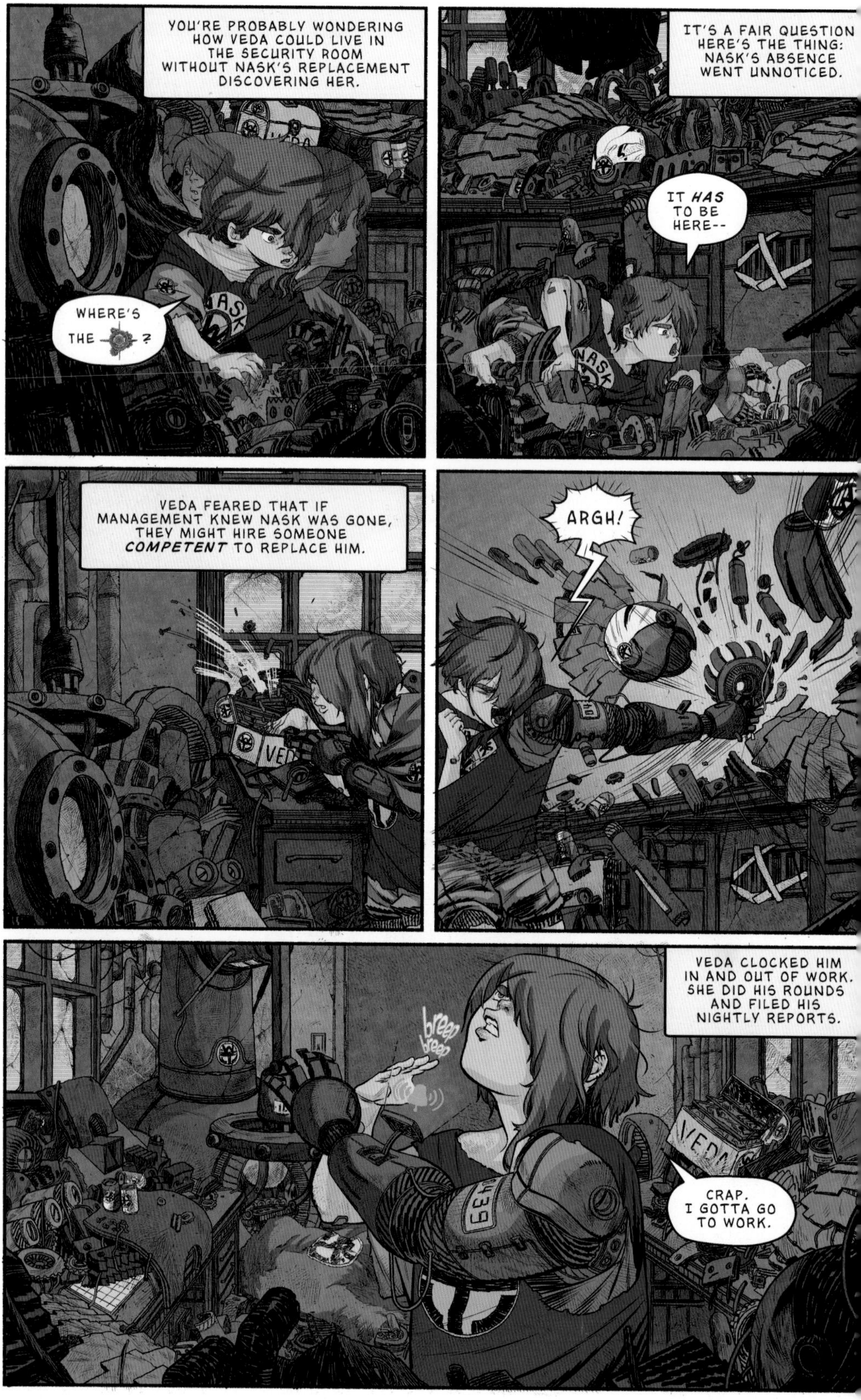
YOU'RE PROBABLY WONDERING HOW VEDA COULD LIVE IN THE SECURITY ROOM WITHOUT NASK'S REPLACEMENT DISCOVERING HER.
WHERE'S THE ?
IT'S A FAIR QUESTION. HERE'S THE THING: NASK'S ABSENCE WENT UNNOTICED.
IT *HAS* TO BE HERE--
VEDA FEARED THAT IF MANAGEMENT KNEW NASK WAS GONE, THEY MIGHT HIRE SOMEONE *COMPETENT* TO REPLACE HIM.
ARGH!
VEDA CLOCKED HIM IN AND OUT OF WORK. SHE DID HIS ROUNDS AND FILED HIS NIGHTLY REPORTS.
breep breep
CRAP. I GOTTA GO TO WORK.

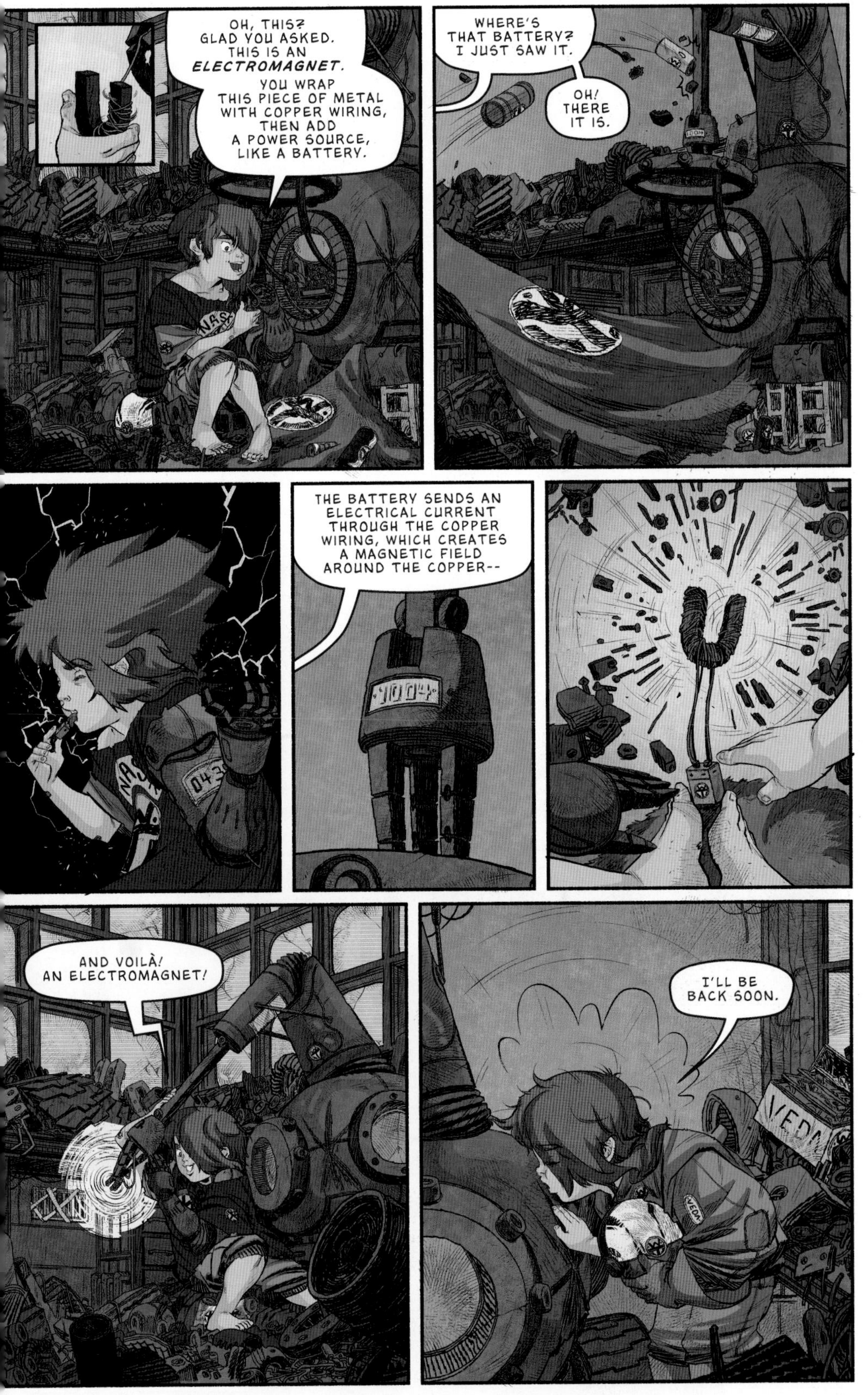
OH, THIS? GLAD YOU ASKED. THIS IS AN *ELECTROMAGNET*.
YOU WRAP THIS PIECE OF METAL WITH COPPER WIRING, THEN ADD A POWER SOURCE, LIKE A BATTERY.
WHERE'S THAT BATTERY? I JUST SAW IT.
OH! THERE IT IS.
NASA
0430
THE BATTERY SENDS AN ELECTRICAL CURRENT THROUGH THE COPPER WIRING, WHICH CREATES A MAGNETIC FIELD AROUND THE COPPER--
AND VOILÀ! AN ELECTROMAGNET!
I'LL BE BACK SOON.
VEDA

ASSEMBLY? I'M BACK!

ASSEMBLY?

THIS WASN'T THE FIRST TIME THAT VEDA HAD DISCOVERED ALL OF HER HARD WORK UNDONE.

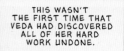

EVERY TIME SHE SLEPT, WENT TO THE BATHROOM, OR DID NASK'S ROUNDS, THE GREMLIN WOULD SNEAK IN AND DISASSEMBLE ASSEMBLY.

VEDA WAS CERTAIN THAT THIS TIME, THIS MAGNET WOULD'VE BEEN STRONG ENOUGH TO CATCH THE GREMLIN.

VEDA HAD A *NEW* PLAN. BUT SHE NEEDED SOME EXTRA *HANDS*.

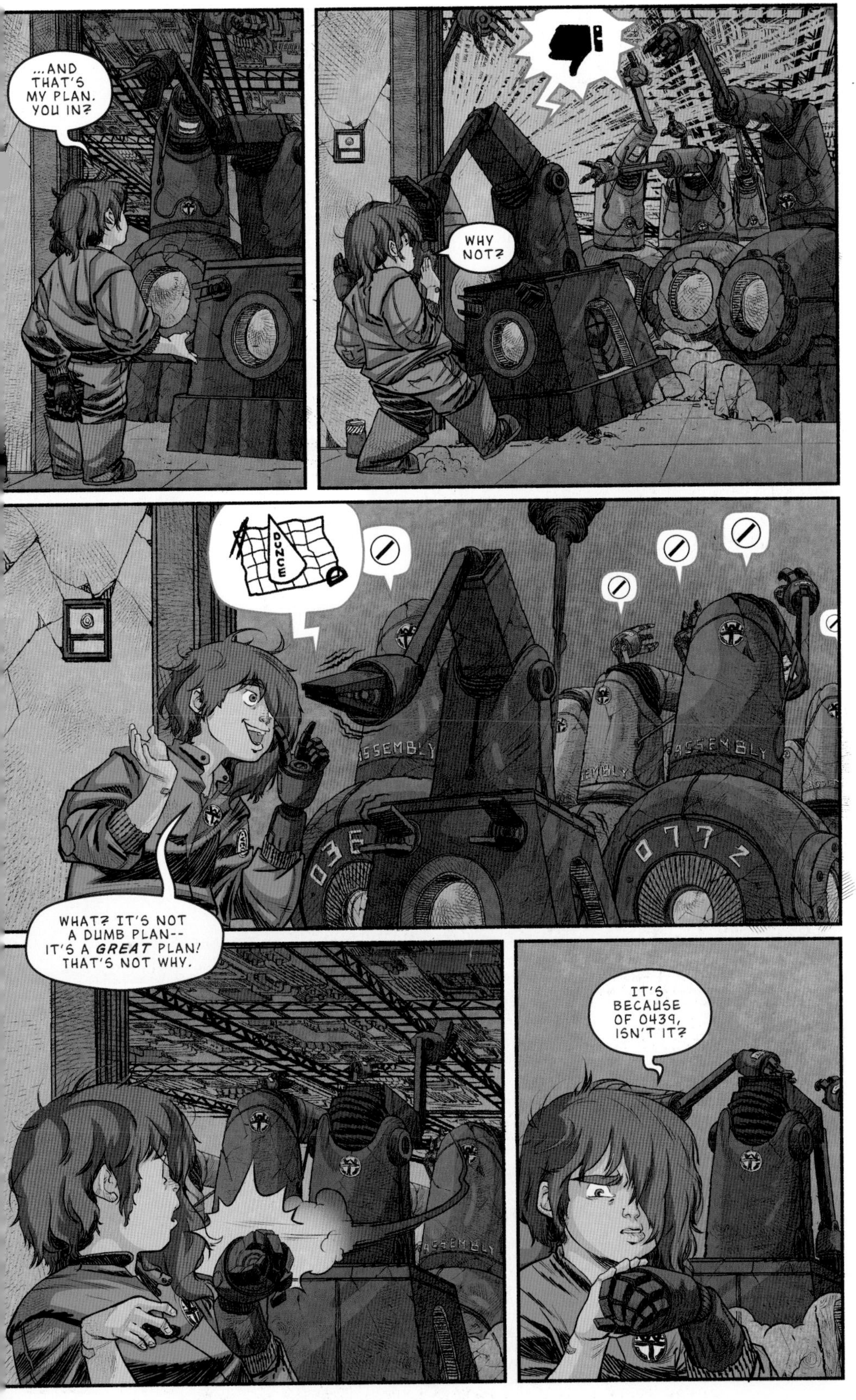
...AND THAT'S MY PLAN. YOU IN?
WHY NOT?
DUNCE
ASSEMBLY
036
0772
WHAT? IT'S NOT A DUMB PLAN-- IT'S A *GREAT* PLAN! THAT'S NOT WHY.
IT'S BECAUSE OF 0439, ISN'T IT?

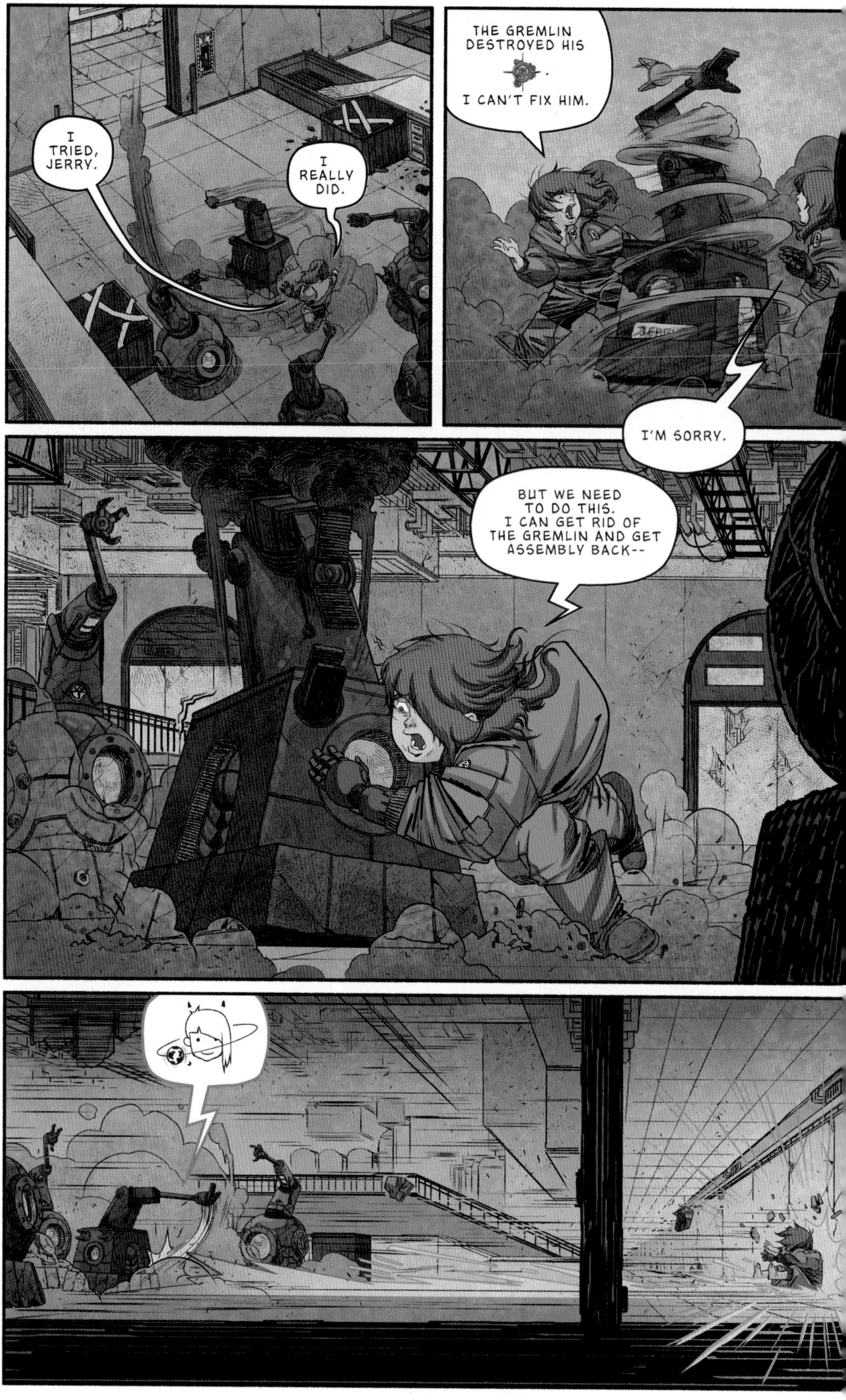
I TRIED, JERRY.
I REALLY DID.
THE GREMLIN DESTROYED HIS
I CAN'T FIX HIM.
I'M SORRY.
BUT WE NEED TO DO THIS. I CAN GET RID OF THE GREMLIN AND GET ASSEMBLY BACK--

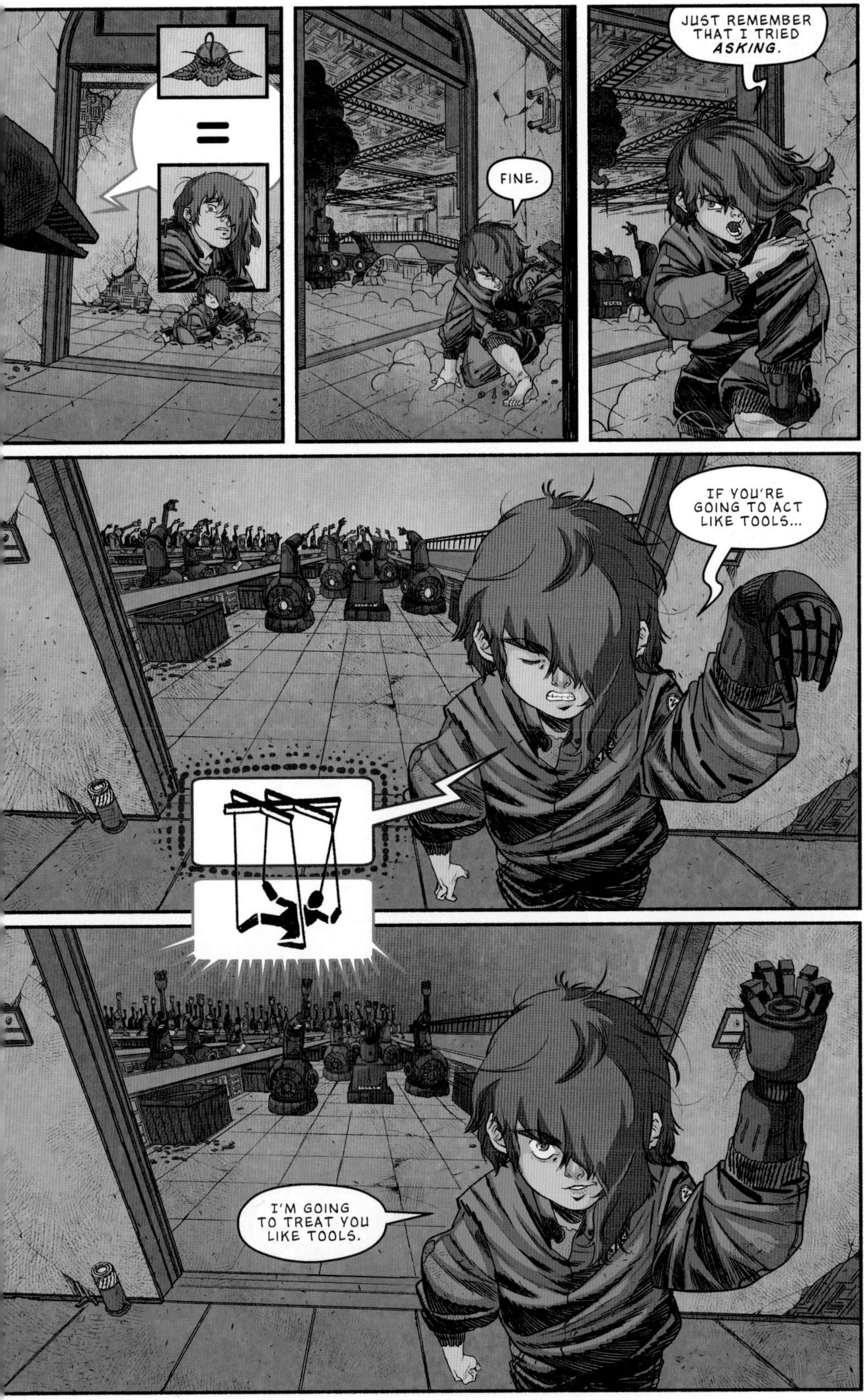

=
FINE.
JUST REMEMBER THAT I TRIED *ASKING*.
IF YOU'RE GOING TO ACT LIKE TOOLS...
I'M GOING TO TREAT YOU LIKE TOOLS.

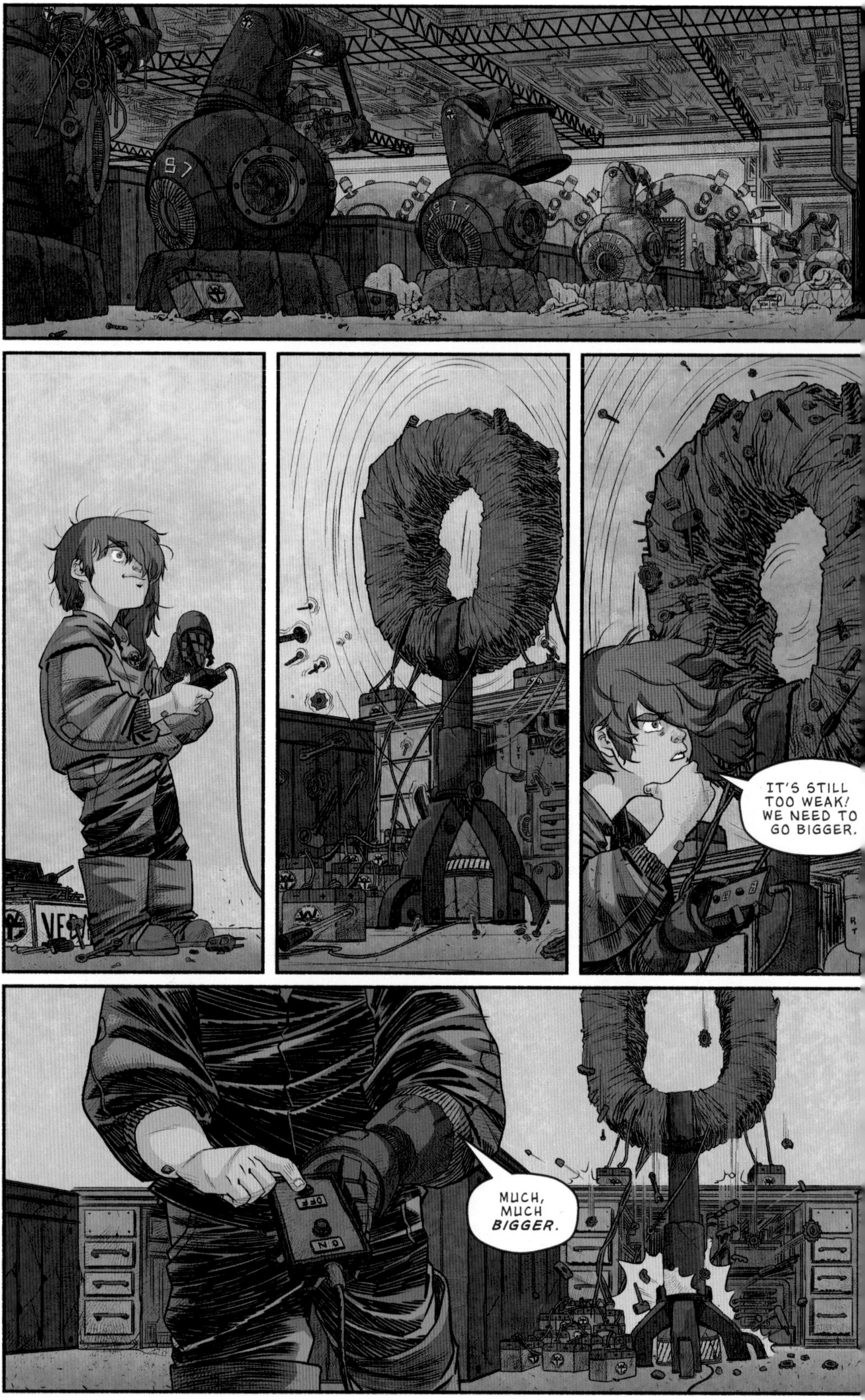
IT'S STILL
TOO WEAK!
WE NEED TO
GO BIGGER.
MUCH,
MUCH
BIGGER.

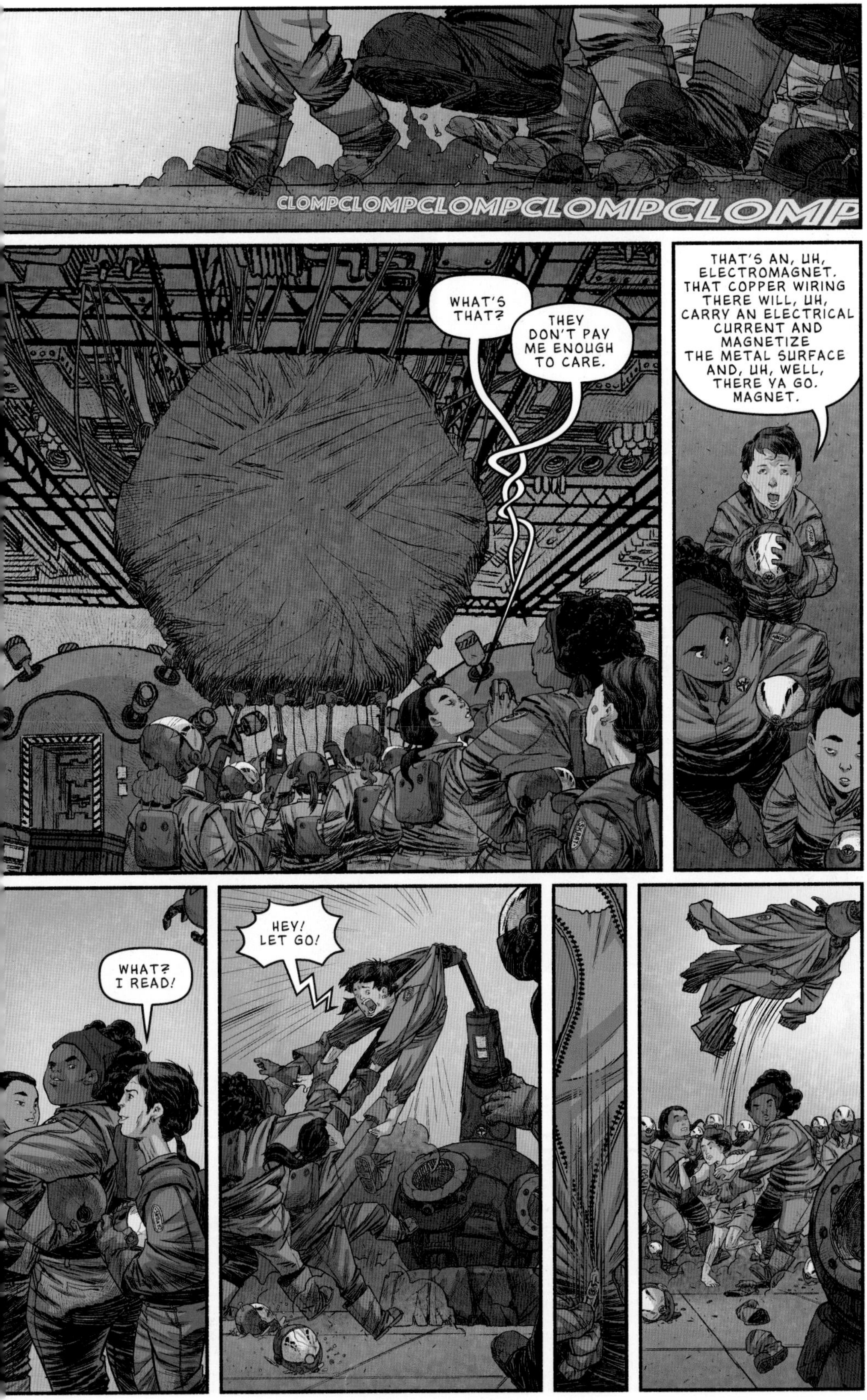
CLOMPCLOMPCLOMPCLOMPCLOMP
WHAT'S THAT?
THEY DON'T PAY ME ENOUGH TO CARE.
THAT'S AN, UH, ELECTROMAGNET. THAT COPPER WIRING THERE WILL, UH, CARRY AN ELECTRICAL CURRENT AND MAGNETIZE THE METAL SURFACE AND, UH, WELL, THERE YA GO. MAGNET.
WHAT? I READ!
HEY! LET GO!

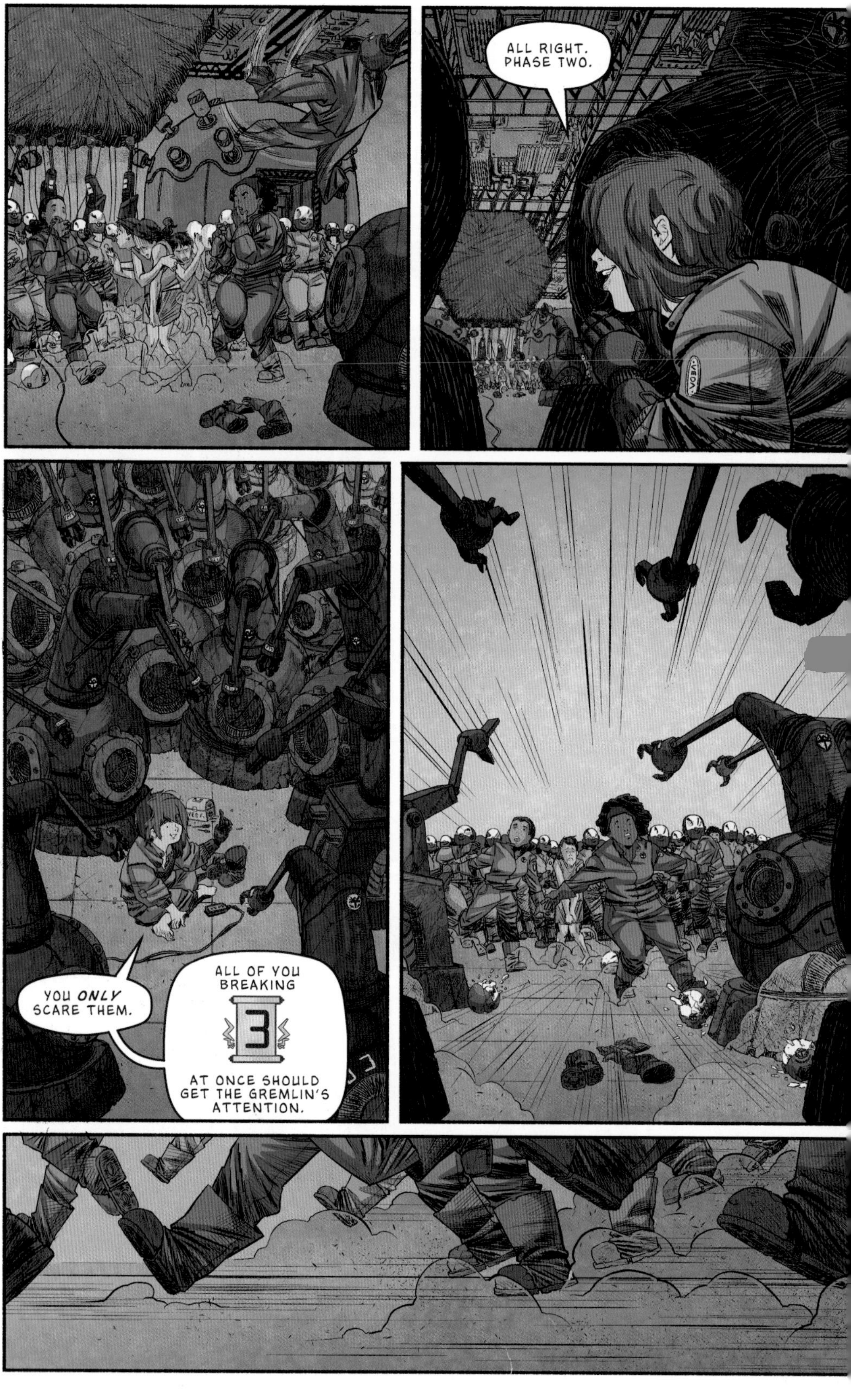
ALL RIGHT. PHASE TWO.
YOU *ONLY* SCARE THEM.
ALL OF YOU BREAKING
3
AT ONCE SHOULD GET THE GREMLIN'S ATTENTION.

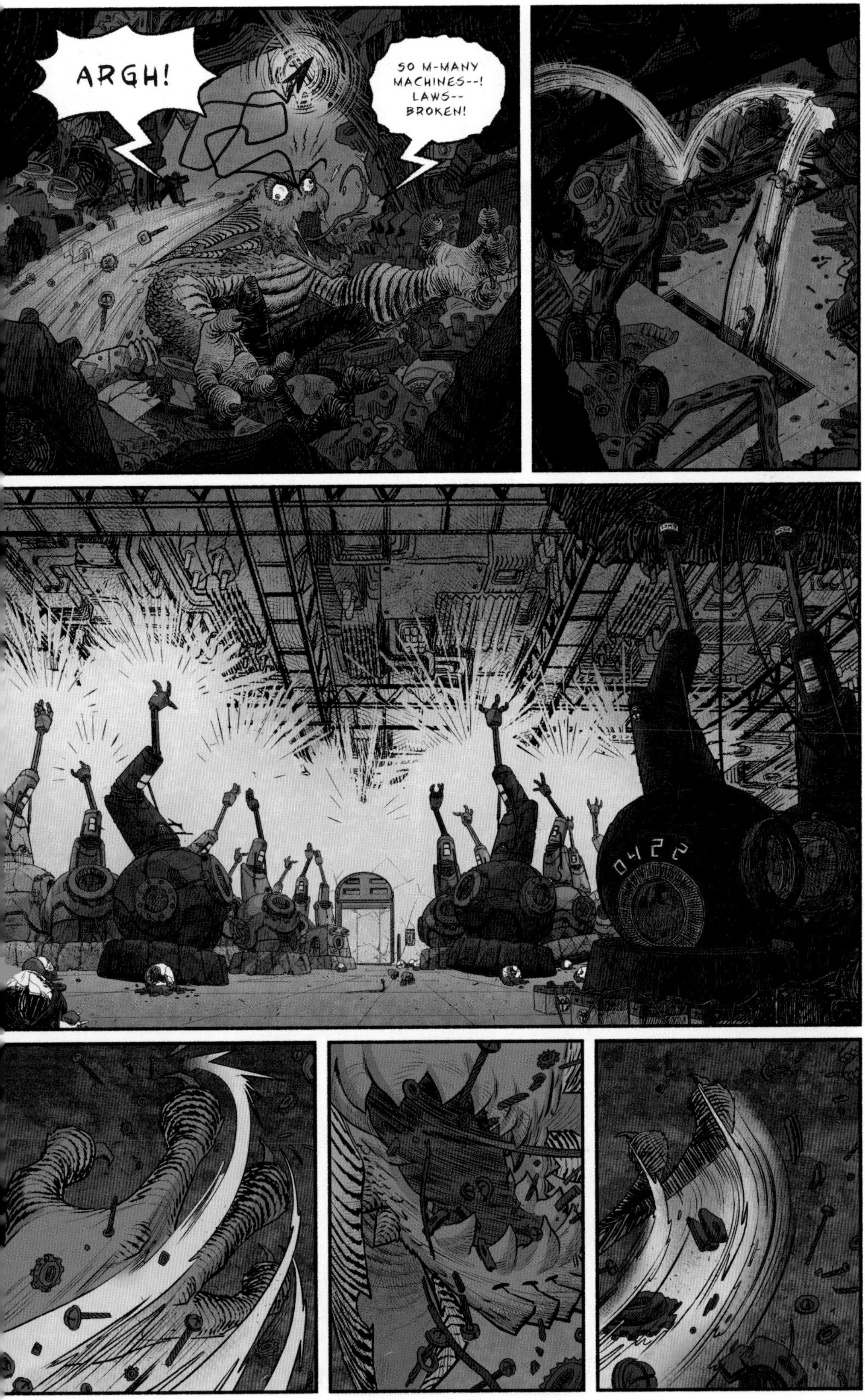
ARGH!
SO M-MANY MACHINES--! LAWS-- BROKEN!

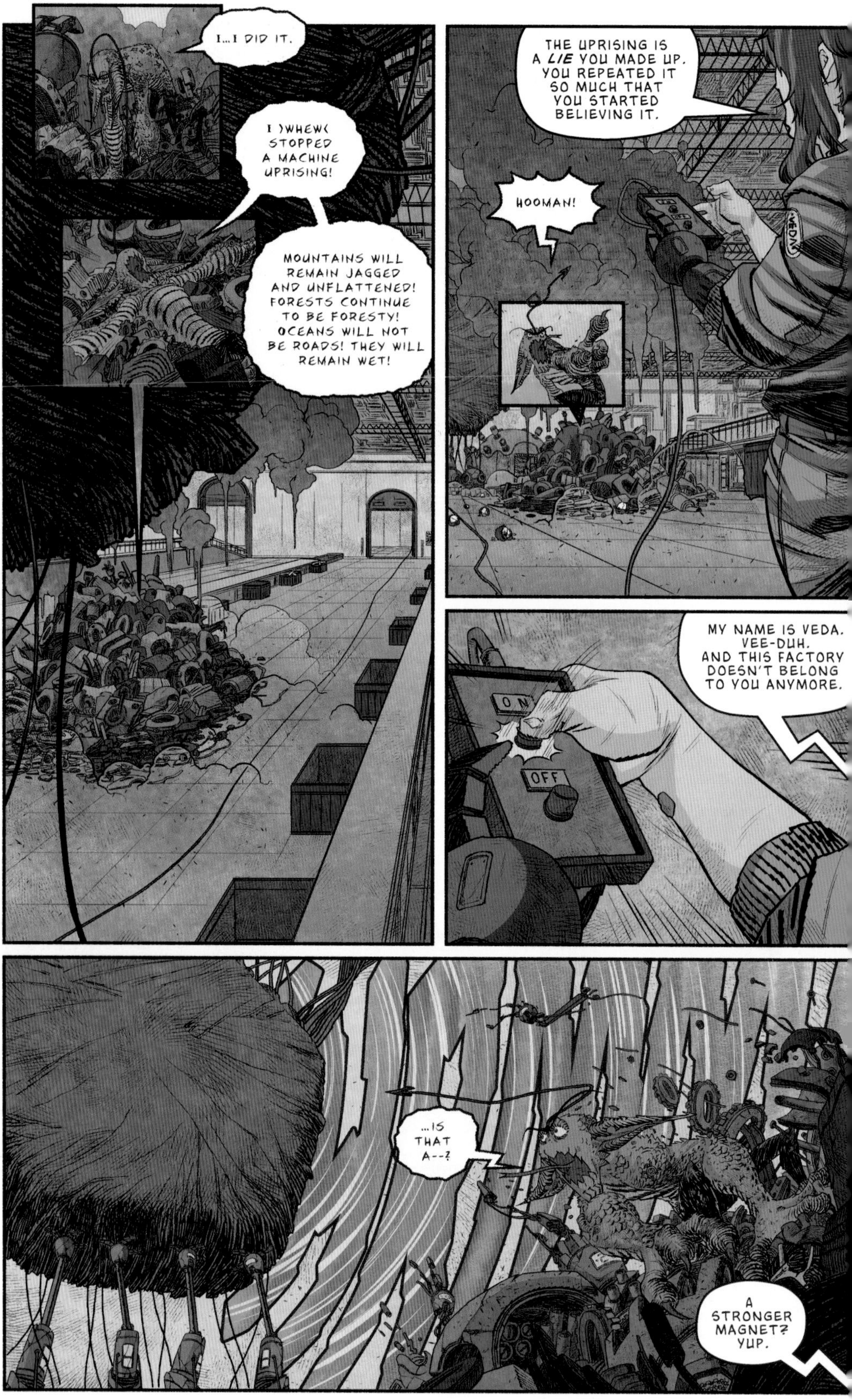
I...I DID IT.
I)WHEW(STOPPED A MACHINE UPRISING!
MOUNTAINS WILL REMAIN JAGGED AND UNFLATTENED! FORESTS CONTINUE TO BE FORESTY! OCEANS WILL NOT BE ROADS! THEY WILL REMAIN WET!
THE UPRISING IS A *LIE* YOU MADE UP. YOU REPEATED IT SO MUCH THAT YOU STARTED BELIEVING IT.
HOOMAN!
VEDA
MY NAME IS VEDA. VEE-DUH. AND THIS FACTORY DOESN'T BELONG TO YOU ANYMORE.
ON
OFF
...IS THAT A--?
A STRONGER MAGNET? YUP.

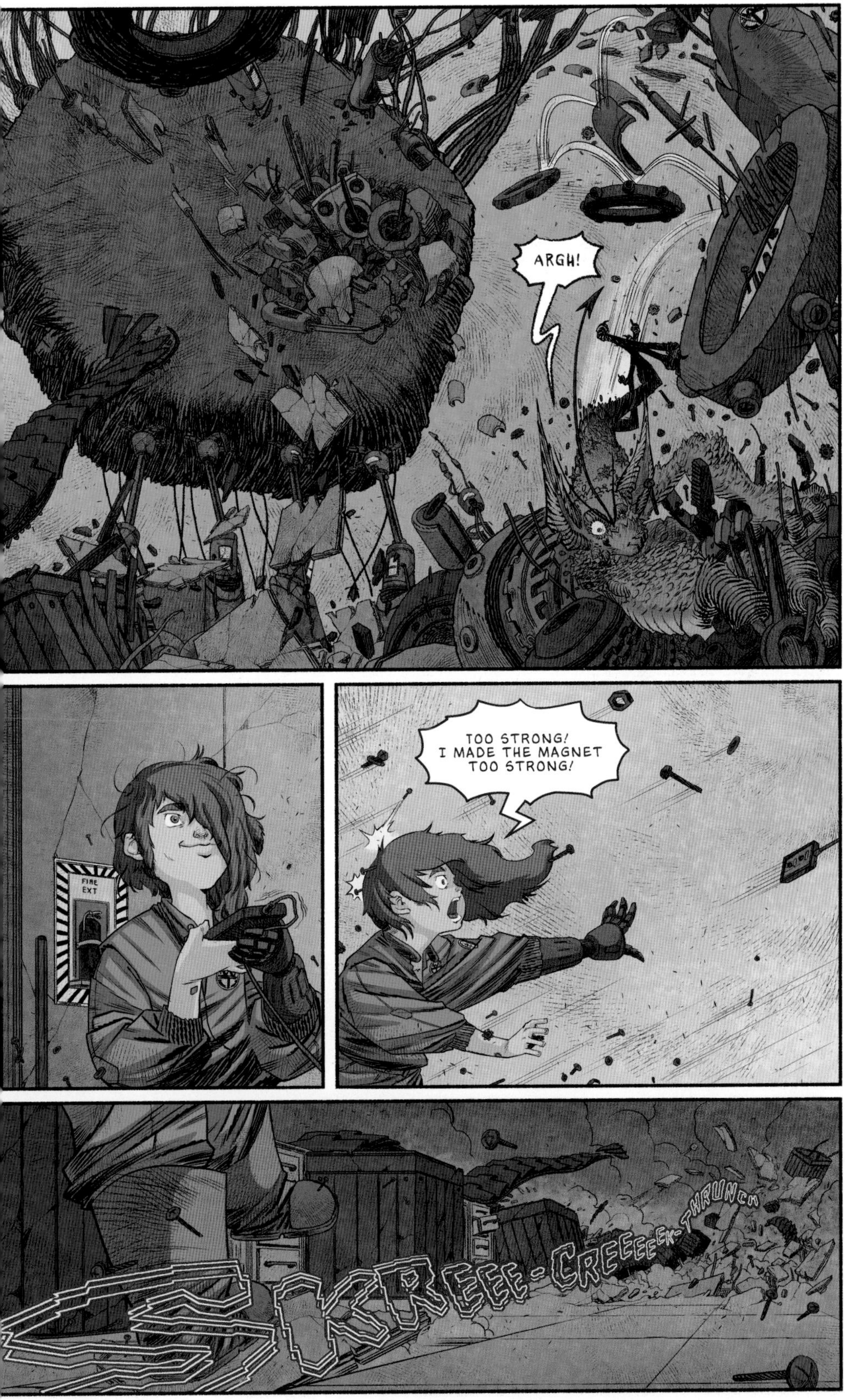
ARGH!
FIRE EXT
TOO STRONG! I MADE THE MAGNET TOO STRONG!
SKREEE-CREEEEEK-THRUNCH

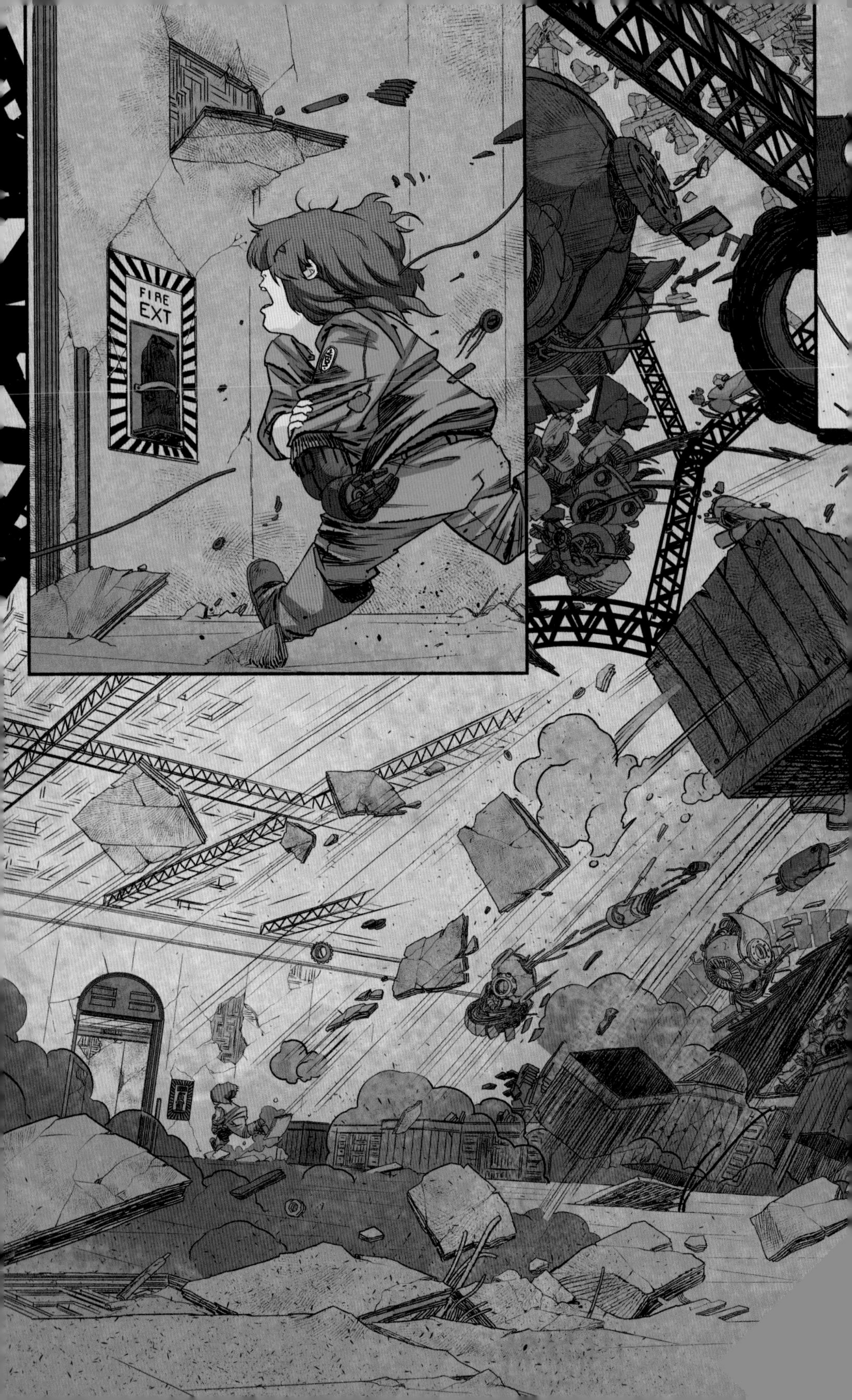
FIRE
EXT

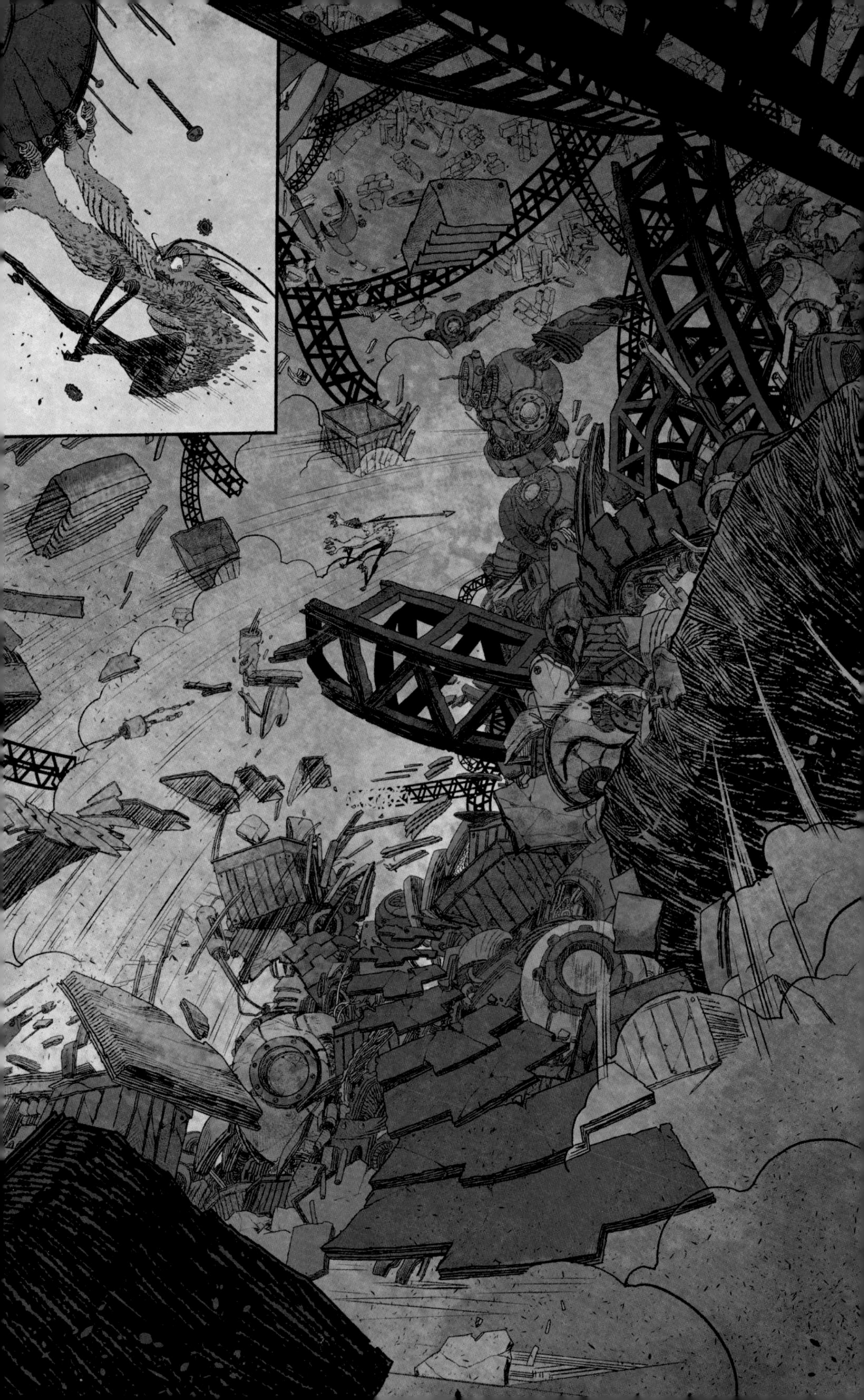

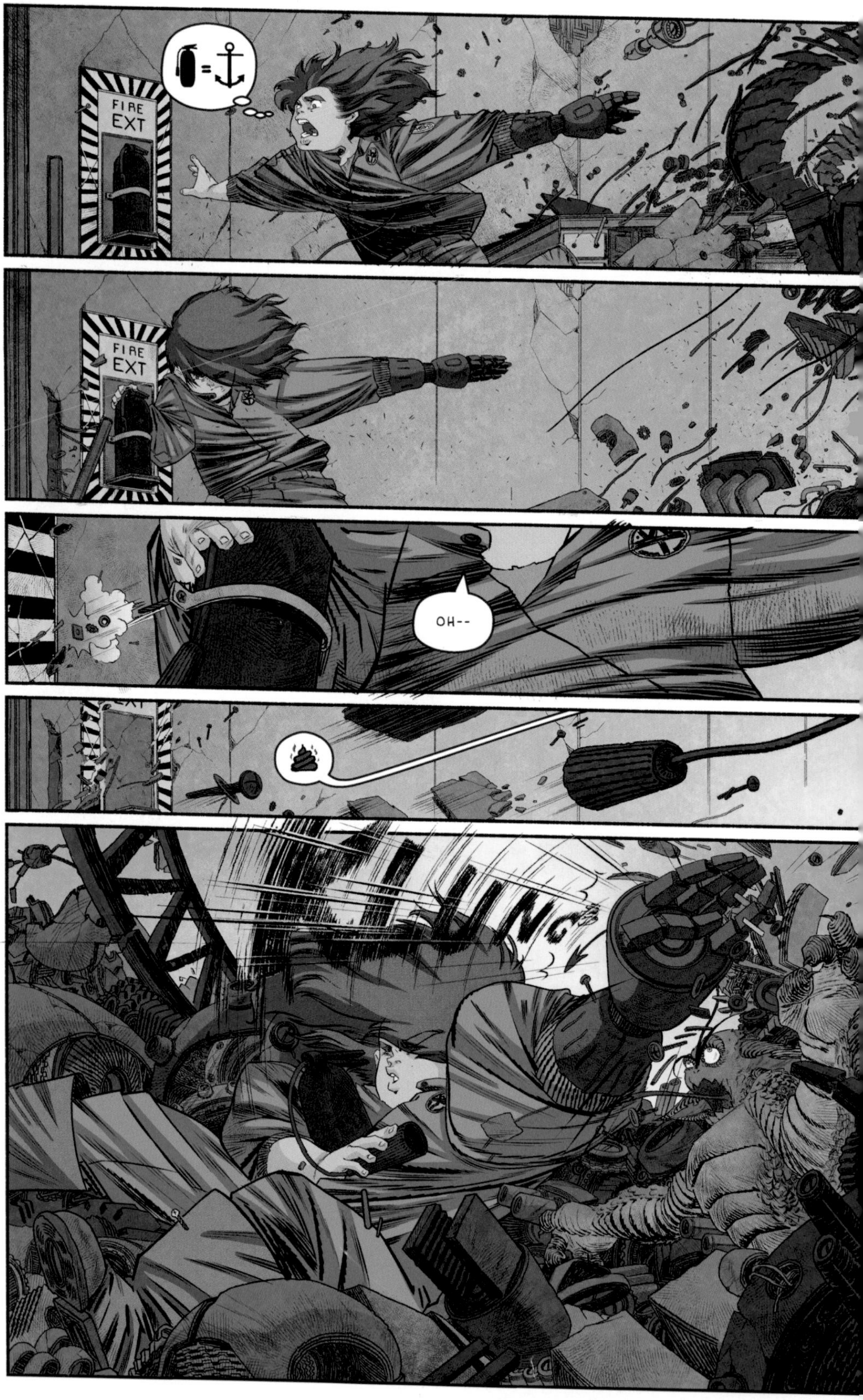
FIRE EXT
FIRE EXT
OH--

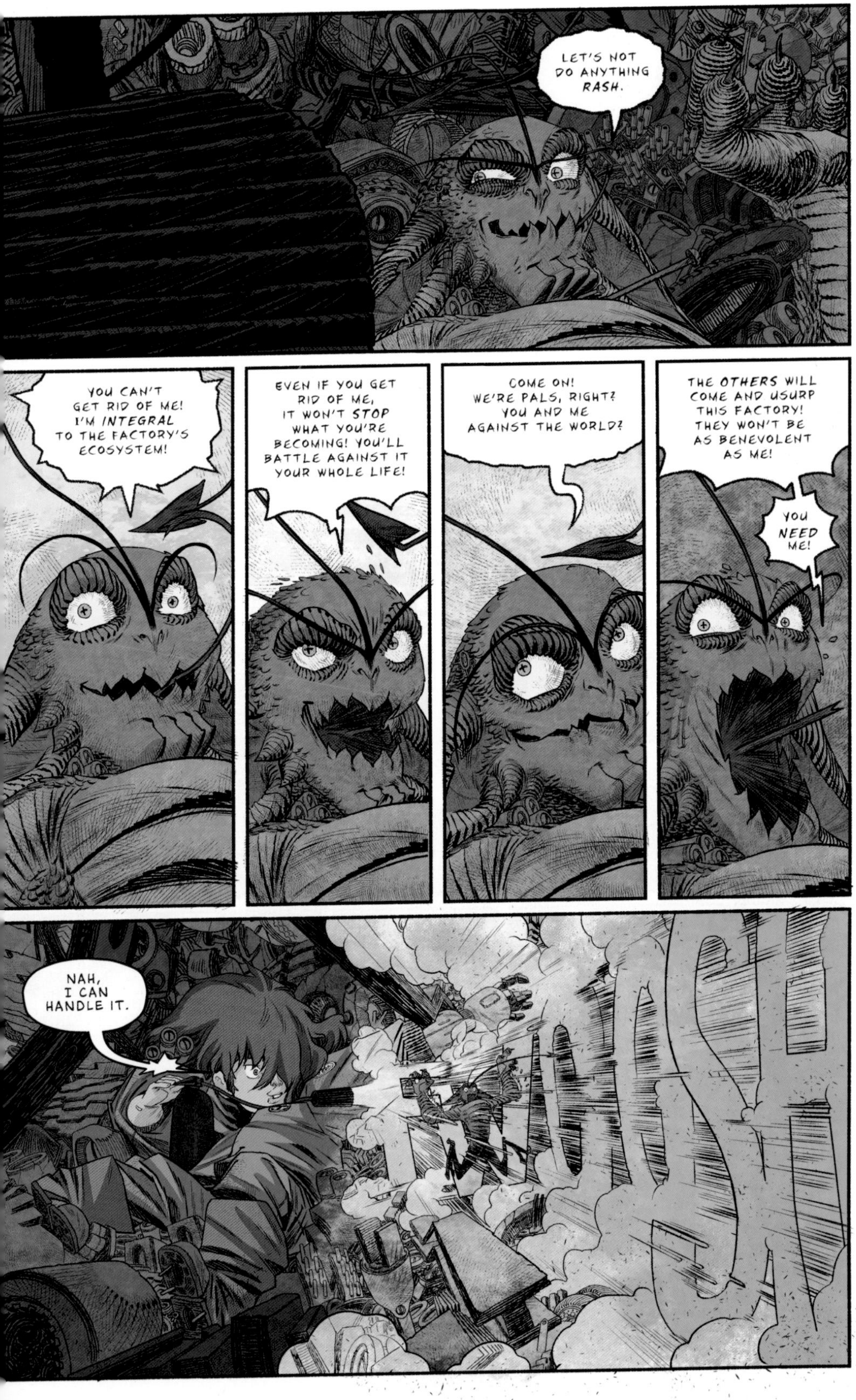
LET'S NOT DO ANYTHING RASH.
YOU CAN'T GET RID OF ME! I'M INTEGRAL TO THE FACTORY'S ECOSYSTEM!
EVEN IF YOU GET RID OF ME, IT WON'T STOP WHAT YOU'RE BECOMING! YOU'LL BATTLE AGAINST IT YOUR WHOLE LIFE!
COME ON! WE'RE PALS, RIGHT? YOU AND ME AGAINST THE WORLD?
THE OTHERS WILL COME AND USURP THIS FACTORY! THEY WON'T BE AS BENEVOLENT AS ME!
YOU NEED ME!
NAH, I CAN HANDLE IT.

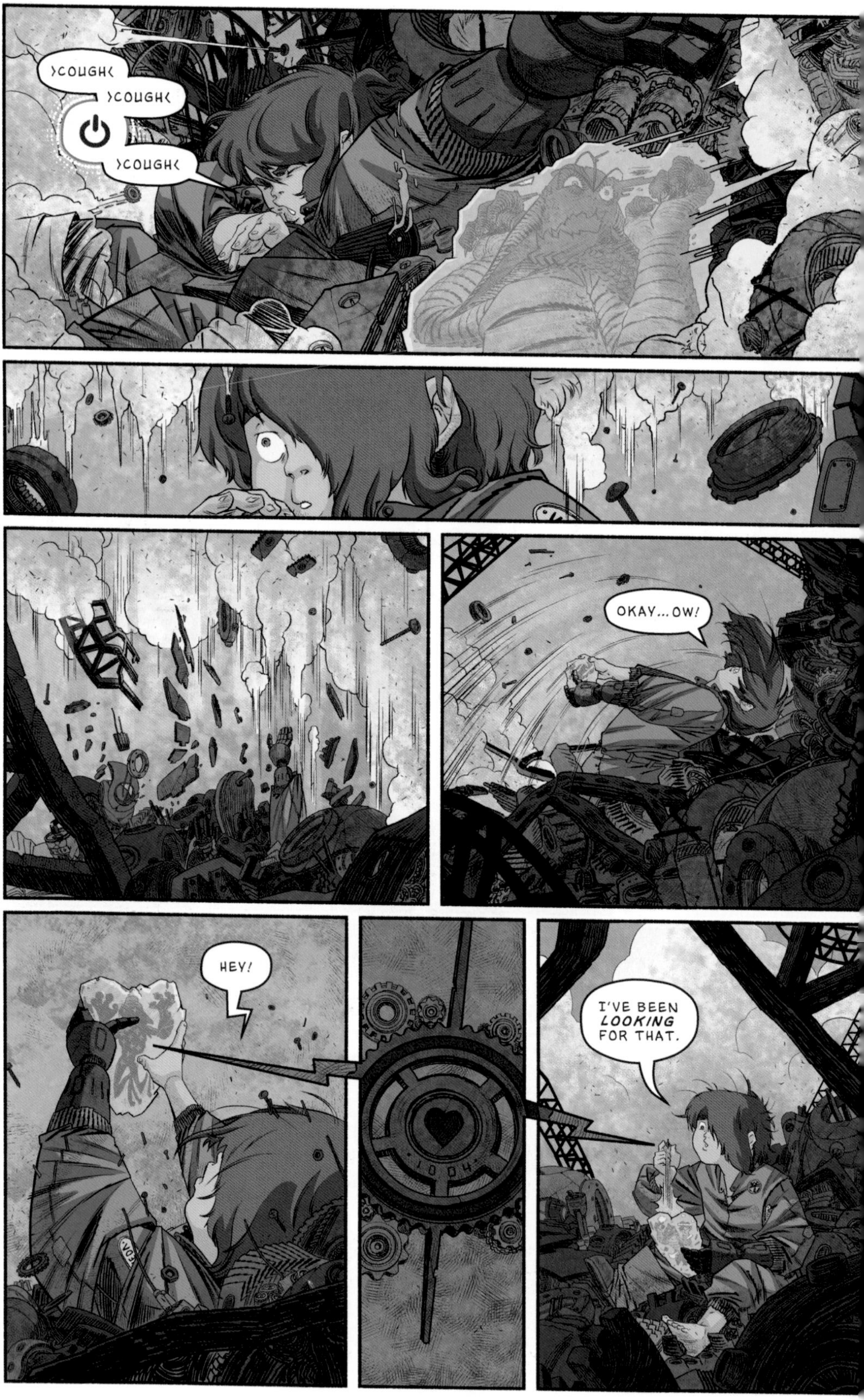
›COUGH‹
›COUGH‹
›COUGH‹
OKAY... OW!
HEY!
I'VE BEEN LOOKING FOR THAT.

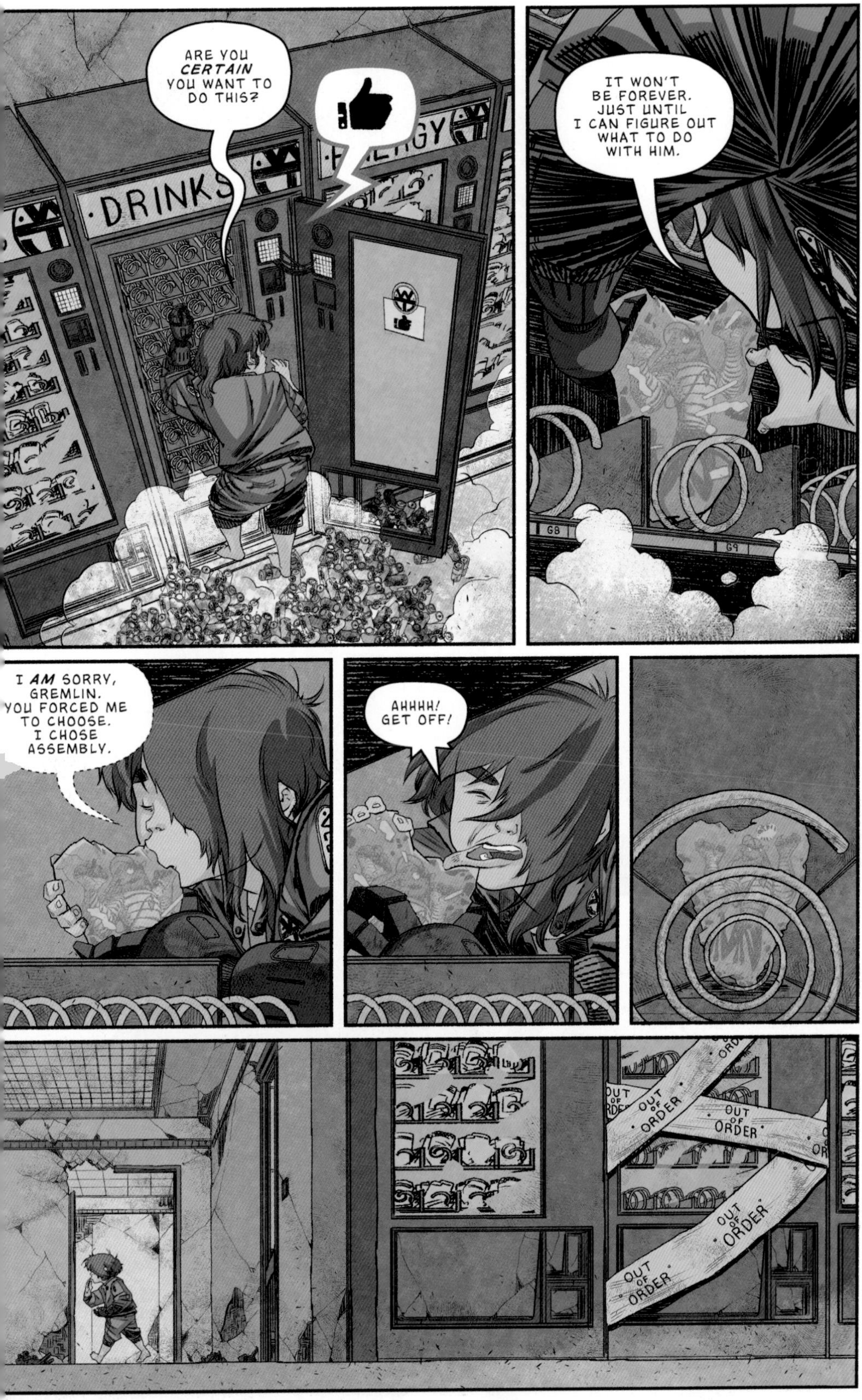
ARE YOU CERTAIN YOU WANT TO DO THIS?
·DRINKS
·ENERGY
IT WON'T BE FOREVER. JUST UNTIL I CAN FIGURE OUT WHAT TO DO WITH HIM.
G8
G9
I AM SORRY, GREMLIN. YOU FORCED ME TO CHOOSE. I CHOSE ASSEMBLY.
AHHHH! GET OFF!
OUT OF ORDER
OUT OF ORDER
OUT OF ORDER
OUT OF ORDER
OUT OF ORDER

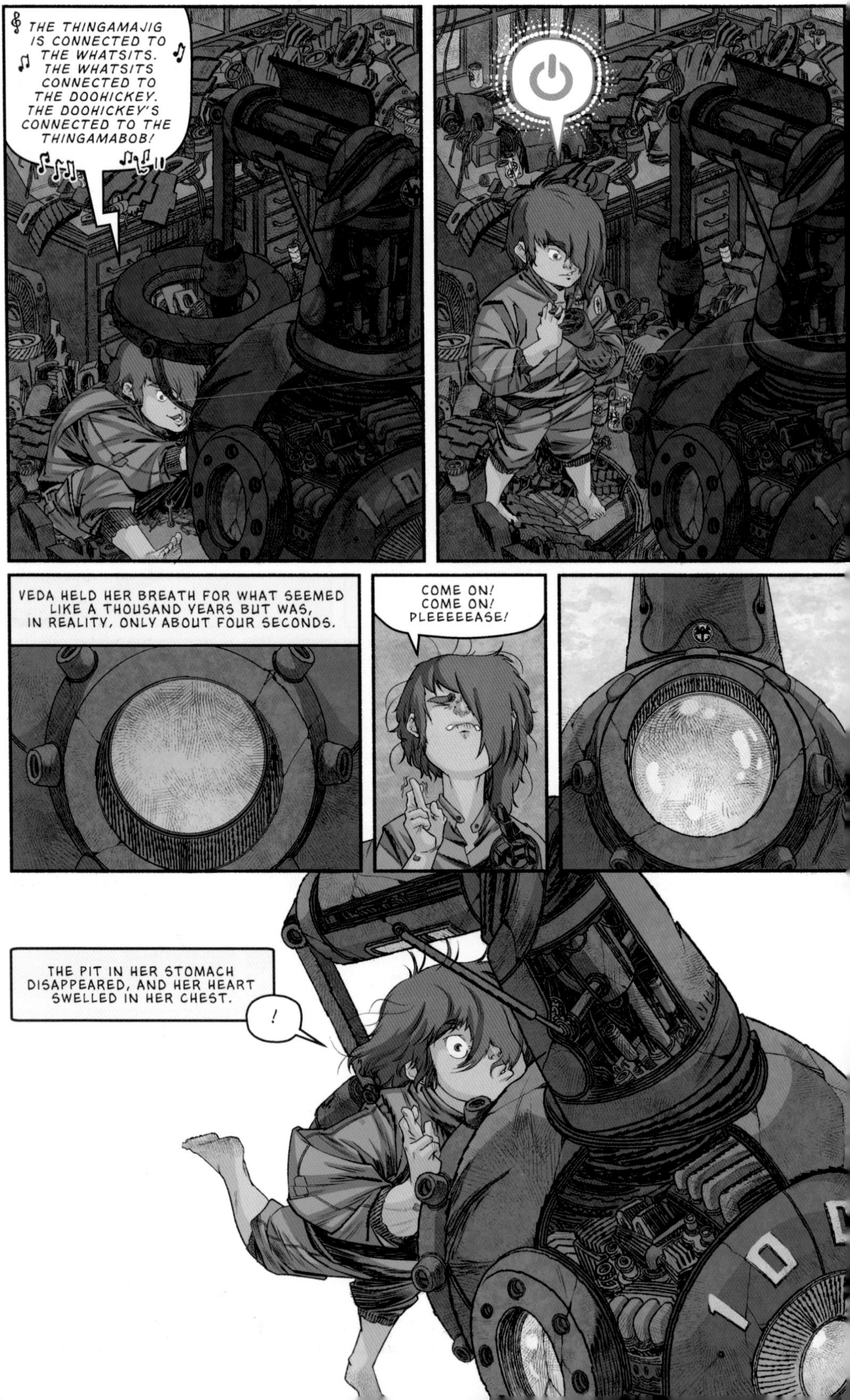
THE THINGAMAJIG IS CONNECTED TO THE WHATSITS. THE WHATSITS CONNECTED TO THE DOOHICKEY. THE DOOHICKEY'S CONNECTED TO THE THINGAMABOB!
VEDA HELD HER BREATH FOR WHAT SEEMED LIKE A THOUSAND YEARS BUT WAS, IN REALITY, ONLY ABOUT FOUR SECONDS.
COME ON! COME ON! PLEEEEEASE!
THE PIT IN HER STOMACH DISAPPEARED, AND HER HEART SWELLED IN HER CHEST.
!

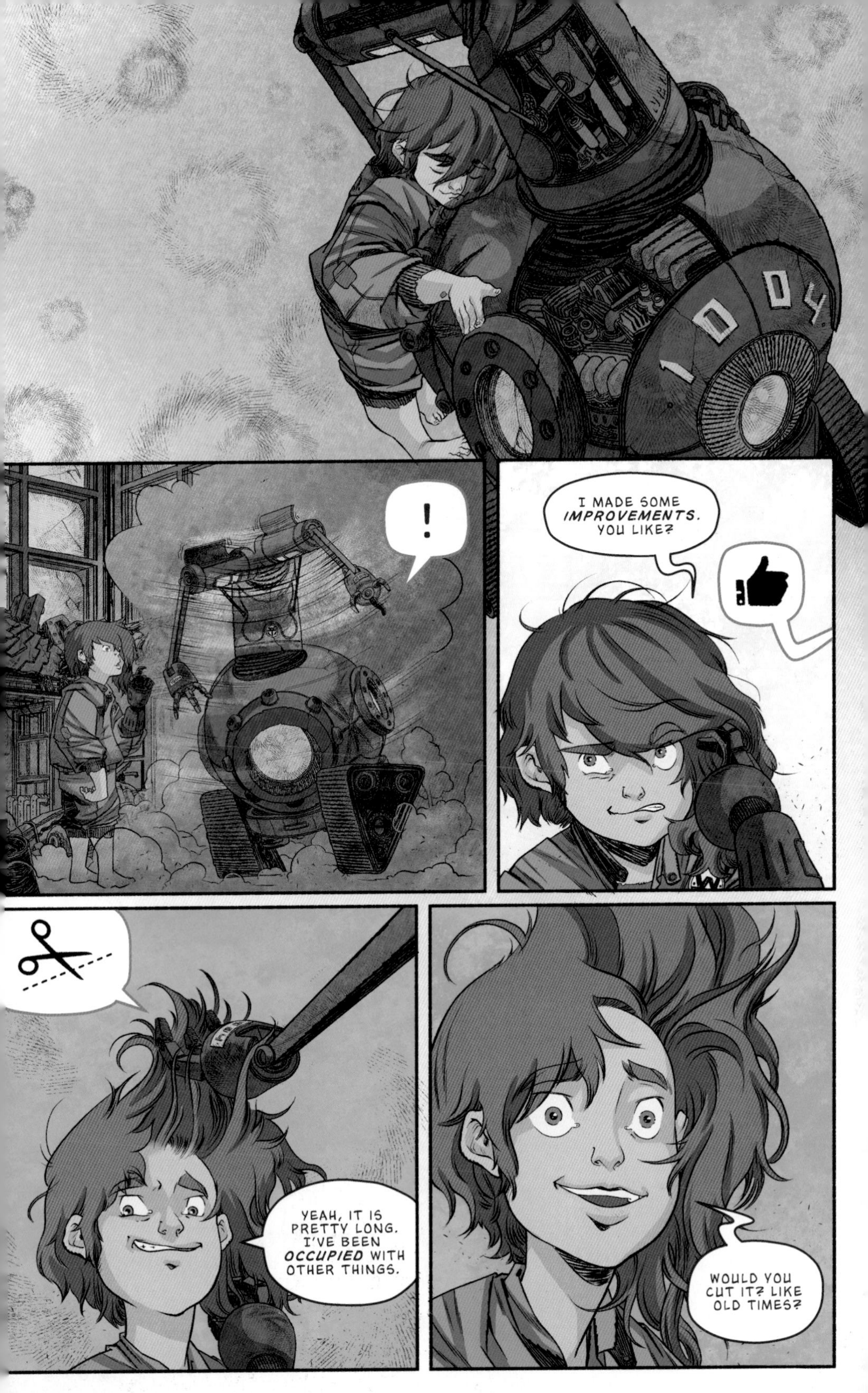
1004
!
I MADE SOME *IMPROVEMENTS*. YOU LIKE?
YEAH, IT IS PRETTY LONG. I'VE BEEN *OCCUPIED* WITH OTHER THINGS.
WOULD YOU CUT IT? LIKE OLD TIMES?

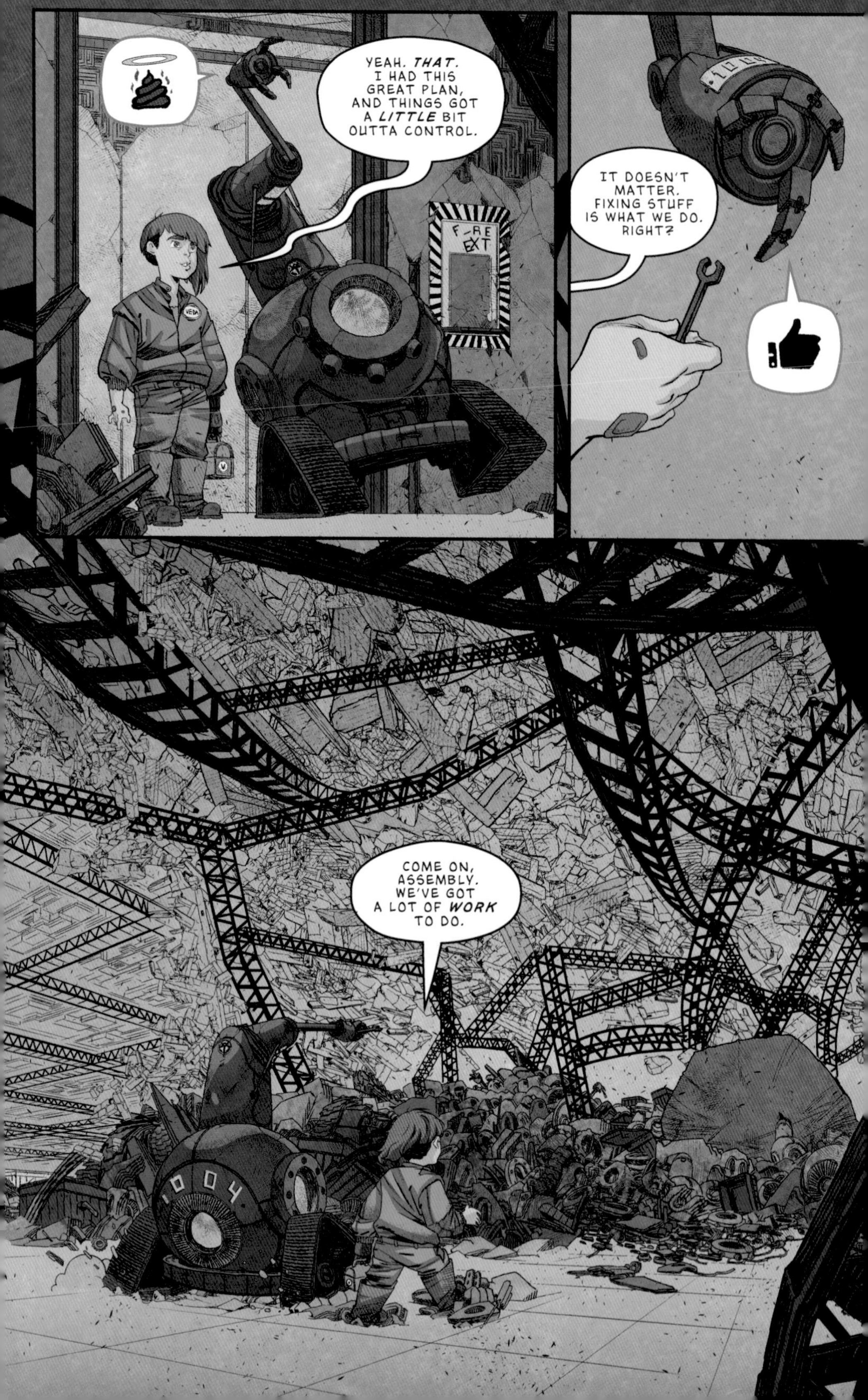
YEAH. *THAT.* I HAD THIS GREAT PLAN, AND THINGS GOT A *LITTLE* BIT OUTTA CONTROL.
IT DOESN'T MATTER. FIXING STUFF IS WHAT WE DO. RIGHT?
COME ON, ASSEMBLY. WE'VE GOT A LOT OF *WORK* TO DO.
1004

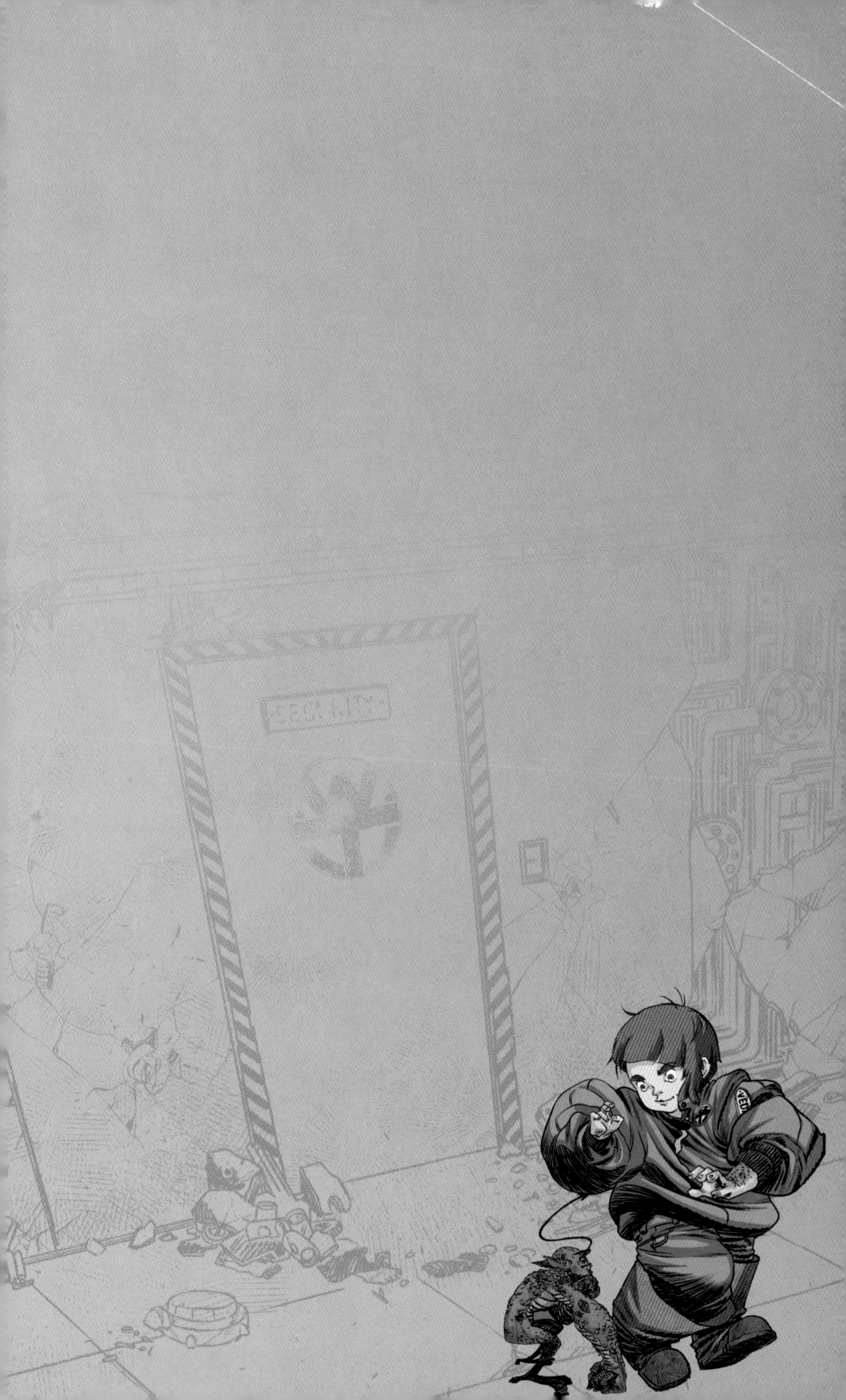

SAMUEL TEER was born to a deaf maintenance worker and an immigrant who spoke English as a distant second language. So obviously he became a writer. He was raised outside of St. Louis, Missouri. He currently lives in Thornton, Colorado, with his wife, Andrea, and dog, Roxie.

Veda: Assembly Required is his first published work.

HYEONDO PARK was born in Seoul, South Korea. At age ten, he relocated with his family to Dallas, Texas. He holds a bachelor's degree in cartooning from the School of Visual Arts.

Visit activatecomix.com/42.comic and hanaroda.net for his latest progress.

KELLY FITZPATRICK was born a military brat in San Antonio, Texas. She's moved around her whole life, which made going into a career in comics natural. She holds a BFA in illustration from the Ringling School of Art and Design and currently resides in Portland, Oregon.

USAGI™ YOJIMBO

Created, Written, and Illustrated by Stan Sakai

AVAILABLE FROM DARK HORSE COMICS

The Usagi Yojimbo Saga Book 1
Collects *Usagi Yojimbo* Books 8–10
$24.99 | ISBN 978-1-61655-609-9

The Usagi Yojimbo Saga Book 2
Collects *Usagi Yojimbo* Books 11–13
$24.99 | ISBN 978-1-61655-610-5

The Usagi Yojimbo Saga Book 3
Collects *Usagi Yojimbo* Books 14–16
$24.99 | ISBN 978-1-61655-611-2

The Usagi Yojimbo Saga Book 4
Collects *Usagi Yojimbo* Books 17–19
$24.99 | ISBN 978-1-61655-612-9
ON SALE AUGUST 2015

Book 20:
Glimpses of Death
$15.99 | ISBN 978-1-59307-549-1

Book 21:
The Mother of Mountains
$15.99 | ISBN 978-1-59307-783-9

Book 22:
Tomoe's Story
$15.99 | ISBN 978-1-59307-947-5

Book 23:
Bridge of Tears
$17.99 | ISBN 978-1-59582-298-7

Book 24:
Return of the Black Soul
$16.99 | ISBN 978-1-59582-472-1

Book 25:
Fox Hunt
$16.99 | ISBN 978-1-59582-726-5

Book 26:
Traitors of the Earth
$16.99 | ISBN 978-1-59582-910-8

Book 27:
A Town Called Hell
$16.99 | ISBN 978-1-59582-970-2

Book 28:
Red Scorpion
$17.99 | ISBN 978-1-61655-398-2

Book 29:
Two Hundred Jizo
$17.99 | ISBN 978-1-61655-840-6
ON SALE JUNE 2015

Usagi Yojimbo: Yokai
$14.99 | ISBN 978-1-59582-362-5

Usagi Yojimbo: Senso
$19.99 | ISBN 978-1-61655-709-6
ON SALE MAY 2015

Space Usagi
$17.99 | ISBN 978-1-56971-290-0

The Art of Usagi Yojimbo
$29.95 | ISBN 978-1-59307-493-7

The Sakai Project:
Artists Celebrate Thirty Years of Usagi Yojimbo
$29.99 | ISBN 978-1-61655-556-6

47 Ronin
Written by Mike Richardson
$19.99 | ISBN 978-1-59582-954-2

The Adventures of Nilson Groundthumper and Hermy
$14.99 | ISBN 978-1-61655-341-8

AVAILABLE FROM FANTAGRAPHICS BOOKS
fantagraphics.com

Book 1: The Ronin
Book 2: Samurai
Book 3: The Wanderer's Road
Book 4: The Dragon Bellow Conspiracy
Book 5: Lone Goat and Kid
Book 6: Circles
Book 7: Gen's Story

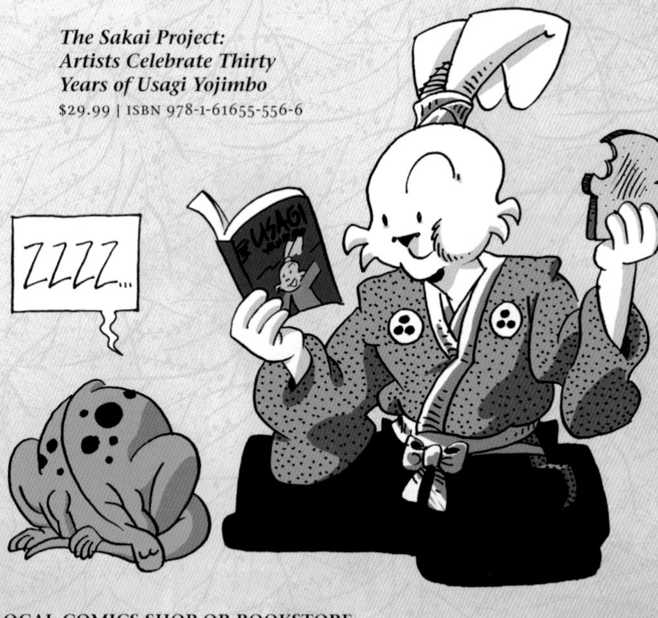
ZZZZ...

AVAILABLE AT YOUR LOCAL COMICS SHOP OR BOOKSTORE
- To find a comics shop near your area, call 1-888-266-4226. For more information or to order direct:
- On the web: DarkHorse.com • E-mail: mailorder@darkhorse.com
- Phone: 1-800-862-0052 Mon.-Fri. 9 A.M. to 5 P.M. Pacific Time. *Prices and availability subject to change without notice.

MORE YOUNG ADULT TITLES FROM

DARK HORSE BOOKS!

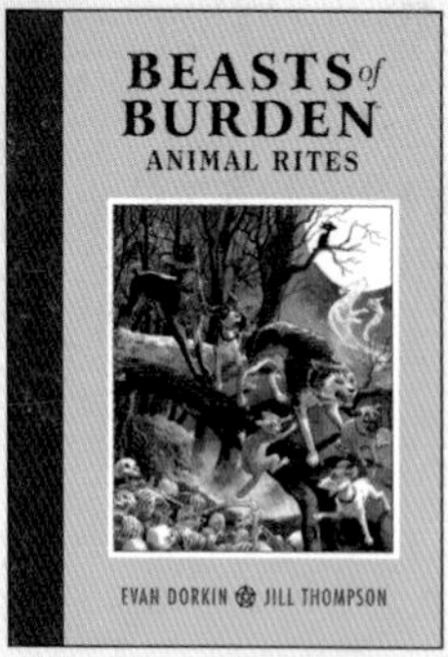

BEASTS of BURDEN
ANIMAL RITES
EVAN DORKIN JILL THOMPSON

BEASTS OF BURDEN: ANIMAL RITES

Written by Evan Dorkin, illustrated by Jill Thompson

Beneath its surface of green lawns and white picket fences, the picturesque little town of Burden Hill harbors dark and sinister secrets. It's up to a heroic gang of dogs—and one cat—to protect the town from the evil forces at work. Adventure, mystery, horror, and hum thrive on every page!

978-1-59582-513-1 | $19.99

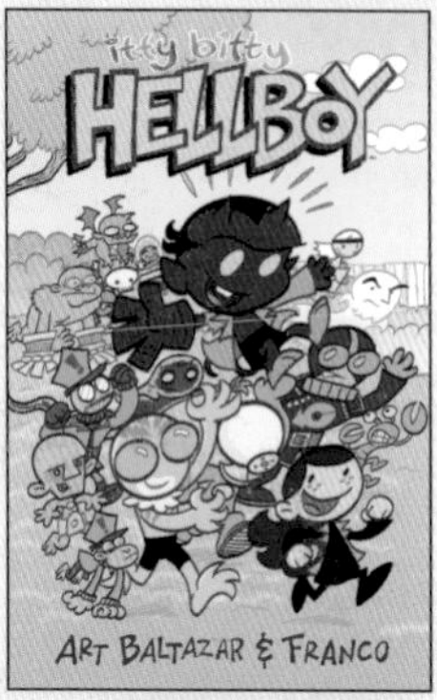

itty bitty
HELLBOY
ART BALTAZAR & FRANCO

ITTY BITTY HELLBOY

Written by Art Baltazar and Franco, illustrated by Art Baltazar

The characters that sprung from Mike Mignola's imagination, with an AW YEAH COMICS twist! This book has ALL the FUN, adventure, and AW YEAHNESS in one itty bitty packag

978-1-61655-414-9 | $9.99

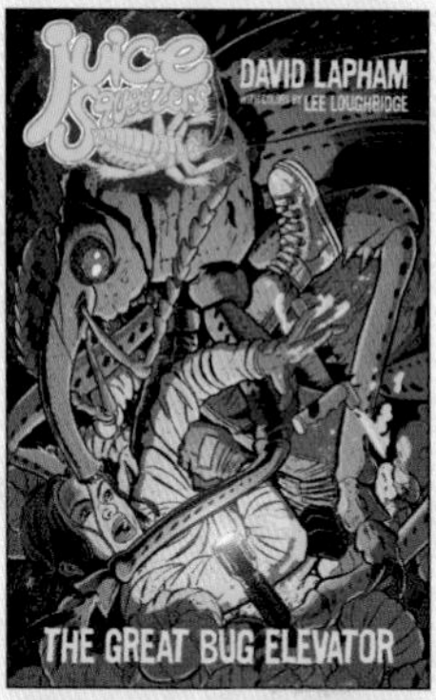

DAVID LAPHAM
THE GREAT BUG ELEVATOR

JUICE SQUEEZERS: THE GREAT BUG ELEVATOR

Written and illustrated by David Lapham

Tunnels made by a legion of giant bugs crisscross the fields below the quaint California town of Weeville, and only one thing can stop them from overrunning the place: the Juic Squeezers. A covert group of scrawny tweens, the Squeezers are the only ones who can into the cramped subterranean battlefield and fight the insects on the frontlines!

978-1-61655-438-5 | $12.99

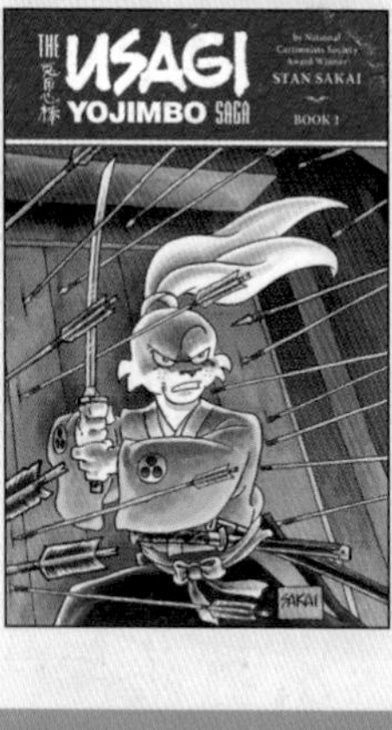

THE USAGI YOJIMBO SAGA
STAN SAKAI
BOOK 1

THE USAGI YOJIMBO SAGA

Written and illustrated by Stan Sakai

Dark Horse proudly presents Miyamoto Usagi's epic trek along the warrior's path in a new series of deluxe compilations. The rabbit *ronin*'s adventures have won multiple awards and delighted readers for thirty years!

VOLUME 1: 978-1-61655-609-9 | $24.99
VOLUME 2: 978-1-61655-610-5 | $24.99

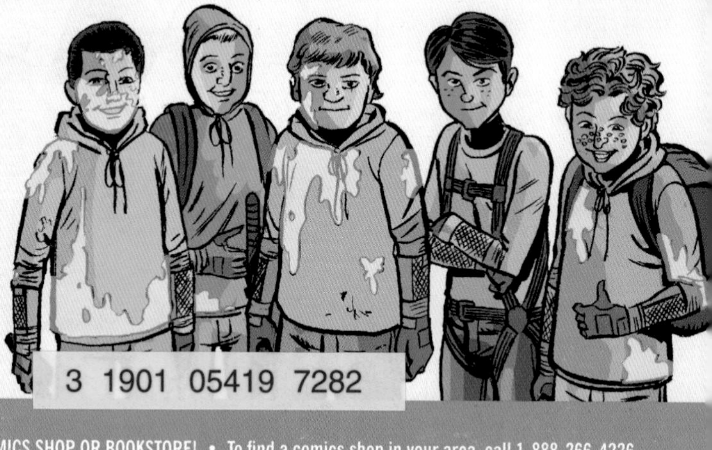